"I got that spot in the ... ... New York—hey! Asshole! Stay in your own lane!—and neither of us wants a long distance relationship, so... Besides, really, you're gay. Admit it and be happy. Con's cute."

His mind shut off. He was *gay*? They were breaking up because she thought—He hung up and speed-dialed her number.

"Cassie," she chirped.

"I'm not gay!" he yelled into the phone.

"Okay, whatever." Her tone was breezy, uninterested. "I'm still going to New York."

"Fine, but I'm not—"

"Gay, right. Just repressed like crazy."

Tim wasn't sure he was supposed to hear that last part. "Cass!"

She laughed. "Relax, Tim. Look, fine, you're not gay. I'm sorry I said it. But I am going to New York."

He sat for a minute, glaring at the cracked tile between his sneakers. Brilliant end to a shitty day. "If that makes you happy..." He was vaguely surprised at how much it didn't hurt.

"It will. And, hey, you and Con would be cute together. Walking wet dream. Seriously."

"Cassie!"

Laughter rang from the other end of the line. "I'm sorry, Tim, I can't help it. Look, I have to go. Call if you need anything, all right?"

"Yeah, sure." The line had already cut. Cursing under his breath, he flipped his phone closed and let his head sink into his hands.

"So," a voice drawled as the door opened. "You're not gay."

This is a work of fiction. Names, characters, places, and incidents either are the product of the author's imagination or are used fictitiously. Any resemblance to actual events, locales, organizations, or persons, living or dead, is entirely coincidental and beyond the intent of either the author or the publisher.

By Degrees
TOP SHELF
An imprint of Torquere Press Publishers
PO Box 2545
Round Rock, TX 78680
Copyright 2009 JB McDonald
Cover illustration by Alessia Brio
Published with permission
ISBN: 978-1-60370-774-9, 1-60370-774-3
www.torquerepress.com

First Torquere Press Printing: August 2009
Printed in the USA

**If you enjoyed By Degrees,
you might enjoy these Torquere Press titles:**

The Broken Road by Sean Michael

Chiaroscuro by Jenna Jones

In the Rough by JB McDonald

The Long Road Home by BA Tortuga

OC Pride: Crossing the Line by Stephanie Vaughan

By Degrees

By Degrees
by JB McDonald

Torquere Press Inc.
romance for the rest of us
www.torquerepress.com

By Degrees

Dedication

Many thanks to Stacy, who read and critiqued it first, gave me lots of help, put up with my ranting and whining, and pushed me into making it better. Couldn't have done this without you. :D

And many thanks to Dr. Danny, who not only gave me cool drug names and told me what they did, but never blinks twice at my odd requests. (In fact... he kind of encourages them.) All the right hospital stuff is his, all the bad is mine. DJ—two decades, man. Thanks for the love. Love you back.

By Degrees

Chapter One

And men are *supposed* to keep growing until they're twenty-five." Tim glared out the car window, his feet slipped out of their flip-flops and braced on the dashboard.

Con grinned, glancing again at his best friend. He hadn't been able to *stop* grinning since he'd flown in the night before. He'd been afraid that he would look at Tim, and Tim would look at him, and they'd realize that something had changed since the last time they'd seen each other—over a decade earlier. They'd just been kids, then, tossed into the same boarding school before circumstances had pulled them apart not even a year later.

Somehow, they'd kept in touch.

But more than a decade without seeing Tim had made Conner anxious, worried that things might be different. They were; his boyhood friend had grown up. It was awesome. Suddenly, moving to a new state to start a new job wasn't quite so terrifying—at least he'd have one friend here already. Tim was quieter than Conner remembered from their school days, more reserved, but that was all right. Solemn lines fit him, somehow. They matched the person Con had grown to know through email and phone calls.

In an odd sort of way, this sudden outburst about height fit, too.

"Well..." Con dragged his mind back to the conversation. "You're more than twenty-five, so of course you're not growing anymore."

"But I stopped when I was *sixteen*!" Tim protested. "That's just not fair! I should have a growth spurt now to make up for it."

Personally, Con thought Tim was just about perfect. Short, yeah, but not a shrimp. He had black hair and blue eyes, fair skin, a strong jaw. A body that was compact and well toned, testament to hours spent in a gym. Con really appreciated those hours. *Really* appreciated those hours.

"Stop your bitching." He grinned out the windshield as he maneuvered the rental through downtown San Diego traffic. "It's not like you're five-six or something."

Silence from the other seat pulled his attention around as surely as a scream. Tim's cool gaze regarded him steadily.

"Oh," Con said after a long moment. "Uh, sorry. Well, you look taller."

With a small noise, Tim went back to glaring out the window. After a while he frowned, glancing over. "Why were we talking about this again?"

"Because I outgrew my pants."

The statement had Tim off and running once more. "Yeah! You're twenty-fucking-eight! You're not supposed to be growing!"

Con chuckled.

"Swear to God, you stole my tall genes."

"Timmy, you never had tall genes."

"Fuck off." The words were a grumble, Tim's head turning as they passed a man and a woman walking hand in hand down the sidewalk, both of them half-naked.

Both were extremely attractive. Con adjusted the rearview mirror to catch the man's rear view, and hummed in appreciation. Living in San Diego was going to be great.

"Here," Tim said suddenly. "Turn here."

Con swerved into the right lane, pulling into a parking lot. It took a moment for his heart, hammering after his dart through traffic, to calm. "Why don't *you* drive on the way home?"

"Hate driving." Tim opened the car door before Con had finished parking. Slipping sunglasses on, he stared off at the outdoor mall while Con closed and locked the door.

Only in California would an outdoor mall stay busy all year. Con grinned. "All right." He clapped his hands before rubbing them together. "Let's find me some California jeans. Money is no concern. Only style."

Tim gave him an unreadable look, then snorted. "Welcome to Fashion Valley."

It had been a long day of shopping—an activity Tim wasn't fond of at the best of times—before they'd gotten back to his apartment. He was almost sorry Con had flown in, though he couldn't quite say why. He didn't like someone else in his little place. Yeah, that was it.

Except that wasn't it, and he knew it.

Maybe Con was just too big. He took up too much space. All eight foot twelve of him.

"What's with the scowl?" Gigantor asked, sprawled on the other end of the couch, feet up on the battered coffee table. Tim had gotten the couch from Rick, his Big Brother, who'd gotten it from a friend, who'd gotten it— hell, he didn't know. Probably off of the sidewalk.

"You're too tall." It was the first excuse that came to mind.

Con snorted. "Someone woke up on the crabby side of the bed this morning, huh?" He went back to his magazine.

Tim flipped through television channels and ignored Con.

God, what was *wrong* with him? They'd known each other since he'd been just ten and Con an oh-so-cool twelve. Even then, Conner had been bigger, rougher, more outgoing. Tim had shadowed him for days before Con took him under his wing, smiling with dimples that bracketed both cheeks.

Nine months later Con's father had been convicted of embezzlement, and Conner had gone to live with his grandparents. Two months after that, Tim's parents had died. The state took decent care of kids with money, but nothing had felt really stable afterward. Nothing except knowing that he could open the mailbox, pick up a phone, or, later, turn on a computer, and Con would be right there on the other end.

He'd cheered Conner on when the other man had decided to become a firefighter, and then told Conner first when he passed the MCATs. When Con had announced that he was moving out of Chicago and had gotten a job with the San Diego fire department, Tim had suggested he fly down for a week and check out the area.

Then Con had stepped off the plane. Big, tall, broad-shouldered, with the stereotypical muscular firefighter's physique and thick brown hair. His dark eyes seemed to sparkle with cheer no matter where he looked. He still had the dimples, even had small lines from them when he wasn't smiling. He had straight, white teeth, and snug clothing.

Tim's heart had dropped right into his feet. It wasn't a sensation he was either familiar or comfortable with. The fact that Con stood a full head taller than him didn't help.

"Damn, Timmy," Conner said from the other end of the couch. "If you hate the show that much, why not just change the channel?"

Tim blinked and realized he was glowering fit to shatter the screen. With a shake of his head, he turned it off and stood. "Look, I'm just a little stir-crazy. I'm gonna hit the gym. You'll be okay here?"

Con nodded, expression wavering somewhere between concerned and amused.

That, Tim didn't need. There was nothing to be concerned about, and he sure wasn't here for anyone's entertainment. Then he mentally rolled his eyes at himself: maybe he *had* woken up on the wrong side of the bed. He headed down the hall to change. Fresh air would make him feel better. Con was just a surprise, that was all.

It was two hours before Tim returned. Con watched him head straight to the shower and wondered if Tim remembered that Con was gay. Because Con was as gay as a double-dicked tree frog, and Tim had come back from the gym sweaty and sexy.

He tried not to stare, keeping his gaze fixed on the television as Tim wandered from bedroom to bathroom, black hair sticking to his neck, naked chest damp with sweat. God, the guy might not be huge, but he was gorgeous. Compact and well put together. Something made Conner think that if Tim tackled you, you'd go down, regardless of his height.

Tim vanished into the bathroom, closing the door. A moment later, the shower turned on.

Con did his best not to think about water sliding over bare skin, or soap lathering between fingers and—

He got up and plucked his headphones out of his

backpack so he couldn't hear the water running. It helped, marginally.

When Tim emerged in sweatpants riding low on slim hips, toweling his hair dry, Con took the headphones off.

"Find something to do?" Tim padded into the little kitchen, opening the pantry and staring inside.

Yes, Conner didn't say. *I imagined you in the shower.* Oh, Lord, this week might be harder than he'd expected. "There's always television." He smiled, trying not to let his thoughts show on his face.

Something small and wry touched Tim's mouth and was gone in a blink. "Hungry?"

He could nibble on those little toeses... Con lifted his gaze from Tim's bare feet. "Uh, no." He cleared his throat when Tim gave him a funny look.

"You're not getting sick, are you?" There was a warning in the light tenor.

"No, Doctor Timmy." A teasing smile danced over Con's lips.

Tim rolled his eyes. "Wish you wouldn't call me that." He bent, peering into the fridge. After a moment's consideration, he closed it and turned around. "The Chinese place down the street delivers."

Con laughed. "I'm up for whatever." And he meant that in any way Tim wanted to take it.

Tim, however, seemed oblivious. He called the restaurant, placing their order and hanging up, then tossed the towel in the bathroom.

"You still seeing what's her name? Tiffany?" Con asked, trying to distract himself from smooth skin and perfect biceps.

"Cassie." Tim smiled blandly. "Yeah." A frown darted over his face and was gone, little more than a shadow. He started to say something, then shook his head and turned away.

"What?" It seemed Con got more from Tim over IM and email than in person. As if, with a screen between them, Tim could pretend he wasn't talking to a real human.

"I—" Tim looked at him, then frowned again. "She's talking about finishing her Masters in New York."

Con winced outwardly, but inwardly cheered. "You gonna do the long-distance thing?"

Tim's narrow shoulders lifted and fell as he perched on the arm of the couch, about as far away as he could get without sitting on the floor. "I guess not. We'll see, though, right?"

"Sure." They both knew he meant, 'Get real.' "Hey," Con said, changing the subject, "when are we going to the beach? I mean, this is California." Grinning, he spread his hands. "We've *got* to go to the beach."

Tim shrugged again. "Tomorrow, if you want. I have a couple of days off. Then I'm on rotation Tuesday, but I have Wednesday afternoon open."

"Cool." Con relaxed back into the comfortable couch. Half-naked people, half-naked Tim... life didn't get better. "This'll be awesome."

Tim might have been dating—temporarily—Tiffany or Cassie or whoever the hell she was, but there were plenty of other attractive people at the beach. Con didn't bother hiding his interest, grinning openly when one jogger caught him ogling.

The jogger winked back, flashing a set of pearly whites and adding an extra bounce to his step.

"I love California." Con sighed, walking backward through the sand. Another three steps and he turned, grinning down at Tim. "Body conscious much?" He yanked off the ball cap that Tim had donned earlier and used it to fan his face. So much for half-naked Tim.

Tim made a grab for it, then stopped, a little bundle of fuming ire. Even with a folding chair in one hand and a cooler in the other, he somehow managed to cross his arms and glare.

"Relax." Con laughed, tossing the hat in the garbage. "Seriously, you're one of the hottest guys here and you're seriously overdressed."

"Seriously?" A hint of sarcasm colored Tim's mild voice.

Con resisted the urge to grab the other man and kiss him silly. Tim probably wouldn't take it right. Or rather, he'd take it too right, and Con would be finding an earlier flight home.

"That guy," Con began, pointing to a man near seventy doing yoga in the ankle-deep water, "is less body conscious than you." Every wrinkle was proudly displayed, the yellow Speedo doing nothing to hide anything.

Tim looked at Con doubtfully. "Thank you," he deadpanned at last. "Now I feel full of self-confidence. And I'm not overdressed. I just don't want to burn."

Con snorted.

"I burn!" Tim nearly shouted. "And skin cancer—"

"Whatever!" Con's laugh was dismissive, the wave of his hand equally so. "You just don't want guys scamming the goods."

Tim flushed bright red, mouth shutting so fast his teeth clicked. Glowering at the ground, he dropped the chair and the cooler, shrugging so that the towel he'd slung over one shoulder hit the sand.

Con's smile faded. He'd just been teasing. He hadn't meant to upset. "Tim?" He reached a hand out tentatively, but stopped short of touching him. "Hey, man, I was just kidding around."

Tim shrugged robotically. "Don't worry about it. Here good?"

"Yeah, sure." Con barely glanced at their surroundings. The whole beach was sandy and filled with people; one spot was as good as another, in his opinion. "Look, I just talk without thinking, you know?" Of course, he wasn't sure what he'd said to upset Tim. Just that he had. Surely Tim wasn't upset at the thought of guys checking him out? "You know I wouldn't let anything happen," he said slowly, a thought that he didn't like at all crawling up his spine. Body consciousness and obvious discomfort at being checked out combined in his head, and suddenly he remembered hearing horror stories about foster care, and—

"Oh, for God's sake, Con." All of Tim's discomfort washed away with annoyance. "I could probably take you in a fight."

Con straightened, looking down at the other man. "Please. It's nice that you can defend yourself and all, but there's no way—"

Tim did *something*. It was too quick for Con to see, just one moment Tim was there and the next he wasn't, and then the *ground* was there and Tim was kneeling over him, looking like, "See?" Con's head rang.

"Ow."

Tim snorted and stood. "Size isn't everything." No one could do supercilious like Tim could.

"No, it's the motion of the ocean." Con sat up and rubbed his throat. Then his head. Then he stood and rubbed his ass. "Man, you bruised my tailbone."

"Doubt it." Tim blithely settled on the beach towel he'd spread out.

"If you did, I'm gonna make you doctor it," Con warned.

"Take two aspirin and call me in the morning."

Con looked at him for a long moment, at the smug self-assurance the man radiated. Swim trunks hung nearly to his knees, and a baggy T-shirt covered the rest. He looked immoveable, sitting there on his towel. With a snort, Con walked toward the water, threading through picnic blankets and giant umbrellas, nearly tripping over a small child. A Sunday at the beach was crowded, but he basked in the life.

At the ocean's edge a group of kids were digging in the salty mud, gleefully filling buckets with cold sea water and big shovelfuls of sand.

"Can I borrow this?" he asked one of the little boys, grinning impishly and pointing at a purple, mud-filled bucket.

The boy eyed him, ascertaining honesty, then nodded once. "But bring it back!"

"Sure thing!" Con picked the bucket up.

Tim was leaning on his hands, blue eyes hidden behind dark glasses, the breeze lifting and tossing his black hair. Con walked right up to him and overturned the bucket of mud on that blue-black head.

"Jesus fucking Christ!" Tim bellowed, leaping to his feet.

Con wasted no time gloating; he'd not-seen the smaller man move just an instant before, and wasn't going to end up flat on his ass again. He turned and bolted for the ocean, tossing the bucket to the kids as he raced past.

"God! Fuck! They're *wriggling*, you asshole!" Tim yelled, hot on his heels into the spray.

A small body pounded into his lower back, wiry arms locking around his waist as Tim dragged him down into the surf. Con got a mouthful of sea water, laughing too hard to hold his breath. They were waist-deep when he surfaced a moment later, wiping water off his face and out of his eyes, catching sight of Tim shaking his head furiously. Shiny hair flung more liquid, then clung to Tim's face and neck, wrapping around his fingers when he tried to drag it out of the way. The T-shirt was plastered against him, outlining pectoral muscles, twisting around his waist.

"You ass!" Tim pulled a small rock out from the neck of his shirt. "That was *full* of sand crabs."

"Sand-what?"

"Sand crabs!" Tim held out his hand, and the small rock began to twist and scuttle, tiny pincer-less legs carrying it off to plop into the water.

Con grabbed for the critter, but it was already gone. "Oh, man. That's wild."

"Wild, yeah," Tim drawled. "You just threw a bucket of *sand crabs* on me. I should kick your ass."

Con laughed and splashed him. "Try."

Water closed over Con's face for the tenth time. He thrashed and came up sputtering. Feet firmly on the sandy bottom, he turned to watch Tim floating on his back, rising and falling with the swell.

"It's not that hard," Tim said, eyes closed. "I mean, salt water's more buoyant than fresh water."

"Yeah, but it *moves*."

Somehow, Tim managed to convey a shrug without actually shrugging. "You just have no talent."

Con ducked under the water, slicking his hair out of his face, then rose up again. With Tim's eyes closed, he could ogle as much as he wanted.

Of course, Tim was *still* wearing his T-shirt, and it floated around him, hiding firm muscles. Con sank until his chin was just under sea level, then glided silently toward the other man.

"Don't," Tim said, just as Con reached out.

He hesitated, wondering how Tim had known. Then he reached out anyway, slipping his hand under the floating edge of Tim's T-shirt and grabbing swim trunks, giving him the wedgie to end all wedgies.

"You ass!" Tim kicked upright, prying his shorts out of his butt as Con killed himself laughing. "What is *with* you? God, you're like, twelve!"

Con kept cackling, nearly gleeful. Tim was so self-contained that getting a reaction out of him was becoming Con's favorite pastime.

"Going to put sand crabs down your fucking pants," Tim muttered, squirming under the water.

"Poor baby. What, can't beat me up in chest-deep water?"

Tim glowered, but Con could see the amusement just under the surface. "That's what this is? You're annoyed that I can kick the crap out of you on land, so you're picking on me in the ocean? I get it now."

Con grinned madly. "You know, you're just proving me right." He waited until Tim lifted a single eyebrow in expectant query. "It's the little guys you've gotta watch out for in a fight."

One corner of Tim's mouth twitched up. "Damn straight."

"Gaily forward, never straight," Con corrected automatically.

Tim looked at him, that eyebrow lifted again.

Time for a subject change, Con decided. "That's a neat trick. I never could manage it."

"What?"

"The single eyebrow thing." He gestured with one hand, water droplets sparkling through the sunshine before plinking back into the ocean.

Tim lowered the one eyebrow and lifted the other. "This?"

"Yeah," Con laughed. "Show off."

Tim smiled, one of those rare ones that actually showed his teeth. "I spent my thirteenth year in front of a mirror, learning how."

"You are *such* a geek." Despite the words, Con's tone was fond.

Tim rolled his eyes, tossing his head once to flip his hair back out of his face. "Ready to go in? I'm getting cold."

Con manfully resisted offering to keep Tim warm and just nodded instead. He followed, enjoying the view as Tim walked out of the ocean, his clothing hugging him tight and water running off his skin. God, now there was a wet dream.

Tim sat wrapped in his towel, watching Con play in the sand with the kids. The tide was coming in, occasionally high enough to splash over their feet and knock down budding sandcastles. They were currently digging for crabs, and Tim had a sneaking suspicion that if he wasn't careful, he'd end up with little crabby pets when they got home.

He shivered and shifted his towel, trying to cover the little bit of skin that the breeze was plucking at. He was pretty sure that the water dripping from his hair was going to keep wetting the area, and the wind was just going to keep making it cold. Lying down would put him out of the blast and flat out in the sun, but it would also take Con from view. Given the man's current crab-finding pastime, keeping him in sight seemed the better idea.

Kids screamed in glee as Con emptied a bucket of crabs over one of the children's heads. God, the man was a big kid himself.

Sand scuffed across Tim's toes, and he glanced up to see the cause. A blue disk lay by his feet, half buried. Not a moment later a girl came trotting over, all legs and stomach. "Sorry." She offered a dimpled smile. "Frisbee got away from me."

Tim risked the wind to snake an arm out of his cocoon, and handed the Frisbee back.

"Thanks." The girl tucked a strand of curly blond hair behind her ear. Beads hanging on the ties of her bikini clicked together, drawing attention to hips and breasts. "You want to—?" She gestured behind her, and suddenly Con dropped to the sand beside Tim, flecking him with grit.

"Careful," Tim muttered, edging around to try and brush the sand off. He only left streaks of finer dust behind.

Con ignored him. "Hey," he said to the girl, smiling up. "Timmy, you brought drinks, right?"

"In the cooler." Tim wasn't sure whether to be amused or annoyed at the interruption. It wasn't coincidence, not with all the tanned skin the lady was showing. Guys always flocked around tanned skin. Even gay guys, apparently. "Don't call me Timmy," he added.

Con grinned, shrugging as he popped open a soda and chugged.

"You guys want to join us?" The girl cocked one hip and smiled.

Something lurched in Tim's stomach, making a sour taste in his mouth as he waited for Con to leap up and escort her off. He stared at his toes, buried in the warm sand—his towel hadn't been big enough to cover them.

"Maybe later." Con shaded his eyes with one hand. "Thanks."

"Sure." She trotted away, somehow managing to bounce less than when she'd first shown up. Tim tried not to feel relieved at her retreating back.

"You *still* cold, dude?" One side of Con's mouth quirked up.

"Dude?" Tim snorted.

"Just answer the question."

Tim felt the tips of his ears warm under Con's scrutiny, and decided he was probably getting sunburned. "Yeah, I'm still cold. The Pacific is *freezing*, man. The ocean currents," he pulled an arm out, gesturing, "bring the water down from the north, so it's colder than you'd think." He slanted a look at Con, big and broad, covered with muscle. "Not all of us have a freakishly large body mass to keep ourselves warm."

"Wuss." Con grinned and stretched his legs out in the sun. He didn't even bother with a towel, just scooted his butt into the sand with a little wiggle that Tim purposely didn't notice. "Why don't you lie down? Sunbathe. Lots of people doing it."

"Yeah, right." Tim's ears went brighter, but after a minute he did so, towel still wrapped around him. The wind flew over him harmlessly, the sun slowly heating his skin. Noises rose and fell like the crash of waves not too distant, the babble of voices a soothing drone. Before long he was dozing fitfully, hair drying and going crispy with salt. He pushed the towel to one side, cracking an eye open to see Con still sitting there, braced on his hands, water glistening in little droplets on his chest.

Tim swallowed and closed his eyes again, feeling his heart thump erratically. It was just odd to be around someone as big as Con. And it wasn't just that he was big—half of Tim's friends were bigger—but everything he did was big. He sprawled, he gestured, he even spoke *big*. Tim wasn't used to it, that was all.

He tried to ignore it, to just doze off again, but every time Con shifted, he heard it. There, Con was drinking

23

something. His neck muscles would be moving, tendons standing out and vanishing again. That was the sound of skin against sand, or a little sigh of contentment.

He shouldn't have been able to hear those things over the sounds of the people around them, the kids playing and adults talking, all the volleyball nets full and teenagers running across the beach and into the water. But he could. He even thought he could feel Con next to him, as if the man had moved closer and was sitting near enough to touch if Tim just shifted a little.

Tim slitted his eyes and peered through his lashes. Con hadn't moved toward him. He wasn't really close enough to feel body heat. It was just Tim's imagination.

He closed his eyes again and let himself drift. When he opened them, the people next to them had moved on and the crowd grown heavier. He rubbed the corners of his eyes and sat up, surprised to realize he'd fallen asleep. The kids down by the surf had vanished, replaced by a group of teens wake-boarding.

"Welcome back, sleepyhead." Con's voice was soft and amused.

Tim turned, remembering belatedly that he had company. He flushed, ducking his head and looping his arms around his knees. How he could have forgotten was beyond him; Con wasn't exactly dismissible. A can appeared at his elbow, and he turned to see Con holding it out for him. He took it, popping the tab and drinking.

"How long was I out?" He pressed chilly aluminum against his over-warm cheek. Now that he was upright, the breeze was cooling him down, but the sun had already done its work.

"Maybe an hour? Not too long. You looked like you needed it."

Tim resisted the urge to squirm. "I haven't been sleeping well," he admitted in a mutter, surprising himself with the confession. "I just—" Unsure how to explain it away, he paused. "Never mind." Muscles tensed as he waited, expecting Con to make some wisecrack or push too hard.

Instead, after a moment of weighted silence, Con simply said, "Want to go play volleyball?"

Tim looked up and around, catching sight of a group just forming at the nearest net. "Sure." It was a relief to escape the too-personal topic of his sleeping patterns. He didn't know what he'd been thinking when he'd said that.

Con pushed to his feet and Tim followed, kicking free of the towel and brushing sand off his arms.

"Room for two?" Con called as they neared, smiling brightly.

"Yeah, cool." The ringleader was a guy just younger than the two of them, Tim guessed. "We need one more, then."

A quick search turned up a lanky teenager willing to play, and they divided themselves rapidly into teams.

Tim, for all he complained about his size, was a fair athlete. The first time he spiked the ball over the net, no one was anywhere near enough to stop it.

"Shit!" one of the guys on his team said, laughing. "He's like a flea!"

"Very funny," Tim snorted, but pleasure at being good overrode his annoyance at the reference to his size.

"You gotta watch that one, guys," Con said from the other side of the net, dark eyes twinkling. "He's like a little bulldog. Tougher than he looks."

Tim made a face, waiting for the ball to be sent back over to his side.

The second time he spiked the ball into the sand, his team declared him the net-guy, and the other team put someone directly across from him in defense.

The rest of the game went similarly, Tim's team winning nine to seven. They all headed away laughing, Tim rubbing his chest, letting the cotton of his T-shirt soak up the sweat.

"Is this some form of little-man syndrome?" Con asked, still complaining about the two hits Tim had gotten past him. "I mean, you can't compete size-wise, so you make up for it by getting all athletically butch? Or is this more like a first strike? You hit them while they're still underestimating you?"

Tim snorted. He'd always been good at physical activities, having never hit that really clumsy stage most guys seemed to go through.

"Soda?" Con knelt beside the small cooler.

"I think we're out." Tim looked out over the sand at the water, past the swimmers and the boogie boarders. The sun sank lower, making the swell sparkle and glitter almost blindingly bright.

"Damn," Con murmured. "Well." He stopped, as if that was the end of his sentence.

Tim glanced back, but Con just sat in the sand, staring out at the Pacific. After a moment's regard, he looked up to meet Tim's gaze. He smiled, lopsided. "It's big."

Tim laughed quietly, feeling relaxed and at ease for the first time in—well, a really long time. "Oceans are like that," he teased.

"Man, I could totally get used to this. Nice weather, pretty people, good friends."

Tim lifted one eyebrow. "What friends do you have here?" He knew full well Con didn't know anyone.

Con rolled his eyes, then balled up his beach towel and threw it. It hit Tim's ribs and flopped to the ground, scattering grit. "You, idiot!"

"I'm one." Tim brushed sand off fastidiously. "Singular. You said friends, plural." The ocean breeze washed over him, lifting his hair, brushing cool fingers along his scalp.

Con snorted. "Oh, what, you're not going to let me meet your friends?"

Tim hesitated, then smiled slightly. "They don't count until you know them."

"Dork." It was said with a quick flash of teeth and no real heat.

Still smiling, Tim turned to look out at the water again. He heard Con stand and shift closer, but didn't bother looking around. When he felt Con's body heat prickle along his skin, tension coiled in his stomach. Just nerves, he told himself, frustrated with his reaction. "Tickle me and die," he grumbled.

Con's chuckle danced over his skin, and a moment later an arm settled casually around his shoulders, hand hanging off the far side. Con's skin was warm, even through the cotton of Tim's shirt. His body tightened, muscles tensing. He wasn't used to being touched, but somehow his usual reaction to take a step away didn't kick in. Standing perfectly still, Con's arm heavy and warm over him, he waited for distaste to arrive. It didn't.

He took a breath, and only then realized he'd been holding it. He took another breath, smelling sand and salt and Con's sweat. Another breath through his open mouth, and his muscles began to relax, centimeter by centimeter. They must have been standing there forever, and yet Con hadn't moved, hadn't said anything, just stared out at the ocean like this was the most natural thing in the world. The urge to step away was suddenly overpowering.

Tim didn't touch. Didn't really like to be touched. While Con's arm felt—he hesitated to even *think* the word 'nice'—it was still an arm on him, around his shoulders, lying heavy, warm, safe—

He shook his head slightly and began to step away,

27

only to feel Con move first, arm dropping off. "Want to go back in the water?" Con asked, heading toward the ocean and smiling over his shoulder.

Tim swallowed, trying to clear his head, not really wanting to know what had just happened. "Yeah," he said at last. "Sure." He headed down the beach, staring at the sand rather than the muscles rippling under the skin of Con's back.

"Hey! Timmy!"

Tim scowled at the name and looked up.

"We should see if we can borrow a boogie board!"

His gaze skidded down Con's outstretched arm, followed the length of his finger, and shot off in the indicated direction. A cluster of pre-teens were sprawled around a tangle of blankets and towels, several boards scattered between them. With a nod meant for Con, Tim changed directions and headed toward the group.

Chapter Two

Con dragged himself away from the television at the knock on the door, gaze remaining glued to the screen until a wall blocked his view. Then he reached the front door and opened it, staring down at a curvy blond digging through her purse.

She glanced up at him, blue eyes sharp. "You must be Conner."

He flashed a smile automatically. "The one and only. And you are...?"

"Cassie." She brushed past him, dropping a set of keys back into her purse and hanging it over her shoulder. "I just needed some things. Don't mind me."

Nodding, he closed the door behind her. So this was the girlfriend. She had keys to Tim's apartment, and left stuff here? He frowned, then shook it off. He guessed that they were more serious than he'd hoped.

The last few days had catapulted him from happy with being a friend to wanting something more. He liked Tim, enjoyed his company; liked the way he dressed, moved, smelled. He loved the brain on the man, and the fact that Tim was aware of his intelligence only in an absent sort of way. The day at the beach had been followed by a day of lazing around and doing nothing, wandering downtown San Diego for a few hours and watching the shoot-'em-up movies that Con had rented. Tim's knowledge of movie pop culture was disturbingly nonexistent—and Con even liked that.

It had been nice, just the two of them, and Tim had relaxed a little more with each passing minute. He had finally stopped tensing when Con found excuses to touch him, to reach past him to get a glass and let his arm rub over the slender chest, or to bump shoulders teasingly as they walked down the sidewalk.

The entrance of The Girlfriend was, he supposed, a good thing. It gave Con a reality check. Damn her.

He followed Cassie idly into the living room, expecting her to be in the bedroom already, getting her things. Instead, she was crouched in front of the almost-bare DVD shelves, picking through movies. "See, he borrows this stuff and then never watches it," she said, facing the television and waving several thrillers in the air.

He tipped his head. "Is that *From Hell*?"

Cassie looked back at him, rolling her eyes. "He's a big Johnny Depp fan."

A smirk danced over his face. "Really?"

"He even has a bootlegged copy of the last *Pirates* flick. *And* a copy he paid for."

"He has all the *Ocean* movies, too. Or are those yours?" he asked, realizing she was taking most of the suspense films as well.

Cassie picked up the rented *Jurassic Park* DVD—Con had been horrified to learn Tim had never seen it—and glanced back. "Yours?"

He nodded.

She put it down. "The *Ocean* movies are his. He likes Brad Pitt."

It was things like this that convinced him all over again that Tim wasn't as straight as he seemed.

"Give him five minutes, he'll explain all his reasons

why Jennifer Aniston is the world's biggest bitch." Cassie turned to look at him. "He'll also insist it has nothing to do with her break-up with Brad, but really..." She shrugged, then pushed to her feet and headed into the kitchen.

Con chuckled, leaning against the counter that separated the living room from the tiny kitchen. "So, how long have you been dating?"

"I'm not sure we're *dating* so much as seeing each other occasionally." Opening a cupboard, she pulled out two margarita glasses, wrapping them carefully in plastic bags before putting them in her purse beside the movies. "And I'm going away to school, so it's a moot point."

He nodded slowly. "Sorry to hear it," he lied.

"Yeah, well..." The words trailed off. She glanced around, then turned and shot Con a smile. "So. You're Con."

He laughed, rocking back on his heels and stuffing his hands in his pockets. Hadn't they already done this part? "Yeah."

Her narrowed eyes traveled over his body like a prospective show-dog buyer sizing up a hound. "Huh. That explains a lot." She breezed toward the door, leaving him to follow, caught in her wake.

"Explains what?" He stopped at the doorway, watching as she bounced down the stairs.

She just lifted one hand in a wave without even looking back.

He watched her go, half bemused and half annoyed, then finally went back inside and closed the door. This was why he was gay. Women made no sense at all.

Tim rubbed his eyes, phone glued to his ear as he listened to his messages. One rambling one from Con asking where he kept bread, then another to say he'd found a loaf. One from Rick, checking in to make sure he hadn't been murdered in his sleep since he hadn't returned calls in a week.

He shifted on the couch in the doctors' lounge, wishing they'd get something comfortable for the room. Rubbing his eyes again, he ruffled his hand back through his hair, dragging it out of his face. He hadn't slept well, and every patient on his shift had been crabby, bitchy, or sick. On him. He'd changed scrub pants three times already. Luckily, his shift was over and now he just had to drive home.

The last message was from Cassie. He fingered a hole in the hem of his shirt.

"Hey, Tim," she said, voice cheerful and slightly distracted. "I got that spot in the Master's program in New York—hey! Asshole! Stay in your own lane!—and neither of us wants a long distance relationship, so... Besides, really, you're gay. Admit it and be happy. Con's cute."

His mind shut off. He was *gay*? They were breaking up because she thought—He hung up and speed-dialed her number.

"Cassie," she chirped.

"I'm not gay!" he yelled into the phone.

"Okay, whatever." Her tone was breezy, uninterested. "I'm still going to New York."

"Fine, but I'm not—"

"Gay, right. Just repressed like crazy."

Tim wasn't sure he was supposed to hear that last part. "Cass!"

She laughed. "Relax, Tim. Look, fine, you're not gay. I'm sorry I said it. But I am going to New York."

He sat for a minute, glaring at the cracked tile between his sneakers. Brilliant end to a shitty day. "If that makes you happy..." He was vaguely surprised at how much it didn't hurt.

"It will. And, hey, you and Con would be cute together. Walking wet dream. Seriously."

"Cassie!"

Laughter rang from the other end of the line. "I'm sorry, Tim, I can't help it. Look, I have to go. Call if you need anything, all right?"

"Yeah, sure." The line had already cut. Cursing under his breath, he flipped his phone closed and let his head sink into his hands.

"So," a voice drawled as the door opened. "You're not gay."

He looked up without moving, only his gaze traveling the room. "You heard that, huh?"

Peter laughed, not entirely nice. "Man, I think the whole hospital heard that." He poured himself a cup of coffee and added four sugar packets, then leaned back against the counter, ankles crossed, and watched Tim speculatively.

"Fuck off, Peter," Tim muttered. He didn't like the other man at the best of times, and this certainly wasn't the best of times.

"You change your mind about that whole 'not gay' thing, you let me know." A slow smiled eased across Peter's mouth. "I'd be happy to initiate you into the world."

"Jesus Christ," Tim muttered in disgust and stood, yanking his backpack up with him. He left the room and the bad coffee to Peter.

Con could see from the moment Tim walked in that something was wrong. It wasn't hard to tell, what with the storming through the apartment and slamming the bathroom door.

He hesitated, then knocked softly. "Hey, man. You okay?"

"Great." The shower turned on.

Con decided drinks were in order. Tim had nothing alcoholic in the house. A quick trip to the corner market fixed that, and he returned triumphant with a six pack of Corona and a bag of limes. He set about cutting while Tim got dressed. Knife in hand, blade sliding through fruit, Con didn't glance up until the other man reappeared, scrubs gone in favor of soft flannel pants and a black T-shirt. His wet hair dripped, soaking the collar, but Tim didn't seem to care.

"Here." Con twisted the top off of a bottle and stuffed a lime in. He clamped his palm over the top, tipped the bottle, and then set it upright on the counter with a decisive thunk. "Drink."

Tim eyed the beer like it might leap up and start dancing. "Do you have any idea how bad—"

"Just drink it." Con took a swig from his own. "You look like you could use it."

Tim took the bottle and sipped, then eyed the gold liquid as he swallowed.

"I ordered pizza while you were showering, too. Just to make this night *really* unhealthy." Con grinned, trying to lighten the mood.

It earned a reluctant smile from Tim, who turned and flopped down on the couch, curled into the corner.

"You look like you've had the shittiest day imaginable." Con came around the counter with his beer, leaning back against the tile.

Tim took another sip. "I had two people vomit on

me, and one with explosive diarrhea. Some idiot came in because he'd shoved the handle of his razor up his ass and then sliced his fingers trying to get it out, so we had to bandage his hands *and* get it out for him. And then I got chewed out by a mother who didn't like the fact that I couldn't give her daughter anything for her cold. Fuck, they don't *make* antibiotics for colds! There are signs all over the damn hospital saying that a cold is a virus and we can't do anything about it!"

Con nodded sympathetically.

"And to top it off, Cassie broke up with me!"

Con winced. "Aw, man, I'm sorry."

Tim's head fell back against the headrest, blue eyes staring sightlessly at the plaster above. "Did you say there was pizza?" He sounded forlorn.

The urge to smile was huge. Con resisted. "It'll be here in a few."

"I can't afford pizza," Tim muttered. "I have student loans."

"I'll pay for the pizza." Con gave in, smiling. "Drink your beer."

Tim lifted the bottle to his lips and drank. "And do you know *why* Cass broke up with me?" he asked, barely swallowing before he began to talk again.

Con perched on the arm of the sofa, as attentive as he could be.

"Because she thinks I'm gay! *Gay!*"

Keeping the glee off his face was difficult, but he managed. "Aw, man. I'm sorry." Hesitating, he flipped the bottle cap through his fingers before asking as casually as possible, "Are you?"

"What?" Tim muttered.

"Gay." Con glanced sidelong. Tim was unwinding further and further, sinking into the couch. With his legs stretched out along the floor, he was as relaxed as Con had ever seen him.

"No." A frown slid across his features and vanished a moment later.

Con scratched at the paint on his bottle, tossing the cap toward the counter. The frown had been too quick for Tim to be upset at the question. At least, Con thought it had been. But facial expressions, especially ones people weren't aware of, were often the key to figuring folks out. Maybe Tim was wrong. Maybe the thought of saying he wasn't gay upset him. Which might mean he was gay.

Con sighed, wondering if he was reaching. Probably.

A knock on the door heralded the pizza delivery guy, and Con set his bottle down on the scratched coffee table to stand, digging his wallet out of his back pocket. He opened the door, smiling distractedly at the teenager there.

"Fourteen fifty-three, man," the kid said, looking bored as he pulled the pizza out of its warmer.

Con nodded once, juggling pizza and money until the kid took the cash. "Keep the change." It was only a buck and half.

The teenager snorted and headed down the apartment stairs. Con took a step back, kicking the door closed. A glance at Tim showed him eyeing the lime slice morosely as it floated in his beer.

"Hey, Timmy, things'll get better."

Tim took another swallow of beer.

Shoving papers and dishes on the counter aside, Con put the pizza down and opened the box. The scent of tomato sauce slathered with greasy meat and cheese wafted upward. He took a deep breath and stared down at it, not seeing the food before him, but thinking about whether or not Tim knew he was gay, and what the man's reaction to that news might be if he didn't.

"You just gonna stare at that, or you gonna bring it

here?" Tim asked from the living room.

Con jumped, then smiled self-deprecatingly. "Sure, sorry." He grabbed the roll of paper towels and the box. "Hey, Timmy?" His voice was unusually hesitant, but if Tim noticed he didn't show it.

"Don't call me that," Tim muttered, sitting up and leaning his elbows on his knees, beer dangling from his fingertips.

Con ignored the words, too worried about Tim's possible reaction. "You know I'm gay, right?"

The look Tim shot him was so full of 'of course, you moron,' that Con couldn't help but smile. "Man, you talk about the guys you've slept with. Now give me some pizza."

Setting the box down with the lid open, Con flopped on the couch. Tim pulled a slice free, grabbing cheese between thumb and forefinger and tugging until it finally tore loose. He piled that on his pizza, then folded the slice and took a large bite.

Con sprawled in the corner, arm along the back of the couch. He swirled the liquid in his bottle, watching Tim chew and swallow and take another bite, apparently oblivious to Con's gaze. Then, without looking over, Tim grumbled, "What?"

"Nothing." He leaned down to grab a slice for himself. He didn't add, 'You're cute, that's all,' because he didn't figure Tim needed *that* after being reminded Con was gay.

They ate in silence, licking grease off their fingertips and drinking beer. Con finished his drink and got another, twisting the cap from a second one for Tim as well. Jamming limes in both necks, he carried them back to the coffee table. Once there, he tipped his head and eyed Tim's bottle. A little over an inch sloshed in the bottom. "You going to finish that?"

Tim picked it up and drank the rest without looking, burping once. The tips of his ears went pink. "'Scuse me."

Smiling, Con set the new bottles down and picked up the empty.

"I really don't need any more."

He glanced back over his shoulder. "Well, I already opened it, so you might as well drink." The empty one rattled into the trash.

Tim was looking at the full beer like it might bite. "Bottles go in recycling," he muttered absently.

With a snort, Con pulled the empties out and stuffed them in a paper bag filled with other glass and plastic things.

Tim was still just staring at his beer.

"You don't like it?" Maybe he preferred vodka drinks or some fruity, girly thing.

"It's just—well..." Tim frowned, and Con sat back down, studying the pale face. Slightly flushed cheeks, too bright eyes.

"Dude, are you *drunk*?" He started to laugh. "Off *one* beer?"

Tim's cheeks turned pinker. "I said I don't drink!" A grin slipped free, was smothered as he regained control, and slipped free again. "Shit," he chuckled softly, rubbing a hand over his face and through his hair. "I'm not drunk. Just... feel a little weird."

"That weird feeling would be drunk." Con grinned teasingly. Tim probably wasn't drunk, but definitely relaxed. He tipped back his second.

Tim snickered, tried to stop, apparently couldn't, and hid his mouth behind his hand.

"Good God, you are drunk."

Tim curled into the corner of the couch, pulling his feet up under him and studiously not looking at Con. One finger traced patterns on the arm of the sofa, the other rubbing up and down his shin, flannel pants dragging along his flesh. "Just *tipsy*," he murmured with a smile.

Con stared as an ankle appeared, then vanished beneath cloth. He took another sip of beer and reminded himself that Tim didn't like to be touched. "So," he said, trying to anchor his thoughts in something other than seduction, "is it so bad breaking up with Cassie?"

Sighing, Tim leaned on his arm, flexible enough to fold over his own legs and brace his chin on his hand. "I guess not." The words sounded slightly crushed. "But I hate finding someone new to date. It's so... unpleasant."

Con snorted. "Unpleasant. Yeah."

Tim came to his feet in one graceful motion, pacing the room. His fingertips slid along the bottom of a picture frame, then brushed over his computer screen. He paused to feel Con's leather jacket left lying on the back of a barstool, then picked the coat up and sniffed it clinically, set it down, and picked it up again. He rubbed it between his fingers, compact body going still, and lifted it once more to smell. Eyes half-lidded, thumb skimming back and forth over brown leather, his chest rose as he inhaled softly.

Con dragged his gaze away, feeling blood stir in places that weren't going to be getting any attention from Tim tonight. Not even, sadly, if he were interested.

"You're fidgety." Con stared hard at his beer to keep from standing up and pressing against Tim instead. He could think of all *sorts* of ways to burn off fidgets.

"Yeah. I guess." Tim put the jacket down and walked to the window, staring out at the dark sky. "I keep thinking I should be more upset about Cassie. You know?"

Con stared at the way Tim's T-shirt fell, soft and supple from narrow shoulders, pooling briefly around his hips. "Maybe you're ready to move on. Maybe you never really liked her that much." Then a thought hit him, and he frowned. "Do you have anyone around here that you do like that much?"

"I only date one girl at a time, Con." Laughing, Tim glanced back over his shoulder, his blue eyes bright. "Some of us can't lure several people at once."

Con snorted. "You obviously think highly of my skills," he said into his bottle. He drank, then continued, "I mean, do you even have close friends around here?" He couldn't remember Tim talking about anyone—not the way people talked about those who meant something, anyway.

Tim frowned. "Cassie."

"But you're not upset about her," Con pointed out.

His hands slid over the windowsill. "Rick. Ricky."

"Your Big Brother, right?" Con clarified. If that was the case, then Tim had known Rick for almost ten years, when the older man had joined the Big Brother group and they'd been paired together.

"Yeah." Tim shrugged, tense. "I've been busy. You know, school, work..."

"Yeah, sure," Con agreed, mostly to placate the other man.

Still standing at the window, Tim relaxed, then finally turned to face Con, hands braced on the sill. He smiled. It flickered away, came back. "And you. I mean, I've known you *forever*."

He lifted his bottle in a silent toast. "And I will always be here, man. You're not getting rid of me easily."

For an instant, he could have sworn he saw relief flicker across Tim's pale face. Then the instant was gone, and Tim flopped back onto the couch, one leg over the side and his arm along the back, bicep resting partially on Con's hand. "I know. You're annoying, but I'll keep you around."

Con leaned in, smelling the clean scent of shampoo and soap, the light mint that was Tim. He could just wrap his hand around a muscular shoulder and tug him those last few inches, close the distance between them. He didn't. "Good." He purred the word into Tim's ear, and saw him go very still. "Because I'm not leaving." His breath whispered over pale skin, tickling the tiny hairs that grew soft around the hairline.

Tim looked up at Con slowly, just his eyes moving. Then, still hesitantly, he slid back, putting a little more space between them. He swallowed, tongue peeking out to lick his lips, pupils dilating. "Well, uh, good. Because... Yeah."

He looked confused. The tiny voice that served as Con's conscience managed to nag him enough that he shifted back, giving Tim space and easing up on the sex appeal.

Tim broke eye contact, swallowed again, and blinked at the far wall. "I mean," he repeated after a minute, "that's good."

With a smile, Con finished his beer.

Tim spent a restless night, blood feeling too hot in his veins, the sheets rasping against his skin every time he moved. Masturbating in the shower the following morning only helped slightly, and all he could think about that afternoon was getting home to Con.

He had no idea what they had planned, or even if they had anything planned, but every time he thought about Con his mouth went dry and he began to sweat. He couldn't decide if he liked it or hated it, but one thing was certain: he was obsessed with his best friend.

He was sitting in the doctors' lounge trying not to

think about Con when a nurse came in, her face flushed and her hair sticking to her temples. "Dr. Shelton?" she asked, looking straight at him. "Dr. Westfall said you'd be in here—"

"Yes, that's me." His words came out warily.

"There's a man in the ER asking for you. You'd better hurry."

He put aside his sandwich and followed her down the stairs—they were faster than the elevator—wondering who it might be and why. When she pointed to the OR, he dragged on yellow surgery scrubs and went in, confusion swept away by concern.

Then he saw the man on the table, blood smearing naked flesh and still pumping out of a chest wound. He didn't see much more before the identity registered.

Brown hair. Dark eyes. A strong jaw, broad shoulders trimming down into a slim waist— "Con," he said.

A nearly black gaze focused on him, hazed with pain or drugs. Probably both. People moved, hurrying around, requesting things as someone pushed a syringe of fluids into an IV. Tim ignored all of it. "What happened?" He darted around a tray of instruments to get to Con's head.

"Hey." Con's eyes didn't quite focus as he smiled up. "I think someone got shot."

"He got *shot*?" Tim nearly shouted, looking up.

"If you're going to act like a civilian, you'll have to leave," the surgeon snapped.

"Sorry." Chastised, he looked back down.

"You've got thirty seconds, Dr. Shelton." The anesthesiologist was already prepping.

"You'll be fine," Tim murmured, looking down at Con. "And I'll be here when you wake up."

"Sure." Con's words slurred. "But you might want to see to the guy who got shot." Then the drugs took effect, and he was under.

They shoved Tim out of the way, closing off veins and arteries, opening Con's chest to yank out bullets.

Tim left to give them room. Much as he wanted to stay, to do it himself and make sure that it was done right, the other surgeon was experienced at emergency surgery, and Tim wasn't. Con had a better chance without him taking up space.

He yanked off the yellow scrubs and stuffed them in the trash, realizing he was shaking as he went back into the hall.

"Dr. Shelton?"

He jumped, head snapping up. A uniformed officer stood there, waiting patiently. "Yes?" he managed.

"Do you know," the cop paused, opening a wallet, "Mr. Lemor?"

"Yes," he said again. Mr. Lemor was in the emergency room, bleeding all over the table, skin too pale, size not helping him at all anymore. He wondered if the doctors had taken shock into account, then reminded himself that they knew their jobs.

"We've been trying to track down his family—"

He shook his head, trying to rattle thoughts into moving. "I—they're in Florida. We're friends. I have their phone number..." He started to pat his pockets, then frowned and tried to focus. "At home. I can get it...?"

"Please do," the officer said. "I'd appreciate that." After a moment, the man added, "Do you need a ride?"

He stared blankly at the hospital corridor, at people hurrying to and fro, where Con wasn't. Because Con was in surgery. "Yeah," he said finally. "That might be best."

"This way, then." With a hand on his elbow, the policeman escorted him out of the hospital.

Tim hovered in the doorway of the ICU room, gaze traveling over the tubes that snaked into Con. None of the lines indicated he was in serious danger. There were antibiotics, to stave off possible infection. An IV carried saline and pain meds. An oxygen tube threaded under his nostrils, but it was only supportive.

Surgery had gone well; they'd gotten the bullet out, then found a few bone fragments and pulled those out, too. Con was going to have an interesting scar, but he'd live.

His grandparents were coming to get him. They'd already boarded a plane. They'd told the police that Tim could have all the information, so the cop had filled him in.

A robbery. A couple of teenagers had held up a convenience store. Con had been buying batteries for the smoke detector. Tim had let it run down, and the beeping drove Con buggy. When the teenagers started waving around guns, the clerk had emptied the register while the customers ducked for cover. The robbers had just about left when a little kid spooked—they didn't know why, or how he'd gotten away from his mother—and bolted past Con, into the main aisle. The teenager had already panicked at the child's movement, whipping around. Con made a bigger, more threatening target.

The boy was all right. Con was shot. One teen had been caught five minutes later, the other turned himself in. Both were in jail.

Con had just been in the wrong place at the wrong time.

He stared at his best friend, drugged and bandaged and frighteningly pale. Con's vitals were good, and that was something. He was young, strong, he'd be just fine. Bounce right back.

Another officer and another accident kept

superimposing other memories over this one. Tim remembered staring up at the police officer, looking from the woman to his headmaster and back again, saying only, "I don't understand."

The cop had looked frustrated, uncomfortable. It was his headmaster who had dropped down to one knee, down to Tim's level, to explain that his parents wouldn't be coming to get him for summer break. To explain about the drunk driver, what that meant, talking to him like he was five instead of eleven. They'd been in the wrong place at the wrong time.

His vision wavered. He blinked rapidly, startling when someone called his name. A glance into the hall showed Grace, her dark hair pulled back into a severe knot, leaving olive-colored skin tight across high cheekbones and a delicately pointed chin.

"Are you all right?" she asked, pausing with a hand on his arm, glancing into the room where Con lay.

"Yeah. Sure." Tim shrugged, twisting so her hand fell away. "I'm just not used to being on this end of a patient."

Grace's eyes searched his face. "Call if you need anything," she said, and continued down the hall, scrubs swishing with every step.

The intercom scratched to life, paging a doctor. Machines beeped softly, echoing against tile and plaster. Footsteps were muffled; soft-soled shoes, so the patients could rest.

"Yeah. Sure," he heard himself say again. He stared at Con, at the sheet so white it was almost blue. Con snuffled, eyes opening.

"Tim?" His voice was less than a croak.

Tim took a single lurching step into the room, as if the power of his name alone could force him forward. "Yeah."

Con blinked, trying to look around. "Oh, ow." He relaxed against the pillow, his face pale.

"Here. I'm here." Tim walked forward into Con's line of sight. He checked the EKG read-out, then pulled his penlight out of his pocket and flashed it in Con's eyes. Familiar movements made him feel safe, in control of the world again. Con's pupils contracted normally, though his heart rate was slow.

"I hurt." Con swallowed twice before he got the words out.

Tim fussed with the morphine drip, not caring that it was going to make Con more woozy.

"What happened?" Con whispered, dark eyes falling closed. Heavy lashes lay on his pale skin.

"You were shot. No more heroics." Tim did his best to keep his tone brusque, and suspected he more than succeeded.

Con's eyes opened again, glassy and unfocused. "I died."

"No, you didn't."

"I saw a bright light."

"That was the ambulance."

"It hurt."

"That," Tim said, voice desert-dry, "was the bullet." He thought, then added, "And the surgery."

Con stared at him as steadily as a drugged man could, as if trying to discern truth by eyes alone. "I had to tell you something." The words were almost a question.

Tim waited, hands still at his sides.

"I—are you sure I'm not dead? I don't feel anything..."

Rather than point out that Con had been complaining of pain a moment before, Tim reached out and put his hand on a muscular forearm. The arm shifted, twisting, until a large hand caught his fingers.

"Oh." Con smiled, relieved. "That's good."

Tim stood very still, skin warm and tingling, trying to make his heart beat normally.

"Timmy." Con sighed, eyes closing.

"Don't call me that."

Con's lips twitched, curling lazily into a smile. Lifting his hand, he pulled their interlocked fingers to his face. Tim took a step forward, half wincing as he expected the injury to stop his friend's movement. Apparently, though, he'd given Con too much morphine. It didn't matter. The drug would knock him out and he'd stop moving, anyway.

"Timmy," Con murmured again, lips moving against their fingers. "Had to tell you..."

Tim swallowed, watching Con's mouth slide against his knuckles, breath warm and damp over his skin.

"...love with you."

For a long moment, the words didn't quite register. Then they did.

Tim yanked his hand back, nearly skidding across the room. Con was unconscious, breathing even, heart rate slow. Tim stared at the sleeping man, trying to erase the words from the air, trying to convince himself that it was just the drugs talking.

People said crazy things when they were drugged. That was all it was. Drugs.

Shaking, sweating, his stomach in knots, he backed toward the door and fled from the room.

Chapter Three

Rick folded another mat and shoved it into one of the cupboards that ran along a wall of the dojo, keeping half an eye on the young man echoing his movements. At some point, he'd figured Tim would break and talk. So far, though, Tim had proven decidedly unbreakable. It had to be something bad. Something worse than the shooting, which Tim had been willing to talk about right away. Rick headed toward the thermostat, turning the air conditioner off for the night, then wandered into his office. "Want a drink?" he called out onto the floor.

"Sure," Tim answered.

Rick pulled two bottles of Gatorade out of the little refrigerator and kicked back in his chair. A moment later Tim walked in, obviously feigning nonchalance. He caught the bottle that Rick tossed, then dropped onto the futon against one wall.

Rick waited.

Tim twisted off the cap and drank.

Rick waited.

Tim peeled the label free and let the shreds flutter into the trashcan.

Rick waited.

Tim sighed and stood. "I guess I should be going—"

"Sit your scrawny ass down," Rick growled, giving up. No one could outwait Timothy. "What is wrong?"

"Nothing." The word was spoken only grudgingly as he lowered himself back onto the folded futon. "Why would you think something was?"

"Because you just spent three hours helping me teach beginning martial arts to kids under twelve," Rick pointed out. "You don't even *like* kids under twelve. Don't insult my intelligence."

Tim sulked. It was hard to tell the difference between his 'leave me alone' face and his 'sulking' face, but Rick had gotten good at it over the years.

"Just a long week." It was barely even a mumble.

Rick frowned. He sipped neon-red Gatorade and pondered Tim. Maybe it was the shooting. God knew that'd be enough for anyone, and it'd be just like him, Rick thought, to try and ignore the whole thing. "You still freaked out over your Internet friend getting shot?"

Tim glared up, then back down at his bottle. "He's not an Internet friend, I didn't freak out, and no. His grandparents picked him up two days ago. I'm sure he's fine."

Rick's eyebrows rose. "You don't know?" It wasn't like the little control freak not to know if someone he cared about was all right or not.

Tim shrugged again. "I think I would've heard if something bad happened."

Rick pondered that tidbit, and wondered what to ask next. Tim saved him.

"Have you ever had someone say something, and you were pretty sure they were serious but you weren't positive, and you really wished they hadn't said it?" The tone was casual, but Tim's intent study of his bottle suggested the question wasn't.

It took Rick a moment to translate that sentence. Then he thought, trying to remember a similar case. "Yeah," he said finally. "I have."

Tim looked up, blue eyes meeting Rick's from under thick lashes. "What did you do?"

"What happened, Tim?" Rick asked quietly.

"Con—" Tim stopped. Frowned. Started again. "He was high on morphine, so who knows what was going on in his brain, right? He just... said... this thing. I didn't like." Suddenly, he was very interested in scratching something off the plastic bottle.

"What did he say?"

Rick almost didn't catch the mumble. From the way Tim's ears turned pink, he was already wishing he hadn't said it. Rick sat for a while, letting his mind process, until the words percolated into his brain. Rick's eyebrows rose. "Oh."

Tim's ears upgraded from pink to red.

"Well," Rick said, treading carefully, "I suppose there's just one important thing."

Tim eyed him.

"Do you like him back?"

Rick supposed he should have anticipated the explosion. Tim's head snapped up, fire crackling in his clear blue eyes. "I'm not gay!"

"Who said anything about being gay?" Rick put his hands out, palms up.

"If I like Con, then I like guys, then I'm—"

"You know, there was this guy in the seventies who did this sexual study—"

"Kinsey, and it was in the forties." Tim glowered.

"Yeah, that's it," Rick continued blithely. "He said that sexuality is on a sliding scale and everyone is a little bisexual. Maybe you just like Con." He thought it was brilliant, himself. Besides, Tim was gay. Everyone knew it but Tim. Hell, the very few movies he owned were an almost complete collection of Johnny Depp films. Tim thought *Benny and Joon* was the ultimate date flick. If that wasn't gay, Rick didn't know what was.

"I'm not gay," Tim repeated softly, staring into the middle space.

"So, what are you going to do?" Rick asked, somewhere between annoyed and resigned.

"Repress," Tim muttered. "Repress like never before."

Rick laughed helplessly, standing and sauntering to the mini-fridge. "Yeah, because you need to be wound tighter. Mark my words, Tim, you're going to pop if you don't relax a little." He opened the door and peered into the pristine white shelves. "Beer?"

"Why is everyone trying to get me drunk lately?"

The question was rhetorical. Rick raised both eyebrows; Tim just shook his head. After pulling out another Gatorade and closing the door, Rick wandered back to his chair. There had to be a way to get around Tim's gay-block. "How's Cassie?"

"Broke up with me," Tim said forlornly. "She's headed to New York."

"She's, what? Your fifth girlfriend in four years?"

He nodded, shrugging. "Something like that."

"And what's your longest relationship?" Rick watched as Tim's eyes narrowed, suspicion entering them.

"Three months. Cass."

"And you don't think that's a little odd?"

"Fuck off." Tim muttered it into the mouth of his bottle.

Rick chuckled. "Did you even have sex with any of them?"

Tim's ears turned pink again. "I was respecting their wishes! God! A guy can't be nice without being accused of being gay?"

"Did any of them actually wish to not have sex?"

Tim's mouth opened. Closed. Opened. "I thought all women wanted to wait or something."

"Jesus, Tim." Rick snorted. "How far *did* you get?"

His ears went brighter.

"You *have* kissed a girl, right?" Sometimes, the kid was just *so* amusing.

"Fuck you!" Tim yelled. "Yes, I've kissed girls!"

"Felt 'em up?" Rick asked cheerfully.

"I—I—yes!" Slouching back into the corner, Tim looked like he couldn't decide whether to be belligerent or mortified.

"Got a hard-on at the thought of titties?"

"I'm not talking to you about this." Tim crossed his arms over his chest, fuming. "And 'titties'? Who says *that*?" He took a sip, then continued almost before he'd swallowed. "Besides, maybe I'm frigid. Did you think about that?"

"Do you have sexual fantasies?" Rick shot back. "Wake up with a hard-on? Masturbate?" Tim's ever-deepening blush spoke volumes. "Then you're not frigid," Rick finished. He started to drink, then put his bottle down. "When you do jerk off, what do you think of?"

"Rick!"

"No, really," he said calmly. "It's healthy to talk about this stuff, you know. Breasts? Lips? Girls? Another guy? Multiple people?"

Closing his eyes, Tim clenched his teeth and swallowed, jaw muscle popping. "What people fantasize about isn't always what would turn them on in reality."

"Huh." After a moment, Rick added happily, "I fantasize about multiple people. I used to have bondage fantasies—where're you going?"

Tim stood, glaring at him. "Thanks for the Gatorade."

He headed for the door.

"Hey! Tim!" Rick called, unable to quench his laughter.

The young man stopped.

"Email Con. If he was talking drugged, he probably never meant to say it, or doesn't remember that he did. Give the guy a break, huh?"

Narrow shoulders stiffened. Then Tim nodded, once, and headed out of the dojo.

Rick sighed and leaned back in his chair, feet on the cluttered desk. He didn't know if he felt worse for Tim or for Con.

"I fucked up."

"Language, Conner," his grandmother chided, fussing with dinner in the kitchen. "It can't be that bad. You've been friends for years; whatever you said might put a wrinkle in your relationship, but Tim'll return your calls eventually."

Con didn't bother arguing with Grams. Once she'd decided something, nothing could sway her. "Where's Papa?" He glanced idly around the little house.

"He's out watching the transvestites," she informed him cheerfully. "So he can understand you better."

Con blanched. "Grams! I'm not a *transvestite*, I'm gay!"

"I know, sweetheart," she laughed, "but you're also his excuse. He's really fascinated with the trannies."

"Trannies?" Con echoed, disturbed. "Where'd you hear the term 'tranny'?"

"Oh, television, I'm sure." She paused, wooden spoon to her mouth. "Or maybe from Ed. Down the street." The spoon fluttered, dismissing the topic. "He's a tranny like you."

"I'm not—" Con stopped, seeing the wicked twinkle in her eye. "You're very funny," he grumbled.

Grams chuckled.

Con stared out the window at the cars passing by down the little residential street, everything dripping green. Florida was nothing if not *wet*. And not in a fun way, either. He missed Chicago. He missed San Diego. He really wished he'd gotten to see Tim before his grandparents had flown him to their home to recuperate, but Tim hadn't returned his calls even when they'd both been in the same hospital. There was nothing as frustrating as knowing that, somewhere on a floor above you, your best friend was completely ignoring your calls.

He'd debated blaming his words on the drugs. Lying, saying that he hadn't meant it, that of *course* he didn't love Tim. But he wouldn't lie. He wouldn't betray himself like that. On the other hand, Tim wasn't speaking to him, so maybe lying would be worth it. Fuck it all to hell and back.

Two inches to the right and the bullet would've killed him, solving all these problems. Stupid bullet. Stupid Tim. Stupid robbers. Stupid morphine. Really, really stupid Con. He picked up his cell phone and started to punch in a text message.

Tim's phone beeped twice. He ignored it.

Gay. He wasn't *gay*. Not even remotely. So the girls he'd dated had never really done it for him—so what? He was picky. Really picky. And sure, sometimes he looked at other guys, but that was just aesthetic appreciation. It wasn't like he walked around ogling asses. Or crotches.

He dropped the weights into their rack, glowering

at steel as if it were responsible for his thoughts. A man walked past, muscles bulging out of everywhere, and Tim found his eyes dropping lower, to hip-level—

Shit! He yanked his gaze back up, realized it was lingering on broad shoulders and the sweat-slick line of a spine—

He closed his eyes. Okay, but that didn't prove anything. It was just because he was thinking about it. Besides, everyone looked. Right? Right. He was spazzing out, and over what? Nothing! The opinions of someone else—okay, a few someone elses—and a stupid, drugged statement made by his best friend.

Rick's response kept floating through his mind, pinging him at inopportune moments. *"Do you like him back?"*

He didn't want to think about that. It made his stomach flutter. Besides, he wasn't gay.

Rick jumped when the voice started shouting at him over the phone. "You stupid asshole!" Tim yelled, louder than Rick had ever heard him.

"What did I do?" He tried to keep the question neutral, but suspected Tim could hear his near-laughter. An angry Tim was always amusing. Even though he really could be deadly, his size made it hard to take him seriously. Rick always thought he looked like an enraged hamster on the rare occasions when he actually got upset.

"Thanks to you, I keep checking out guys! It's driving me crazy!"

"Oh, no," Rick laughed. "You're not pinning this on me. I just made you aware of what you'd been looking at, that's all."

"Bullshit. Open your fucking door."

Frowning, Rick got up and walked to his front door,

pulling it open.

An old Mazda rocked to a halt inches from his garage. Tim got out, storming around the back of the car, closing his phone as he came. "Now what? Now what the hell am I supposed to do?"

Rick hung up his phone, seeing what Tim wouldn't want him to see: not anger, but panic.

"How am I supposed to know if I'm gay or straight or—or—fucking bisexual!"

"Come on." Rick stepped aside to let the other man in, regretting that he'd pushed quite so hard. Tim didn't do things by halves; he took an idea, looked it over, and if it had merit, he embraced it wholeheartedly. Everyone else in the world took baby steps, but Tim always jumped into the deep end. He looked first, sure, but looking didn't stop him from diving. When the deep end changed the entire way you lived, viewed yourself, and identified, it had to be scary.

"Beer?" Rick offered, walking through the small house and back toward the kitchen.

"Fuck, no." Tim stalked into the living room, bringing his own personal storm cloud with him. He crashed down onto the couch, arms crossed over his stomach.

Rick reached the refrigerator and opened a bottle anyway. "Help you relax," he said as he wandered out to Tim, clinking the beer down on the coffee table.

Tim didn't even acknowledge it was there. "I spent forty-five minutes just walking through the gym. Just wandering, staring at people. Men, women." He frowned. "Not children, obviously..."

"What did you decide?" Rick asked before Tim could sneak off on a tangent.

Elbows braced on his spread knees, Tim ducked his

head far enough to rub the back of his neck, nearly burying his face in his arms. "The guys are more attractive. I look at them more," he mumbled. "But the girls are attractive, too! And how do I know I'm not just looking to see what my competition is? Or to compare myself to them? Or maybe I just think they're attractive, but when it comes right down to it there's no way I'd be interested in handling someone else's dick!" He looked up, black hair falling in pleading blue eyes.

"Is the thought a turn-off?" Rick leaned against the door between the kitchen and living room.

Tim's eyes slid away. "I don't know."

"You could try." He could practically see the emotional recoil in the slant of Tim's shoulders.

"What, go have sex with some random guy? I don't think so."

"Rent gay porn." Rick grinned. "If it's hot..."

Tim's ears turned pink. "Just... just walk into an adult movie store and... and..."

"Rent porn," Rick finished for him. "And yes, walk. They look down on it when you skip."

Tim shot him a dirty look. "I can't do that."

"What, skip? It's easy," Rick teased.

"Rent porn," Tim growled.

"Poor, repressed little man." With a mocking sigh, Rick shook his head. "Get it off the Internet. That's what the Web's there for."

"And put spyware on my computer?" Tim looked aghast.

"Okay, fine. Live in uncertainty and frustration. See if I care."

Tim stood, his car keys in one hand. "Fuck it. I'll figure something out," he muttered, his brow furrowed. "I'm smart. I'm a fucking genius. I can figure this out."

"Keep telling yourself that." Rick followed Tim to the door and watched him get into his car. The headlights came on and the Mazda pulled carefully out of the drive. "And good luck," he added with a sigh.

Tim never did anything without a plan. So while he continued to ignore Con's calls (and text messages, and emails, and instant messages—which was a shitty thing to do and he *knew* that, but he just didn't know what to say), he researched. He started with 'gay.' He looked at theories on why and how it happened, and the different lifestyles of gay people throughout history, then recently, then locally. He researched 'the gay scene' and discovered there was a whole culture. It seemed as confused and frustrated as the straight culture, once he got past the hullabaloo. He checked out message boards, and finally decided that gay people seemed to make connections through gay bars, just like straight people made connections through straight bars.

He also realized he'd known all this just from being alive for twenty-six years. Still, the researching made him feel somewhat in control.

Tim didn't drink, and he didn't like crowds, but at least a gay bar was a place to start. Maybe something there would give him a definitive, "Yes! You're a flaming homosexual!" or a, "Hell, no! Get out of here and find a vagina!"

Of course, he should have known it wouldn't work so well after he'd spent fifteen minutes staring at his closet, wondering what the hell he was supposed to wear at a gay bar. He finally went with roughed-up jeans, artfully torn, and a slim, long-sleeved T-shirt. Then he got in his car and drove to downtown San Diego. Specifically, Hillcrest.

He regretted his decision half an hour later, crushed against a crowded bar, hoping a table would open up and he could at least sit somewhere where he wasn't constantly drawing inward, away from the other people. He'd forgotten how *much* he hated bars: the noise, the press, the drinking.

"Buy you something?"

He didn't even bother to glance over. "No. Thanks." Okay, so obviously this wasn't the way he needed to be meeting people.

"You sure? What are you drinking? You waiting for someone?" The man slid onto the barstool beside Tim, crowding him.

"I'm sure." Boy, was he ever sure. He stepped down and pushed away.

"Aw, c'mon, Tasty."

Tim turned around, both eyebrows lifting incredulously. For a moment he considered telling the guy off. Then he just shook his head, elbowing through the crowd toward the door. It wasn't worth the fight.

The night air was cool, almost too chilly. He leaned back against the brick building, dragging his hands through his hair and leaving them braced on his head. This had been a rotten idea. There must be another way to figure out if he was *really* gay or not. He was pretty sure he was at least a little gay—could you be a little gay?—or he wouldn't be here, but... hell.

"Tim?"

He put his hands down and glared up.

A blond was standing in the doorway of the bar. Tim nearly cringed as the blond smiled slowly.

"I thought that was you." Peter walked out, putting his hands in his pockets. "I didn't think you were into the bar scene. Or gay."

Tim stood, staring out at the dark. "Apparently, I'm

not," he grumbled.

Peter laughed. "Hey, man, you look miserable. Why don't we go get coffee? You can tell me what's wrong?"

The last thing in the world Tim wanted was to tell Peter what was wrong. But then, he didn't want to be standing there talking to Peter either, and he was. Fuck it all. Figuring out this whole gay thing meant he had to talk to *someone* gay. At least he knew Peter wasn't a serial killer—just a mediocre doctor.

"Sure." Tim kept glaring at the sky. "Coffee."

"So, you need to find someone to screw around with."

Tim stared levelly at the other man until Peter looked up. "No," he said firmly. He already wished he hadn't told Peter as much as he had—which was almost everything, leaving out Con. "And if you make the offer, you'll be proving me right." When Peter looked confused, Tim added, "About how much of an ass you can be."

Peter snorted and stirred his nearly untouched drink. "Well, my piece of advice? You're gay. I mean, if you're contemplating it, then you are. It almost always works out that way."

Tim frowned and looked away, glaring out the window at the dark street. "It's not that easy. What if I start dating someone and then realize I'm straight?" He thought of Con, and tried to banish the image. His mind supplied images of playing volleyball at the beach, Con bare-chested across from him, sweaty and grinning, muscles hard under smooth skin— Fuck.

"So date someone who already knows the risks," Peter suggested. Then he grinned, smirking. "I volunteer."

"You're a dick," Tim muttered under his breath.

"But an available dick. You can at least see if it interests you, right?"

Tim stared at his coffee. He sipped, then set it back down. He didn't even like coffee.

"Timm-mmy," Peter laughed. "It's perfect!"

Tim pointed with his spoon, eyes hard. "Don't call me that."

Hands up in surrender, Peter whistled quietly. "Sorry."

Tim returned to glaring at his coffee. He needed to know, and soon. One way or another. Con was coming back to San Diego—assuming his plans hadn't changed—and Tim needed to know by then. He needed an answer.

"Love with you," Con sighed.

"Do you like him?" Rick asked.

"Tim?"

He flinched, eyes snapping up. "Sorry. Just thinking."

"Yeah, you do that a lot." Peter smiled. "What were you thinking about?"

Tim couldn't tell him the truth. He hesitated a moment, then said, "We could try it. Dating. But I'm probably not gay."

Leaning back, Peter smirked and tucked his hands behind his head. The movement showed off slim muscles. "I'll change your mind."

"And if you're an ass, we stop," Tim snapped.

Peter just laughed.

To: T.dot.Shelton@yahoo.com
From: superdude2467@gmail.com

Tim—i'm sorry. please call me.
-C

Con hit 'send' and sat back, looking gloomily at the screen. The footsteps behind him were soft, but not soft enough. "Hey, Grams."

Her hands settled on his shoulders, one on each side. Her tone was almost sad. "You don't have to go to San Diego. I'm sure they need firefighters here in Florida."

He smiled humorlessly. "Yeah, but Florida's not for me."

His grandmother was quiet for a long moment. When she spoke, he barely heard her. "But a friend who ignores you because of a slip... that's for you?"

Con didn't answer.

Tim closed his locker, banging the latch until it held. "So."

He glanced sidelong at the blond who thumped up against the row, blocking an easy exit.

"Yeah?" Warily, Tim glanced around. No one was there except for him and Peter; the other doctors were already either on shift or gone.

"What do you want to do tonight?"

Tim edged away, wanting more personal space than Peter seemed to think was necessary. "I have martial arts tonight." He pulled his lab coat on over his shirt.

"I'll pick you up after."

He stepped around Peter, but the man dogged his heels. "I don't get out until nine," Tim said dissuasively.

"Nine it is. Where should I come get you?"

Irritation surfaced, and he tossed a look over his shoulder. "Don't."

"Hey, you're the one who wanted to try dating, remember?" Peter said, annoyance clear.

Tim stopped before they entered the main office, not

wanting their coworkers to be privy to this conversation. "Fine," he said at last. "You can get me at the Keeton Dojo at nine-thirty. Not before."

"Yes, sir." Peter gave a mock salute and grinned.

Tim ignored him, hurrying off.

"So... New girl?" Rick leaned against the doorway of the little bathroom in the back of the dojo, watching Tim's reflection as he whipped a brush through still-wet hair. The place was too small for a full-sized locker room, but the bathroom had a standing shower.

"No," Tim said expressionlessly.

Rick thought about it. "New guy?" he asked curiously, one eyebrow rising.

Tim's expression got a little bit blacker. Not enough for any normal person to notice, but Rick had made an art out of reading Tim's expressions. "Sort of. Just to see."

"To see? To see what?" Then Rick put the pieces together. "Tim! You can't just go out with a random guy to see if you're gay!"

Tim's reflected gaze met his for an instant, then broke away. "He's not random. I know him from work."

"Do you like him?" The lack of an answer was answer enough. "Tim," Rick groaned, "being gay is just like being straight. You can't expect to be attracted to *every* girl you meet, and you can't expect to be attracted to *every* guy."

"It's at least a place to start." A frown creased the skin between Tim's brows.

Rick was going to continue arguing, half afraid that if Tim didn't find himself attracted to this guy he'd just declare himself straight, whether or not he was, and that would be the end of it. Then the chimes above the front door rang, and a voice called out, "Hello?"

"That's Peter." Tim buckled his watch on. "I'm leaving my car here. I'll be back for it later."

Rick stepped aside to let him out, then followed behind. Peter wasn't much bigger than Tim, a little taller, a little more rangy. Blond hair and blue eyes. A mouth that fell into a smirking leer before straightening into a smile. Rick didn't like him. He could see from the way Tim didn't relax, tension still riding in his shoulders and spine, that Tim didn't particularly like the guy, either. Rick resisted the urge to hit something.

"Have fun," he said as the two men walked out the front door.

Peter looked back at him curiously, and then the door closed between them.

Rick cursed and began picking up mats.

Tim supposed the date had gone well. He had spent most of the night looking at other people, trying to decide if they were staring at him, out with another guy. In San Diego he was as likely to get catcalls as insults, but he couldn't stop himself.

"You could probably afford a nicer car," Peter remarked, pulling up beside Tim's Mazda.

"Or I could pay down my student loans faster." Tim unbuckled his seatbelt. The mythical doctor wealth hadn't shown up yet, and while what his parents had left him had paid for most of his tuition, there hadn't been enough to cover living expenses as well as medical school.

The government took good care of rich kids, right up until they weren't legally kids anymore. Very careful budgeting had stretched his inheritance a while longer; he hadn't had to get a job until the last year of medical school, and then he'd started his internship. He couldn't keep a job while working as a student doctor, so student loans had been necessary. The Mazda, while a bit beat up, ran well and was cheap to fix. In fact, Rick had a friend who did most of the fixing. Jay had been a lifesaver more than a few times.

"You're gonna pay down your student loans when you start making money, and you *will* start making money." Peter turned his car off—a silver BMW that he'd bought used and probably still paid too much for—and climbed out.

Tim shrugged, sliding out of the two-door and digging his keys out of his pocket. A glance toward the dojo showed a light on in the back office. Rick was still there. The man practically lived in the office, sometimes. When he'd first started the dojo he actually had, unable to pay rent on an apartment and the building. It was a nice place, though, with the futon in the back.

Tim paused a moment, knowing that if Rick was still around he'd appreciate Tim poking his head in to say he'd returned safely. Of course, if he didn't poke his head in, Rick would just look out the window and see his car was gone, and he'd settle for that, too. All in all, Rick was fairly easy-going.

It seemed like a better idea to go inside, if for no other reason than that Tim wanted to see a friendly face. He took a step away from his car, then realized Peter had moved closer. The other man's presence prickled along his skin unpleasantly. He glanced over.

Peter looked from him to the dojo and back. "What, is he your keeper?" He laughed.

"Not exactly." Tim didn't bother to explain that Rick was the closest thing to family he had. That would require explaining the whole orphan thing, and his personal business was none of Peter's.

Peter's gaze sharpened, then relaxed. He gave a resigned shrug and started walking toward the dojo.

Tim hesitated, unsure why. Then he chided himself on being stupid and stepped forward, catching up in two long strides and arriving at the door with Peter.

Reaching out, Peter tried the handle. "Locked."

Tim fussed with his keys, sorting through them. Car key, spare key, apartment key, locker key, key to the medical supplies, key to a padlock he'd long since lost, key to Rick's house—

"Christ, Tim," Peter snorted. "What are you, the key master?"

—key to his last foster home even though he hadn't been there in six years, and—he pulled the important one free—key to the dojo. Tim fitted it into the lock, gave the special twist-and-jiggle it needed, and felt the bolt slide open.

Peter chuckled. "Does that mean I get to be the gate-keeper?"

Tim turned to look at him, annoyance carefully hidden. "Well, thanks." He wondered why Peter was still hovering, and what exactly he should do to tell the guy to go away.

Peter smiled slightly. Tim had a disconcerting moment where he thought the smile hadn't reached Peter's eyes, but he gave himself a mental shake.

"Don't I get a goodnight kiss?" Peter's voice was low and smooth. Too smooth; like silk sheets, it sounded good, but when you laid down you slipped right off and banged your ass on the floor.

Tim glanced around, half looking for observers, half stalling for time. Peter, to his credit, waited for an answer before coming any closer. One hand still on the keys in the door, Tim traced the outline of the knob with his thumb. He supposed if he were out with a girl he'd figure on a kiss by the second-ish date, even though coffee hadn't really been a first date. It wasn't an unreasonable request, though.

"Sure," he mumbled, still staring out at the parking lot. Looking at Peter was too hard, too intimate, somehow, in a way a kiss didn't have to be. He felt Peter shift, heard a humorless laugh, and fingers brushed along his jaw, pulling his face around. Peter's mouth closed over his, hand still a whisper touch on his skin.

It wasn't unlike kissing a girl, Tim thought clinically. Not quite as soft, nor as poofy. Girl lips had always seemed inordinately swollen to him, like squishing up against a damp pillow. Peter's lips were dry, without the benefit of moisturizer and lipstick, and thin.

The angle was odd; Peter was a few inches taller than Tim. Not noticeable when they were talking—Tim was used to looking up at people—but strange when kissing. He'd only dated one girl taller than he was.

Peter's mouth opened, his tongue sweeping over Tim's lips. Tim jumped. Chuckling, Peter pulled back until his mouth only brushed softly, without pressure. "So tense." His fingers curled until his knuckles brushed up and down Tim's jawline. "Relax."

The hand along his face only made him more tense, though. He took a deep breath, willing his muscles to release. It worked marginally, might have worked better if his deep breath hadn't included Peter's scent. It was like sour apples and martini olives, neither one a smell he was particularly fond of.

"That's better." Peter's tone implied it was only a *little* bit better.

Peter stepped closer, close enough so that when Tim inhaled he could feel another chest. He resisted the urge to back up. Putting his hands on Peter's waist gave him control over just how close he'd let Peter come.

Peter kissed him again, tongue sliding over his lower lip. After a moment's debate Tim opened his mouth, allowing the kiss to deepen. It was okay, he supposed, but no better than with a girl. Then Peter tried to edge closer again, and Tim dug his thumbs in just above the man's hipbones. Peter pulled back, and for a moment Tim saw consideration in those blue eyes. His guard went up, expression carefully neutral so as not to give anything away.

Peter smiled ruefully and took a step away. "You've gotta learn to relax, cutie."

Despite the urge to curl his lip at the name, Tim didn't move. Peter took another step away, and Tim's hands slipped off the man's hips, dropping to his sides.

"You on shift tomorrow?" Peter jiggled his car keys.

Tim just nodded once.

"Then I'll see you then." Hand lifted in a farewell, Peter smiled and headed toward his car. "G'night."

"Yeah," Tim murmured. "Good night." He waited until Peter was actually in the car and driving away before turning and walking into the dojo.

In the entryway he paused, hand on the knob still, listening to voices rise and fall from the back office. He waited a moment, checking for tone. The closed door muffled the words, but the tone would tell him if it was safe to bother Rick.

Two men, he realized, talking lazily. He dropped his keys on the front counter, turning to close the door and throw the deadbolt, then headed to the office. He knocked once before walking in, gaze sweeping the room.

Rick was kicked back in his desk chair, feet up beside the computer. Jay sprawled across the folded futon, red hair falling in his face, a beer in one hand. "Hey, kid," he said, lifting the beer in greeting.

Tim nodded, closing the office door and leaning against

the wall. "You're here late." Curiosity as to why ate at him, but he was too polite to ask.

Jay answered anyway, rolling expressive brown eyes. "Bad date. Bad, bad date. Chick was a dingbat."

Tim's voice was wry. "Maybe you should stop picking up at bars."

Jay laughed. "Maybe I should!"

"How'd your date go?" Rick's feet thumped to the floor as he leaned over.

Tim hesitated, glancing toward Jay. He wasn't sure he wanted to talk about his experimentation. Wasn't sure he wanted Jay to know, even if Jay was blatantly bisexual.

Jay took the option away. "A guy from work, right?"

Tim shot Rick a dirty look for blabbing, but passed over a comment in favor of reviewing his night. He was reluctant to call it a success, though it hadn't been bad, either. Eventually, he just shrugged.

"That good, huh?" Jay chuckled. "I've been on those. You come with me, kiddo, I'll introduce you to some hotties who like 'em small."

Tim leveled an annoyed gaze toward Jay, debating various responses. Rick beat him to it with, "Jay, he doesn't want to sleep with prostitutes."

Jay clutched his chest, mock-wounded. "You kill me. You really do. As if I'd let one of yours sleep with a carrier monkey."

Tim lifted a single eyebrow. One of Rick's? Now that was annoying. He didn't belong to anyone, thanks. "As riveting as this conversation is," he drawled, "I have to work tomorrow."

"What, and I don't?"

Tim looked at Jay blandly. "I don't know, do you?"

The redhead grinned, lifting his beer again in a toast. "Got a new one."

"Only the fifth this month," Tim said in deadpan congratulations.

Jay laughed, brown eyes twinkling. "I like the brat, Rick. Even though he is a wise-assed little snot." He turned and winked at Tim. "You just let me know when you're ready to date a halfway decent guy. I'll set you up."

"Don't believe him, Tim," Rick said wryly. "He doesn't know any decent guys."

Jay grinned at Rick. "I know you."

Tim twitched. "And on that incestuous note," he said, "I'm leaving." In the beat of silence that followed, he opened the door and stepped out.

Then he heard Jay's howl. "I wasn't setting you two up! Get your mind out of the gutter!"

Tim snorted. He was halfway down the hall when Rick caught up to him, matching him stride for stride. "Everything went okay?"

Tim shrugged. "All right. Nothing great, nothing disastrous." He glanced sidelong at Rick, picking up his keys. "You told Jay?" He didn't need to specify what he was talking about.

Rick smiled apologetically, apparently sensing Tim's unease despite Tim's attempt to hide it. "It kind of slipped out. I knew he wouldn't care, and he was wondering why I was here so late."

"Waiting up for me?" Tim asked dryly, confused himself as to whether he was annoyed or amused.

Rick smiled. "Someone has to make sure you're not raped and left to die by the side of the road."

"As if anyone could." They reached the door and paused there. "Besides, I told you I know this guy."

"I know," Rick said. "I worry anyway."

Tim just nodded, accepting that fact. "I do need to go, though." He waited for Rick to step out of the way.

Rick did, shoving both hands into his jeans pockets. "Call if you need anything."

It was ritual: Rick said it, Tim just nodded, and they both knew Tim wouldn't. He might show up at Rick's house or the dojo, but he rarely called.

The night was cool, damp ocean air coming in off the bay. Tim paused at his car door, looking up at the stars. His thoughts drifted, mind unwinding from the day at long last. His muscles relaxed, tension easing out of his body.

He wondered what Con was doing. Then he remembered the confession, followed quickly by an image of Con at the beach, splashing around like a whale as he tried to backfloat, laughing as he failed.

Tension coiled in Tim's stomach again, spreading hot through his chest and legs, making his heart speed. He swallowed and banished the images, the memories. It was too stressful. Too alarming. His reaction was too much, too intense. Scary, he thought, and shoved that word away, to be replaced with a more acceptable 'uncomfortable.'

He didn't understand it. He'd never felt it before. He didn't like it.

Tim got in the car and slammed the door, starting the engine with a violent twist. He ignored the stars overhead.

Con sat in a lawn chair outside, staring up at the sky, at stars nearly hidden by the glow of lights from the city. Days were running into weeks, and he still hadn't heard from Tim. The San Diego Fire Department had contacted him to say they didn't mind delaying his start day for another few weeks, given his injury. The Chicago Fire Department had sent him his final paycheck with a 'get well soon' card signed by the staff—a card that included notes like, "get burned, not shot, you moron" and "next time, dodge." Grams had been horrified at the lack of compassion. Con and his grandfather, an ex-cop, had thought it was hilarious.

Everything was set for him to move to San Diego. Everything except Tim.

Con stretched his legs out, pondering the apartment key that sat safely in his wallet. Tim's apartment key, given to him his second day visiting. Tim had offered to let him stay a while when Con moved out there, to sleep on the couch until he found a place. It would make it easier; he wouldn't have to rent somewhere sight unseen, or live in a hotel for a week while he searched. Now, though, he wasn't sure the offer still stood. For all he knew, Tim hated his guts. Maybe the guy was homophobic. Slightly homophobic, so the idea of gay guys didn't bother him, but the idea of gay guys scamming his ass was terrifying.

They said that homophobes were oftentimes gay themselves.

Con dragged himself back to pondering the key in his wallet. The way he figured it, he had two choices. The first one was to respect Tim's wishes and wait until Tim contacted him. The second was to realize that, as well as he knew Tim—and after all these years, he liked to think he knew Tim very well—the man might never contact him again. Con would be damned if he'd let his best friend ignore him over a stupid comment. They'd get over it. He could look past how much he liked Tim, and Tim would eventually forget about it. If he could get Tim to stop ignoring him.

There was a key in his wallet.

He could get Tim to stop ignoring him.

Chapter Four

After nearly a month, Tim arrived at the conclusion that he was more gay than not.

He slid into the driver's seat of his Mazda, reaching up to pull his tie loose before tossing half a dozen wrappers from medical instruments into the cup holder. Someday, he'd start remembering to toss those in the garbage rather than pocketing them. In the meantime... He eyed the cup holder. He really needed to empty it.

Starting the car, Tim checked the rearview mirror and pulled out.

He'd finally realized he looked at men with more interest than women. It was a realization he was still coming to grips with, but one that seemed to fit. Telling himself he didn't have to look at women if he didn't want to had released something, and now he barely noticed them at all unless someone pointed a girl out. The discomfort he'd always felt, like he was two steps behind everyone else, was gone.

He still wasn't sure *how* gay he was. After five outings with Peter—he didn't want to call them dates, as he still wasn't sure he liked Peter—it was obvious men turned him on, and just as obvious he still didn't want to be touched. He knew Peter was frustrated, though they'd gotten as far as making out in the front of the car. Tim never initiated it, and he always grew uncomfortable quickly and put a stop to things. Was it possible to be only kind of gay?

He changed lanes, merging onto the freeway and coming to a stop in rush hour traffic, his thoughts making him glower. Maybe he *was* frigid.

Peter had told him one night, with great ire, that he was still seeing other people.

Tim had answered, "Okay," and only realized when Peter looked even more annoyed that he was supposed to be upset about that. He couldn't quite bring himself to care, much like he hadn't been able to care when one of his girlfriends had said the same thing two years before. Maybe it was a symptom of something. Maybe he was just too far on the asexual side to really be either gay or straight. After all, if he was attracted to men, but then didn't want to be touched, did that count as gay?

He was so fucking confused. In an effort to avoid his thoughts, he listened to the radio the rest of the way home.

The answering machine light was blinking when he got in, and he punched 'play' before heading into the bathroom for a quick shower. He paused, half undressed, listening as Peter came on.

"We still going to that party tonight? Call me," Peter said, and hung up. It was the only message.

Tim showered, dried off, and pulled on loose jeans. Then a green T-shirt, snug without being tight, and a quick dig through a box to find his watch with the heavy leather band.

When the phone rang he picked it up, bracing it between his ear and his shoulder.

"Hey. Party?" Peter asked.

"Sure." Tim stood in front of the mirror to finger-comb his hair back.

"Pick you up in fifteen."

The line went dead before he could say he'd just meet Peter there. He frowned and hung up, staring at the steady red three on the base. Three messages saved, waiting to be deleted. He'd played them so often he knew them by heart, even the last one. The deep breath, followed by a single huff of hopeless laughter and Con's voice. "Timmy... Fuck. Never mind."

He didn't listen to it again. He didn't delete it, either. Tim looked down at his watch, adjusting it needlessly. At what point did 'a long time' become 'too long'? It had been more than a month since Con's confession, weeks since the man had called, e-mailed, or text-messaged. In theory, Con would be moving to San Diego soon, joining the firefighters, looking for friends and... other things. Tim didn't know if he still counted.

Avoiding Con because of uncertainty about what had happened had mutated into avoiding Con because of Tim's uncertainty about himself, which in turn had mutated into avoiding Con simply because it was habit. What was Tim supposed to say? "Hey, sorry I haven't spoken to you, I was figuring out my sexuality? By the way, I think I'm gay but I might also be frigid, and I don't know if I could love you back regardless. Oh, and I hope you weren't just drugged and meant 'love' as in 'good friends,' because that would mean I was conceited enough to misread it and *really* make a dick out of myself."

Yeah, right.

A knock at the door interrupted his thoughts, and a glance at the clock told him that more than fifteen minutes had passed. He grabbed up his wallet as Peter called, "Hey, cutie!"

Tim yanked open the door, glowering. "Don't call me that."

Peter gave his best boyish grin—the one that annoyed

Tim—and stepped aside. "Sure. You ready?"

Tim stepped out, closing and locking his door behind them.

He regretted ever inviting Peter in. He'd known better. He'd done it a time or two before, and always ended up feeling like he was fighting off an octopus. But people at the party had been making out, and with his thoughts earlier in the day about being frigid, he'd needed to prove that he wasn't, even if he was only proving it to himself. He wanted to be normal. So he'd invited Peter in, and they'd both known why, and he couldn't pretend he'd just meant to play video games and watch movies or something stupid, even if ten minutes into the evening found him wishing he could.

"Hey, chill." Tim crowded into the corner of the kitchen sink, his fingers firmly on the tile behind him.

"I am chilled." Peter laughed, pressed up against him, hands sliding around Tim's waist and up his back. "You're the one freaking out."

Tim bit his tongue against the instant denial, knowing Peter was right.

"Still so tense," Peter murmured, leaning in to kiss him. "You really need to find a way to de-stress. You're going to give yourself a heart attack by the time you're thirty."

Tim scowled, felt Peter's chuckle, and knew the man was probably right. Again.

"Just enjoy yourself, cutie."

"Don't call—" The rest was cut off by lips and tongue, and Tim closed his eyes and tried to just enjoy sensations. It was why he'd invited Peter in, right? To prove he wasn't asexual.

Hands slid under his shirt, skimming over flesh. He focused on the touch, attempting to force his body into a reaction he wasn't having. He could feel Peter's erection through their jeans, pressing into his hip. Kisses slid over his jaw, lips and teeth moving carefully over his skin, his earlobe pulled into a hot, wet mouth. All Tim could think of was that it was kind of gross, having someone's spit all over his skin. Like a big hound, drooling and dripping over everything.

"C'mon, Tim." Peter's breath was hot and humid against Tim's ear. "Do something."

Right. It was a two-person thing. He pried his hands off the edge of the sink, putting them on Peter's arms. He petted awkwardly, really wishing the other man would just back off a little bit, give him some breathing room. All he could smell was Peter, sour apples and martini olives combined with the sickly sweetness of arousal and the spike of alcohol. Peter tasted like old beer, not like the cool and citrusy stuff Con had bought, but like a drink gone flat and acidic.

Tim gave himself a mental shake, trying to think of what he *did* like. Focusing on what he didn't like certainly wasn't going to help him cure any frigidity problems. He liked—he liked—hands. There was nothing that tasted bad about hands because he wasn't tasting them. Lips on his neck should be good, if he could stop fixating on drool. He couldn't. He went back to the hands, remembering belatedly to rub his own up and down Peter's arms, imagining rounded muscles instead of Peter's slim build. Rounded muscles and dark hair, broad shoulders—

Peter's hands slid over his hips, one coming around to fondle his crotch. Tim jumped. "Peter—"

"Re*lax*, Tim. This is supposed to be fun, remember? What's with you?"

Tim struggled internally for a moment, feeling Peter's

hand rubbing against him, reaching down between his legs and back up again in long, slow strokes. If he was gay, shouldn't he be responding to this? Thrusting back, like Peter was doing against him, and not wishing he could pull further away into the sink?

"Come on," Peter coaxed, his free hand wrapped around the back of Tim's neck as if he could sense Tim's desire to flee.

Tim tried to enjoy it. He really did, but all he could think about was Peter's dick rubbing up against him and Peter pissed out of it and, in a minute, if Tim didn't stop this, Peter was going to ejaculate and liquid would seep through denim and onto him, and he really wasn't getting hard and he really *didn't* like Peter's hand where it was—

"Stop." He shook his head at himself, frustrated.

"You kidding?" Peter asked incredulously, sliding his hand down Tim's torso until both hands were at his pants, unbuttoning his jeans.

Tim set a palm flat on Peter's chest, gathering all the intensity he could—which, when he focused, was a fair amount. "I said stop," he repeated, quietly and firmly.

Peter froze. "You've got to be fucking joking." Anger began to spill through.

"No. I'm not."

Peter took a step back, face pink and turning pinker, eyes bright. "You are something else, man." He shook his head. "You invite me in here, start fucking around, and tell me to stop only *after* I'm set to go? Jesus Christ."

Tim's whole body tightened as anger, guilt, and frustration mixed. "I'm sorry," he said through nearly clenched teeth. "It was a mistake."

"Mistake, my ass!" Peter shouted. "You're a fucking tease!"

"I didn't mean—"

"Bullshit, you didn't mean! You were standing here two minutes ago encouraging me, and once I'm rock hard you tell me to stop? We've been going out for how long, and you *still* won't get into it. You're cold, man." Sharp eyes raked up and down Tim's body, assessing. "Look at you. Not even half hard. What is this, a game?"

Tim's jaw tightened. He forced it to relax. "You should leave," he said, after a moment spent regaining his composure.

"I should—" Peter stopped. He looked disgusted. "Yeah. Maybe I should." He stormed out of the kitchen, yanking his jacket off a barstool. "There is something wrong with you." Shoving his arms into sleeves, he stalked to the doorway. After wrenching the door open and starting into the hall, he stopped and turned back. "Maybe you should see a doctor, Tim," he said snidely. "Because, speaking as a professional, you just aren't normal."

Tim stood, silent and unmoving, until Peter slammed the door and his footsteps faded. Then he swallowed bitter frustration, turning and leaning his elbows against the sink, head in his hands. Fuck.

He couldn't keep from seeing Peter the next day, though he did his best. Eventually, Peter cornered him in the lounge.

"Hey," Peter began, and Tim felt himself tense. "Look, I wanted to apologize." He leaned against the counter where Tim stirred sugar into coffee. "I was out of line."

Tim hadn't slept for thinking about the night before. He shook his head, refusing to look up. "It's all right," he said woodenly. "Besides, I think you were right." He felt Peter's stare, but kept his eyes on his Styrofoam cup.

"At least, partly right. I'm not gay. I should've realized it before this. I mean, what we do doesn't get to me like it should." He braced himself and looked up at Peter, taking in the man's exasperated expression.

"That's not—" Peter began, and Tim interrupted.

"I'm sorry. I didn't mean to string you along like that." He turned and left the room.

He wasn't gay. Or he was gay, but not gay enough. Or he was asexual. He didn't know. He'd spent the night re-learning about frigidity, and that didn't fit, either. The symptoms weren't right. He got erections, and he had sexual fantasies, and men seemed to trigger them more than women, but... Fuck. He just didn't like being touched. Could that be a sexual dysfunction? He didn't know. He wished he did, and then maybe there'd be a pill or something.

Tim picked up the next patient folder and tried to put the whole thing out of his mind.

"So... You want to tell me what's wrong?"

"Not really." Tim picked at the plate of warmed-up leftovers Rick had put in front of him. After a minute he dropped all pretense, along with his fork, and leaned his head in his hands. His fingers spiked his black hair into wild disarray. "You are seriously missing some key nutrients here," he muttered, staring down at canned corn, boxed mashed potatoes, and a slab of charcoaled mystery meat. "As in, any nutrients."

"That's what vitamins are for." Rick flopped into a battered kitchen chair. "So tell me what's wrong."

Tim didn't answer. He couldn't explain frigidity to Rick. Besides, Rick would just tell him he wasn't frigid, and that was true, too. So... what was he? Other than hopelessly miserable and confused. "Do you have any good movies in here?" He shoved away from the table and wandered into the family room, which held the only expensive piece of equipment in the whole house: the entertainment center.

"I just bought *Die Hard: With a Vengeance*."

Tim snorted. "I said *good* movies."

"What, you'd prefer Barbara Streisand?"

He turned to glare at Rick, who just grinned irrepressibly.

"Boy, you *are* in a mood," Rick commented. "How's Peter?"

"An ass." Tim crouched to paw through Rick's DVDs.

"Ah."

It was an awfully knowing 'ah.' Tim turned to gaze at the other man, his eyes narrow. He had to lean to see around the recliner and into the dining area, but it was worth it. "What's that supposed to mean?"

"Lover's tiff?"

The word 'lover' made his stomach knot. His ears turned red, and he shifted away from Rick again, pretending to peer at the shelves.

"Tim," Rick sighed, but didn't continue. There was a long moment of silence before he spoke. "He's not for you."

"Yeah, I know," Tim snapped over his shoulder. "And I'm not seeing him anymore." He heard Rick stand and walk closer, and tensed as if for a fight. He'd never fought with Rick. He'd never actually gotten in a fistfight with anyone, but he tensed anyway, a prey instinct that crawled up his shoulders and waited.

"Just because you don't like one person doesn't mean you aren't gay."

"I know." His words were barely even ground out.

His hand tightened on the shelf, knuckles going white. He relaxed forcibly. Liking or disliking one guy wasn't the problem. Not wanting to be touched, not getting turned on by another person—that was the problem. He couldn't explain that to Rick. It was personal and embarrassing, and Rick wouldn't know what to do anyway. Rick wasn't a doctor; he wasn't even a psychologist.

Tim wanted to beat his head against something hard. He controlled the impulse, and stared at the movies instead.

He'd gotten home by eleven, movie unwatched, and put himself to bed. There, he lay awake, staring at the ceiling while his mind raced round and round in circles. It was near midnight when he heard a fumbling at the front door.

At first, he thought it was his imagination. Then he realized it wasn't, that someone was actually trying to get inside. Silently, he crawled out of bed, grabbing his cell phone and dialing in 911 without hitting 'send.' If it was just someone at the wrong apartment, he didn't want to bring out the cops. He padded down the short hall, through the living room, and paused to watch the entry.

Metal slid against metal, like a key sliding into the lock. The bolt turned. The door swung open. Tim wished suddenly he'd grabbed a weapon. He hadn't expected a *key* to work, after all.

As he started forward, prepared to attack now while he could surprise the intruder, the shape cursed quietly and nearly staggered over two large, rectangular objects. Suitcases, Tim realized with confusion, and halted his forward step. What kind of robber brought luggage? He stared as the figure came inside, close enough to make out features. Dark hair, broad shoulders, muscles filling out a snug T-shirt, a trim waist—

"Con?" he asked incredulously.

The shape jumped. "Fuck! Jesus, Tim, you scared the shit out of me! What are you doing, lurking in the shadows?"

"I thought you were a robber. What are you *doing* here?"

Con turned around and closed the door as Tim took a step back, flicking on the living room light. They both spent a few moments blinking. Then Con straightened, leaning casually against the door, one foot propped up against the wood behind him. "You said I could stay here while I found a place." He smiled and shrugged, seemingly at ease. "So, here I am."

Chapter Five

Ll right, sheets, blankets, um, you know where the
food is." Tim was frazzled and babbling, but he
didn't know what to do. If he were honest, he'd
have to admit that he was afraid Con wanted something
more than just friendship, and he couldn't *do* that.
"So." He scrubbed his hand through his hair. "So, that's
everything. And I'm not gay." His voice rose on the last
words, nearly broke. He blinked into the sudden quiet,
wondering where that declaration had come from. He
certainly hadn't meant to say it.

Con wasn't looking at him, but somehow Tim could
see the hurt those words caused. The broad shoulders
went still, the line of long spine freezing. Tim flinched.

"Tim," Con said slowly, "I was high, all right? I'm
sorry."

Tim struggled for a moment, then finally bit out,
"Morphine doesn't make you lie."

Con laughed humorlessly. He still hadn't looked over,
his dark eyes shaded by thick black lashes. Tim could
see them in profile, curling away from smooth skin. The
sudden urge to touch was almost overwhelming, and he
took a step back in reflex.

"No." Muscles shifted under Con's thin T-shirt.

"But it makes you blab things you'd know not to say otherwise. Tell secrets you shouldn't be telling. Admit to inappropriate emotions." He glanced up then, the hard planes of his face somehow softer. "I shouldn't have said it. I don't expect anything from you. I'm sorry."

Tim shifted, awkward and uncomfortable. In the many scenarios he'd imagined, he'd never imagined this. "Me, too," he said at last.

Con nodded. Then he took a deep breath and summoned a smile, showing off the dimples in his cheeks to match the one in his chin. "You probably have to work tomorrow, and I'm beat. We should hit the sack."

It took Tim a minute to realize Con was heading toward the couch. Separate sacks. Right. He relaxed. "Yeah. I—Okay." Nodding once, he tried to rally his thoughts into something approximating their normal orderly process, and headed for his bedroom. He walked in, closed the door, opened it again, and called out, "Sleep well."

"You, too," came Con's disembodied voice.

"Right," Tim muttered to himself, and closed the door. He stood there for a moment, feeling the spastic way his heart pounded in his chest. Just the fright at a possible robber, that was all. The shaking, that was adrenaline, both from a break-in and from what could have been an ugly confrontation. Same with the way his muscles felt warm, and, well, he couldn't explain away his sudden fascination with Con's shoulders or his new obsession with the way muscle swelled under the man's T-shirt, but adrenaline could explain the cottony feel to his mouth.

He rested his forehead against the door, letting his breath gather between his skin and the wood. He could already tell he wasn't going to sleep again tonight.

Con couldn't sleep. He stared at the coffee table, gaze tracing scratches and cup rings in the wood, arms curled under the throw pillow he was lying on.

The tension in Tim, obvious from the moment Con had seen him standing there, had gotten worse over their conversation rather than better. Tim had kept that unreadable expression plastered across his damned face, the only indication of his true feelings showing in the way he babbled. And then, when Con had suggested going to bed, he'd gone breakably rigid.

Something had changed. Con supposed it could just be stress, or that Tim had reacted worse than Con had suspected to the drugged confession. But that didn't feel right. It didn't quite explain everything, either. Tim seemed aware of him now, in a way he hadn't been before. Con had purposely dressed casually, wearing baggy jeans and a looser T-shirt than he normally would. But he knew that he was attractive, had grown used to people looking. He'd learned how to play to it, and when to notice it.

Tim had been looking. Con had felt eyes on him from the moment he'd entered. Sliding across his shoulders, examining his face, straying down his back. He'd been careful not to look at Tim, not to acknowledge it in the slightest. He was afraid it might scare Tim off. Again.

But something had changed.

"Hey, cutie—" a voice said behind him, quiet and quick.

"Stop." Tim wasn't in the mood for Peter or his 'cutie's.

"Look, I was out of line the other night. It doesn't mean you're not gay, it just means—"

"Stop it," Tim repeated, shoving through a doorway

and down the hall. "I'm not interested, Peter. It was a mistake. I'm not gay."

"But—"

Tim halted, turning on his heel in the same fluid motion. "I am not interested," he said, slowly and clearly. "I am not gay."

Peter looked like he wanted to argue. Before he could find the words, Tim turned and went into the exam room.

It wasn't that Con wasn't looking for a place to live. It was that he wasn't looking anywhere he'd be interested in living. He could view apartments in a shitty area all day, know that there wasn't going to be anything suitable, go back to Tim's, and still manage to say he hadn't found a place. It was perfect. It gave him time to make sure that Tim wasn't going to start avoiding him again.

"Maybe I should look closer to the beach," he said thoughtfully, digging though broccoli to find more steak.

"Rent's more expensive there." The frown that had been hovering over Tim's face all evening deepened.

"Well, maybe I should look around here. I've already found some take-out places I like." Con grinned broadly, doing his best to pretend like Tim's overall bad mood wasn't stressing him out. He poked at his Thai again.

"You can't live on take-out," Tim muttered.

"Ha. You underestimate my abilities." Silence hung, dark and grumpy. When he was unable to bear the quiet any longer, Con asked, "What's wrong?"

"Nothing."

That was bullshit and Con knew it. He stabbed at his food, then set it down on the coffee table. "Is it something I did?"

"No." Tim didn't move.

"Something I didn't do?"

That earned a snort. "No."

"Is it organic?"

Tim blinked and looked up. "What?" His guard dropped, overpowered by confusion.

Con almost smiled at the man's befuddled expression, simply because it was an emotion other than irritation or a flat wall of nothingness. "Isn't this twenty questions?" He grinned slowly, trying to lure Tim into a better mood. "Because it feels like twenty questions. I just thought I'd narrow the field to organic or man-made."

The confusion melted away, narrow face softening into amusement. "Man-made." Tim's lips twitched upward. He looked down at his food, and the walls rose again, locking Con out. Then he spoke, shrugging it off. "There's this guy at work who's been on my case. It's just bugging me."

Con nodded slowly. "What's he on your case about?" Either Tim was getting worse at keeping the walls in place, or Con was getting better at reading them. He liked to think it was the latter. That expression was definite annoyance.

"Nothing."

"Must be some nothing."

Tim didn't answer.

"You used to talk to me about this stuff. Maybe we should go back to email," Con added in an undertone.

Tim stood, movements sharp. He set his take-out container down on the counter with carefully controlled motions, then strode toward the bedroom. "I can't deal with this." It was quiet enough to almost go unnoticed. Almost.

"Deal with *what*?" Con snapped, sitting up and forward.

"Nothing. I have martial arts tonight. I need to go."

Trying to bank his frustration, Con took a deep breath and exhaled. "Can I come?"

"No." The bedroom door closed.

"Why not?" he yelled down the hall and through the wood.

Tim opened the door a crack and answered, "Because."

"That's a childish answer!" Con shouted. There was no response. He hated that answer. 'Because.' You couldn't even argue with it. It wasn't a reason, or it was a reason in and of itself, and he was never sure which.

Tim came out, a white T-shirt and drawstring pants thrown over one shoulder.

"I took karate in second grade." Con stood up and leaned against the counter.

Tim grunted.

"It lasted a whole month."

Tim snorted.

"I took ballet in high school to meet chicks..." He trailed off thoughtfully.

That earned him a dubious look. Con smiled and shrugged. A look was better than nothing. "It only lasted a week. The chicks all thought I was gay."

"You are," Tim pointed out.

"Well, yeah. Maybe that was why I quit. If there had been other cute guys..."

Tim rolled his eyes.

"Are you sure I can't come?" Con asked, trailing his friend to the door.

"I'm sure."

"I might get bored."

Tim shot him a look over his shoulder and headed down the hall connecting the apartments.

"If I get bored," Con called, "I might change the

settings on your computer."

Tim stopped, turned, dead serious. "You change the settings on my computer," he warned, "and I'll kick your ass, then make you change them *back*." He faced front again and bounded down the stairs.

Con sighed and stepped inside, closing and locking the door. Little squirt thought he could kick Con's ass, huh? Con was a full head taller than Tim, and much more muscular, and now he knew Tim was a fast little bugger. No surprises left. Con booted the computer up and started looking for porno pictures to use as the desktop background.

Dawn light filtered through the blinds as Tim flicked on his computer, half a bagel stuffed in his mouth. He studiously didn't look at the half-naked man sprawled out on his couch. He didn't need to look to know what he'd see. Blankets had been kicked off, pooling on the floor. Dark hair mussed across a throw pillow, falling across eyes lined by lashes, thick and heavy on broad cheekbones. Full lips parted in sleep, the dimple in Con's chin easing the almost too-strong look of his hard jaw and square face. The skin on his neck was slightly darker than that on his chest, the paler flesh stretched taut over clearly defined pectorals and abs. Shadows were highlighted by curls of black chest hair, sprinkled lightly and coalescing into a thin line down Con's stomach, vanishing under boxers riding low on his slim hips. Arms sprawled, legs cockeyed, his whole frame was wrapped in muscles and hard planes.

Tim had gotten a quick look before he'd fled to the kitchen. He was trying to forget, and failing miserably.

His computer chimed, drawing his attention, and the

screen came up.

He bellowed.

Con jerked awake, blinking eyes that were smoky with sleep, his broad, long-fingered hand gripping the back of the couch. "What? What?"

"You put gay porn on my computer!" Tim shouted, pointing to the screen. "I'm not gay!"

Con blinked several times, then grinned slowly. "So, you wouldn't have objected to straight porn?"

"Fix it!" Tim refused to be softened by dimples or that lopsided smile. "Before I get back from work!"

"Yes, sir!" Con gave a mock salute, already starting to laugh. "But I'll have you know, that's my favorite image."

Tim glared at him again, snatching up his backpack and storming out the front door.

Rick knocked on Tim's door, knowing full well the kid wasn't home. He also knew from a tirade after Tim's martial arts class that Con had shown up unexpectedly, and Rick was hoping for a look at this mystery friend who'd single-handedly turned Tim's life upside down.

He wasn't disappointed.

It was the first time he'd actually *seen* Conner, though he'd heard stories for the past several years. He was more, well, *male* than Rick had expected. Bigger, broader through the chest and shoulders, baby fat long since stripped from a square jaw. From the way Tim had described him—never describing the way he looked, just his personality—Rick had expected someone younger, not so tough looking, someone softer around the edges. Someone shorter.

He realized all of that in the moment between the

door opening and Con smiling, brown eyebrows lifting fractionally. "Help you?"

Rick met his gaze squarely, surprised to realize that the man had given him the same assessment that he'd given Con. There was steel in that look, cool and slightly impersonal. Rick smiled broadly. Con viewed him as a threat. Now, *that* was funny.

"Rick," he said, and stuck out his hand. "I'm—"

"Tim's Big Brother," Con finished, the steel in his dark eyes melting away. He grinned, posture softening, dimples appearing. His grip was firm but not crushing. He wasn't trying to prove anything through it, Rick was pleased to note. "Come on in." Con stepped away from the door, gesturing to the little apartment. "Tim's not here right now, but—"

"I actually came by to see you," Rick said easily, sliding his hands into his pockets as he wandered inside, stepping past Con and taking up space near the computer desk. "You seem to have given Tim quite the jolt. Thought I'd check it out for myself."

"You mean, check *me* out." Con's wry smile matched the tone of the words.

Rick nodded amiably. No reason to pretend like he wasn't here to play Big Brother, irony aside. He looked around the living room, noting the dishes in the sink and the suitcase open by the couch. The clothes inside looked like they'd never been folded in the first place, though the mess remained mostly contained. There were boots by the door—much bigger than Tim's feet—and an open can of pop beside the keyboard. He caught a glimpse of an IM conversation in progress, then averted his gaze so as not to snoop. Not that he was above snooping, but it seemed extra rude with Con standing right there.

"My grandmother," Con said, catching the direction of Rick's gaze and leaning forward, tapping a quick set of keys as he spoke. "She learned how to chat a year ago, and now we can't pry her off Instant Messenger without a crowbar and the promise of a Long Island Iced Tea."

Rick chuckled, glancing over to read Con's typed, *company. be right back*. "Well," he said after a minute, when Con straightened up and leaned toward the door as if hoping Rick would take the hint and leave. "I can understand why Tim's all up in arms."

Con frowned. "What?"

Smiling, Rick tossed hair out of his face. "You've put a Coke on the computer desk. Completely freaks him right out."

Con snorted and plucked the can up, drinking from it. "So, do I meet with your approval?" The question wasn't quite sarcastic, conveying vague annoyance but stopping shy of rudeness.

Rick tipped his head and eyed the other man. Con was nearly as tall as he was, and broader across the chest. "I don't know," he said finally. "I haven't had a conversation with you yet."

One side of Con's mouth turned up in something just short of a smile. "You going to ask me my intentions?"

Rick laughed. "I might. Are they honorable?" He deepened his voice and looked mockingly stern.

Con snorted, brushing by to toss the can in the trash and open the refrigerator. "This isn't the seventeenth century, and he isn't a woman." Looking over his shoulder he asked, "You want a soda?"

"Sure." Rick dropped down into the computer chair, back to the desk. "And he might not be a woman, but that doesn't mean I can't look out for him." He waited a beat, then said, "It's not like there's anyone else around to do so."

He saw Conner's shoulders straighten, stiffen, then relax. Muscles flexed and a can opened with a pop and a hiss. Crossing the room, Con handed Rick the Coke and shrugged. "Yeah. I guess. So..." He dragged the word out as he lowered himself onto the couch and promptly sprawled, taking up nearly the whole thing. "What did you want to talk about?"

Rick sipped, smiling. "What *are* your intentions?"

Con laughed, rolling his eyes, and Rick caught sight of the man Tim had described: friendly, gregarious, easy to like. "Jesus, Rick. We're just friends." He lifted his drink, thick lashes covering his dark eyes, and muttered almost to himself, "Tim's not gay."

"Bullshit."

Con glanced sharply upward.

"Tim's confused, and it's because of you. So, what I want to know is, are you going to push him into realizing he likes you, or are you just going to back off?" Rick wasn't sure what answer he was hoping for.

Con frowned into his soda for a long moment. "If you're right and I push, then I become the cause of still more stress as he has to work through whatever shit he has to work through. And that's the best case scenario. I'd rather just..." He shrugged, smiling slightly as he looked up. "I'd just rather go back to being friends. If he's not ready, he's not ready. And if he's not gay..." He shook his head, looking back down, slouching down into the couch. "Then he's not gay."

"But we both know he is." Rick found it hard to believe Conner was just going to back off. He didn't know many people who would do that; let someone find his own way rather than trying to force an opinion or view onto him.

"It's not my call to make." Con looked up sharply, his dark eyes narrowed. "And you shouldn't be pushing him around, either. He'll figure it out, or not, when he's ready. He's smart. Have a little faith in him, huh?"

Rick smiled slowly, nodding. He liked the guy. Most

people looked at Tim, at his smaller stature and quiet, solemn demeanor, and assumed he needed to be led. Con apparently knew better.

"Hey," Con said suddenly, sitting up and bringing his legs in, elbows on his knees. "Tim didn't—I mean, he wasn't—" He colored slightly, then shook his head and fell back. "No, never mind."

"What?"

Con slid a glance toward him, then away. "It's just... He's so anti-touch, you know? I just wanted to make sure... I mean, he said nothing happened, but..."

Rick smiled wryly. "I met him when he was sixteen. He was anti-touch, as you put it, even then. I think that's just Tim, and the more people try to touch, the more stand-offish he gets."

Conner rolled his eyes. "Digs in his heels just out of sheer stubbornness."

"Exactly." Rick laughed, rocking back in the computer chair. Obviously, Con knew Tim well. "I don't think it came from anything bad. I mean, I doubt there was a whole lot of touchy-feely-ness going on in his family. Anyone who'd send a ten-year-old kid to a *boarding school*..." He didn't bother to hide the derision, and only realized his mistake when Con looked at him, eyebrows raised. "Annnd, you were sent to boarding school as a kid." He felt like an utter heel. "Look, I didn't mean—I'm sure your parents were—"

Con laughed softly, shaking his head. "Relax. You're probably right. My mom died when I was a baby, and my dad was a piece of work." He frowned briefly, and Rick wondered what memories had triggered it. Then Con continued, "My grandparents on my mom's side pretty much raised me from thirteen on. They're good people."

As if on cue, the computer chimed. Rick turned to look, Con standing and leaning forward, their heads drawn around to the screen as if by a magic power.

Mary_J342: Your grandfather just came down in a sarong Ed the tranny gave him. He says it's much more comfortable than pants, and cooler, too. He's going out to buy more. I'll send pictures.

Silence stretched. Rick bit the inside of his cheek, trying hard not to laugh at the mental image of an old man in a sarong.

"They're kinda weird," Con said after a moment, "but they're good people."

Rick grinned, then laughed, then laughed harder when he turned and saw Conner's pained expression.

"God love 'em." Con snorted a rueful chuckle, shaking his head.

"So, let me get this straight." Jay watched with arms crossed as the first set of Rick's students warmed up on the mats. "You're going to try and set Tim up with... an Internet friend?"

Rick gave him a warning look. "It's not an Internet friend. He's known the guy for years. And this kid's perfect for Tim. He's why Tim got all hot and bothered in the first place."

"Right. But Tim's not gay."

"Tim has some hang-up." Rick shrugged. "But I don't think it's that he's not gay."

Jay snickered and shook his head, tossing a stray lock of hair out of his eyes. "I am *so* glad you're not my family. You meddle worse than a stepmother."

"You'd know," Rick shot back, and headed out to the floor to help with stretching.

Jay watched for a moment, absently critiquing various kids' forms, then finally shook those thoughts free. Rick had done a good job here. Solid basics to build from, and the advanced students, Tim among them, moved with clean and rapid precision.

Rick hadn't bothered teaching them the minutiae of fighting, the kind of stuff you couldn't use in a competition, or even in a normal street fight. Rick wasn't the sensei he and Jay had shared, and that was probably a good thing. As a bitter little street punk wannabe, Jay had gloried in knowing how to be devious, how to read body language or throw someone off using simple gestures or touch. These kids, clean and smart and eager to learn, weren't him.

Thank God.

Then the door opened and another kid who wasn't him, who would never be him, entered. A smile lit her face when she caught sight of Jay and she sprinted across the mats, skirting the other students.

"Dad! I got a B in math!"

"Hey, congratulations, Emmy!" Jay lifted her effortlessly and planted a noisy kiss on her cheek. "Now, go change; Rick's starting."

"Okay!" Once her feet were on the ground again she raced for the lockers, pink and yellow backpack in tow.

He watched her go, then let his gaze wander back around to Rick. Meddling Rick. Meddling Rick who didn't know when to butt out, who would pick and pluck at poor, perfect little Tim's perfect little life until the kid was so turned around he wouldn't know what had hit him.

It was gonna be hilarious.

Chapter Six

"Cutie."

Tim nearly flinched, then carefully contained the urge to punch his locker. It was no way to end a day. He turned on one heel. "Peter."

"Tim, sweetie," Peter began.

Tim felt his lip curl and forced it back down. "I am *not* your sweetie."

"What can I do to make this better?" Peter stepped closer, inches from Tim.

Tim resisted the urge to pull back, knowing he'd only end up pressed into the locker. "There is no 'this.'" His words were slow and clear, carefully enunciated. "I'm sorry I gave you the wrong impression. There is no 'this,' and you can't make anything better. Leaving might help. Go. Away." Then he did step back, sliding out and away, striding down the hall.

"Whoa, easy, boys." Grace dodged as Tim hit the door at a fast clip. "Everything okay?"

"Just peachy," Tim muttered in a tightly controlled undertone, and brushed by.

"I did something stupid, and Tim overreacted."

Tim's stomach tied up in knots, and anger pulsed through him, hot and choking. He took a deep breath, then another, and continued down the hall. Let Peter say what he would. It didn't matter. Hell, Grace didn't like Peter, either.

He reached the outdoors and realized he'd gone out front, rather than down into the parking garage where his car was. He stood there for a long moment, then finally decided it was a subconscious thing. The thought of going home and seeing Con made his stomach clench. The man stirred up more emotions that Tim didn't know how to handle.

He turned and headed down the street, hoping that a walk would at least burn off some of the anger. He'd gone to work, glad to get away from Con and the confusion surrounding him, then spent the entire time trying to avoid Peter, who seemed to appear every time he turned around. Leaving work meant going home, where Con would be waiting. Tim could go to the dojo, but he knew Rick would be there with his questions and his prodding, saying things that just made the confusion worse. He hadn't been to the gym since the day he'd wandered around, looking at sweaty bodies flexing and stretching, and realized he was gay. And he was gay; he knew that. Easier, though, to say he wasn't than to explain he didn't like sex.

He had no refuge anymore. It wasn't possible to run from yourself, anyway.

He stopped, taking in his surroundings. Dusk was falling, and the park he found himself in was cool and secluded. Quietly, he wandered to a bench and sat down, staring at the empty playground. A swing drifted back and forth in the air, recently vacated. He watched the empty arc, trying not to think about the stressful things that kept shoving to the front of his mind. The empty movement was oddly hypnotic, even restful. He watched idly, thoughts spinning slower and slower.

His mind drifted until the darkness and a chill off the ocean roused him. The chest-crushing stress had eased, the tension in his shoulders slacking off a little. Not gone, but at bay again. Tim took one last, deep breath, then stood and began the trek back to his car.

The three heads in Tim's little apartment all swiveled as one when the door opened. Rick grinned. "There's the man we've been waiting for!"

Tim stood framed, blinking at them in apparent confusion. "What?"

"Eloquent." Jay laughed from the corner.

"We're going out." Rick watched as Tim composed himself and glanced around the apartment, taking them all in. "Give poor Conner here something to look at other than these four walls." He was still waiting for Tim to unscrew himself from the doorway.

"Oh. Right." A frown marred the skin between Tim's eyebrows. "Sure. Well, uh, Con has a key..."

Rick and Jay exchanged looks. Sometimes, Rick thought, the genius was really dumb. It was another thing to add to the list of things that made up Tim: perfect at ignoring all problems and emotions, and really dumb for a smart guy. "All of us. You, too."

"I can't." Tim didn't even stop to think about it, just shook his head once. "I have things to do—"

"No, you don't," Rick interrupted. "You're just being anti-social. C'mon. We're going." He stood, putting his beer down and heading firmly toward Tim. Getting out would be good for him, anyway.

"Guys." Con laughed from the couch, halting Rick's progress. "You can't just drag him out the door."

"*Thank* you." Tim shot Rick a dark look. It didn't

faze Rick in the slightest.

"You have to let him change first."

The dark look shifted to the sprawled figure on the couch. Rick laughed. He knew he liked Conner. "Of course. Tim, go change."

"I don't know what to wear to a bar!" Distress streaked across his face.

"Wear that blue T-shirt," Jay suggested from the kitchen. Rick stepped back, turning to see both men.

Tim stared uncomprehendingly at Jay.

"The old one," Jay clarified. "Oh, c'mon, you wear it to the dojo sometimes."

"That's practically worn through." Tim crossed his arms over his narrow chest and looked immovable.

"I know. It's all soft and practically translucent. It's perfect. Has that scuffed look people pay good money for." Jay grinned, brown eyes wicked. "Brings out your baby blues."

Tim glowered, his baby blues throwing sparks.

"Trust me," Jay said blithely. "I'm a lech."

Rick choked back his snicker. "And wear those old jeans." When Tim's gaze turned to him accusingly, he shrugged and said, "They make your ass look good."

Silence was difficult. Most people wanted to fill it, wanted to do something with it. Rick let the silence hang, the weight of it a pressure on Tim to comply. After several breaths longer than most people would have held out, Tim cursed softly and dropped his backpack in the corner. He didn't even flinch at the bang, just stormed into his bedroom.

Rick turned to look at Jay, miming a whistle. Then he looked at Con, who'd curled up in the corner of the couch.

"Look, if he doesn't want to go—" Con began.

Jay interrupted. "Fuck that. Kid needs to get out. He's

just gonna sit here alone and brood, otherwise."

"Remember, you're not on the other end of a phone line to help him vent anymore." Rick felt only marginal shame for guilting both men into going out together. It would be better for them in the long run.

"Yeah," Con mumbled. "I guess."

"Trust us." Jay smiled so beguilingly it would have been impossible not to.

"Hey, I didn't know they were going to strong-arm you into this," Jay heard Conner say in an undertone as he leaned close to Tim's black hair. "If you want to leave..."

Jay looked around the two of them, catching Rick's eye with a disbelieving, 'is he really that stupid?' expression. Here they were, working hard to give Con half a chance, and he was sabotaging their efforts. The twerp.

"Drinks all around!" Rick waved a hand at the bartender.

"I don't think this is a good idea." Conner turned to Jay. "Look, we're gonna head out—"

"Here's the rule," Jay said before the kid could totally ruin things. "Three shots and a dance. And then, if we're not having fun, we leave." He caught Rick's eye and shouted, "Right?"

There had never been such a rule, but Rick went along with it, nodding as if everyone knew that. Jay smiled at Conner, saw the indecision in the man's eyes, and let his own gaze soften. He leaned in so close his mouth brushed Con's ear. "Hey, we want Tim to have fun, too."

He felt the shiver run through Con, and did an inner lech dance. God, guys ruled by hormones were *so* easy to manipulate.

Con looked at Tim hopefully. Tim's gaze was on Jay, eyes narrowed. He nodded once.

"Here!" Rick pushed them away from the bar, three shot glasses held in one large hand and a Coke in the other. He passed the glasses around, grinning. "Try it."

"I'll pass." Tim attempted to hand his glass back. "Someone has to drive, anyway."

Jay lifted the Coke. "That would be me." He grinned broadly.

"*You're* the designated driver?" The incredulous tone was impossible to miss.

Jay's brows rose, vaguely annoyed. "I think I've just been insulted."

"Bitch slapped!" Rick cackled. "Now, drink!" He put his glass to his lips and tossed his head back, Con mimicking the motion. Tim hesitated.

"One shot won't make you vomit." Jay grinned.

Tim gave him an evil look and drank, though it took three swallows. When it was gone, he peered into the glass as if more might be hidden. "What was that?"

"Yours was chocolate mint," Rick answered. "An easy shot, since you don't drink. Tastes like candy, huh?"

Tim nodded slowly.

Jay hid his laugh behind his cup. Easy shot, tasty for beginners. Also incredibly alcoholic. This was going to be an interesting night.

"Your friend is hot." Jay leaned across the table and shouted into Tim's ear to be heard over the pulsing beat.

Tim's head swiveled, blue eyes fixing on Rick and Conner on the dance floor. "Yeah." The word barely made it past his drink.

Jay tapped his shoulder, and when Tim looked around,

said, "No, I mean *really fucking hot.*" He waited a breath, saw the flash of irritation across Tim's features, and added, "You're not interested, right? 'Cause he's a little young, but hell."

Tim squirmed, turning to look at Conner. "No. I'm not interested."

"Good." Jay grinned when Tim turned.

"What's that supposed to mean?" The look in Tim's eyes was sharp, wary.

Jay peered at him. Three shots into the kid and he loosened right up. Said all those things that he normally kept hidden behind an overly controlled façade. "It means," Jay enunciated, just to make sure the inebriated little brat didn't mishear him, "that if you're not interested, I sure am."

Tim's face darkened. He turned again to stare out at Rick and Con, both laughing as they danced, cheeks flushed from alcohol. Then Tim looked back at Jay, attempting to shrug nonchalantly and failing. "Sure. Whatever."

Jay grinned and watched Rick and Conner closely, standing up when they started back to the table. "Hey!" He grabbed the belt loop of Con's low-slung jeans. "Dance?"

Con snatched his beer and slugged half of it back without answering. Then he turned, slapping a hand on Jay's chest, his fingers curling into cloth to drag the man out to the floor. Well, Jay reflected, laughing, the kid certainly wasn't shy.

The dance floor was crowded with writhing bodies, most of them half naked and all of them sweaty. It meant everyone danced in everyone else's space, bumping and grinding away. Jay glanced toward their table and, sure enough, Tim was ignoring Rick completely in favor of glowering at them. But Tim wasn't gay. Riiiiiight. Jay smirked and put a hand on Con's waist, pulling him close when he started to drift off with another cute guy. Jay gave the interloper his best 'mine' look, and the man bumped and ground in a different direction.

Con turned, looking a little surprised. He said something, but over the heavy bass Jay couldn't hear him. Jay leaned in, hand on the kid's back, pressing him chest to very nice chest. "You know I'm not interested, right?" Con bellowed.

Jay snorted. "Man, way to inflate my ego." Shaking his head, he leaned in, dark hair tickling his nose. "I'm trying to create jealousy, here."

Con reared back and turned to look at their table. Tim and Rick watched them, heads together, Rick talking and Tim glowering.

"Ohhhh." Con laughed. *Finally*, the kid was getting it. His hips rocked, body pushing up against Jay's.

Jay wrapped himself up in the slightly-shorter man. At six-three, nearly everyone was smaller than he was—Rick only an inch shorter, and Con maybe two. He appreciated Con's height; he always felt like he was going to break little people. He could never, ever have dated someone Tim's size.

"Jesus, you're too fucking tall." A glower flickered over Con's expression, settling into something awkward.

Jay laughed. "You like little guys?"

"Hell, yeah." Con's gaze twitched up. "What, you like 'em big?"

"Oh, yeah," Jay purred, and glanced toward their table, feeling Con do the same. Jay's gaze hesitated over Rick, then purposely skipped past to land on Tim.

Damn it, Tim wasn't looking anymore. Jay waited until the kid glanced over, then he turned and pressed into Con, wrapping his hand around that strong neck and kissing him thoroughly, tongue and all.

He felt surprise rock through Con, and the instant, almost automatic response to kiss back. He resisted the urge to laugh: this guy was a womanizer. Manizer? Something like that.

Christ. In fact, the kid could *kiss*. Jay swept his tongue over Con's teeth and felt him respond, hips grinding up. Jay pulled back, panting. "Tell me you're not twenty-one." The words were groaned; he felt rather like a dirty old man.

"Twenty-eight," Conner laughed.

"Oh, thank God. You're back in the respectable age range." Only a seven-year difference; he wasn't an old lech yet.

He also really, really needed to get laid.

"I need beer." With that announcement, Con staggered off.

Jay pretended to watch him go, letting his gaze slide over Con and back to their table. Tim was fuming. Perfect. Rick was talking to a woman at the next table. Jay started back, felt a hand on his elbow, and turned to see a pretty girl smile up at him, hips moving, hands over her head. He smiled and obliged.

"You guys okay?"

Con spun to answer, grinning broadly as the world kept turning. "I'm totally sober enough to get us into bed."

Jay snickered. Con blinked rapidly, hearing the vague leer in the laugh but unable to figure out why. Then Tim got the apartment door open and fell inside.

Con swiveled to look at his friend. He had to look way down. "Duuuuude," he laughed. "That looks like it hurt."

Tim lifted one arm off the rug. "'M good!"

Grabbing Tim's wrist and hauling upward, Con dragged the smaller man to his knees, laughing drunkenly. "That's a good look on you."

"Oh, Jesus." That was one of the older guys, but Con had long since lost the ability to tell which one of the two was speaking. "Save me from drunken double entendres."

Tim just looked confused, then shook his head as if inwardly bemoaning being surrounded by friends who made no sense. He grabbed Con's jeans with one hand, his shirt with the other, and climbed until he was upright, swaying.

The motion brought them closer, Tim's thighs and chest brushing up against Con's. Con inhaled the clean scent of Tim's shampoo, black hair tickling his chin, and tried not to move. He didn't want to scare Tim off.

"I think," Tim whispered into the hollow of Con's collarbones, "that I'm drunk."

Jay and Rick both started cackling. "And on that note, we're gonna head home."

Con's hands hovered just off Tim's arms, wanting to steady him and somehow afraid that if he moved too much, Tim would dart away. Tim didn't seem aware that he was clinging to Con's shoulders and shirt, pressed up against him so close their body heat mingled.

"Bye," Tim said to the closing door.

"Yeah, bye," Con echoed. The latch clicked. They stood for a moment in the quiet, the world around them muffled and soft. "Tim?" He almost breathed the word, lowering his head until he could brush Tim's soft hair with his nose.

Tim staggered away. "I need another drink." He crashed toward the kitchen. "Do you want another drink?"

"There's beer." Con nearly fell into the room. His legs moved at the last moment, saving him from face-planting on the carpet. Then he sank to his knees, shoving the coffee table aside so he could lie down on the floor beside the couch. The floor, at least, was easy to find. It didn't move.

"I want one of those minty things."

"We don't have the stuff for a minty thing." The carpet absorbed the mumble. Con rolled over onto his back, one hand playing with the hem of his shirt.

"That was fun. I liked the dancing." Tim stumbled into the living room with a beer in each hand and then, as if to demonstrate, he hopped up and down on both feet, hair flopping in his face.

Con laughed and took a beer. "You didn't dance." He lifted the bottle to his lips, tonguing metal. Frowning, he pulled the bottle away. The cap was still on. He sat up with the help of the couch, covered his hand in his shirt, and twisted the cap off.

"Mine, too." Tim handed him the other beer, still hopping.

"You're so drunk." Con opened Tim's, setting both bottles on the coffee table.

"Am not." Tim stopped hopping, humming tunelessly under his breath, body still moving in what *could* have been dancing, if you bludgeoned a monkey and called it graceful.

"You didn't dance." Con leaned his head back against the seat of the couch and watched Tim bobble around the room.

"I like *watching* the dancing. It's all—" Tim squirmed, rubbing his stomach. "All sexy."

Con grinned, eyes half-lidded as Tim jiggled around, all movement and no coordination. After a little while Tim stopped, laughing, and licked his lips. He paused, then did it again thoughtfully. He lifted a hand and rubbed his mouth with his fingertips, eyes almost crossing to watch.

"What are you doing?"

"Feels funny," Tim said in all seriousness. "Tingly." He rubbed again, lost his balance, stumbled sideways, and in the way of the drunk, somehow remained upright. "Kinda all of me feels tingly." His hand drifted down to slide along his neck.

Con's fingers itched to reach out and help with that. He reached for his beer instead, and took a swig. When Tim started looking around, seeming oddly dissatisfied, Con nearly did offer to help.

He put the beer down and decided maybe he'd switch to water. At least then he wouldn't jump Tim in a drunken stupor.

When he came back to the living room, carrying his water in both hands because it kept sloshing out of the cup, Tim was holding Con's hoodie. Smelling it, actually; his body still, all his attention on the scent as if it were the greatest thing in the world.

Something tightened in Con's chest. He drank his water. "Do you like that?"

"Smells good." Eyes closed, Tim's lashes were thick on his pale cheekbones.

"Like detergent?" Con chuckled.

Tim tipped his head, rubbing his cheek slowly back and forth over the cloth, cat-like. "No. Something else."

Something like Con. He'd slept in that the night before. He sat down on the floor near the end of the couch before he could walk over to Tim and do something he might regret in the morning. Then he drank *all* of his water, hoping it might clear his head, or cool the desire knotting in his groin. "Me?" he suggested, trying to sound casual.

"Hm?"

"Does it smell like me?"

109

Tim blinked and took a moment to focus. Then he stumbled forward, fell across the couch, and scooted up.

It took Con too long to realize what Tim was doing. When he did realize it, it took him longer to figure out what to do about it. Around the time his drunken brain told him that moving away and offering an arm would probably save both of them some embarrassment, Tim's face ended up near his, cheek pressed against cheek. Tim inhaled, his eyelashes brushing Con's temple. "Yeah." The word ghosted over Con's neck. "Like you." He inhaled again, face turning under Con's jaw, nuzzling closer. Tim shifted, sliding against Con's neck and shoulder. "Feels funny. I like your hair."

Con swallowed the lump in his throat, trying to work up some spit in his mouth. Then Tim flopped back onto the couch, sprawling out over the whole thing. Relief and disappointment waged a bitter war in Con's chest, then finally melted away under the onslaught of alcohol. He slid to lie on the carpet, inch-worming until he was lengthwise along the bottom of the couch, scooting again until a few feet separated him and Tim and he could look over to see the other man.

Tim lay on his stomach, a hand caressing the edge of the cushion.

"You like soft things?"

Tim smiled and nodded, then stretched like a feline against the sofa. When he relaxed again his shirt was rucked up, giving Con a glimpse of a trim waist, skin pale and smooth. Tim's legs moved slightly, playing the same touching game with the couch that the rest of him seemed to be doing.

Con's inebriated mind leaped through hoops that his sober one wouldn't have, and his eyes narrowed. "Rick says you are, too, gay."

Tim's eyes closed. He smiled a little, like he had a secret

no one else did. "Uh huh."

Con frowned. "Then why do you keep saying you aren't?"

"'Cause I don't like the touching part."

Con watched him for a moment, saw his hands still sliding over material, the occasional shift of his head to rub cheek against cloth. His shoes were gone, though Con couldn't remember that happening. His toes flexed against fabric, one foot sliding over the other ankle, over and over. "Liar," Con said narrowly.

"No. I don't like touching girls—" Tim began.

"If you don't like girls, that makes sense."

Tim continued as if he hadn't spoken. "And I made out with Peter. Didn't like that, either."

That stopped Con, making him think for a while. Jealousy curled. He worked past it. He'd heard the name 'Peter' in various conversations, but couldn't remember more than the vague feeling that Tim hadn't liked him. "I thought Peter was scum." He couldn't be sure, but his emotions insisted on that.

"He's an ass," Tim agreed cheerfully, eyes still closed.

"Then of course you didn't like touching him."

"I didn't touch him. He touched me."

Con thought about what Tim had said. "Maybe you just don't like people touching you." He pondered that, deciding, finally, he was right.

Tim's eyes opened. "That's what I've been *saying*."

"*But*," Con continued loudly, annoyed at being interrupted, even though he'd been finished a moment before. "Maybe you like to touch other people. Maybe it's a control thing. You just don't want someone else making the rules. " Con gloated a little, pleased with his logic.

When the silence stretched he blinked, focusing on Tim with a little less effort than it had taken earlier. The water was kicking in, maybe. Or the lack of alcohol. He figured that between last call at the bar and the drive home, it'd been a good hour since he'd had anything more than a sip of his beer, and he'd always metabolized liquor quickly.

Then he blinked again and re-focused on Tim.

Tim was looking at him thoughtfully, fingers still sliding back and forth over the couch cushion. His gaze wandered up and down the length of Con's body, an almost physical caress.

"Tim?" The word was hesitant.

"I could try touching you." Tim's words were slow, considering.

Con had a suddenly sober moment in which he realized his reaction could make this go either very, very well, or very, very badly. He wished he knew which reaction could do what. Then, in a flash of inspiration, he remembered that Tim liked control. Con linked his hands together and put them behind his head, stretching his body long, shirt tight against his chest. As nonchalantly as possible—he didn't want Tim feeling pushed—he said, "Go for it." Then he held his breath.

Tim half slid, half fell off the couch, landing in a giggling pile of limbs and cloth. He straightened himself out, pushing up until he sat cross-legged beside Con's torso. Con waited for awkwardness, but it never came; Tim was apparently too drunk to feel self-conscious. He stretched a hand out, fingers drifting feather-light over Con's chest, down his pectorals, skimming over his ribs and abdomen. Where Con's shirt had come up and flesh was exposed, Tim lingered, his thumb rubbing from cloth to skin and back as if enjoying the change in texture.

"Did the bullet scar?" Tim looked thoughtfully at Con.

"Want to see?"

Tim nodded, and Con moved just enough to pull his

shirt up and off. He tossed it aside and lay back down exactly as he had been.

Tim reached out, his fingers sliding over the puckered scar that was slowly fading. For a moment he looked distressed. "How long did it take to heal?"

"A while. Lots of physical therapy."

"You should still be doing it." Tim's touch was soft, brushing over the spot again and again.

"I am. The San Diego Fire Department has someone they recommended, even though I haven't started yet. And I do stuff here, while you're working. And my new boss said I have to get counseling, to make sure I'm not going to panic or something in an emergency." He wished he hadn't said it as soon as the words were out; a shadow fell into Tim's eyes, bringing a crease and pressing it between his brows.

"That must have been scary."

Con wondered how they could get back on the sex-track. Talking about injuries was less than fun. "It was. But I'm all right. I grew up around guns. And it's not like I expected never to get hurt, in my line of work."

"Not shot, though," Tim mumbled darkly.

Con gave him a lopsided smile. "No, not shot. But it's okay." He tipped his head a little, catching Tim's gaze. "It's really okay."

Tim was quiet for a long moment. He traced the mark, the skin around it, and finally spoke. "Don't get shot anymore, all right?" He was completely earnest.

Con nodded, just as serious. "All right."

Tim looked a little relieved, and turned his attention back to Con's chest. His thumb brushed over the scar once more, then down, following the edge of pectoral muscle, over a flat nipple.

Con struggled not to react, not to bring his hands up and pull Tim close like he really, really wanted to. His fingers tightened behind his skull as Tim's calluses slid over his bare skin, the slightly rough pad of a thumb grazing over his nipple again. Then Tim's hand moved on, across to whorls of chest hair. Fingernails scraped lightly through black curls. Tim's fingers flattened out as he followed the line of hair to where it smoothed down the center of Con's stomach.

Con inhaled slowly, trying to bank his arousal. His muscles tightened, shuddering against Tim's hands.

"Are you ticklish?" Tim asked, sounding surprised.

"Not... exactly."

"You shivered." It was almost an accusation. Con could practically hear the wheels spinning in Tim's head: you shivered, you must be ticklish.

"Yeah," Con said.

Tim traced idle patterns on Con's stomach, looking at him thoughtfully. Then his fingers caught on Con's belly button, distracting him again. His hand slid lower, stopping where the little trail of hair vanished under the waistband of Con's jeans. His fingers skimmed along the edge, thumb flicking at the button.

Oh, God, Con had to stop *that* line of touch right now. "Do I smell like my shirt?" It was the first thing that popped into his mind.

Tim started to lean over, lost his balance, rose up on his knees, and swung across so that he was on all fours, hands on either side of Con's head, knees on either side of his waist. Then he lowered himself, leaning down until they were tantalizingly close, his face inches from Con's neck and shoulder. Heat coiled, trapped between them. Tim's shirt brushed against his stomach. Con's muscles tightened. Breath whispered against his neck with each of Tim's exhalations. As distractions went, Con thought it was effective—on both of them.

"Yeah." The warmth between them went damp with

the word. Then Tim sat up, his rump coming down on Con's hips a hair above his erection. Con considered wiggling and, at the last moment, decided against it.

Tim's hands skimmed over Con's chest, shaping his torso, rubbing back up again in long, sweeping motions. "You have big muscles."

"They're for carrying people out of burning buildings." Con smiled.

Tim returned it absently, then caught his lower lip in his teeth. He swallowed, pupils dilated, breathing shallow. Con had guessed right, then: Tim got off on men, but didn't like giving up control. He nearly laughed. Hell, he didn't mind letting someone else set the pace.

Tim squirmed against him, thighs rubbing against Con's hips, butt against his crotch briefly. Con bit back a sigh of appreciation and wondered how he could get Tim to speed things up a little. Tim leaned closer, skimming a finger along Con's jaw, up around the cup of his ear, into his hair.

"Soft."

"Does your mouth still feel funny?" Con stared at Tim's lips, not terribly far away.

Tim's tongue slipped out and back in. "Kinda." It wasn't the kiss Con was hoping for.

"Timmy," he murmured, trying to seem soft and harmless—not easy when you were over six foot and built with muscle. "Can I touch you, too?"

Tim sat up, resting on his heels, hands withdrawing. Caution filled his eyes, an uncomfortable wariness. "I don't think I'd like that."

Con cursed mentally, trying not to let it show on his face. "If you don't like it, then I'll stop." He'd eat his jacket if Tim didn't like it. The way Tim kept feeling things, lips parting at changes of texture, he was practically *begging* to be petted.

But Tim still looked uncertain. "But then if I don't like it and you have to stop, you'll get upset." He shook his head, gaze dropping. "I don't want to tease."

Something clicked in Con's mind, something in the back of his brain where the sober bits of him were hiding. Things made sense, but he wasn't sure why. Anger sizzled, hot and prickly in his stomach. For a startled moment he thought he was angry at Tim, but that didn't feel right. Angry about the statement, somehow, and whatever had clicked in his head that he hadn't quite realized. "Timmy, I wouldn't get upset over something that silly. Especially not at you."

Tim's gaze came up, then flittered away again. He swallowed, Adam's apple bobbing. "But if I don't like it—"

"I'll stop," Con promised.

"And I probably won't like it."

"Okay."

Tim looked everywhere but at him, too drunk to school the anxiety off of his face. "Okay. But you can't get mad."

Con nodded, leaving his hands behind his head, waiting for Tim to settle again. It took a little bit, but Tim did, nerves unable to beat all the alcohol in his system. Con slid his hands out, letting them rest on Tim's denim-clad knees. "You going to touch, too?" he asked when Tim didn't move.

Tim laughed quietly, then put his hands back on Con's stomach, thumbs rubbing over the abdominal muscles.

Con traced tiny circles, feeling the jeans rough under his hands and the hard-soft impression of skin sheathing muscle. It didn't take long for Tim to truly relax, distracting himself by sliding his hands over Con's chest, stroking the line of hair, and scratching hardened nipples.

Con enjoyed the sensations, letting them drift pleasantly

through the back of his mind as he paid closer attention to touching Tim and the reactions he got. He kept the circles up, edging ever higher on Tim's thighs until he reached the man's hips. Those he skimmed over, trying to keep to safer boundaries. He was more than willing to wait and make sure Tim was comfortable. It would really, really suck to have to stop because he'd moved too fast and scared Tim off.

Tim's shirt was old and worn, slipping over his slender shoulders and compact torso like a lover's hands. Con stroked slowly, hips to shoulders and down again, feeling the shift and play of sinew as he ran his palms downward. Tim's eyes shuttered closed, lips parting slightly, goosebumps lifting on his arms. Sliding his fingers around, Con stroked along the edge of Tim's nipples gone hard under the thin T-shirt. Tim made a noise in the back of his throat, hands stilling as he shivered.

"Good?" Con was pretty sure of the answer, but wanted to be certain.

Tim nodded without opening his eyes, licking his lips again.

Con slid his hands around, his palms grazing Tim's nipples, fingers stroking down to the edge of the shirt. Con skimmed under it, feeling the warm, elastic flesh and the hard planes of his abdomen. "Can I take this off?"

Tim opened his eyes, blinking, and sat back. For a disappointed moment, Con expected a definite no. Then Tim grabbed the hem of his shirt and pulled, exposing pale skin stretched taut over his ribs.

Con's heart hammered in his chest, breathing shallow. "If you lean closer, I can reach you easier," he pointed out in a husky murmur.

Tim hesitated, looking a little like he didn't understand the mechanics of leaning forward. Then he did, nearly falling to his hands and bracing there, his face less than a foot from Con's. "Now I can't touch you so easily." He sounded put out.

"That's okay. I'll just touch you for a while. You tell me what you like." Con smiled persuasively. His hands slid up Tim's back, over his shoulder blades, then down the long line of his arms.

"I like that." Tim's eyes closed. He took a deep breath, shifting slightly so his hips rubbed against Con's. Con felt the ridge of Tim's erection and resisted the urge to slide his fingers around for a good grope. Slow. He was taking things slow, damn it, and then they'd have a happy ending all around, with no one pulling away. "No one" meaning Tim, of course.

"You're warm." Tim let his head droop until his nose tickled Con's chest.

"Yeah?"

"Yeah." Tim was so close that his mouth moved against Con's skin, and Con bit back a groan. Then he didn't bother as Tim's head dipped a little more, lips skimming over his collarbone, sliding back and forth, feather-light.

"Tim." Con's head turned as Tim looked up, skin burning where their chests met. Con didn't reach up and pull the other man in for a kiss, much as he wanted to. What he did do was to lift himself a little higher, brushing his lips over Tim's mouth. The angle was awkward; he couldn't do much more than that, but hoped the message was clear enough when he lay back down.

Apparently, it was. Tim shifted, moving up, hands sliding around Con's neck as their lips met again. Con opened his mouth, tasting Tim and groaning when a tongue slid wet and hot against his. He smoothed his hands up the muscular back, pressing Tim closer, shuddering at the feel of Tim's dick through his pants and moving slightly so it rubbed against his stomach.

Con felt tension coil through Tim's body, giving way to

trembling muscles. Tim's hips slid over Con. Pulling away slightly, Tim opened his eyes. He looked a little surprised at himself. Then he leaned in again and Con arched up, catching Tim's lower lip in his teeth, sucking it into his mouth, and swallowing the groan his movement elicited. Con's hand skimmed down over the curve of a firm ass, his fingers flexing into the muscle. His other hand rose, threading through Tim's soft, black hair, grip tightening briefly.

Tim whimpered and thrust downward with tiny little movements of his hips as if he wasn't really aware of what he was doing. His chest hitched against Con's.

Con shuddered as Tim's lips and teeth ran along his neck, nibbling and tasting skin. Tim's tongue flicked out, catching the lobe of Con's ear and following it up along the curve. "That's good." Con returned the favor, movements a little more steady, slowing the pace and drawing out arousal like a musician with a harp. He kissed the soft skin of Tim's jugular, feeling the heartbeat pounding there. Carefully, he scraped his teeth along the edge of a sharp jawline, then nuzzled at the hair behind Tim's ear.

"Oh, God." Tim's hands stuttered over Con's ribs, starting and stopping as if unsure of what to do next.

"Good?" Con purposely breathed across Tim's ear, thrilling at the shudder that went through the body pressed against him.

"Yeah." Tim kept trembling. "Don't—don't stop—"

"No," he promised with a throaty chuckle. "Don't worry." He slid his hands down Tim's spine, over his denim-clad hips, fingers trailing down the crease to his crotch, over the distorted shape of balls and dick covered by jeans. He felt Tim tense, stilling, and wasn't sure if that was a good thing or not. He slid his hands to the outside of Tim's thighs—arousing, but less intimate. Con struggled to remember something significant, something he should be remembering, then asked, "Anything you'd rather I do?" in an attempt to give back the all-important control.

"Dunno," Tim mumbled against his shoulder, kissing warm flesh.

"What do you like?"

"None of it." Tim's tongue licked out, tasting, and then he squirmed as Con turned to gently bite the tip of his ear.

"You must have liked something, at some point." Con knew Tim hadn't liked Peter, so didn't bother asking. "Something a girlfriend did?" he suggested instead, then inhaled quietly while waiting for the answer, enjoying the warm, musky scent of sex and arousal and Tim.

"You already did all that."

Con snorted a laugh, mentally rolling his eyes. So Tim liked control right up until he had to *vocalize* what he wanted. Figured. Con slid his hands up Tim's spine again, dipping his head to suck a mark onto a slender collarbone. Mutual jacking off seemed like a good place to start, he thought happily. You didn't have to worry about oral sex hang-ups or who preferred top or bottom, and—

He paused, Tim's words sinking into his addled brain. He'd already done all that? "Tim?"

"Hm?"

Con wrapped an arm around Tim and rolled, careful not to actually loom, but really needing to be able to control the movements for just a minute. If Tim was on the ground, it made things easier; it was harder to move up to kiss and grope, and he might actually be able to get Tim to stop shifting and look at him for a second. "Tim," he repeated, serious.

Tim blinked, glanced around at his new position, and frowned slightly. "What?"

"You've had sex, right?"

The tips of Tim's ears flushed pink and, encouraged by the alcohol, the rest of his face followed suit. "Well... not exactly." Then he shifted, arching up, hand around the back of Con's neck and tugging none too gently.

Con kissed him thoroughly, more than willing to comply. His tongue slid into the warm, willing mouth, licked slowly along teeth, and rubbed against Tim's tongue. Then he pulled back and looked down again. "What does 'not exactly' mean? Jacking off?"

Tim shook his head, still blushing.

Con closed his eyes, forehead leaning against Tim's. "Mutual rubbing? Tell me you've gotten off with *someone* besides yourself." Because, oh God, he was looking forward to having sex, but you didn't have sex—not even rubbing off—with a drunk *virgin*. Even his muddled brain remembered that.

"No," Tim mumbled, obviously embarrassed. He rubbed his hands up and down Con's arms uncertainly.

When Con opened his eyes, Tim looked like he was ready to have a mental meltdown. Con smiled reassuringly, leaning in to press a gentle kiss against Tim's mouth. Tim's leg moved, shifting up the outside of Con's in an unconscious invitation.

Con took a deep breath. Maybe Tim had sobered up somewhat. God knew Con had. He leaned back a little to look into Tim's blue eyes and realized they were still glassy and only half-focused. *Fuck.* You just didn't have sex with a drunk virgin! Not unless you'd both known the night was going to end like that, and since, until the alcohol hit his system, Tim had been distinctly anti-touching, that obviously wasn't the case.

"Con?" Tim asked warily. "I—" He stopped, licked his lips. "That is—"

Con offered up a soft smile. He was freaking Tim out

with the sudden retreat. The *last* thing he wanted was for Tim to think he'd done something wrong—not now that they'd finally gotten over this touching-control thing. "You are really, really sexy." He leaned in to nuzzle kisses along Tim's neck, stroking down his body with one hand. He licked a wing-like collarbone, feeling the uneasiness slide out of the body under him once more.

Shifting, he left open-mouthed kisses down Tim's torso, licking a nipple thoroughly. Tim made a soft noise, hands tightening in Con's hair. He did it again, dragging his tongue over the hard nub before sucking.

Tim arched away from the floor, breath shallow, muscles shaking. Con smoothed a hand over Tim's waist, trying to calm them both down a little without completely withdrawing. Sex was just not going to happen tonight.

Tim squirmed, leg rubbing up and down Con's hip.

Maybe jerking off would be all right. That wasn't really taking advantage, was it? Con groaned, resting his forehead against Tim's slim chest, cursing alcohol and virgins and drunken making out.

"Timmy," he said into firm muscles, "we have to stop."

"Because I haven't had sex?" Tim sounded so forlorn it was almost comical.

Con swallowed his rueful laugh. "Because I really, *really* want to have sex with you, but I want you to be aware of what you're doing the first time we do it. After that, I'll happily have drunken sex with you as often as you want."

"I'm aware of what I'm doing."

"Yes, but you're doing things you might regret tomorrow," Con said. "And I don't want you to regret this." He took a deep, bracing breath, and looked up.

Tim frowned, eyes narrowing. "That's stupid logic."

Con smiled wryly. "Sorry."

"What if I promise not to regret it?" His expression turned sly and speculative.

"Then when you're sober you can tell me you wouldn't have regretted it," Con answered, "and we'll have sex that instant."

Tim pouted. Con leaned in and kissed him, running his tongue along Tim's lower lip.

"Do we have to stop totally?" The words were wistful.

"Stop what? Touching?" Con skimmed his hand up and down Tim's ribs again in demonstration.

"Yeah."

"No. We definitely don't have to stop touching." Christ, maybe he couldn't have sex with Tim, but he could make out all he wanted. He had no inner voice telling him *that* was wrong, thank God.

Tim sighed. "All right." He glanced down at their bodies, at Con leaning over him, then made a fist and punched Con lightly in the chest, scowling. "Get off me."

Con snorted and rolled so they lay side by side, propping his head on one hand and sliding his other down Tim's body, hooking the man's leg and drawing it up his waist again. It brought them crotch-to-crotch, the sensation both heady and incredibly frustrating. He pressed his hand into Tim's lower back, snugging their erections even closer, a glutton for punishment.

Tim groaned quietly and started to squirm, stilling when Con shifted his grip to stop the movement. Much more of that and Con's morals were going to go right out the window. Then Tim would hate him, and he'd hate himself, and everything would be fucked up.

When Tim looked at him plaintively, Con smiled and leaned in, leaving soft kisses along Tim's reddened lips, deepening the kisses slowly until his tongue slid into warm heat again. If mouth-to-tongue action was as close as he was getting to sex tonight, then damn it, he was going to make sure it was thorough.

Chapter Seven

Con sat gingerly on the edge of Tim's bed, a glass of water in one hand and two aspirin in the other. "Hey," he called softly. "Timmy. Gotta get up."

Tim grumbled something and rolled over, taking his pillow with him.

"C'mon, man, you're gonna be late for work."

That pulled him from sleep, eyes opening blearily.

Con smiled. "Hey."

"Ugh." Tim pushed his way upward.

"How're you feeling?"

"Like someone's playing bass in my head." Tim leaned over, resting his skull on his hand. "Ohhh, fuck," he breathed.

Con chuckled. "Here. It'll help." Handing over the water and pills, he watched as Tim took them and drank it all. "Keep sipping liquids all day. Hangovers are mostly dehydration—"

"I *know* that. I *am* a doctor."

"Right." Con waited a beat, needing to ask the next question but nervous about the answer. "How much of last night do you remember?"

Tim frowned. "Everything. I think." The frown deepened, and he glanced around as if aware of his surroundings for the first time. "I don't remember going to bed." His gaze flickered down as he apparently realized he was still wearing jeans. "I remember falling asleep..." He went pale. Slowly, he looked up at Con.

Con smiled, suspecting his expression wasn't as nonchalant as he was hoping for. "I put you to bed after you conked out." He waited in the hope that Tim would say or do something other than stare at him as if he didn't know what to think. When the silence stretched and Con's heart couldn't take it anymore, he spoke. "Regretting it yet?"

Tim swallowed. He opened his mouth, closed it, and swallowed again. The tips of his ears went pink. "Um... not yet."

"Freaking out?"

"Maybe a little."

Con nodded, trying not to feel upset. At least Tim wasn't regretting it, even if it had been a 'not yet' rather than a 'hell, no.' "Well, I should let you get up and get dressed. You said you have to work at noon today, right?"

Tim nodded wordlessly.

"Get moving." Con left the bedroom.

Tim ended up pulling a thirteen-hour shift, getting home long after Con had gone to bed, and leaving the next morning for another shift that started at eight. The second shift ended at a more respectable six o'clock, and with time to stew over what had happened after the night at the bar, he went straight to Rick's dojo rather than going home.

Rick was in the middle of a class when he got there. Tim

headed to the back, showered, changed into sweatpants and a T-shirt—both Rick's, and entirely too large—and crashed on the futon in the office.

He hadn't expected to sleep. Honestly, he'd figured he would be too worked up over everything to be able to sleep. So when he awoke two and a half hours later, he was a little surprised.

"Feeling better?" Rick asked, pulling a clean shirt on.

"Ugh."

"So, how'd things go the other night?"

Memory came crashing back. Tim sat up, his face heating.

"Oh-ho!" Rick laughed. "That good, huh?"

Tim shook his head, trying to rattle loose his thoughts. "Jay is a complete asshole." That was why he'd come—or at least, one of the reasons.

Rick blinked. "What?"

"He was totally hitting on Con! You're not supposed to hit on friends of your friends!"

"Why not? If you're not interested in him..." Rick let the sentence trail off with an evil little smile.

"No." They both knew it was a warning to keep Rick from twisting the subject. Then again, switching to Jay's behavior, "No. You don't *do* that. It's a rule. Doesn't it bother you?"

For a moment he thought Rick was going to admit that, yes, it bothered him. Then the moment was gone, and Rick just shrugged. "Tim, Jay's a slut. Swear to God, he needs to join sexaholics anonymous or something. If you don't want him hitting on Conner, just tell him." Rick smiled sweetly. "Of course, he'll need a better reason than 'he's my friend'..."

Tim's ears went pink. He could feel the blood as warm

as Con's mouth on his flesh. The memory made his skin heat, breath catching in his throat. "Con's mine," he mumbled, then repeated it louder, firmly, when Rick's eyebrows rose. He lifted his chin defiantly, daring the other man to comment on his sudden attitude change.

But Rick only smiled slightly and inclined his head, acknowledging the claim. "Does Con know that?"

Tim faltered. "He will as soon as I screw up the courage to tell him." He sank into the futon. "What if he doesn't like me back?"

"He likes you."

"What if we don't suit each other and it ends badly?" Tim blanched at the thought. "My God. We could totally fall apart and never even *speak* to each other ag—" Fingers snapped in front of his face. He jumped, then scowled and looked up. "What?"

"Get a grip, Tim." Rick leaned back against the desk. "Don't be a drama queen. If it wrecks, I'm sure you'll sort it out. Beat each other up, feel better, go back to being friends."

Tim stared at him for a long moment. Then he laughed briefly, shaking his head. "Thanks. I think."

"Go home. Talk to Con. I'm betting you haven't," Rick added, as an afterthought. "God, I have to do *everything* for you two..."

Tim gave him a snide look, then stood and headed toward the doorway. "Right. Home. And talk. And no being a drama queen."

Rick laughed behind him, but he kept walking. By the time he'd fought traffic back to his apartment, Tim's courage was screwed to the breaking point. He stormed up the stairs as if he were going into battle, then forced his steps to quiet, respectful of the other occupants, and slunk down the hall. He opened the front door, braced himself, and stepped inside.

The apartment was empty.

Tim glanced into the kitchen, the bathroom, and the bedroom. No sign of Con.

Damn it. That bastard. He crossed his arms over his chest and glared.

"Hey." Con caught a passing doctor by the sleeve of his labcoat, stopping him. "I'm looking for Tim Shelton? He's a doctor here?" He knew Tim hadn't been avoiding him exactly, that sometimes doctor work meant long hours and this happened to be one of those times. But, Christ, he was going to give himself an ulcer if he didn't find out soon whether or not Tim hated him. And if he didn't find out before he started work, which would happen within the week, then he'd have fewer chances to make things right. If they needed to be made right. Maybe they didn't. He was giving himself a headache.

The doctor he'd grabbed looked him up and down out of watery blue eyes, then lifted gold brows and said, "And you are?"

Con buried the flash of annoyance, already prepared to slap the asshole. In his line of work—in any line of work where there were emergency situations—you learned how to assess people. He knew that look, knew that in another twenty years it'd be finely honed for putting people down and keeping them in check.

"Conner Lemor." He kept his tone civil.

The smile leveled at him was just short of a sneer. "I meant, who are you in relation to Dr. Shelton?"

Con wanted to tell the man that it was none of his business, but given how reluctant hospitals were to give out personal information, he decided to play nice. "I'm—" he paused, wondering if he was speaking the truth or if things had changed. "—his friend. I'm staying with him."

That gaze raked him again, down and back up. Con resisted the urge to slam the scrawny asshole into the wall.

"I see. Dr. Shelton's off-shift. He left a few hours ago."

"Right. Thanks." Frustration laced the word as Con turned away. Maybe Tim *was* avoiding him.

"I assume you'll see him again at some point," the doctor said, "since you're staying with him. Tell him I said to call me when he's ready."

Con turned and glanced back. "And you are...?" He was mockingly close to the tone the man had used.

"*Doctor* Peter Wiggs."

Con nearly snorted at the emphasis. As if he couldn't see that for himself. He smiled, knowing full well that the man was using his title as a status symbol. "Well, Dr. Wiggs, I'm sure I'll see you again. I just transferred to the San Diego Fire and Rescue Department. Hopefully, though, if I end up here for treatment, I'll get someone a little..." His gaze traveled over the weedy figure, giving him an unimpressed look of Con's own. He let disdain creep into it. "A little more experienced."

There. Con turned and headed out of the hospital, feeling the glare on his back the whole way.

He was in the car when his cell phone rang. He thumbed it open, glanced down at the caller ID, and felt something in his chest release when he saw it was Tim. Con hit 'send' and put the phone to his ear. "Hey."

"Where *are* you?"

Con smiled. Obviously, Tim wasn't avoiding him. "I was just at your work, looking for you."

"Why? Is everything okay?"

"Yeah, of course," Con assured him. "I just hadn't seen

you in a few days and... well..." He was too embarrassed to admit that he'd been getting paranoid. "I met your friend Peter."

Tim snorted. "He's not my friend."

"Thank God. He's a complete dickhead."

"I know!"

"Hey, I'm headed back now. Do you want me to pick up dinner on the way home?" It sounded so domestic that for a moment Con's heart thudded in silence.

There was a long pause. "Yeah. No more pizza."

"All right. Indian? I saw one on the way here..." He thought he could find it again.

"Okay. See you soon."

"Sure." Con hung up, tossing the phone onto the passenger seat. This was good. He'd get to talk to Tim, and stopping to get dinner gave him some time to compose himself before the possible relationship talk. Con focused on breathing and tried not to panic at the thought.

Con fumbled with his key, nerves making him shaky. He finally got the door open and stepped inside, only to stop in the entrance.

Obviously, he was the only one freaking out. He couldn't decide if he was glad Tim was calm enough to sleep, or annoyed. Then again, he figured Tim had gotten no more than eight hours of shut-eye over the last couple of days, so maybe it wasn't so much calm as it was exhaustion. He guessed that it had to be exhaustion. Tim hadn't even lain down, just passed out curled into the corner of the couch. His skin was pale, even for him, his normally tidy hair mussed. Con smiled slightly.

He tiptoed into the apartment, setting bags of food on the counter, keeping half an eye on the slow rise and fall of Tim's chest. Trying to let the man sleep for as long as possible, he pulled out dishes and spooned food onto them, figuring that if it got cold there was always the microwave.

Midway through, however, Tim took a sudden breath, jerking awake. He blinked, leaning on the arm of the sofa, then turned toward Con.

"Oh, hey." Tim straightened up and rubbed the heel of his hand against one eye. "How long was I out?"

"Not long. I just got home a few minutes ago." Con dug two forks out of the drawer. "Dinner?"

"Um." Tim looked around, befuddled. "Yeah." He picked the stack of magazines Con had been collecting up off the coffee table, then looked around for a moment before setting them on the floor.

"I'll find a place for those," Con promised, smiling sheepishly. He walked around the counter to hand Tim a plate, then sat down on the other end of the couch.

The silence between them stretched, straining with the unspoken things they needed to say. Tim broke it, staring intently at the beans he wasn't eating. "Okay, I'm not freaked out." He glanced up, then back down. "Well, not completely."

Con took a deep breath and nodded, relief making him dizzy. "Cool. I mean, good."

"Do you like Jay?"

Con's mind stuttered at the non sequitur, trying to figure out where that leap had come from.

"I mean, you guys were dancing... and kissing..." The last two words were muttered darkly as Tim glared at nothing.

Con grinned. His heart did a happy little flutter in his chest. "You're jealous?"

"No," Tim snapped. "But there's no point in starting something if—"

"So we could start something?"

Tim frowned, flustered.

Con loved flustering him. Over the last few weeks he'd stopped provoking Tim, trying instead to get everything back to the way it had been before. He'd forgotten how much fun teasing him was. "No. I'm not interested in Jay. He was trying to make Rick jealous."

Tim looked up doubtfully. "I don't think so."

"Trust me." Con laughed. "Now, can we go back to that part where you suggested we start something...?"

The tips of Tim's ears went pink, and he suddenly became very interested in his food. "This isn't Indian."

"I couldn't find the Indian place. Mexican was easy."

"Oh."

Con waited. Tim said nothing else. "Timmy?" he prompted at last.

Tim set his plate on the coffee table, leaning back and bringing one leg up between them. He sat sideways on the couch, facing Con. Creating distance, Con suspected. That didn't look good.

"See, here's the thing." The walls were solid behind Tim's eyes, and his tone was matter-of-fact. "I really enjoyed the other night. But I don't know that... I mean, I was drunk, and the fact is that I don't normally like—" He hesitated.

"Touching?"

Tim nodded, seeming calm and composed. One foot bobbed, giving him away.

"Okay," Con said slowly. "Well, we should try again when you're not hammered and see if you like touching when you're in control." He smiled pleasantly. "That was the trick, right? Control?"

Tim looked like he wasn't sure whether to be insulted, annoyed, or relieved. "Yeah," he muttered at last. "Apparently."

"We could try now." Con did his best to seem like he wasn't hoping that Tim would say yes.

Tim's gaze darted away, flashed around the room, and came back. "Maybe later."

Con nodded, ate a bite of chile relleño, then chewed and swallowed. Out of the corner of his eye he watched Tim pick his plate back up, pushing food around without actually eating anything. There was something missing between them. Con took another bite and chewed thoughtfully. Things were too strained right now. Awkward. They were never going to do anything if they couldn't even be friends.

"When's your next day off?" he asked casually.

"Friday."

He nodded. "We should go do something." Couples dated. Friends did things together. If they could reaffirm that everything was all right, it might sort out the tension between them.

"Sure." Tim seemed distracted.

Con nodded again. He'd look into it.

Chapter Eight

Con leaned against the far wall, watching the teenagers and young adults spin and kick and in general do things that looked like they'd come from *The Matrix*. When the class was over, Rick walked right up to him, sucking water out of a sports bottle.

"Conner?"

Con smiled and lifted his hand. "Hey. Tim and I are going somewhere on Friday, but I have no idea where that should be. Thought maybe you'd know where a relaxed date place is. Something with no pressure."

Rick stared at him for a moment, then tilted his head. "Why didn't you just call me?"

Con shrugged. "Didn't know your number."

"But you knew where I worked?" Rick sounded slightly bewildered.

"No."

There was a beat of silence as Rick glanced around. "Then how did you find me?" he asked finally.

"I pretty much just drove to every martial arts place in the phone book." It was an admission Con made only sheepishly, but he faked nonchalance well.

Rick stared at him. "You didn't think to phone?"

"Of course I did," Con said, mildly offended. "I didn't

go to the places that picked up."

Rick just stared at him some more. "Jesus. Obsessive much?"

Smiling slowly, Con hooked his thumbs in his belt loops. "You're just jealous because you're not sleeping with an obsessive."

Rick's eyebrows rose. "How do you know I'm not?"

"If you were, you'd be too tired from all the orgasms to be leaping around like you just were."

Two students standing nearby stopped talking to gape. Then they laughed and edged away. Rick closed his eyes, not quite wincing. "Well, now that I have a nice lawsuit for inappropriate behavior to look forward to... What was your question?"

Con repeated it, grinning.

"There's a festival going on at the San Diego Bay. You can hit Seaport Village, too, since it's in the same area. Head there." Rick took half a step closer and lowered his voice. "So, you and Tim...?

"What about us?"

"*Are* you sleeping together?"

Con grinned. "Not yet." No one could have mistaken that 'yet' would happen soon.

"Oh, God, Tim!" Con wrapped his hands around the safety bar of the Ferris wheel and swung their box. "We're gonna fall!"

"Jesus fucking Christ, you asshole," Tim snarled through gritted teeth, his grip white, one hand on the side of the enclosure and the other on Con's arm, his feet braced against the floorboard. "If you get us kicked out, I'm going to..." He let the sentence hang in the air, unfinished.

"Is that a threat?" Con laughed.

"It's a *promise*." Tim's eyes hadn't left his knees.

Con cackled and stopped rocking, sitting back and stretching an arm out over the back of the seat. "Aw. Don't worry, Timmy, I'll save you," he said patronizingly.

Tim let go of Con's arm to punch him in the chest, a quick little pop that left Con's skin stinging.

He chuckled, rubbing the spot, and looked up and out at the ocean. From this high, it looked like it stretched forever. "This is nothing like the Great Lakes." He sighed happily as the sun warmed his face, chasing off the chill that the breeze brought up. "People said the Lakes were similar, but they're not."

"That's because it's an *ocean*." Tim kept staring at his knees. "Whereas the Lakes are *lakes*."

Con looked at him, amused. "You could have said you were afraid of heights before we got on, you know."

"Then you would have just wheedled until I got on anyway, and I'd still be sitting here thinking about how badly we'll be hurt if we fall and somehow survive the drop, the rails, and the ground."

Con laughed again, sliding his arm from the seat back to Tim's shoulders. "We won't fall." The muscles under his arm were strong, if tense. Tim was apparently so busy concentrating on his little list of doom that he wasn't being bothered by public displays of affection. That was nice. Maybe they needed to ride more Ferris wheels. "You must just be a blast on roller coasters."

"Do you know what kind of whiplash roller coasters can cause?" Tim shot back. "If you're going to do something for thrills, go skydiving. At least then, you either die or you're fine."

Con grinned, flashing straight teeth. "Timmy, if I went skydiving, would you go with me?"

"Only if you promise to stop calling me 'Timmy.'"

"Done."

Tim blinked and pulled his gaze from his knees to fasten it on Con's face. "Wait. What?"

"We're going skydiving." Con smiled benignly.

"Let me think about it."

"You think too much." Con leaned back and the box began to rock slightly. Tim tensed again. "We are *not* going to fall." Con's words were firm and quiet as he closed his eyes to enjoy the sun. "Here, lean back."

Tim didn't budge.

Con smiled, wrapped his hand around Tim's far bicep, and tugged until Tim edged cautiously back. One hand clamped on Con's knee, the other hand grabbed his fingers in a vise.

"Okay," Tim breathed. "Okay."

Con tugged Tim more snugly against him, part of him trying to comfort, but another part of him just enjoying the feel of the small body pressed up tight, neither skittish nor wary. The wind off the ocean picked up, setting them swaying, and Tim stiffened. Con tightened his hold around Tim's shoulders, squeezing the fingers holding his. "Just relax. Lean back. There you go. Close your eyes. Imagine we're on a porch, one of those big bench swings." His voice was calm and soothing, the same one he'd used to talk people away from their burning houses, or out of wrecked cars. "It's a wooden swing, and you can hear the creak of the chains holding it up. A little push with your feet against the ground makes it move, just swaying back and forth over the floorboards." He could feel Tim relax marginally and kept talking, turning his head until the black hair tickled his nose. After a while he stopped, enjoying the view and the man against him. "I didn't mean to scare you," he said softly.

Tim snorted, completely unromantic. "Yes, you did."

Con grinned broadly before placing a kiss on the

temple so tantalizingly close. "Yeah. I did. But I didn't mean to scare you that badly."

He could feel the shift and play of muscle under Tim shirt. "I wasn't that scared." The words were a grudgingly-spoken mutter.

Con didn't laugh at him, tempting as it was.

The ocean crashed below, a distant roar that faded into the background. Seagulls cried, pinwheeling overhead. The sun sparkled on the water like glitter on satin, flashing and ever-moving. Look at one sparkle, and it was already gone. "When we get down," Con said after a long while, "we should get ice cream."

"You just had ice cream." Tim sounded amused.

"Like, two hours ago!" Con protested, though he smiled as he did so.

"Like, thirty minutes ago!" Tim mimicked.

"Well, still, I need more."

Silence fell again. The wheel circled, bringing them closer to the ground, closer to the laughter of the crowds. Then it went back up, carrying them over the sea and into the sky.

"What are you thinking about?" Tension crept slowly back into Tim's muscles as they rose.

Con turned his head slightly, brushing his cheek over soft, straight hair. Tim had said it was getting shaggy, but Con couldn't tell. He liked it mussed, anyway.

"Hey." Tim shifted to nudge him with an elbow. "What are you thinking about?"

For a moment, Con tried to think up a lie. Then he stopped, keeping his voice soft and low, calming. "I like having you here. On an honest-to-God date."

Tim chuckled, a single huff of air out of his narrow chest.

"I was thinking," Con added, "that I'd really like to kiss you, but I didn't want to freak you out."

Tim shifted—not away, Con noticed—and the box rocked. He jerked, hands clamping down once more on the side and Con's knee. "Jesus! No kissing if it's going to cause that!" His eyes opened, staring wide at the view spread out before them.

Somehow, Con doubted that Tim thought it was pretty. He laughed, tightening his hold. "Kissing didn't cause that, doofus, you moving around did."

"And kissing would cause more moving around!" Tim bit off. "No kissing!"

Con grinned, nuzzling into Tim's hair again. "Does that mean I can kiss you on solid ground?" His voice dropped to rumble along Tim's skin.

He felt Tim shiver, and nearly crowed. Anti-touch, his ass.

"Only if you don't rock the box anymore." Tim enunciated through gritted teeth.

"Deal." Con gloated, happy in the sun with his gorgeous best friend. "Know what I'm thinking about now?" The wheel began the start-and-stop motion that signaled people unloading.

"What?"

"Kissing you." He could almost feel the mental eye-roll, but Tim didn't tense. Suddenly, Con couldn't wait to get off. It seemed like the longest time of his life, but finally they were both out, the ground firmly under their feet.

Tim started away. "Ice cream's this way."

Con caught his hand and pulled him aside, so other people could flee the Ferris wheel. "You promised me a kiss." He tugged until Tim came closer.

Tim gave him a narrow-eyed look. "I didn't *promise* anything."

Con started to object, then paused. "You agreed to a kiss." He was half prepared for some kind of excuse and was already getting annoyed at the thought.

For a moment, Tim looked like he was going to argue. Then something in his posture softened, and he stepped forward. "Yeah." He gave a faint smile. "I did." Another step brought him closer, his hands sliding up Con's arms, stopping just short of lifting up onto tip-toe. "You have to bend down, though." He looked vaguely aggravated. "I am *not* standing on my toes for you."

Con laughed and leaned in, brushing his mouth softly against Tim's. When Tim didn't pull back, didn't hesitate, he circled a hand around the back of the slim neck to bring Tim in. Con nipped at his soft bottom lip, keeping the kisses mostly light—they were in public, and *he* never really wanted to see tongue from other people—but thorough.

Tim didn't pull away until Con did, though the tips of his ears had gone pink and his breathing was shallow. "People are staring." Tim ducked his head and stepped away, stuffing his hands in his pockets. Blue eyes glowered around.

"Let 'em." Con pulled one of Tim's hands out and threaded their fingers together. "San Diego has one of the largest gay populations in North America. If they're not used to it by now..." Then he grinned wickedly. "Besides, they're all just looking at you."

"Oh, thanks." The words dripped with sarcasm, and Tim shoved hard into Con to send him staggering.

"Hey, I can't help it if you're hot." Con shoved back and nearly sent Tim into a flower vendor.

"Did you want ice cream or not, you dickhead?" Tim snapped, but his gaze was amused.

"Ice cream." Con lifted his hand—and consequently Tim's, since they were still linked—to his chest. "The way to my heart."

"I'll keep that in mind." Tim smiled.

Con grinned, lifting their hands higher to kiss Tim's fingers, earning an amused look. With one last squeeze Con released him, trying hard to remember that Tim wasn't touchy-feely, as Rick had put it earlier.

"Do you know how to surf?" Con took a spot in the ice cream line and looked out over the ocean.

Tim followed Con's gaze, then shook his head. "Never interested me."

"Afraid of sharks?" Con asked curiously, but Tim only gave him a disdainful look. "Afraid of falling?" he hazarded next. "It's just water."

"You've obviously never been tumbled through the ocean." Tim looked at him wryly. "And no, not that either. Just..." He shrugged. "Not interested."

"I'm gonna learn." Con grinned. "Then I'll teach you."

"You can learn." Tim didn't even comment on the second part of Con's statement.

"Surfers are hot." Con leaned close to his boyfriend, getting a little thrill out of applying that label to Tim.

"You'll be deadly." The words were bland. "Firefighters are hot, too. You'll be doubly dangerous."

Con grinned, taking the compliment at face value despite the tone in which it was delivered, and pulled out his wallet as they neared the front of the line. "You want ice cream?"

"No, thanks."

Ten minutes later, Tim had apparently changed his mind. Con watched, amused, as his boyfriend took the stick and stole a careful bite, then handed it back. "You sure you don't want your own?"

Tim slid on the wraparound sunglasses he'd just bought. "No, I'm good."

Not only good, Con reflected, but oblivious to facetiousness.

A bicyclist passed them, a man wearing a helmet, bike shorts, and nothing else. They both turned to watch him go.

"So, if someone cheated on you—" Con began.

Tim didn't even let him finish. "I'd break both their legs and leave the rest for Rick."

Con laughed, more at Tim's matter-of-fact tone than the words. "Good to know. You're secretly bloodthirsty, aren't you?"

Tim smiled without answering. "You're sunburning."

Con frowned, glancing at his arms. "I put sunscreen on..." But only after a twenty-minute lecture on skin cancer from Tim.

"Missed your nose." Tim didn't even look over.

Con poked his nose. "It doesn't sting." His skin felt a little tight, but that was all.

Tim gave him a dubious look over the edge of his sunglasses. "It will."

"We've been out all afternoon. I guess I'm not surprised." The day was fading, and beside him Tim wandered, relaxed and moseying. "Ready to go home?"

Tim nodded and shrugged all in one motion. "I'm hungry."

"We could stop and get food." Con handed him the rest of his ice cream.

Tim took it wordlessly, nibbling the chocolate coating off with careful lips and tongue. A slide here, a taste there. Catching it with his teeth and drawing the coating into his mouth. Then Tim's tongue danced out, skimming over ice cream, licking it off the stick. Con watched, knowing Tim didn't have a clue that what he was doing was really damn erotic. Maybe, he pondered, the trick was to smear ice cream all over himself, and then Tim would nibble on *him* like that.

When Tim looked up questioningly, Con realized he'd

made a noise at the image. He just smiled and shook his head. "C'mon. I still haven't had Indian." He headed toward the car.

Tim followed, tossing the stick in a trash bin as they passed, then caught up and brushed his shoulder up against Con's. Con smiled softly and wrapped his arm around the other man, not bothered that Tim kept his hands in his pockets. They walked like that for a whole fifteen feet before Tim pulled away, and Con let his arm drop back to his side wordlessly.

The day out had done exactly what Con had hoped: hit the relationship 'reset' button. They'd both needed a reminder that they were friends, even if they were becoming more.

"You make killer Indian food." Con leaned back on the couch, one foot propped on the coffee table.

Tim glanced over the counter separating kitchen and living room, standing with their now-empty plates in hand. "Absolutely," he agreed, deadpan. "You need anyone to dial the take-out number, I am your man." He put the dishes in the sink with a clink of glazed clay on stainless steel, then wandered back and sat down again.

The television played, filling the silence with an inane sitcom neither of them were paying attention to. Con reached out, picking up Tim's hand and idly rubbing his fingers. From the corner of his eye, Con watched Tim watch the massage, while Tim's hand warmed and softened, muscles loosening.

"You still anti-touch?" A smile lurked at the corners of Con's mouth.

Tim's gaze came up, a little wry. "I guess not as much as I thought."

Con dropped his own eyes back down to what he was doing, wondering how to get back into make-out mode without actually making the first move. This control thing could be a pain in the ass.

"We could—" Tim's eyes fastened on his hand, but he stopped speaking, ears going pink.

"Oh, thank God." Con pulled Tim closer, taking the aborted suggestion for what he hoped it was. "You still don't regret the other night, then?" He wrapped an arm around Tim's waist and dragged him up to lean over Con's lap.

"No." Tim chuckled, fussing until he wasn't so sprawled. He finally sat on the couch facing Con, one leg on the floor and the other curled beneath him. "But we're getting tested before we have sex," he added firmly.

Con sighed. "How about condoms?"

There was a slight hesitation, then Tim smiled and said, "How about we just see how far this goes?"

Con nodded, ducking in to kiss the lips that had been tempting him all day. This time, there was no audience. Tim's hand circled the back of his neck, pulling him closer, and Con happily obliged. He slid his arm around Tim's waist to bring him in. Con started to press down before he felt muscles flex beneath him, halting the movement. Tim pushed, and Con gave way. When Tim kept pushing, Con happily leaned back, pulling until Tim's leg shifted to straddle him. He had no problems being on the bottom, if it meant they got to keep making out.

Con knew things about drunken sex. Things like how alcohol made a person less sensitive, and he'd read that being less sensitive made drunken sex less satisfying than sober sex. He figured that was just a rumor to keep people from sleeping around—he found any kind of sex satisfying, himself. But what he hadn't thought about was the possibility that Tim had been *less* sensitive before.

Everywhere Con stroked, Tim shivered, goosebumps rising on his skin. Con's hands slid up and down Tim's ribcage, feeling the shift and play of muscle. His tongue rubbed slowly over Tim's thin lower lip, grazing across teeth when those lips parted. Tim opened for him, breath fast and hot, mingling with Con's. Then Con slipped his tongue inside, stroking, tasting curry and something smooth that was just his boyfriend.

Tim groaned softly, rubbing down Con's chest, his fingernails scratching nipples. Con jerked, tightening his grip on Tim's slim hips and pulling him down, crotch to crotch. An erection pressed up against his, hard and hot. He thrust slowly, long, languid motions that sent shreds of pleasure up his spine. From the way Tim trembled, he guessed it was good for them both.

"Nice?" Con pulled out of the kiss enough to murmur against the pale skin.

Tim just nodded, hovering over Con's chest before sliding his hands across Con's stomach, smiling slightly when he shuddered.

Con chuckled, low and deep. "You like getting that reaction, don't you?"

Tim's smile grew. He nodded. Then his fingers found the hem of Con's shirt and tucked underneath, just enough to tease, to feel the first slide of skin on skin. Con tightened his grip on Tim's hips and pulled him in, pushing up at the same time, watching blue eyes fall closed and hearing Tim's breath hitch unsteadily.

"I like that reaction, myself." Con thrust up again, cock pressing against denim and Tim. Then he leaned up, nuzzling under Tim's jaw, licking around the edge of his jawbone, teeth scraping over flesh. This close, he could *feel* little noises he couldn't otherwise hear, feel the tightening of ribs and throat as Tim caught whimpers before they broke free. He bit down on the lobe of Tim's ear, released it, and blew across the shell.

Tim ducked away, arousal masked by annoyance. "That tickles," he muttered darkly.

Con chuckled and sat up higher. His stomach muscles strained as he tried to capture that annoyed half-pout in a kiss. He pulled Tim back down with him, sliding a hand up Tim's spine to press him close, feeling Tim's hands edge around his own ribcage, higher under his shirt. With his other hand, Con felt the shape of Tim's ass beneath his pants. He curved his fingers around the inside of Tim's thigh, rubbing just a thumbnail across the shape of testicles.

Tim jumped, then groaned, moving his face until it was cradled between Con's neck and shoulder, planting feather kisses along the skin. Con rubbed his thumb over Tim's crotch again, feeling the man's fingers curl into the pads of muscle over his ribs.

"Good?" Con tried to think past a hesitant tongue tracing the line of his neck, leaving a warm, damp trail.

Tim nodded quickly, pressing back into the touch on his crotch.

Con abandoned using just a thumb, instead rubbing his hand up Tim's thigh, between his legs, to caress balls and cock despite the jeans. Tim didn't do anything so loud as groan, but his breath cascaded over Con's shoulder in broken waves as he thrust up with tiny little shivers.

Tension built in Con's muscles, heat radiating out from his cock. Every time Tim reacted it made the tension worse, better, more intense. He had the distinct impression from Tim's tiny movements, shifting like he couldn't decide if he should push back into Con's hand or down into Con's crotch, that the feeling took the other man by surprise.

"Here." Con wriggled until he could get his fingers between them, sliding the tips under the waistband of Tim's jeans and popping the button. Tim jumped, going still when Con touched him, face still buried in his neck.

Pausing, Con slid his free hand up and down Tim's back, teasing at his ear with lips and tongue, inhaling the scent of his hair. Con waited, not wanting to move too fast or scare Tim off.

Then Tim shifted again, the smallest thrust against Con's hand, and Con took it as agreement. The zipper was easy, sliding down with a rasp of metal muffled by their bodies. Tim's boxers were damp, his dick hard inside them.

At the first touch of Con's fingers against his thinly-sheathed erection, Tim hesitated again.

"S'okay." Con willed him to relax, using his free hand at Tim's nape to guide his head up for a kiss. He waited until Tim eased again, kissing back. Con teased, tongue sliding out to touch before withdrawing, leaning back until he was flat so that Tim, if he wanted the kiss, had to come closer. Tim did so, shuddering when his weight put pressure on his cock. Finally, Con relented, opening his mouth, thrusting his tongue slowly into Tim's mouth. A prolonged shiver ran through Tim as he shifted restlessly.

Con tasted, fingers moving a little, thumb brushing over the slit in the head of Tim's dick, the material still between them. Tim jumped and whimpered, pulling out of the kiss, and Con looked hard at the other man's face before smiling slowly. "You're blushing."

"Am not." The blush deepened.

"Yeah. You are." Con grinned, leaning up to kiss Tim again, to dip his tongue slowly into the heat of the other man's mouth. He withdrew and murmured against damp lips, "It's cute."

"Fuck you," Tim grumbled.

Con shifted his hand between them, finding the opening in Tim's boxers and sliding his fingers in. Callused skin against overheated, sensitive flesh. He brushed carefully around the flare of the head before sliding up, his thumb rubbing again over the slit in Tim's cock. The skin was smooth, almost soft, and hot. It was perfect.

He watched as Tim's eyes closed, brows drawn in, breath shuddering. "It's *adorable*," he teased gently, words whispering over Tim's flesh.

Tim opened his mouth to say something else and Con stroked his dick again, sabotaging the attempt. Then he shifted, scooting his hips around until he could feel the rub of his wrist along his own cock every time his hand slid up Tim's erection. He groaned, balls tightening, thrusting up slightly for a better angle. Tim tensed against him, curling in, forehead pressed to his chest.

"Conner—" Tim's knees braced on either side of Con's hips.

"Yeah," Con bit out. "I know." He stroked faster, grip tightening on Tim's shaft. Con sighed softly, almost a moan, when Tim started thrusting into his hand. Short, sharp little motions slid hard flesh over his palm, from the base of the cock to the flared tip. Tim shuddered, semen sliding hot and slick over Con's fingers, hands scrabbling briefly against his chest. Con stroked several more times, feeling Tim's open mouth against his collarbone, teeth biting down as he dragged Tim's orgasm out almost painfully long. Con's hips pushed up, arm wrapping around Tim to pull him down, feeling heat and pressure against his cock and thrusting hard and fast. The desire to be inside the other man was intense, but he ignored it. This would do for now—hard and fast rubbing, cock between them, smelling Tim and feeling the weight of him, lax and sated, and the scent of sex in the air.

He tightened, feeling the cry that was choked off as his throat closed, diamond bright pleasure shivering through him. Then he collapsed back, one hand on Tim's spine, the other still down Tim's pants.

They were *so* going to have to do laundry.

Tim lay, still trembling with aftershocks, his forehead pressed against Con's shoulder. He could hear the jackhammer heartbeat under the muscles of Con's broad chest, and feel his own pulse pounding in his throat. He swallowed, trying to wrestle his body's reactions back under control, fighting emotions that had been safely hidden behind walls—walls his orgasm had torn down.

He'd masturbated. He'd had orgasms. He knew the biology of it, and even the psychology of it. He knew that people often experienced feelings they'd been blind to. He'd never felt it himself, never having had an orgasm strong enough to blow his walls down.

He breathed and tried to stop shivering, tried instead to focus on the calming stroke of Con's hands down his back. Tim shoved the threatening tears behind tight eyelids and forced back a mind-numbing desire to curl into a ball and sob. This wasn't right. He shouldn't be reacting like this. He didn't care what the psychology of an orgasm was.

"You okay?" Con asked sleepily.

Tim nodded, blinking his eyes open. Sure. He'd just had mind-blowing sex, followed by a mind-numbing emotional swamping. Of course he was okay. "Is it always like that?" he found himself asking, and listened carefully for the answer. Because, Christ, that was... too overwhelming. He shivered and forced himself to breathe slowly, calming, banking the stress like he'd done so many times before.

Con chuckled. "Pretty much. Gets better."

Better? Tim closed his eyes. He rubbed his forehead

against Con's shirt, wishing he'd thought to pull the damn thing off. He hadn't expected things to progress so quickly.

"You're awfully quiet," Con said after a long moment.

"Just thinking." There must have been something in his voice, though, something in his tone. Con shifted to free his hands, wiping the messiest one off on his jeans before sliding both palms up Tim's back. Fingers feathered around his jawline, encouraging him to look up without forcing. Tim did, letting Con's strong arms tug until he was in a better position. Con kissed him slowly and softly.

"You sure you're okay?" Dark eyes searched Tim's face.

Tim managed a smile, still a little shaky, and nodded. "Just startled." That was true enough.

The confession made Con give him a sultry smile. "Oh." He kissed Tim again, sliding his tongue into Tim's mouth. Tim closed his eyes and just enjoyed it, trying not to worry about loss of control or battering emotions. The orgasm was rapidly fading, and with it, the moment of fear he'd felt at the vulnerability.

It was an *orgasm*, for God's sake. He was just overreacting.

Chapter Nine

You're in a good mood." Grace fell into step beside Tim as he picked up a patient folder and headed down the hall.

Tim smiled at her, then looked back down at the contents.

"You look like..." Grace trailed off thoughtfully. A moment later, Tim heard her gasp.

He stopped and looked up and around quickly, then realized that she was gasping at him. He turned to her, taking in her wide eyes. "What?"

"You and Peter didn't—" She paused, then made a circle with the thumb and index finger of one hand, jabbing a finger on her other hand crudely through it several times.

"God, Grace!" Tim strode away. "First off, I think that only applies to straight couples, and second off—Peter? Give me some credit."

Grace snorted, catching up easily with her longer stride. "First off, it applies to any penetrative sex—such as butt sex—and second off, *you* dated him."

"We went out a few times," Tim corrected, stopping at an exam room doorway. "And I learned my lesson."

"Then who?" Grace's voice lowered and her dark eyes sparkled.

Tim smiled smugly and ducked into the exam room.

Con looked up hopefully as the door to the doctors' lounge opened. A doctor had said he'd send someone to find Tim, but surely it hadn't been long enough to have done so.

He nearly backpedaled when two people—the doctor from before with another woman doctor, judging from the lab coat—entered the lounge. "Uh, hi." Two sets of eyes pinned him like a bug.

"Hi." The woman's dark gaze intensified. "So, you're the guy Tim's banging?"

"Grace!" the man in scrubs hissed.

Con's eyebrows slowly rose toward his hairline. "Somehow, I don't think you got that from Tim."

Grace waved a hand. "No, of course not. The little runt won't admit to anything. But he's walking funny."

Con frowned.

The male doctor turned to stare at Grace, then looked at Con speculatively. Specifically, at his crotch.

Con resisted the dual urge to shield himself with both hands and snap that if Tim was walking funny, it didn't have anything to do with Con's dick. Besides, even if they'd gone that far the night before, he had more skill than that, damn it.

Grace apparently caught her co-worker's stare. She rolled her eyes. "Not that kind of walking funny, you perv," she said. "Like, cute. Prancy." She thought, then nodded once. "Yeah. He's prancing."

"Tim's... prancing?" Con asked doubtfully. He couldn't even see Tim skipping, much less *prancing*.

Grace stalked closer, like a cat preparing to pounce. "So, are you Tim's beau? Because he kept saying he wasn't gay."

"You'll have to talk to him about that." Con purposely didn't back up. Any sign of weakness and she might leap. Women were like predators that way.

"Why are you here, if you're not seeing him?" She eyed him suspiciously.

Con held up a white dress shirt like a shield. "Apparently there was an accident with a coffeemaker. He asked me to bring him a clean shirt."

"So you have a key to his apartment!" she crowed.

The door opened. For a moment, he thought he was saved, but it wasn't Tim—it was the asshole he'd met before, Peter. "Christ." He felt distinctly ganged up on despite being the biggest person in the room.

Peter's eyes narrowed. He sneered. "What are you doing in the doctors' lounge?"

"He—" Con pointed at the man in scrubs, "—said I could wait here while somebody found Tim." Of course, then the man had shown up with this *girl* doctor who *wasn't* Tim, and there was no sign anyone had been sent to *get* Tim. Con glared.

The man shrugged apologetically. "Grace was in the hall," he said, as if that explained everything. Actually, looking at her, Con thought maybe it did.

"Peter, back off." Grace shifted until she stood solidly in front of Con, arms crossed like some sort of immovable guardian. "Brad, go find Tim."

Brad left swiftly.

Peter gave them one last disdainful look and poured old coffee into a Styrofoam cup. "He isn't supposed to be in here."

"It isn't going to hurt anything if he waits for a few minutes."

Con didn't mention that 'he' was standing right there. Instead, he did his best to melt into the surroundings, something he'd never been very good at. As if trying to blend had drawn attention to him rather than taken it away, Peter turned and glared over the edge of his cup. Grace looked thoughtfully at Con. Con smiled weakly under their dual regard.

After the longest three minutes and twenty-nine seconds of his life—the clock in the corner ticked away each instant—the door opened and Tim walked in.

Tim glanced around at the little tableau, then ignored everyone and walked straight across the room to Con. "Thanks." He took the shirt and shrugged out of his lab coat.

"Your boyfriend's cute," Grace said. "But he hasn't given us a name."

Tim glanced at her, glanced at Peter, and turned to look at Con. "These guys giving you a hard time?" There was an underlying threat in his voice.

Con just shook his head, both grateful and amused that Tim, all five foot six of him, was coming to Con's rescue. "We've just been... standing. Staring. You know. Good fun."

Tim huffed a laugh, pulled his shirt off, slipped the new one on, and shoved his arms back into his lab coat. "I probably won't be back at the apartment until late." He ignored both Grace and Peter.

Con nodded. "I'll scrounge up some food. I have some errands to run, anyway." In two days he started his first shift at the department, and he had a few last-minute things to finish up first.

Tim smiled slightly, nodding once.

With a final glance at the other doctors Con headed out of the lounge, calling back, "Later."

As the door closed he heard Grace say, "That's your

boyfriend? He's *cute*!" and Tim's answering, "He lives in Chicago, and hasn't found a place here yet. He's just crashing on the couch until he does."

Con frowned at that description, but tried not to let it bother him too much. It was all new for Tim, and he hadn't expected the man to tell all his co-workers that he was gay, and... well... fuck. It sucked. He stopped in front of the elevator, Tim's dirty shirt balled in one hand. It smelled like coffee.

A shape stepped up beside him, and with a sidelong glance he saw Tim standing there.

The elevator opened and they stepped inside, still quiet. The doors closed. Tim took a breath. "I'm sorry. About the ambush. I didn't tell Grace anything earlier, and she's primed for information now. I'd hoped to get you in and out without them noticing you..."

Con nearly flinched. Tim didn't seem to catch it.

Tim frowned, then took another breath. "And I'm sorry for making it sound like we're not together. Peter's still bugging me about—well, I dated him, and..."

The annoyance washed away. Con turned, looking at Tim's profile. Straight nose, narrow jaw, high cheekbones. As solemn as ever, possibly more so—geared for something unpleasant. "That's the guy that's been harassing you?"

Tim hesitated, then nodded once and finally looked over. "I just figured, if he knew we were dating, it might get worse."

"Are we?" Con murmured. "Dating?"

The tips of Tim's ears went pink. He frowned down at his shoes, leaning back against the elevator wall. "That's what that was, right? A date? I mean, that's what people interested in each other do, right?"

Con laughed quietly, then leaned in and stole a quick kiss. "Yeah. Dating." He stepped away just as the elevator doors opened to the parking garage. "I'll see you later."

Tim nodded. "Thanks for the shirt." He vanished as the mirrored doors slid shut.

Two weeks after dating officially began, Tim found himself on the living room floor, shuddering under hands and skin and lips. Somehow, he and Con almost never made it to the bedroom. Things started in the living room, and just kept going. Hell, when he wasn't on-call at the fire department, Con was still sleeping on the couch.

Tim was beginning to suspect that Con wasn't looking for another place to live at all. He didn't particularly mind.

What he did mind was the sexual frustration. Something was wrong, and had been wrong ever since the first night they'd had sex. He didn't know what, but it made him want to scream. It wasn't that the foreplay wasn't good because, oh God, it was good. And it wasn't that he didn't get hard. He got hard, so hard he hurt, and he could jack off in the shower perfectly fine. Just perfectly fucking fine.

But somehow, with Con, sex never seemed to work.

He wanted to snarl.

They didn't bother with condoms—not after test results on both of them came back clean. One of the perks of being a doctor was that he hadn't had to wait on those. Without rubber to dull sensitivity, that wasn't the problem. And it wasn't lube, or lack of lube, or anything like that.

The problem was—this.

He felt his body tighten, his testicles draw up, and panic hit. He shivered, breath catching, the orgasm suddenly pushed off. Not gone entirely—he could feel it there, waiting. His body ached, muscles on the brink of cramping because they'd drawn so tight. And he knew that when he got close again, that same moment of panic would hit and drive it off. Again. The foreplay was great. It was fun and easy and good. But then things got serious, and the anxiety built, and suddenly he was here—hard and wanting and unable to actually come.

"Timmy." Con read his reaction with frightening ease. "Relax. You're over-thinking this."

Tim took a deep breath, fighting embarrassment and frustration, neither of which would help. Con stroked the hair off his face. Tim shivered as calluses slid carefully up and down his cock, the mouth on his neck leaving quiet, soothing kisses. Since the first time, they'd tried doing it fast. They'd tried slow. They'd tried rough and tried soft and now—apparently—were back to trying easy and soothing. None of those things were working. The panic still hit. The orgasm still retreated.

Tim shoved at Con's shoulders, anger at himself needing some kind of outlet. "Stop." Just that and Con did, backing off with his own look of exasperation.

"Tim—"

He shook his head sharply, rolling away and up, stalking into his bedroom and closing the door before he really did begin to scream. He stood there, naked, trying to breathe with long, slow inhalations to calm his pounding blood. It wasn't working.

"Fuck," he snarled, and turned, punching the door.

His knuckles throbbed to the same tempo as his heartbeat.

There were footsteps in the hall. They paused and he stood there, feeling Con on the other side, breath warming the paint between them. "Tim?"

Tim leaned his forehead against the door. "Go away." There was a long beat of silence, and then the footsteps retreated. He turned, pressing his shoulders against the wood, and slid to the carpet. Knees drawn up, arms looped around them, he rested his head and stared at the floor between his feet. He didn't know what the hell was wrong.

Con was pretty sure he'd fucked something up. He didn't know what, and Tim kept saying it wasn't him, but when you had sex with a virgin and then suddenly they stopped being able to orgasm, that was a bad sign.

As freaky as it was to talk to them about his sex life, he ended up calling his grandparents while Tim was at work. With Grams on one line and Papa on the other, he explained with as few details as he could about what was going on.

"He's impotent?" Papa asked the question loud enough to make Con wince.

"Papa!"

"No, dear, I think he's just uninterested," Grams said.

"Grams!"

"Well, Conner, if you're going to be vague—"

Con stared at the ceiling and prayed for death. He continued breathing. "Tim's not impotent." His cheeks burned. "And he's still interested. We're just... having some bedroom problems."

"Can't decide who should be on the bottom? That's the term, right? 'Bottom' and 'top'? Or—what was that other one, Mary? The Japanese one Ed was talking about?"

Con closed his eyes painfully. "Papa..."

"Well, is it your problem or his problem?" Grams asked.

Con squirmed. "I don't know. He says it's his problem, but..."

"There's always Viagra. Those little pills are a godsend,

let me tell you." His grandfather sounded like he was trying to reassure.

It wasn't reassuring. "Tim gets hard just fine," he snapped, then wished he hadn't.

"Well, sweetheart, most bedroom problems stem from emotional problems," Grams said calmly. "Why don't you talk to him?"

"He's a *guy*. Guys don't talk about their emotions."

His grandmother sounded exasperated. "Well, then you'll just have to do some sleuthing, won't you?"

Con sank into his chair miserably. "Yeah," he muttered at last. "Maybe."

After four days of having Tim avoid him—which wasn't too hard, since he worked for two of those days, but it was still the principle of the thing—Con went back to Rick's dojo, found out when Tim's classes were, and showed up at the appropriate time.

Rick seemed to think it was all amusing, but wouldn't let Con wait in the main room. He said it was vaguely creepy to have an unattached male hanging around and watching kids practice martial arts.

Con couldn't argue with that, and Rick promised to send Tim into the office as soon as he arrived.

A few minutes later Tim walked in, and stopped dead in the doorway. Con remained seated on the folded futon, hoping he looked less threatening.

There was a beat of silence. "Hey." Tim closed the door behind him. "What are you doing here?"

Not the warm welcome Con was hoping for, but kind of the one he'd been expecting. "Well, you're not ever at the apartment anymore." He smiled dryly.

"Did you need something?" Tim asked, as if Con

would have shown up because they'd run out of milk.

Irritation flashed. "Yeah. I need to talk to you."

"I have class." Tim put his hand on the doorknob. "Can't it wait?"

The room fell quiet, strain gathering. Con pleaded silently, and was relieved when Tim let go of the knob, though he didn't come any farther into the room.

"What's so important?" Tim stared at his feet.

Con struggled with words, knowing Tim *wasn't* that obtuse. "Look, I know something's wrong between us, but I can't figure it out on my own. Tim, we've only been dating for three weeks." He laughed hopelessly. "Are we just... done? I mean, I'm pretty sure the foreplay isn't bad, though I could be wrong..." He almost hoped he was. If he was just doing something—or not doing something—that Tim didn't like, that was an easy fix.

"No." The single word was soft. "The foreplay isn't bad."

"Then *what* is going on?"

Tim didn't answer.

"Do you know?" Con was half desperate. "Because I—look, I poked around online, and I'm no doctor, but this seems like it's probably a mental thing."

Tim's sharp gaze flicked upward. "So now I'm crazy? Thanks."

"That's not what I said," Con snapped. "Look, if you want to run away from this—fine. But tell me to leave, don't treat me like an ass to push me away."

Tim gazed at him steadily, blue eyes hard. "All right." His tone was cool, almost brittle. "Leave."

Con's chest lurched. He stared for a moment, uncomprehending. Too comprehending. Out the window, a car raced by. "Oh." He withdrew, pulling away from the overly controlled man at the doorway. "Okay." He licked his lips. Swallowed. Tried a smile and found it hurt. "I didn't expect that." Standing, he looked around as if he meant to gather his things, then remembered that he hadn't brought anything with him.

That was it, then. Friends for sixteen years, only to fuck it all up over a couple of weeks of no sex. Con couldn't imagine life without Tim. He'd been a major part of everything for so long...

In aching silence, he walked to the doorway. Paused, looked down, hoping to see a teasing smile. Tim was staring at the floor, arms crossed over his compact chest. Wordlessly, Con swung the door open. He stepped into the hall, heard the chatter of voices and the thump of bodies in the main room. He started to walk.

"Wait." Tim's voice was strangled.

Con turned as if yanked. Blue eyes met his, the walls between them gone for just an instant. For that instant, he saw pain and fear and horror.

"I didn't mean that. I'm sorry. I didn't mean that."

Con took a deep, shaky breath, and stepped back into the room. He closed the door without thinking about it, reaching out for Tim. Tim stepped away, curling in on himself.

"Don't."

Hands up as if trying to placate someone hysterical, Con backed off. "What is going on?" Hurt crept into his voice, despite his attempts to keep it out. His relief was so great he was nearly shaking, but anger swirled in to replace the pain of a moment before. Sixteen years, and Tim was fucking around with his emotions now?

"I don't know." Tim flattened himself against the far wall. "I don't know. Con, I'm *sorry*." He looked up, pleading. "Don't go."

Con just shook his head; he wasn't leaving. "You have to tell me what's going on," he said softly but firmly.

"I don't know." The words were nearly a frustrated

shout. Tim dropped down onto the futon, arms still wrapped around his chest. His fingers gripped his biceps as if he could hold himself together—or keep from grabbing Con. "If I knew, I would fix it." He leaned down over his legs. "I don't know what's wrong with me." The last was a whisper, hands releasing his arms to link behind his neck, his position almost fetal.

Con fumbled behind himself until he found the desk. He slid down it to the floor, not wanting to loom, then leaned back and waited. He didn't know what else to do. With any other person, he'd sit down beside them, pull them close, and hang on—but Tim didn't want to be touched.

His knuckles so tense they'd gone white, Con watched Tim wrestle with emotion. He watched Tim battle it back, fight for control. When Tim finally sat up, he was implacable once more. He took several deep breaths and looked at Con. "I'm sorry. This would be easier if something traumatic had happened, but nothing did." He spread his hands, lifting his shoulders in a heavy shrug.

Nothing had been solved. But they weren't breaking up. It gave Con the strength he needed to deal with this— whatever 'this' was. He propped his arms on his raised knees, resting his head on top. "Dating you is like having a five hundred piece puzzle," he muttered unhappily, "only the picture is all black, and I'm missing three of the pieces." When Tim looked uneasy, Con added, "I know you don't do it on purpose. But it's really driving me crazy."

A black puzzle with missing pieces. The comparison annoyed Tim. It took him a full day to screw up his courage enough to approach one of the senior doctors, one he knew and respected.

He knocked softly on the woman's open office door, then stepped inside when she looked up. "Dr. Ferguson?" He closed the door behind him. "I have a question about—a patient."

If she noticed the hesitation, she didn't say anything.

"It's a sexual dysfunction." Somehow, it was a little easier to talk about this once he'd distanced himself. "When he and his partner begin intercourse he's able to gain an erection, but he can't seem to orgasm. It doesn't fit the symptoms for the normal dysfunctions—" He stopped when she shook her head over her hands, linked in front of her face. "No?" he echoed faintly, confused.

"For something like that, refer him to psychiatric. I assume you've done all the screening tests?"

He nodded.

"Everything's within average ranges?"

He nodded again.

"That's a head problem. He needs a shrink, not a doctor."

Tim wilted. "Oh." Great. He *was* crazy.

Dr. Ferguson looked at him for a moment, then sighed. "How long have you been seeing him?"

"My patient?" Tim tried to think back to when this started.

"No. Your partner." Ferguson's voice was laced with quiet compassion.

Tim ducked his head, studying the floor. He didn't know how he'd given it away—maybe just because it was so clichéd. Embarrassment burned hot in his chest. "About three weeks."

"Dump him."

Tim's head snapped up. "What?"

"Look," she said, waving a hand, "he obviously has issues. At three weeks, you aren't in this for the long haul yet. Don't get yourself wrapped up in someone who needs help right off the bat—you have enough problems to deal with in a relationship without starting out with them. I know it's not advice you want to hear, and I understand he's really attractive and he's probably a great guy—I have all the compassion in the world for him, and I hope he gets help. But dump him."

Tim blanched. "But it's not—" He stopped when her eyebrows rose, unable to bring himself to admit it wasn't Con who had the problem, especially in light of her little monologue. "Okay," he said weakly. "Thanks."

"Tim?"

He paused at the door.

"Think about what I said, okay?"

He nodded miserably. Great. Now he was crazy *and* ought to be dumped. His week just kept getting fucking better.

"Hey, Tim."

Tim paused warily in the apartment doorway, braced for the worst after his conversation with Ferguson. "Yeah?" He looked at Con on the couch, then blinked and frowned. "You wear glasses?"

Con whipped them off so fast it was like they'd never been. "Just for reading," he mumbled. "Just occasionally. Anyway," he continued louder, "I've been thinking." He paused.

Tim's stomach wound itself into knots.

"What if we stopped having sex?"

The relief was heady. "Stop?" And in the next moment he panicked. Maybe Con had come to his senses. Maybe they were breaking up.

"Just for a while," Con hurried to assure him. "I

165

mean, I've been doing some reading, and..." He trailed off, sliding the little rectangular glasses back on as he flipped through pages of print-outs. "Damn it, it was here somewhere..."

Tim walked slowly into the room, calming as he realized that he wasn't being dumped at all. He felt drawn despite himself.

"Well, in one of these articles it was talking about, like, sexual hang-ups and stuff, right? And it was saying how sometimes, if a person feels pushed they can't, uh, you know. And then there was this message board and this girl—I know you're not a girl, but still—and she was talking about how when she has sex with people she doesn't know very well, it just doesn't work for her."

Tim let his backpack slide to the floor, then settled down on the edge of the couch and thumbed through papers. Most of them looked like they came off the Internet, and Tim didn't own a printer. "Where'd you find all this?"

"Mostly online," Con said, frowning at all the pages. "Some of it was in journals."

"I mean—where did you go?"

"Oh." Con smiled sheepishly and pulled his glasses off again. "The library."

Tim's eyebrows lifted slightly, surprised. He couldn't even imagine Con, the one-time high school drop-out, setting foot in a library. He supposed he shouldn't judge. Con had gotten his GED despite dropping out, and his Associate's degree for firefighting after that.

"So..." Con took a deep breath, obviously winding himself back up. "So this doctor was saying that stress just makes the problem worse, right? And there's a lot of stress surrounding the whole—" He waved a hand around. "—sexual act, and then even *more* stress because we're both anticipating something going wrong, and then this girl on the message board I was telling you about, she had a link to this study about how sometimes people just can't do it with strangers, and we've known each other for forever, but not in person, you know? I mean, scent and body language and everything, our biology thinks we've only recently met, so—"

Tim leaned in and kissed Con, just to get him to shut up. It worked. Con blinked at him, not even reacting beyond the basic press of lips in return.

"Yeah," Tim said. "Okay."

"Okay." Con looked poleaxed. "So, we can just date." The words were almost, but not quite, a question. "And go out. And stuff."

Tim nodded. He wasn't being dumped. He didn't have to stress about sex anymore. God, it was a relief. He smiled for the first time in what seemed like forever—though it had probably only been a few days, and it wasn't like he was a smiley person anyway.

Con smiled back, hesitantly at first, and then with growing warmth. "We'll figure this out. Don't worry about it."

Tim nodded, projecting the assurance Con seemed to feel, even though he was skeptical. A break in sex didn't mean all their problems—his problem, if he was honest—would go away. But if Con was willing to wait... Suddenly, Tim was hopeful.

"So, what did you do?" A mixture of horror and fascination colored Con's voice as he watched the play of sunshine over Tim's blue-black hair.

Tim popped another cherry tomato into his mouth, and went back to picking through the little plastic container. As far as Con could tell, Tim only ate the perfect ones. "I told him that it was his little shits making the messes, not me, and if he wanted a maid, my going rate was thirty dollars an hour."

Con choked off a laugh. He couldn't even *imagine* talking to an adult like that when he was a kid. His grandmother would have tanned him. "You didn't say it like that."

Tim smiled wryly and shook his head. "No. I said 'brats,' not 'shits.' I was only twelve. Not swearing yet."

Con stared, laughed, and stared again. "Didn't he *kill* you?" He couldn't decide if it was the funniest thing he'd ever heard, if he was horrified at the thought of speaking to an elder that way, or if he was just plain amazed at Tim's balls.

"Oh, he threatened to swat me." Tim snorted. "I called my social worker. You don't so much as look cross-eyed at foster kids without catching heat." He found another perfect tomato and munched calmly. Con could watch him pop things into his mouth *all day.* He'd been trying not to stare too obviously.

The breeze picked up for a moment, blowing off the ocean some miles distant, rustling the leaves of a maple nearby. It cooled Con's skin, gone pink from the sun. He settled himself more comfortably on the blanket they had laid across the park grass.

"You must have been a terror as a foster kid." There was only a little bit of envy in his voice.

Tim slanted him a laughing look, one cheek puffed for an instant before he chewed the fruit into mush.

Leaning back on his hands, legs stretched out in front of him and crossed at the ankles, Con basked in the afternoon light. "So, did you move to a new foster home after that?"

"Hell, no. Once he knew I'd call in the big guns, he treated me *really* well. You get paid for keeping foster kids, you know. If I'd complained, he'd have had all of them taken away, and he really wasn't a bad guy. So, I told my social worker that I'd just been mad at him, she gave me a lecture on calling her needlessly, and then I got to live like a king for the next few weeks." Tim sighed and shrugged. "Eventually the guy told my case worker that we weren't a match, and she found me a new home. But until *then...*"

Con laughed, shaking his head. "Look at you, pimping the system at the ripe old age of twelve." His eyes twinkled, teasing.

Tim grinned, flicked a wrinkly tomato into the grass, and ate another one. A crow hopped down from one of the nearby maples, plucked the fruit up, and fluttered off.

"How many foster homes did you go through?" Con asked speculatively. He was getting good at reading Tim's moods, and saw the almost imperceptible stilling of the man's shoulders, the fewer movements that meant strain creeping into muscles.

"I dunno." Tim shrugged nonchalantly. "A few."

"A few? C'mon, Tim." He nudged the other man with his foot. "The first year. How many?"

Tim chewed slowly, gaze distant. "I guess... maybe three?"

Con reviewed the stories that had been the bulk of their conversation for the afternoon, and shook his head. "More than that. I'm sure of it. Count."

Tim frowned. For a moment, Con thought he was just going to sit there stubbornly, but then he drew his knees up and linked his hands around them, relaxed. Blue eyes squinted up into the cloudless sky. "Well, that first home. I don't even remember their name. I was only there for about a month. Then the Albertsons. The Roberts, with their dog who hated me. Tried to bite me, and I got moved... The Reynolds, but they were going through this divorce and three of us got taken out of there after just a few months... I was with the Owens for Christmas... then the Taylors, the Wallaces, but I was only at the Wallaces for a few days. Doesn't count," he added. "And then the Drakes, I ended up there and I lived with them for almost twelve months." He glanced back. "How many was that?"

"Seven." Con looked at his boyfriend, disturbed. "Christ. Your parents died and you went through seven homes in a year?"

"It was probably a few months more." Tim said the words with an awkward shrug. Plucking grass, he tossed it into the light breeze, watching it settle back to earth scattered and newly dead. "And that's not normal. I was kind of a pain in the ass. Plus, y'know, it's hard to find homes for older kids."

Con watched the line of Tim's back, the muscles rigid beneath his T-shirt. "How didn't I notice? I was sending you letters—"

"You had my social worker's address."

That explained it. "So, every time they moved you... you switched schools, had to make new friends?"

Tim tore up more grass, plucked the longest stem, and began to strip it. "They try and keep you in the same school district."

"You can't tell me that they succeeded. That there were *seven* homes that could take you, all in the same school district."

Tim gave another jerky shrug. "Well, the boarding school let me finish out the year there. Then I switched, I dunno, twice, I guess."

Con watched Tim attempt disinterest. "Must have been hard." He spoke cautiously, trying to feel out the other man's mood.

Tim frowned. "They did the best they could."

"Yeah, but as a kid you don't always understand that. All you know is your parents are gone and people keep passing you around."

The narrow chin lifted, defiance settling around him like a shield. "I can take care of myself."

"Now, sure." Con nodded, keeping his tone carefully inoffensive. "But you were eleven when your parents died."

For a moment Tim didn't respond. Discomfort stretched. "I had Rick."

"When you were sixteen. Don't give me that." Even if Tim was just trying to make him feel better, Con didn't like that shady sort of truth.

A muscle jumped in Tim's jaw, his eyes gone hard. Con looked away, trying to settle the anger that curled up in his gut at the thought of his boyfriend being bounced around. Being angry at Tim for trying to make the memory better wouldn't help anything. "I'm just saying, it must have been hard." Con's words were quiet.

That periwinkle blue gaze locked on a daisy, glowering.

Nudging him with his toe, Con smiled a peace offering. "No wonder you're a control freak. Everything else went crazy on you," he teased gently.

For a long moment, Tim glared. Then he softened, lips tipping up ruefully at the corners. "Yeah, well..." He brushed a bug off Con's shin. His fingers were dry, rubbing just below the hem of the long shorts. Tim sighed and leaned back on his hands. "Do you ever see your dad?"

"I got a couple of letters from him, when he got out of jail," Con said, giving it a moment of thought. The man had been eager to start a relationship back up. But after years of dubious contact, and the hurt of everything being torn away because of his father's embezzlement,

Con hadn't been receptive. "Grams and Papa *really* didn't like him, and frankly, I didn't care for him, either." He shook his head, trying not to be bitter and succeeding only marginally. "Did I tell you, when the lawyers took his stuff to pay off the company, we found out he hadn't even paid the boarding school? Grams and Papa had to, and they sure as shit didn't have that kind of dough."

"How'd they manage it?" Tim watched him curiously.

Con shrugged. "Dunno. I do know we ate a lot of cheap food for a couple of years." He grinned. "They managed. They always do."

Tim smiled fondly. "You really love them, huh?"

"'Course. They raised me." Then he laughed, ducking his head. "Well, they raised me through the important parts." He'd been thirteen when he'd gone to live with them, but he felt like they'd been his parents forever. "You should meet them some time." He'd offered over the years, his grandparents more than willing to put Tim up for a summer. There had always been a reason not to—mostly involving foster homes and the social worker being uncertain about shipping Tim out of state.

"Since you're living out here now, I'm sure I will," Tim said neutrally.

"Actually, Grams emailed the other day. She and Papa are already talking about coming out." Con chuckled, shaking his head. They might be pains in the ass, but they were *his* pains in the ass. He figured he must have told them something that made them think he needed help— or maybe that he and Tim were serious.

As far as Con was concerned, he and Tim *were* serious. They'd only been dating for a few weeks, sure, but he'd known Tim for so long that it just felt natural. He couldn't imagine life without the other man, and he rather hoped it'd be as more than just friends. "Hey, babe," Con said, a thought occurring to him.

Tim turned to give him a murderous look. "I am *not* your 'babe.'"

"Babe is a small pig." Con nodded, then continued. "You know I'm not gonna leave, right?"

Tim stared at him blankly, first for the pig comment—he really didn't watch enough movies—and then for the last comment. "Have you completely lost all sense?"

Con tipped his head up to enjoy the sunshine. "That's what I love about you, Timmy."

"Don't *call* me—"

"Your compassionate and nonjudgmental nature. I'm just saying, this whole sex thing is probably a mental issue, right? After all the people who left you, I just thought I'd point out that I'm not."

"You're not... what? Sane?" Tim's tone was caught somewhere between confusion and skepticism.

Con slanted a bland look at his boyfriend. "Leaving."

Tim glowered. Not the look Con was hoping for, but the one he'd expected. He didn't mind.

"I don't think it's a mental problem." Tim turned to stare at a group of kids pouring out of a minivan. "If it were a mental problem, it would have cropped up before now."

"Because you've had sex with *so* many people." Con laughed.

Tim turned to glare at him again. "I do mastur—" He stopped, watching a toddler go staggering past. "Never mind."

Con snickered. "It doesn't have to do with, uh, *that,* though." He gave all the children a look. "I think it has to do with another person."

"I think I'm confused," Tim muttered.

"You can—" Con gave a meaningful 'I'm not saying it' look at the kids and continued, "with yourself, but not with someone else. It has to do with having another person there."

"So, now you're a therapist?"

"Maybe." Living with his grandmother, who had been a therapist, had obviously rubbed off. Con had always been good with people, anyway. "I just think—"

"I think if that were the case, it would've come out in counseling." Tim turned to watch the kids race toward the playground a hundred feet away.

Con frowned. This was the first he'd heard about any counseling. "When did you see a shrink?"

Tim's brows drew in, his shoulders hunching slightly. "When my parents died. You have something big happen like that, they make you see a counselor."

"Why didn't you tell me?" He almost felt hurt.

"I'm telling you now."

"Why didn't you tell me *before*?" That was the kind of thing people mentioned, wasn't it? Important stuff.

The corners of Tim's lips turned down. "It never came up. Besides, it wasn't a big deal. Not like it lasted very long. Big waste of resources, if you ask me."

Con scowled. If Tim had already had counseling... then there went the emotional issues theory. He followed Tim's gaze, watching a couple of kids on the swings shout at each other and pump short legs furiously. He glanced back at Tim, who was still staring at the cluster of children. "You, uh, like kids?" He liked kids. Someday he wouldn't mind thinking about having them—but not any time soon.

"I was just waiting for that one on the monkey bars to fall and break his legs. I figure there's got to be a reward for being a doctor on the scene, right?" Tim gave a wicked little smile over his shoulder.

Con cracked up. "Man, I fell off a slide once. Split my chin wide open. Coulda used a doctor on the scene then."

Tim glanced at him, smiling softly. "Yeah?"

"You can still see the scar." Con leaned forward, tapping his index finger on his chin, waiting while Tim scooted closer to look.

"Oh, yeah." A feather-light touch traced the thin line that ran from the cleft in Con's chin to just under his jaw. "Did a number on yourself, didn't you?"

"It was great. Three stitches. I went as Frankenstein that Halloween."

Tim chuckled, eyes traveling Con's face. His gaze narrowed, peering, and then he reached up and traced the bridge of Con's nose, pressing slightly. "When'd you break that?"

"I broke it?" Con reached up to feel it himself. "I'll be damned! I *told* Grams it was broken! She kept saying I was overreacting..."

"Didn't your face swell up?"

"Yeah! She said that's what I got for slamming head-first into the car."

Tim winced and paled a little.

"I was on a skateboard," Con said quickly, remembering belatedly that Tim's parents had been killed by a drunk driver—hit while crossing the street. "The car was parked."

Tim looked at him, appalled. "That doesn't make me feel any better."

Con shrugged and smiled his best boyish, lopsided smile. "Sorry."

They fell silent, a shout from one of the kids pulling Tim's head around. Con watched them absently, too, enjoying the fact that Tim hadn't moved away after scooting closer, but leaned toward him, braced on one arm.

The toddler was eating mud—Con didn't want to know where the mud came from, since that had been dry sand a moment ago. He couldn't imagine raising kids. Not soon, anyway. Way too much responsibility. But— "I want a dog."

Tim didn't miss a beat. "Would you take a fish?" He looked unimpressed at the thought of a dog.

"A lab, maybe," Con continued, ignoring Tim's comment. "Or a golden retriever."

"If you got a house plant, you could just replace it when it died."

Con laughed despite himself. "Wouldn't you like a pet?"

"Does a tarantula count?"

The negative Con had been prepared with froze on his tongue. He thought about it. "That might count," he said slowly. "Or—oh, dude, a scorpion!"

"That'd be cool. I could deal with a scorpion."

They sat in comfortable silence, Con's mind drifting. The breeze fluffed Tim's hair and Con inhaled, catching the scent of mint and soap that was his boyfriend. He liked that title. Boyfriend. He smiled and breathed again. "You always smell so good."

"It's called showering." Tim didn't bother to look around. "You should try it occasionally."

Con gave him a dirty look, but it went unnoticed. Tim was still staring at the kids. "You know, you really can't take a compliment. You're supposed to just say 'thank you.'" He eyed the other man. "Shall we try that again? Hey, Tim, you smell really good."

Tim turned to face him, a syrupy expression on his face, batting his eyelashes. "Thank you," he said on a whispery, girly breath.

Con started to laugh. "You are such an ass."

"You say the sweetest things," Tim simpered.

"Oh, God. Just stop." Con closed his eyes, the image too painful to look at. When he opened them again, Tim was staring out at the playground, a definite smirk on his face. Con leaned in and kissed him to wipe it away.

Things were just getting good when some brat called, "Ewww, Mom, those guys are kissing!"

Childish shrieks started up, and Tim pulled away. Con sighed.

"If it's so gross," Tim snapped, "why are you looking?"

Con turned to watch a mother scoop the kid—old enough to know better, really—up into her arms and shoot Tim a nasty glare.

"Never go into pediatrics, okay?" Con suggested to Tim with an amused smile.

Tim frowned. "Just annoys me."

"I know. Come on, we should head home anyway. Looks like the schools are getting out." Two more cars had arrived, with the attendant children. He sure as hell didn't want to be around a million little rugrats. He and Tim stood, gathering the grocery bags of food they'd brought, slipping flip-flops back on. There was nothing as attractive as Tim in relaxed jeans with a shirt unbuttoned over a tank top, wearing sunglasses and flip-flops, in Con's opinion.

It took them a little bit to find the Frisbee. The football Con had loaned to a couple of teenagers was missing— they'd apparently taken it with them. He could always get another one.

They wandered toward the car, tossed stuff in the trunk—the back seat was loaded with Tim's crap, accumulated over the last three years from the looks of it—and started out with Con at the wheel. Tim tended to drive as little as possible.

"Hey, what did you and your shrink talk about?" Con asked after a while.

Tim frowned out the window. "My parents dying.

Emotions. The usual."

"What did you tell her?" Con caught Tim's shrug from the corner of his eye.

"Whatever *he* wanted to hear."

Con glanced at Tim, turned his eyes back to the road, then glanced over again. "Doesn't that defeat the purpose of therapy?"

Tim shrugged again.

Con faced front. Maybe the emotional issues theory wasn't out, yet.

Chapter Ten

Con's voice on the other end of the line was hushed and rapid. "Okay, Tim, just don't freak out."

As an opening sentence, it freaked Tim out. "What? Don't freak out about what? What's happened?"

"Nothing! It's fine!" The words were a hoarse whisper over the cell phone. "I said *don't* freak out and that's exactly what you're doing!"

Tim dropped his voice to the same quiet tones. "What am I—" He stopped, shook his head as if he could shake loose the urge to whisper, and said louder, "—supposed to do when you say, 'don't freak out'? Tell me what's going on!"

"Okay, okay!" Con sounded like Tim had spent hours badgering him ruthlessly. "It's just—" His voice got even lower. "Remember when I said my grandparents were talking about flying in?"

"Yes..." There was a warning in Tim's voice, though he didn't know what he was warning against.

"It's just, they called, and they're here. Ed found a flight for cheap—"

"Who?"

"Never mind. But they're here. And they asked me when you got off work and I was so flustered, I told them, so—so we're gonna pick you up and go get dinner. I'm *sorry.*" Con sounded like he'd murdered Tim's dog, only Tim didn't have a dog, and this was worse.

"Coming *here*?" Tim yelled. He flinched, glanced around the empty doctors' lounge, and lowered his voice. "Con, I only have work clothes, and—"

"Shit, they're back. I gotta go." The line went dead.

"Con? Con!" Tim snarled, as if that might help. "Damn it!"

"Boyfriend trouble?" The voice was coolly snide.

He clutched his phone so hard it nearly broke. Then he pasted a smile on his face, relaxed his grip, and turned around. "Hi, Peter." He'd barely seen the man in the last few weeks, and not at all since Con had shown up with the clean shirt. He'd hoped things had been solved, somehow.

Now Peter was looking at him speculatively, intelligent eyes hard and cold. Tim wondered what had ever possessed him to date the thin blond. His complexion was sallow, his eyes too small, his hair stuck up in all directions— okay, to be fair, so did Con's, but on Con it looked good. He didn't have any muscle tone, his arms like little strings hanging from skinny shoulders, and his nose was too big for his face.

Obviously, Tim had been temporarily psychotic.

"Hi, Tim." Peter smiled in what Tim guessed was supposed to be an ingratiating way. He just found it irritating. The man poured himself coffee, stirred in sweetener, watery eyes glancing up with quick, flickery little looks. "You said you weren't gay."

Oh, hell. He should have known anything he told Peter was going to come back and bite him in the ass. Then a thought occurred to him, half theory and half memory of their last date. "I guess you were right." He shrugged. "I was gay. And you said some pretty shitty things." They rose up now in his mind, making bile turn in his stomach. No matter how much he told himself they weren't true—he wasn't a tease, or frigid, and he didn't string people along—they'd insinuated themselves into his subconscious, eating away at what limited confidence he had in his relationship abilities. Or, maybe more specifically, sexual abilities. "Look," he said, trying for civility, "we can play the blame game all we like. The fact is, we weren't right for each other. It just didn't work out." He started to walk, to leave the lounge, and Peter stepped into his path. Short of shoving past him or dancing around like an idiot to get by him, he was stuck. Tim stopped and leveled a cool glare at Peter.

"Damn it, Tim! I tried! I even apologized, despite you stringing me along for months!"

"Weeks," Tim drawled.

"You were playing some fucked-up game, toying with me. You're ice." Peter sneered. "Tired of your new boyfriend yet? Does he know what you are?" A hand rose, an index finger jabbing Tim in the chest. Tim looked down at it, then up, all his walls firmly in place, his gaze flat.

He still had to look *up*. He hated being short.

"Has he gotten sick of celibacy yet, or are you still tying him up in knots? Is that fun for you?"

Tim considered breaking Peter's finger. It wasn't hard, really. When he spoke, he kept his tone soft. "I suggest that you get out of my way."

They hung there for a long moment, still, silent. Then Peter snorted in disgust and stepped back. "I'll be here, you know."

Tim made for the door, trying to get out before he started trembling.

"I forgive you. When you're done with him, you let me know. I might just take you back."

He slammed through, and the door swung closed

behind him. Emotions churned as he strode purposefully down the hall. What Peter said shouldn't matter. Peter was an ass. Tim knew that.

Somehow, though, the words hurt, no matter how much he told himself he didn't care.

Con didn't know how Tim had managed it. He knew that Tim had left that morning in slacks, a plain white button-up, and a gray tie, but somehow when he came out to meet them in the patient waiting room he looked clean and casual, tie gone, hair neatly brushed, sleeves rolled up to his forearms.

"Tim." Con stood, grateful to be out of the plastic seats designed, he was sure, for sheer discomfort. Someone, somewhere, was laughing at all the poor schmucks in the doctor's offices.

"Hey, Con." Tim gave him a real, if somewhat distracted, smile.

Blue eyes flickered to Con's grandparents, and Con grabbed Tim's hand to regain his attention. That steady gaze lit on him again, a question there. He leaned in and kissed Tim gently, smiling. "You look great."

"I practically bathed in the bathroom sink," Tim muttered, breath ghosting over Con's ear. Then he plastered a polite smile on his face and looked beyond Con. "You must be Mr. and Mrs. Lemor."

Con stepped back out of the way as his grandparents came forward.

"Mary and Sam Johnson, actually," Con's grandfather said.

"Lemor was my dad. These are my maternal grandparents. Sorry," he explained in an undertone.

"Mr. and Mrs. Johnson." Tim smiled, slightly apologetic.

"Mary and Sam," Con's grandmother corrected, stepping forward to wrap Tim in a hug.

Tim shot a half-panicked look over her shoulder. Con only shrugged, wincing.

"Oh, relax, you." Grams pounded a hand once on Tim's back. "You feel like a mannequin."

Tim put his arms around her awkwardly, while Papa laughed and Con stood, uncertain and wanting everything to go well.

"Mary, stop that. You're making him uncomfortable."

Grams ignored him. "That's better," she said to Tim when he hugged her back tentatively. "Not great, but better." She stepped away, her hands on his shoulders, her gaze inspecting him quietly. "You'd better learn to hug if you're going to date my grandson." Then she smiled and patted his cheek just a little too hard; Con recognized Tim's wince as one he'd worn often.

"Timothy—it is Timothy, right?—I'm so glad Con was able to meet another tranny!" Wrinkles wreathed Sam's face as he smiled.

"Papa!" Con yelped, horrified.

Tim gave him a mystified look. "Tranny?"

"Transvestite." Grams laughed. "Oh, but Sam, you know they're not trannies. Look, not a skirt in sight! Not even—" She whipped around to Tim, cutting herself off, and bent close to give his eyelashes a narrow-eyed stare. "Nope! Not even a lick of mascara!"

Con wanted to fall through the floor.

"No, ma'am."

Grams looked at him in disgust. "You ever call me that again, and you'll regret it."

"Yes—" Tim stopped, looked at Con for help—he gave another hopeless shrug—and finished, "Mary."

Grams smiled. "That's better. Now, shall we go get

dinner? I'm famished. I hear the Mexican here is great."

"Import 'em and slaughter 'em ourselves." Con's nerves were getting the better of him. He dodged when he saw Tim's fist making a quick beeline for his arm; the little twerp *stung* when he did that.

"I'm sorry?" Grams asked, having missed most of the exchange as she preceded them out the door.

"Nothing." Con gave Tim a half-smile. He wasn't going to risk those hands again.

Tim began to walk slower, the distance between himself and Con's grandparents growing. Con slowed as well, matching his boyfriend's steps.

"Why did he think I was a transvestite?" Tim leaned close, watching the two ahead of them.

Con opened his mouth to explain, realized it didn't even make sense to him, and just shook his head. "It's complicated, and involves being old."

Tim gave him a skeptical look, but lengthened his stride again to catch up. "My car is here," he said as they headed toward the street. "Why don't we meet at a restaurant so I don't have to come back to get it afterward?"

"Taco Palace?" Con's suggestion earned a pained expression from Tim, who insisted it didn't taste like *real* Mexican food. Con couldn't tell the difference.

"Sure."

"I'll go with Timothy." Grams stepped aside and wrapped her hand firmly around his elbow. Tim, Con noticed, only tensed slightly. He doubted his grandmother felt it.

Tim shot Con an 'Oh God, help me' look.

"Sounds like a plan." Con was not about to thwart his grandmother. He knew better. He turned toward his Jeep, waving briefly. "We'll catch you there!"

"So..." Mary waited as Tim grabbed up wrappers, a pair of dirty socks, and his lab coat from the passenger seat and tossed them in the back. "Con says you're an orphan."

Iron control kept him from reacting. "Yes, ma'— Mary."

"And such manners." He couldn't tell if she was teasing him or being serious. He started the car as she pulled her seatbelt across her chest with a zipping noise. "But you have a sibling? Is that right?"

A frown touched his brows, and he smoothed it out. "No," he said slowly. "I don't know why Con thought— Oh." His smile was faint. "Rick. I enrolled in the Big Brother program when I was sixteen."

"And you're how old now?"

"Twenty-six." He glanced in the rearview mirror, pulling out carefully.

"Do you still see your Big Brother?"

"Yeah. He owns the dojo where I do martial arts."

"And what's his name?"

He glanced at her, wondering if the rapid fire questions were going to continue. "Rick."

"And how old were you when you met Con?"

Apparently they were. "Almost eleven." God, this was worse than an interview. More like the Spanish Inquisition. They pulled out of the parking garage, and a quick glance around the outdoor lot showed Con was already gone.

"Did you grow up around here? Before your parents died, I mean?"

Tim tensed slightly. He could answer questions about knowing Con and how old he was—those were innocuous enough. He didn't like talking about himself. "I did. Nearby, anyway. Closer to Laguna Beach." He kicked himself. It wasn't like she knew where Laguna

Beach was.

"That's nice. But you don't have any family in the area? Except your parents?"

He mentally stumbled. They were dead, so surely didn't count as 'family in the area.' Besides, he sure as hell didn't want to talk about them with a woman he barely knew.

"I assume they're buried around here," she added.

He glanced over, wondering if he was being touchy or if she was being rude. Who asked about gravesites? "Um, no. I mean, yes. I—" He paused, rallying his thoughts. "I have no family around here, and my parents are buried nearby."

"Well, that's nice. You can go and see them. I grew up in the deep South, you know, and we used to go visit my Uncle Ian every Sunday."

He made a noncommittal noise.

"If I'm making you uncomfortable, you can tell me to stop." Mary smiled.

No, he couldn't. You didn't tell people they were being rude, because it, in itself, was rude! And this was Conner's *grandmother*, not some random woman he'd never see again. "Oh, no, it's fine." The lie of a reassuring smile came easily.

There was a pause, and then only, "Hm."

He looked at her.

She smiled. "So, do you ever go see your parents?"

"No." He winced internally as he waited for a chastisement. He'd missed the funeral altogether, had only been to the gravesite twice in the last fifteen years. He didn't enjoy it. It made it hard to breathe, as if the control he fought so hard for was slipping away. He hadn't cried when he'd been told they were dead because he hadn't been able to quite believe it. He hadn't cried later, because he hadn't trusted the strangers he'd been living with. That much emotion made you vulnerable, and protecting himself had been too important.

And then, well, too much time had passed. He wasn't a teary person, anyway.

"And you don't have any other family?"

God, the questions just kept *coming*. He looked around half-desperately for the restaurant. "I have a great-uncle on my mother's side in England or Germany or something," he said politely. "He travels. I've never met him."

"Why didn't he take you?"

He frowned. "I suppose he wasn't in the country. Besides, living with him would have been just like living with a stranger. I never met him," he reiterated.

"He would know your family history. It must be hard, not knowing that."

Tim looked at her, trying to keep from seeming as annoyed as he was becoming. Maybe she was clueless as to how much she was prying.

But her eyes were sharp, intent, and not entirely compassionate. "I don't know why I didn't go live with him." He grit his teeth and smiled coolly.

Her eyes narrowed fractionally. "I see." She paused. Then the questions began again. "You don't really like to talk about your family, do you?"

"No more than Con does, I suppose." He pressed on the accelerator.

"He doesn't mind talking about his," she returned. "We're very open."

"Oh." Damn.

"So, why a doctor? Were either of your parents doctors?"

"That was brave."

Con glanced over at his grandfather, who was staring out the window. "What?"

"Letting your grandmother go off with your boyfriend like that. You know she's going to interrogate him."

"Then why didn't you *say* something!" Low-level anxiety about the whole situation finally hit a boiling point. "You just stood there, smiling!" Con's fingers flexed on the steering wheel.

"Hell, boy," Sam muttered. "I have to *live* with the woman. *You* could have said something."

"Like what?" Con snapped. "Hey, Grams, don't grill him?"

"Yeah. Something like that. Oh, hey now. Isn't that a sight." Con's grandfather craned around in his seat, staring out the back window.

Con didn't bother to look.

"Say, your apartment isn't in the gay district, is it?"

Con shook his head. "And it's Tim's apartment."

"Why not? Seems to me two gay boys should live in the gay district."

"I don't know why not, Papa." Con glanced in his rearview mirror in the hopes that he'd catch sight of Tim's car. No such luck.

"Ed says Hillcrest. That's where you should be living."

Con didn't answer. He signaled, pulling over into a streetside parking space, and dug through the cupholder for quarters.

"Oh, hell, I'll get this," his grandfather grumbled, clambering out of the car.

"Thanks." Con waited for traffic to clear before he opened his own door. When he came around to the sidewalk, the meter had been fed and his grandfather was admiring a sporty Miata convertible parked behind them.

"Now, this, son, this is the car you should have." Sam put his hands in his pockets and rocked up and down, toe to heel. "Weather like this, you could leave the top down all year long!"

"Right. Soon as I hit the jackpot." Con snorted. Then he looked up again, scanning the traffic.

"Not like that crap car you have."

Con frowned, looking at his Jeep. "I like my car."

"It's almost ten years old! And look at this—you still have boxes you haven't unpacked. Boy, you need to find yourself a place to live. Unpack your damned boxes. I knew we shouldn't have let you drive all this way…"

Con wasn't sure what driving across country to get there had to do with unpacking boxes, but he didn't say that. "I liked driving. It gave me time to think."

"What in Sam Hill does a man your age need to think about for five days?"

Con smiled wryly and tipped a look at his grandfather. "Tim."

The rant collecting on Sam's face vanished. "Ah." He gave a knowing wink. "He is an attractive young man." There was a pause, and he added, "And successful, too! A doctor. A doctor and a firefighter. You two are gonna drive the girls crazy."

"Neither of us particularly care about the girls, Papa." Despite his determination not to encourage his grandfather, he was amused.

Sam didn't seem to hear him. "When I was your age—"

Con saw Tim's Mazda turn the corner, and relaxed a little.

"Wanna lay odds on whether or not one of 'em's dead?"

"No bet." Con smiled as the car slipped down a side street and parked. "Tim has too much—" His smile turned wry. "—control."

They waited in silence until Tim and Grams had gotten out of the car and crossed the street. Con studied his boyfriend's face as Tim drew near, saw the telltale coolness in his blue eyes that spoke of strain under careful wraps. "Hey. You guys find the place all right?"

"Just fine," his grandmother answered breezily. "Tim was just telling me about living in foster homes."

Tim's polite smile got ever-so-slightly more polite.

"Grams." Con gave her an edged look. "That can't possibly be appropriate dinner conversation." He almost shuddered as he said the words. 'Appropriate dinner conversation.' God, he sounded *old*.

"Tim doesn't mind," she said cheerfully. "Do you, Tim?"

"*I* do." Con caught the way Tim braced himself, the smile both more brittle and slightly harder. The look of relief sent his way him made him ache. He resisted the urge to wrap Tim up in his arms and hold him there until the chill went away.

"Well." She was piqued. Con didn't care. "What would you like to talk about, Conner?"

He turned, leading them into the restaurant, sensing Tim fall back and go in last. "How's Ed?"

Con took his grandparents to their hotel, listening to his grandmother's rant on how she hadn't *really* been interrogating Tim, and if he were halfway emotionally healthy he really *wouldn't* have minded talking about those things.

Only by reminding himself that he loved his grandparents even when he hated them did Con manage to avoid matricide. Grand-matricide. Something like that.

His grandfather followed him back out to the car, wandering alongside him in easy quiet. "She's just worried about you." They reached Con's Jeep, a bulky shape in the moonlight.

"I know." Con unlocked the driver's door, then turned to look at his grandfather. The man seemed to have shrunk in the month since Con had last seen him, though he knew it was impossible. He'd been several inches taller than his grandfather for years, but it always surprised him to look down at the older man.

"I'll talk to her," Sam said. "Find out what has her all riled up."

Con hesitated, then asked because he had to, "Is it just that Tim's a guy?"

His grandfather stared at him for a moment. "What the blue devil makes you think that?" Jowls quivered.

Con shrugged. "She's never met any of my other boyfriends before. I just thought—maybe it's just hit her that I'm really gay?"

Sam snorted and shook his head. "Son, she's Googled every single one of the fellas you've been interested in. More likely she just sees what I see when I look at you and this Tim."

Con waited, knowing his grandfather would continue.

The man smiled softly. "This one's serious. Now go home and make sure he's all right. I'll take care of your Grams."

Con sighed, nodding. "Thanks, Papa."

"Don't worry. I'll tell her to be better tomorrow." He lifted a hand without looking back as he sauntered toward the hotel.

Con made the best time he could getting back to the apartment, stopping only to get flowers and beer. He didn't knock at the door, just walked in and glanced around.

Tim was sitting on the couch, still wearing his work clothes, making notes on a case file. He looked up, his narrow face pale, when Con came in. "What are the flowers for?"

"An apology." Con spoke around them, smiling and wincing all at once. "Flowers are traditional, right? She'll be better from now on. Papa thinks he can control her, but *that's* a joke. I just won't leave you alone together again."

"Great." Tim turned back to his notes.

After a hesitant moment, Con took the flowers into the little kitchen and, when he couldn't find a vase or a pitcher and the water glass almost tipped over, he filled the blender with water and stuffed the bouquet inside.

"Artistic," Tim said wryly.

Con glanced up, saw Tim watching him from the couch, and smiled. "Want a beer?"

The hesitation was answer enough. Con twisted a cap off and walked back around, setting it on the coffee table.

"I don't actually think that's a good idea," Tim said finally.

"Drink some. I'll drink the rest." It could only do Tim good; Con worried about the tension in his boyfriend's shoulders and the darkness under his eyes.

Tim still hesitated.

"I'm sorry about Grams. She can be a little..."

"Bitchy?" Tim suggested mildly.

Con flinched at hearing his grandmother described that way. "I was going to say overbearing."

"Oh. Sorry." Tim didn't sound apologetic in the least. He picked the beer up and sipped.

Con reached out, drawing Tim's hair back off his face. It was almost imperceptible when Tim moved away, but it was enough.

"I've got a lot of work to get done." Tim stared down at his files.

Con withdrew. "Right. Sorry." He knew a dismissal when he heard one.

"Conner's angry with you." Sam flipped through a magazine, his feet up on the bed as Mary came out of the shower.

"I don't like that boy." Lips pressed together, she towel-dried her hair and walked to her suitcase.

Sam didn't pretend to misunderstand. They both knew she meant Tim. "He seemed like a perfectly nice young man to me."

"Of course he did. That's what he's good at." Sitting down on the other bed, she pulled her robe on. "He has a remarkable façade, but he's wound so tightly... When he snaps, and he will, you mark my words, he's going to take someone with him. I've seen the news. These days, boys snap and they don't just sit at home and quietly drink like they did in our day. No, today they take guns and shoot their loved ones."

Sam hadn't looked up from his article. "I'm pretty sure he doesn't have a gun." The chilly silence was response enough.

Eventually, Mary spoke again. "Conner is head over heels for that boy. I just don't want him to end up like his mother—alone in another state, completely unhappy."

"And dead young," Sam added quietly. "I know. But Conner isn't Margaret, and has never acted like her. They'll be all right. Just see."

Con waited until Tim left for work the next morning, then made a beeline for his grandparents' hotel.

"You *have* to be nice," he said when they let him in. "God, Grams, Tim was *completely* freaked out last night!"

She looked almost pleased. "Really? Did he yell at you?"

"No!" Con snarled, her expression making him angrier. "He just got all—all cool and standoffish like he does!"

She looked crestfallen. "Yelling would have been much healthier," she said in an undertone.

"Grams!"

She looked mutinous.

"Just—be nice."

Tim checked his messages, sitting in the doctors' lounge with a mug of tea. They were out of coffee. Grace was calling for mutiny.

The first message was from Cassie, saying she'd left a romance novel at his place and would he please not throw it out. He was pretty sure he already had.

Next, an automated call from the credit card company, offering him a two thousand dollar credit limit at just twenty-four percent APR. Ha.

A message from Con, saying they'd made plans to go to Seaport Village on Tim's day off, and another promise that his grandmother would be good. Tim tensed and deleted it.

A second message from Con, asking where the carpet cleaner was, and telling him not to worry. Which, of course, made him worry.

A third call saying Con had bought some cleaner, and

the stain had come out all right. Tim shook his head as he deleted the calls and debated on what action to take. He'd be damned if he was going to spend an entire day at Seaport Village getting grilled. After a moment, he dialed Rick's number.

Two days later dawned bright and clear, the noon hour finding Tim and Con standing at the entrance to Seaport Village, watching traffic. Tim slipped on the sunglasses he'd bought the last time he had been there with Con, and put his hands in the pockets of his khakis. He forced himself to relax, but the tension didn't quite drain out of his shoulders.

"She'll be good," Con promised. "I spent all day yesterday telling her how wonderful you are, and to play nice."

Tim made a noncommittal noise. All of that had likely only made her more curious. "I invited Rick." He stared out at the parking lot as they waited for people to arrive.

Con turned to look at him. "Yeah?"

Tim nodded.

"Moral support?" Con smiled wryly.

Tim shrugged.

"My, you're so talkative today," Con muttered.

Tim slanted him a vaguely annoyed look, but said nothing. "There he is." Relief filled him as Rick's old TransAm slid into a parking space across the street.

"Tim!" Rick shouted, spotting them. He lifted a hand, looked for traffic, and jogged over to meet them as someone else climbed from his car. "I brought the big guns." He grinned madly.

"The big guns?" Tim had no idea what that meant. He'd explained the situation to Rick, and the man had agreed to come down. What big guns were against grandparents, though...

Then he realized the other person climbing out of the car was Jay, and what was taking him so long was the seven-year-old attached to his neck. "Oh," Tim said. "Emmy."

Rick grinned. "He has her this weekend. I figured she could use some serious spoiling, and grandparents love kids. Right?"

Con snorted and shook his head. "God, this is terrifyingly like a family meeting." He tipped his head, watching Jay carry the girl over, but spoke to Rick. "Are you sleeping with him yet?"

Tim turned to Rick again, interested in the answer.

Rick looked like he'd swallowed the wrong way, except he hadn't been eating or drinking. "I'm sorry?"

"Well, he totally has the hots for you." Con shrugged, broad shoulders rising and falling easily.

"You've lost your mind, kid."

Tim grinned at the irritated look Con shot at Rick. "Kid? I'm almost as old as you, you know."

Rick ignored him. "Emmy!"

She grinned and nearly threw herself from Jay's arms. "Make me Supergirl!"

"There they are," Con murmured, and Tim glanced back into the parking lot to see the rental car drive up.

Rick lifted Emmy and swung her around wildly. Tim tried to focus on that, on the sheer joy in the little girl's face rather than the knotting in his stomach as Con's grandparents got out of the car. His expression remained impassive as he watched the older couple, though his mind stuttered to a halt. "Is your grandfather wearing a sarong?"

Con only sighed heavily.

"Is this Hillcrest?" his grandfather shouted, peering around.

196

Tim looked questioningly at Con, who ignored him in favor of answering.

"No, Papa. This is Seaport Village."

"Too bad," the older man muttered, and gave Con a hug before turning and enveloping Tim.

Tim froze. Then, hesitantly, he patted the man's back. Sam let him go.

"Sam, Mary, this is my Big Brother, Rick, his friend Jay, and Jay's daughter, Emmy." Tim took a step away before anyone else tried to hug him.

When Sam hugged Jay, Jay looked a little surprised before hugging him back, lifting the older man off his feet and plopping him back down. Jay grinned. Sam stared. Then he started laughing, pounding Jay on the back before going to Rick and shaking his hand.

Tim looked longingly at Emmy—the apparent reason Rick wasn't getting a hug. He needed to attach himself to the kid.

"Pick me up, too, Daddy!" Emmy bounced on Rick's hip, arms straining toward her father.

"Anytime, kiddo!" Jay scooped her out of Rick's arms and tossed her lightly in the air.

The plot worked. Mary glossed right over Tim and went straight to Emmy, asking her how old she was and what 'Emmy' was short for. Tim relaxed a little. Maybe this would be all right.

"How long are your grandparents staying?"

Con looked up from the television, eyeing Tim. The question had been asked casually, while Tim stood in the doorway of the bathroom, still wet from his shower, a towel wrapped around his trim waist.

"They haven't bought return tickets yet." Con gave

his boyfriend a small smile. "You okay?"

Tim shrugged, looking vaguely disgruntled. "Of course. Why wouldn't I be?" He apparently didn't expect an answer, turning away and walking into the bedroom even before he'd finished the question.

Con sighed and stared at the television. Aside from the fact that Tim had felt the need to hide behind a seven-year-old girl, Con thought the day had gone fairly well. Grams hadn't tried to grill Tim, focusing her attention instead on Jay. She didn't approve of divorce, and approved even less of a weekend father. Jay, however, hadn't seemed to care. Papa had gleefully told everyone about statistics Ed had given him on how trannies made great dads, and Jay had gleefully told Papa that he was bisexual, and was therefore the best parts of straight *and* transvestite parents. He hadn't even attempted to correct Con's grandfather on the difference between gay and transvestite. Con couldn't decide if he was annoyed or relieved.

Between Jay and Rick, they'd kept Con's grandparents entertained all day. And Tim was still stressed. This, Con thought darkly, was not helping their relationship.

He chewed on his lip and tried to decide what to do.

Chapter Eleven

D r. Shelton?"

Tim looked up from his case file, listening to the hum of the fluorescent lights in the doctors' lounge, his eyebrows raised in question.

"There's someone here for you." Her message delivered, the nurse left.

Frowning, Tim put the case file down and headed out into the waiting area, assuming that if he hadn't been given different directions, then his visitor would be there.

His heart sank when he saw Mary. He pasted on a smile. "Hi. Can I help you?"

She smiled back and lifted a grocery bag. "I brought lunch. I thought maybe we could have some private time."

His smile felt all edges, even to himself. "I'm afraid I have patients—"

"I'll wait." She sat down and pulled out a book.

Shit. Tim looked around, then finally ducked back down the hall. He'd see to his next three patients, and if she was still there... then he supposed he could eat lunch with her.

Con wandered down the cobblestones of the outdoor mall, his grandfather sauntering alongside.

"What are you looking for, exactly?" Papa asked, his hands in his pockets.

Con frowned. "I'm not sure. I'm hoping I'll just know when I see it." He paused outside Bath and Body Works, peering in at the half-dozen people who wandered amidst colorful bottles and bars of soap in overly cute barrel-baskets.

"Is that a fetish shop?" Papa sounded entirely too gleeful.

Con turned to look at whatever had caught his grandfather's attention. "No. That's Hot Topic. This way." He turned and went into Bath and Body Works. He really wasn't sure what he was looking for, and wasn't entirely surprised when his grandfather made some excuse and didn't go in. Sex shops were one thing, girly shops another. Con shifted his Old Navy bag from one hand to the other, feeling too big and too male to be where he was. It smelled like a flower fairy had died in there.

"Hi!" A cheerful girl who looked about twelve appeared at his shoulder, all plastic smiles and bubbly enthusiasm. "Can I help you?"

"Uh, yeah." He held his arms close to his body in an attempt not to hit anything. You never knew what might make you smell. "I'm looking for something relaxing."

"We have bath oils—"

He repressed a snicker. Somehow, he couldn't see Tim in a bath. "Something else?"

The girl frowned, catching her lower lip between her teeth and chewing on it. "For yourself? Or your girlfriend?"

There was a moment of hesitation, then he decided to throw caution to the wind. If his grandfather had the guts to walk around in a sarong, he could admit to being gay.

"For my boyfriend."

Her face fell. "Oh." She took half a step back, caught her lip in her teeth again, and tucked a lock of honey-blond hair behind her ear. "What about massage oil?"

Tim didn't like to be touched. Con frowned. "Anything else?"

"A bottle of wine?" She gave him an apologetic smile.

"Okay," Con said on a sigh. "Let's see the massage oil."

There was an entire shelf crammed with oils. Brown glass bottles, little white tubs, bottles with pumps, bottles with squirters, plastic containers, glass containers, squeeze tubes—he had no idea there were so many types.

The girl looked at him expectantly.

"Uh," he said. "Do you have a suggestion?"

"Well, this one's for sensuality." She pulled down a glass bottle and popped the lid before sniffing and pushing it into Con's face. He pulled back, then sniffed delicately when she just waited.

"Oh, God, that's terrible," he said before he thought better of it. "I mean—I can't imagine him using something that's all flowery. Isn't there something that doesn't smell like... anything? I mean, that has no scent?"

The girl frowned. She capped the bottle and put it back on the shelf, then stood for a long moment staring at the labels. Hands on her hips, she turned to look at him. "No."

He supposed that answer was succinct. He looked around the store, watching people come and go, feeling her gaze on him as he stood there. He imagined Tim, small and compact, muscles hard under his hands, gaze frank but guarded. The clean smell of him, soap and mint. He sighed. "All right." He turned back to the bottles. "So... I can just sniff these?"

The girl nodded.

Hesitantly, he reached up and popped the lid on one. He sniffed. His eyes nearly watered. "Not that one."

"What aftershave does he wear?" The girl unscrewed a lid and ran it back and forth below her nose like a good glass of wine.

"I don't think he does." Not that Con had noticed, anyway.

She looked annoyed. "What kind of soap does he use?"

Con shrugged. "Something white." He sniffed another bottle. It wasn't as bad.

"What about this?" She held it out.

He checked cautiously. "It's all right, I guess."

She hmmm'ed and put it back.

"Grace!" Tim caught his coworker's arm, pulling her aside. "I have a visitor joining me for lunch, but I have a lot to do and I'm afraid I'll lose track of time. Could you interrupt us in about fifteen minutes?"

She looked curious, but nodded without asking him anything.

Tim thanked her and headed down the hall, leaving his lab coat on in the hopes that it might speed Mary away. If he *looked* busy...

She was still sitting in the waiting room. "Mary?" he called, and smiled politely at her when she stood up and followed him through the doors in an odd parody of a patient.

She started talking even before they'd reached the doctors' lounge. "I wanted to apologize for the other day."

"Nothing to apologize for," Tim murmured, even

though he didn't really feel that way.

"Con was very upset with me." Mary chuckled ruefully. "I suppose I can't blame him. I think he's afraid I'll scare you off."

Tim held the door open as she walked in, his gaze flickering around the room. Empty. "You're just protecting him." He followed her to the battered couch and sat down on the edge. "That's admirable."

When she returned his gaze, he had the distinct impression she was measuring him. He held himself still.

"Yes," she said slowly. "And Rick protects you. Right?"

He'd never really thought of it that way. She turned away, obviously listening for his answer as she opened a grocery bag and pulled out Tupperware and forks.

"I suppose he does," Tim said at last. "It's what friends do." The thought rankled, though. He didn't need *protecting*.

Except maybe from grandmothers.

"And your family can't." She pulled the lid off a container and handed it to him. "I'm sorry."

He shrugged, picking up a fork. "It was a long time ago."

"I lost Con's mother almost twenty-eight years ago. It still hurts."

Tim frowned, picking at chicken Caesar salad. "I was young," he said, uncomfortable with the whole discussion. "Kids heal fast."

She was watching him in that way that she had, seeing every little movement and giving them all causes.

"You were young?" Her tone was mild.

Tim nodded, eyes still on his food.

"So, it didn't bother you too much?"

He peered at her sidelong. "As much as it would bother any kid." He didn't trust this line of questioning, though he couldn't say why not. "But I've always been pretty good at handling my emotions. And I had other things going on."

"Foster homes."

Tim shrugged. Yes, foster homes, but he wasn't going to say that.

"Well." The tips of her mouth edged up. "Then it's a good thing you weren't too upset."

There was something there, something in her expression, that made Tim wary. Before he could think of a topic change, or decide if he should agree or defend himself, Mary smiled and pointed at his salad. "Do you like it?"

"What? Oh." He took a bite and nodded quickly, though the taste hadn't quite registered yet.

"My daughter's recipe. Not that there's much recipe involved in Caesar salad, mind, but the dressing is hers." She smiled, all intensity gone. "Seaport Village was interesting. And your friend's daughter was adorable. Spoiled, but adorable."

Tim nodded, trying to keep up. He wasn't sure he'd call Jay a friend... but it didn't matter. What was more important was that she was, apparently, trying to make up. He could try, too, if only because it was Con's family.

"So..." Con warily followed his grandfather into the bright hotel room, the gloom of the evening chasing them inside. "How'd lunch with Tim go?"

Mary looked up from her book and smiled, pulling off her reading glasses. "I didn't interrogate him, if that's what you're asking."

Con relaxed a little, finding a relieved smile. "That's not what I was asking."

"It was exactly what he was asking," his grandfather chuckled. "So, what'd you find out?"

"Well, I think he might be repressing—"

"Grams!" Con shouted, not caring if the people in the other rooms heard him. "You're psychoanalyzing my boyfriend?"

She frowned at him. "Yes. Do you want to hear or not?"

He really shouldn't. For her to pull information from Tim and create theories without Tim ever saying, "Hey, I think I'll talk to a therapist," was in itself unethical. Add to that the shady ethics of *saying* what she'd learned... Wasn't there some sort of patient-client privilege? Except Tim wasn't a patient. Con scowled.

Apparently, his grandmother had waited long enough. "I think he's repressing."

Con edged onto a seat at the wooden table, setting his bags down at his feet. He shouldn't listen. He really shouldn't. Curiosity ate at him. "Repressing what?"

"Everything. He told me today that the death of his parents didn't bother him. That he'd been young at the time. But I thought he was a teenager...?" She looked at Con, waiting.

"Eleven, twelve," Con said uncertainly. "Something like that."

"Old enough to be bothered." Mary nodded decisively. "We had only a short conversation, but even after that, he insisted nothing bothered him." A frown drew a line between her brows. "Do you know if he ever actually mourned? It's possible that he's lying to me, since I'm a stranger. I thought you might—"

Con shook his head briefly. He couldn't remember Tim ever talking to him about it. "But—is that bad? I mean, everyone represses a little. Guys are known for it." He smiled, lips twisting wryly.

"Well, it's not healthy." Grams spoke cautiously, thinking through her words. "But you're right. A lot of people do it. And on a small scale, it's not disastrous. But I think maybe Tim is refusing to feel any emotions that are uncomfortable." She paused. Eyes narrowed, she spun her reading glasses in one hand, holding onto an ear piece. "If he never felt safe enough to mourn, and emotions became a scary thing... You said he's controlling?"

"I said he's a control freak," Con corrected. "He doesn't try to control me, but he likes everything..." He trailed off, poking at the air with his fingers as if that might convey something. Finally, he scowled and shrugged.

"And you can't control how you feel," Grams mused. "I do think he's repressing. It's possible he's ignored his emotions for so long that he doesn't realize he's doing it anymore. That's it's just become habit. Chronic." She glanced at Con. "And, no, that isn't remotely healthy."

Con picked at a rough spot on the table, blunt fingernails chipping through the lacquer. "Can I do something about that?"

His grandmother shrugged. "Short of therapy... I don't know, sweetie."

Con's eyes narrowed on the tabletop. "I'm not leaving him because he represses. I mean, you don't even know that it's a problem."

He felt his grandfather's hand on his shoulder, squeezing. "You wouldn't be the person we raised if you left someone over something so silly," the man said, voice gruff.

Con relaxed a little, looking up and smiling into weathered blue eyes. "Thanks." For a horrible moment, he'd thought that was what his grandmother had been pushing for—that she'd decided she didn't like Tim, and was going to fight Con over his relationship.

"He's a nice boy. You two will work through this."

Papa looked up. "Right, Mary?"

"If you want to, you can work through anything," she said at last.

Con gave her a dirty look, recognizing her form of not-quite-support. "Do you just not like him? Is that what this is?"

She frowned. "No, he's a sweet young man. I just don't want you to be unhappy."

"I'm not unhappy!" Con said, distressed. "But I'd be a lot happier if you could try to get along!"

"I just don't like you being so far from us." Then she brightened and looked at Sam. "We could move to California."

"Ed says Hillcrest is a nice area," Sam said cheerfully.

Con resisted the urge to bang his head against the table.

Con was sitting on the couch, his legs crossed under him, trying not to think about his earlier conversation and reading the label on the massage oil when Tim came home. "Oh, hey." He glanced up, then turned back to the bottle. He stared at it sightlessly for a moment, processing what he'd seen, then glanced up again. "Scrubs?" He knew Tim hadn't been wearing them when he'd left that morning.

They looked really sexy. God, he could look at Tim in scrubs all day. The little V-neck shirt with the drawstring pants that tied around his hips...

"...What?" Tim paused in the entryway, backpack halfway to its corner on the floor.

Con just shook his head, smiling slightly. He uncapped the brown glass bottle and sniffed it, then held it out. "Tell me what you think of this scent."

Tim wandered closer, leaning over the coffee table to sniff. He shrugged. "It's all right."

"It's supposed to be de-stressing."

"You mean relaxing?" Tim asked wryly before bending to sniff again. He straightened. "I suppose."

"And on the back they actually had to write, 'Not for use as a personal lubricant or for sexual activities.'" Con smirked. "And, really, isn't saying one of those enough? I mean, what else do you use a personal lubricant *for*?"

The quip pulled a tired smile from Tim, who was still standing on the other side of the coffee table.

"Here, sit." Con scooted over slightly and patted the couch. "I want to try this."

Tim straightened, crossing his arms over his chest. "That's oily."

"I know. Sit down."

"That's gross."

Con snorted. "Well, you'll notice I'm not suggesting you shower first, since I know you'll want to shower after..."

"You want to put that on me? I could put it on you." Tim looked at the bottle doubtfully, nose wrinkled.

"Would you just sit your ass down? It's not like I'm asking you to strip and lie face-down on the floor." Con's tone was laced with both laughter and impatience; this was pretty much the reaction he'd expected.

Slowly, Tim came around the coffee table and perched on the edge of the couch, looking at the oil as if it might bite. His arms were still crossed, hands tucked under his biceps. Con reached over and tugged one arm free, hanging on to Tim's fingers while he fumbled the bottle with his other hand, trying to get oil out. The movement could have been seductive, he supposed, but it completely fell short. It didn't matter; Tim was chuckling by the time Con had massage oil on his fingers. Con grinned in response, sliding his fingers over the base of Tim's thumb, rubbing at knots of muscle. "So, Grams said she went to see you today? Everything go all right?"

Tim watched Con's fingers on his hand narrowly. "Yeah. She apologized for the interrogation earlier."

Con smiled, chuckling. "Well, that's good. She's just worried." He frowned, wondering if his grandparents actually were going to move to California. It would be nice, but at the same time, he hoped they didn't. Not if Tim and Grams were constantly going to be at odds. He distracted himself, pressing his fingertips up the joints on Tim's hands, rubbing the palm.

Tim slowly started to relax. His gaze remained fixed on what Con was doing, watching the manipulation of muscle and fingers, Tim's hand swallowed in both of Con's.

"Did you have a good day?" Con asked quietly, letting the silence soak in.

"Normal day." The murmur was absent, lilting.

"What happened to your clothes?"

That brought a dark scowl. "I don't want to talk about it."

Con laughed. "Well, you look good in scrubs."

"I know."

He lifted one eyebrow, amused.

Tim's ears turned pink, and he glanced up from under black hair falling over his face. "I mean—"

"You meant, you know." Con grinned.

Tim's ears got a little bit darker. "Well. Yeah."

Leaning in, Con kissed Tim slowly. Tim responded, lips parting, tongue brushing against Con's mouth. For a long moment Con debated deepening things, moving closer and pulling Tim in. But it was only recently that they'd gotten *back* to this point...

He sat back reluctantly and focused on the hand

massage, moving up to Tim's wrist as well. "Why a doctor?"

"Huh? Oh." Tim shrugged. "It's interesting. I like the puzzle."

"Not the helping people?"

Tim smiled, eyes trained on Con's hands as they shifted to his forearm, one of them leaving to get more oil. "That, too. You don't need that much oil."

Con quirked an eyebrow. "Okay." He poured it back into the bottle ineffectually—it didn't want to leave his hand—and kept massaging.

"I'm going to have to take a shower."

"You were going to have to take a shower anyway," Con countered, keeping his tone light. Tim didn't sound particularly upset at the thought anymore, his gaze still on the massage. Con couldn't decide if Tim was studying or fascinated. Either way, he'd finally relaxed. The strong muscles were soft, tension draining out of them. The tendons in Tim's throat, standing out a moment before, had vanished. His head looked almost wobbly on the graceful stalk of his neck. "Take off your shirt," Con said softly, as if he weren't expecting Tim to say no.

Tim took his hand back, twisting both arms into his shirt before pulling it up over his head. The muscles over his torso rippled and flexed.

Con tried not to ogle. "And turn around."

This time Tim was a little more hesitant, nose wrinkling.

"You can shower later." Con poured more oil on his hands. He didn't look at Tim, just paid attention to what he was doing and gave an inward sigh of relief when Tim finally turned. He started on the upper arms, edging over the cap of shoulder muscle and back down, waiting for Tim to stop glancing back at him. "You're jumpy." His smile was wry.

"I don't like massages."

"I don't know anyone who doesn't like a massage."

Tim was silent a beat. "Well, now you do."

Still, despite his words, he was beginning to calm down again. When Con's hands slid up over his shoulders and fingers pressed into his neck, Tim let his head fall forward slightly, giving Con better access. The scent of the oil filled the air between them, a little too sweet but fading quickly. Tim's skin warmed under Con's hands, his muscles growing pliable. Con leaned in and kissed the nape of Tim's pale neck, breathing in the smell of mint and shampoo and oil.

Tim shifted and looked back. "Con, what if... I mean, I might not be able to—to, uh..."

Con placed another kiss on the skin where neck and shoulder joined, brushing his lips over the smooth flesh. "It's okay. We're in no hurry. And I'm not trying to seduce you, honest. You just looked really kissable there..."

The tips of Tim's ears went pink. He turned away again. "But what if I can't ever—"

"We'll figure it out. Stop borrowing trouble." Con slid his hands down the muscles in Tim's back, feeling the dips and hollows where each muscle met.

Tim fell silent. The clock ticked in the corner, marking the time. The sound of a television babbled through the wall, canned laughter declaring it a sitcom. Con could hear Tim's breathing, slow and even, feel the thump of his heartbeat in his neck. He could see the black eyelashes against Tim's cheekbones. The lines of Tim's face softened. Con couldn't help himself. He pressed his lips to Tim's shoulder, murmuring, "I love you," against skin.

"Hm?" Tim turned his head sleepily.

"Nothing," Con answered, his strong fingers working along hard muscles, thumbs rubbing circles. "Nothing at all."

***

Con let his grandparents fend for themselves while he spent the next few days researching. An uneventful shift at the fire department gave him a lot of time to read. Slowly, pieces started coming together in his head.

Tim had always been better at strategy than Con was, but, occasionally, Con held his own. Tim had flashes of inspiration, or sudden knowledge that just came to him. Con had to work for his flashes, but it was worth it.

He thought maybe he'd figured Tim out. Now all he had to do was get around him.

Chapter Twelve

Tim was cooking dinner. And by 'cooking dinner,' Con really meant Tim was heating up take-out. Someday, Con had hopes that Tim would discover he was really a chef at heart, because damn, their take-out budget was going to be huge if he didn't.

"Wouldn't it be neat to learn to cook?" He leaned on the counter and smiled beguilingly.

"No." Tim didn't bother glancing up from the slowly descending numbers on the microwave. "Unless you want to. Then it'd be fantastic."

Con just snorted, then smiled softly, watching Tim tap his fork against the counter. "Hungry?"

"Hm." Tim reached out, popping the front open before it had finished heating. The spoon plopped into dark sauce, giving it a quick turn before he ladled beef and broccoli onto two plates, handing one to Con.

Con took it, shuffling toward the couch, sitting on the end to leave space for Tim. "You working tomorrow?"

Tim shook his head, tucking one leg under himself as he sat down. "No, I'm off." Then he looked a little wary, glancing toward Con. "Why? Your grandparents want to get together?"

The tips of Con's mouth tipped up ruefully. "Actually, I was thinking maybe we could do something. Just the two of us." He was glad to see Tim's eyes lighten, the lines easing away from his face.

"I'd like that."

He grinned.

The day was nice. Tim found himself relaxing—though it took a full hour—and just enjoying Con's company again. No stress, no extra people, just the two of them bumming around the Gaslamp district, wandering into shops, bickering over whether or not smoothies were girly, finding a bench by the ocean and watching people go by. Somehow, with everything that had been going on, Tim had forgotten how much he just liked being around Con.

"Are you ogling my man-bits?" Con asked, staring out at the ocean.

Tim blinked, realized he'd been looking at Con's profile for some time, and felt his ears go pink. "Not unless you really are a dick-head," he said pleasantly, and turned to look at the water.

Con's laugh rolled over him, agreeable and easy. It warmed him right down to his toes, and he felt the last of the anxiety from the past few weeks drain out of his body. He took a deep breath and relaxed further into the bench, slouching slightly and letting his legs stick out, though still not as far as Con's. He wasn't comfortable totally sprawled.

Con smiled at him, stretching an arm around his shoulders, resting his hand on Tim's bicep. Tim leaned into it fractionally. The scent of the man next to him mingled with salt water and brine, the sea breeze keeping them damp and cool. Con shifted closer, leaning to brush his nose softly against Tim's temple. Lips whispered over his skin, a kiss feather-soft. Tim smiled, feeling no pressure to reciprocate, able to simply sit and enjoy the feeling of Con against him, around him, nuzzling into him in a show of affection that was easy and undemanding.

The waves crashed against the rocks a hundred feet away. The crowds were starting to thin out, the sidewalk only occasionally occupied by joggers with dogs, or small groups of teens. People moved along, leaving Tim and Con alone again while the sun set over the water.

"We should head home," Con said quietly. "It's getting cold."

Tim rubbed his upper arms, glancing down to see goosebumps rising up on his skin. "Yeah." He sighed, sorry to see the day end. Together they rose, Con catching Tim's fingers with his own and tangling them as they walked back to the car.

The drive was pleasantly quiet, with the Jeep windows open and Tim's feet propped on the dash. He watched the world go by, content with life in general.

They parked behind the apartment, then headed inside and up the stairs. He could feel his boyfriend behind him, big and warm, awareness prickling along his skin. It was easy to imagine the broad shoulders, the way Con's T-shirt snugged across his chest, showing off pectorals before his waist slimmed, cloth bagging and only hinting at the muscle underneath.

Tim's skin warmed. The hairs at the nape of his neck lifted with awareness. His blood pulsed faster within his flesh. He fumbled the key into the lock and opened the door, stepping inside without looking at Con.

He really wanted—he wanted to be *normal,* so he could grab Con by the back of the neck and drag him down to a reasonable level, a kissable level, and not worry about anything else that might happen later. He wanted—

Con closed the door softly, wrapped a hand around

the back of Tim's neck, and pulled him in. For a moment, anxiety built in Tim's chest. Then he pushed it down and kissed back. Con's lips were soft against his, tongue teasing for entry.

Tim opened his mouth, felt the warm, wet slide, teeth catching at his lower lip. Desire knotted his stomach, tightening muscles. He ran his hands up Con's strong torso, chest, down over ribs and all the glorious little muscles there.

Con broke the kiss, shifting to nuzzle at Tim's jaw. He shivered, Con's tongue sweeping across his skin, lapping at the tendon. Then the wet was gone, breath hot across the hollow of his ear before lips and teeth nibbled at the shell. Con's hands slid down his back, making his skin tighten. He shuddered when strong fingers stroked over his ass, pulling him closer still. He could feel Con's erection through his jeans, hard and insistent. His heartbeat picked up, arousal and nerves mingling equally in his blood.

"Tim." Con's breath tickled his ear. "You used to my scent now?"

He shivered at the feel of lips moving against his skin, then shivered again when Con lipped at his earlobe. "I—I hope so." He winced at his own words. They sounded oddly pathetic. "I mean, I should be." He meant, oh God, he hoped so.

Con's hands on his hips were big, thumbs pressing under his hipbones, fingers wrapping around to squeeze against denim and flesh. Then those strong hands pushed him back, guiding him surely through the small apartment until he hit the couch. Tim sat heavily, Con leaning over him for just a moment before he sat, too, pulling Tim close. Tim shifted, leaning in to lick a stripe along his boyfriend's neck. Warm skin, tasting of Con and salt water, tantalizingly good. When the broad hand tugged on him he straddled Con, one knee on either side of the slim hips.

Nerves twisted in Tim's gut. He was hard, his erection almost painful against his jeans, and that was good—right? But he couldn't stop thinking about all the other times he'd been hard and things had gone wrong, and he really, really didn't want this to go wrong.

"Stop thinking so much," Con chuckled, his hands sliding down the backs of Tim's thighs, up again, catching his shirt and pulling it up, too.

Tim sat back, struggling free from cloth, then watched Con take the shirt and lay it across the back of the couch. He put his hands on Con's broad chest, feeling the muscles under the material, trying not to think about how badly this could go.

"Timmy," Con said longingly, hand sliding down Tim's chest and stomach, tracing quivering muscles and spreading heat.

"Don't call me that," he muttered absently, still sitting up, as far as he could actually get from Con and still be in reach. Muscles flexed under his hands as Con sat up, too, bringing them nose to nose.

"We won't know unless we try." One hand settled on Tim's hip, the other sliding along the back of his neck. "If it works, then the problem is over. And if it doesn't, then we'll figure something else out. Okay?"

Tim nodded because he knew it was expected. Then he leaned in to kiss Con, partly to shut him up, partly because he needed to act.

He stripped Con's shirt off and enjoyed the man's strength, refusing to think. He pressed close, pushing them back down on the couch, lipping at Con's warm, slightly salty flesh, feeling hands travel up his spine. He tasted a collarbone, startling when his erection ground up against Con's and pleasure sparkled up his body. The hands on his back moved, one sliding up into his hair, the other down, fingers edging under the waistband of his pants.

What if it didn't work? He couldn't just expect Con to go celibate because of his issues. So—so what then? Did they break up? Give it another week and then go their separate ways?

Con moved under him, pushing up against his hips, making him tighten his jaw against a whimper as their dicks slid together and sensation shot up from his groin. "Good?" Hands pulled his legs higher and slightly farther apart so that he dropped down, closer to the man underneath him.

"Good," he groaned, sucking on a dark nipple. He didn't think about the anxiety swiftly building in his stomach. He just clamped down on nerves, and ignored the way his hands shook.

What if it didn't happen this time? What if he choked up? He didn't know if he could put himself through that again.

A thumb pressed up against his crotch, sliding over his testicles, making his whole body tighten. Then Con's hands moved, coming between them, and strong fingers undid the buttons on their jeans. Tim shifted, felt fingers dance over his briefs, slide inside, stroking the tip of his cock. He shuddered, pressing his forehead against Con's chest, rubbing his palms down over ridges of lean muscle.

"Here, stand up." Con pushed at him.

Tim stood, untangling legs, watching Con lean up, stomach muscles crunching, and reach to drag Tim's pants off.

What if he got right to the edge and couldn't finish? Could he convince Con that it was all right if he orgasmed and Tim just never did? Could he live with that himself? He wanted to. He wasn't sure he could.

Jeans and briefs hit the floor, and Tim stepped out of them, watching Con wriggle until his own pants were around his ankles, and then kick until they came off. Tim had started to sit back down when Con grabbed his hips with both hands, keeping him there.

His breath caught as a clever tongue flicked out, touching the head of his cock before vanishing. Lips teased down his length, nuzzling against his legs, open mouth wet and hot against his balls. He bit back a groan, fingers tangling in soft dark hair. Con licked a stripe up the underside of Tim's dick. When Con got to the head again he dragged his tongue over it, slowly, before taking it into his mouth and sucking.

Tim curled his hands into fists, forcing himself to relax again, muscles trembling as he watched Con slowly take him deeper. Heat coiled in his stomach, pooling in his groin, something big and uncontrollable raging with it.

He clamped down on that, half afraid of the power that threatened to overwhelm him. It seemed better to focus on what Con was doing, on the heat and warmth of his mouth. The power raged again, a crashing wave of emotion and sensation that wasn't predictable, couldn't be managed, didn't promise to leave him whole when it was done. He crushed it, afraid of being battered and broken, and felt the orgasm back off with the rest of the monster.

He could have screamed. Instead, he tugged at Con's hair until he pulled away, then stretched over him, straddling his knees, and bent to lick the head of his boyfriend's erection. Salt, musk, the taste that was just Con. He took the cock into his mouth, sucking it deeper, trying to focus on the catch of ragged breath and the way Con's erection was both steel and silk. Anxiety and disappointment turned in his stomach, despite his attempts to ignore them.

He wasn't going to be able to do this.

Tim sank down further, letting Con's dick fill his mouth, rubbing his tongue along the underside. Muscles tensed under him and Con groaned. Tim took the cock in as far as he could, massaging Con's balls pulled hot and tight against his body.

"Oh God—Tim—" Con nearly whimpered, legs spreading, heels straining against the cushions. Tim slid his fingers down, dragging them along testicles, sweeping his tongue against the smooth shaft. He pulled away, sank down again, filling his mouth. Hard and delicate all at once, the flared head and rigid shaft against his tongue. He pulled off, lipped at the top, licked moisture off the tip of Con's dick. It tasted salty, sweet, like distilled Con. He moved down, drawing it into his mouth again, sliding down and back up again, tongue pressing against skin.

"Oh, God, Tim, I'm gonna—"

Tim sucked hard, taking it as deep as he could. He felt Con tense and shudder, hands scrabbling for purchase on the couch. Semen poured into Tim's throat and he swallowed, heard Con groan. He waited until he was sure Con was done, then pulled off slowly. Con looked boneless, chest rising and falling.

Tim smiled regretfully, tracing the line of an abdominal muscle with one finger and rubbing his thumb over the hipbone nearly hidden by more muscle. After a moment Con sat up, wrapping his big hand around the back of Tim's neck and tugging him close.

"You didn't have to swallow," he said with a smile.

Tim shrugged. It hadn't seemed like a big deal, really. Didn't taste bad. "I'm pretty sure I won't get pregnant from it," he said, hiding in the deadpan banter.

White teeth flashed as Con grinned. "You sure? You learn that in doctor school?"

Tim shrugged, nodding, blasé. Apprehension curled

in his stomach. It coiled tighter when Con kissed him, a hand sliding down his torso, fingers dancing down the crease of hip and leg.

It wasn't going to work. Apprehension became full blown despair. "Con, don't," he said quietly, catching Con's wrist. He couldn't go through all this again.

"Tim..."

Tim didn't look at his face, but he could hear the distress. "Stop. Don't give me some line about if we don't try we won't know, okay?" He crushed his disappointment and frustration, ignoring them as much as possible. "It almost happened a minute ago, and... and it didn't, and I don't want to—to—" He didn't say, "Try it and be disappointed." Instead, he took a deep breath and forced himself to speak calmly. "This has been a really nice day, and I have to get up early tomorrow, so..." His gaze darted, careful not to meet Con's, playing it off as no big deal.

No big deal.

Happened all the time.

He didn't care.

He was fine with things as they were.

He could give Con blowjobs and just be okay with that. And then maybe they wouldn't break up because of his stupid fucking neuroses.

"Timmy—"

"*Don't* call me that," Tim snapped, yanking his shirt off of the back of the couch. He stood, rigid, and tried to bank the rising anger. This wasn't Con's fault. "I'm sorry," he said into the silence. "I just—I really just want to go to bed." He picked up his jeans and walked off down the hall, listening to the echoing silence behind him.

His room was quiet. He kicked the door closed, dropped his clothes in the laundry hamper, and collapsed into bed. Sheets and blankets were cool under his flushed skin, crumpled into strange shapes.

The door creaked open. "Tim?"

"Oh, God, just go away." He rolled so his back was to the door, closing his eyes against everything. Footsteps traveled the room. His mattress dipped as Con sat down on the edge.

"Tim."

He didn't answer. A hand braced itself in front of him, the heat of Con's body pressing close against Tim's waist.

"Tim."

"What?" he growled. Everything in him wanted nothing more than to scoot back so he was pressed against Con's side. He didn't.

"Do you trust me?"

Tim frowned and rolled, looking up into dark eyes nearly hidden by disheveled brown hair. "Of *course* I trust you." He figured the 'you idiot' was implied.

Con lifted a hand, stroking Tim's upper arm absently. "Well, because orgasming is a scary thing, you know?"

Tim looked at him blandly. "I thought orgasming was a great thing."

Con gave him a lopsided smile, dimples appearing. "Well, yeah. But so are roller coasters. It's just—I mean, an orgasm sort of leaves you defenseless. Sometimes people who are having intimacy issues—"

"Are you quoting Dr. Phil again?" Tim asked suspiciously.

"Yes. Now shut up and let me finish," Con shot back. "Sometimes people who—"

"It's just *so* attractive to have the ghost of a balding, middle-aged man in my bed," Tim said sarcastically.

Con's hand closed around Tim's upper arm, turning him and pinning him to the bed long enough to lean down and kiss him. Hard. "Would you shut up for a minute?"

he asked, exasperated.

Tim banked useless anger at everything—the situation, the conversation, himself—shifted so he was more comfortable on his back, and looked mock-expectantly at Con. "Okay, Dr. Phil. Continue."

Con frowned, his gaze boring into the mattress to one side of Tim's shoulder. "Come on, Tim. You know I'm not good with words."

Tim arched an eyebrow. "Try. And please keep in mind that I have orgasmed before. You didn't invent it for me."

Con ruffled a hand through his hair, sending it sticking up in all directions. "All right. When you orgasm by yourself, it's predictable. You can control it, right? But when there's someone else involved, it gets complicated. You can't control it, and for a minute there you're pretty much helpless." He frowned, hand sliding up and down Tim's arm again. "It can be a whole lot stronger—"

Tim already knew all this. "I'm not—"

"Would you let me finish? I'm gonna lose my train of thought."

Tim shrugged fatalistically, nodded, indicated Con should continue. Vulnerability wasn't his problem, but if Con needed to talk it out he could listen. And glare.

"And—" Con scowled. Tim could almost see him mentally retracing his steps, figuring out what he'd said and what needed to be said. "Okay. Okay, so, when there's another person involved *and* it's stronger than you're used to, it can be scary."

Which wasn't quite what Tim had been expecting Con to say. "I'm not *scared* of orgasming!"

"No," Con assured him quickly. "But you don't like being vulnerable. And—and you would be." His body softened, the look of concentration disappearing as he stopped trying to remember what he'd read. "It's unpredictable, and for a few minutes there you're helpless. You just have to trust your partner to keep you safe while you ride it out. So... do you trust me?"

Tim stared at him. Con thought it was a matter of trust? That Tim didn't want to be helpless? That was a stupid theory.

He remembered that maw of power he'd been faced with before, remembered trying to quash it. Unpredictable, uncontrollable. It had nothing to do with trust, and everything to do with drowning in emotion. Normal people didn't drown in their own fucking emotions. "It's not a matter of vulnerability or trust," Tim said finally. He sat up, Con behind him. "It just doesn't feel right."

Con's broad hand rested between his shoulder blades. "Not right like... what?"

Tim couldn't begin to explain it. He felt like a failure—normal people didn't have this problem. Freaks did. Failures did. "Just not right."

"Like... it hurts?" There was a note of uncertainty in Con's voice that hadn't been there before. This obviously wasn't something he'd considered.

It wasn't quite true, either. Tim rubbed his hand over his face and left it covering his eyes, elbow propped on raised knees. It would be so easy to say yes, it hurt. And then they'd never solve anything. "You know how people feel all happy post-coital? Well, I feel the opposite." Which was about as close as he could bring himself to explaining.

For a long, quiet moment they just sat there. Tim's muscles grew tense, Con's unmoving fingers a brand against his back.

When Con finally spoke, the single word was filled with knowledge. "Oh."

Tim nearly flinched.

"How can I help?"

Back to this. Back to solving it. Tim spoke through nearly gritted teeth. "You can't."

"Emotional meltdowns during or after sex usually mean you have something you haven't dealt with. I could help you—"

"No."

"Tim—"

"*Con.*" He shoved off the bed, pacing the length of the room. The other wall came up far too fast. Bed springs creaked. Footsteps followed him. He could feel Con stop just behind him, feel body heat.

"Tim. It's not bad to feel upset at things. Even sex-things. And I'm not going to think less of you because you're not perfect."

He couldn't decide whether to be angry that Con thought he was that much of a perfectionist, or feel the tiniest bit reassured.

"I could, possibly, help. Letting it happen might help. What won't help, ever, is ignoring it and letting it rule your life."

He glared at the wall. One of Con's broad hands settled lightly on his shoulder.

"Let me help? Trust me, just a little? Can you let me take care of things? And if you get upset, it'll tell us something else. Then we can go from there."

Con was right. The worst part was, Tim knew it. He swallowed anxiety and responded to the first few statements in an annoyed grumble. "You'd like it if I just let you fix things."

Con gave him a small little smile. "Yeah. I would." He leaned forward, settling a gentle kiss on Tim's neck. "Trust me?"

Tim thought about never getting over it. He thought about breaking down in front of Con. He thought about the maw of power he'd experienced before. He didn't know if he could do this, and he didn't know if he couldn't *not* do this. "What if it takes too long?"

"No such thing."

"Bull. What if it takes forty minutes?" They'd get bored and stop.

"Then it takes forty minutes."

"What if I completely freak out?"

Con stepped to one side, bringing himself along Tim. "Then we'll get through it." The hand hadn't come off his back. Now Con's arm wrapped around his shoulders. He let himself be pulled in, leaning against warm muscle. "Yeah," Tim said at last. "Great. So—so what do you want me to—"

"Nothing." Con pressed another kiss to Tim's neck, hand drifting along his torso, his hip.

"Nothing," Tim muttered to himself, trying not to be anxious or fidgety.

"It's okay," Con said against his skin. "We can get through this."

Tim wasn't sure he believed it. When Con tugged, though, he followed the other man back to the bed, sitting down. He kept waiting for things to speed up, get serious. But Con kept it slow, easy making out like they'd done often enough before. Gentle caresses, tongue and teeth at his jaw, his ears, his neck, until he found himself relaxing, turning his head to catch Con's mouth, tasting the salt and heat of warm skin.

Tim shifted, rubbing his leg up against Con's, seeking touch and sensation. Con trailed damp kisses down his torso, pushing him back to lie on the bed, pausing to lick and suck at a nipple. Tim's hands curled in thick dark hair. Con moved lower, callused palm sliding over a lean hip, grazing down Tim's thigh, sucking at his pelvis, tongue flicking over his belly button, all of it calm and careful. Tim trembled, emotions catching in his throat.

Anxiety rose again when Con moved lower, his tongue slow over Tim's cock. He bit back a moan, moved to give Con better access, tried not to think about this failing. Con's mouth closed over his dick, hot and wet and tight. He groaned, head pressed back into his pillow, fingers closing on the sheet under him.

Oh, God, what if this didn't work? What if Con was wrong, and it still didn't happen? At some point they'd get tired of trying, and then—a good deal of breakups were over sexual frustration. Too many to ignore.

He could feel it building, heat in his groin searing through the rest of him, muscles tightening and relaxing all at once. The power rose, threatening to overwhelm him, and he struggled both to let it do so and to keep it back.

Con's hand replaced his mouth and he moved upward, stroking steadily, thumb rubbing the head of Tim's cock, his other hand rising to slide around the back of Tim's neck. "It's okay." He leaned in to press lips against lips, tongue rubbing against Tim's. Tim opened, legs shifting, hips pressing up into Con's hand, wanting the release even as he shied away from it. Con's tongue thrust slowly inside his mouth, running along his teeth, against his own tongue, slick and soft.

He struggled, feeling the tightness in his stomach that meant orgasm, sensing it could overwhelm him easily. Toss him over and break him, dangerous and uncontrollable. He needed to let go, and couldn't quite. He tried focusing on the hand on his cock, big and firm and sliding up and down, teasing his head, the over-sensitive slit in the tip, sending pleasure snaking achingly through him.

Con broke the kiss, keeping his mouth against Tim's temple, his arm behind Tim's head. "It's all right. It's okay."

He wanted to scream, but didn't. He could hear his

own breath, ragged and almost painful. His arms had come up, he wasn't sure when, wrapping around Con as if he could just hold him there, Con's hand pumping his cock, Con's body pressed against him. "I—I can't—" It wasn't happening. He could feel it hovering there, but he couldn't let it break, kept shoving the swarming emotion back down.

"Yes, you can. It's okay. Relax. It's all right. I'm here. You're safe."

He thrust up, heels digging into the sheets, whole body tight. Safe. He was safe. Had always been safe, he told himself, but he hadn't really believed it. Safety was control and predictability and keeping things handled, and he couldn't handle this. Stupid, that was stupid, people weren't afraid of handling orgasms—except he was, alarmed at the accompanying power. He couldn't handle it.

But he could trust Con to handle it, to keep him from breaking. Con was still whispering in his ear, murmuring nothing and everything. "It's all right. It's okay. Let go, Tim, it's all right."

Tim's hands curled into fists on Con's shoulder blades as the wave crashed, shattering through him, dragging him along. He could hear his own voice, his breath catching against a cry as his body sent glittering shards through him. It brought his walls tumbling down, so carefully set up to keep him safe.

For a moment, as it faded, he was aware of Con holding him tightly while he shuddered, chest heaving. Then all the emotions that had been locked so brutally in check came crashing in. He couldn't stop them, body drained and power gone. He tightened his grip on Con, fighting back wave after wave of—

He didn't know what this was. It was crippling, and it hurt, and it was all he could do to breathe through it, focusing on inhaling steadily, on not letting his chest hitch, on ignoring the tears that threatened. Push it back and try to regain some kind of control over a bottomless void.

The emotion ran roughshod over him and he tensed, trying to fight it away.

"It's okay," Con said soothingly, wrapping him close, nearly covering his body with Con's own. "It's okay. Let it go. It's okay."

"Son of a bitch," Tim hissed, hating Con in that moment and needing him desperately as the words cracked the last little bit of his control and the tears came, ugly and harsh and painful. He sobbed wretchedly, clinging to Con, feeling himself gathered up and turned until Tim rested on top. Con smoothed out Tim's hair, rubbing his back, rocking them as Tim sobbed uncontrollably, years of fear and pain unacknowledged now finally released.

Tim curled his hands into fists, pressing against the strong chest beneath him, hiding his face as wave after wave of grief poured over him.

He couldn't see an end to the tears, to the hurt that raged unchecked. Everything he'd done, all of it washed away in a flood he couldn't stop. He felt like he might cry forever.

Con stood in the kitchen in soft flannel pants and nothing else, staring at the gurgling coffeemaker. He'd expected *something* to happen the night before, had read about how orgasming could force emotions to the surface that people weren't aware of, and figured that if Tim *had* been repressing like Grams said, then there'd be some kind of outburst.

He hadn't really thought it would crush Tim quite

so badly. The man had sobbed for more than an hour, shuddering against Con's chest while Con just held him, unsure what else to do. He'd found his own eyes wet when Tim finally dropped off to sleep, body simply too exhausted to continue grieving. And it was grief, Con was certain of it. Not even for Tim's parents, though that was probably mixed up in there, too, but for trust lost and a childhood missed; instability during a time when things should have been rock solid. Grief for a whole life left shaky and uncertain and frightening. A hole left by parents who shouldn't have died.

The coffeemaker stopped percolating. Con stared at it, unable to remember what to do next. Cup. Right. He opened the cupboard and pulled out a mug, set it on the counter and... and... He stared around the kitchen blankly. And what?

Sugar.

He opened the pantry. Closed it without removing anything, turned around, saw his mug sitting there and remembered the sugar. Opened the pantry again.

The bedroom door slammed. He looked up to see Tim race out, his hair disheveled, eyes swollen, face pale with dark bruises under his lashes.

"I'm late for work," Tim began, his voice hoarse. "I forgot to set the alarm—"

"I called you in sick," Con said quietly.

Tim stopped, stared at him, hurt and angry. "You what? You called—how could you *do* that? My life is not yours to jerk around—"

"Tim." Con stepped forward, his hand outstretched.

Tim flinched back. "Don't touch me."

For a moment, Con froze. Had he screwed up that badly? Then he saw the fear in Tim's blue eyes, and realized he still hadn't been able to force the emotional walls back into place. It was touching that had shattered them, touching that had brought them to this point. Con stepped forward.

Tim stepped back. "Don't," he said, obviously trying to be firm, but his voice shook. There was a plea there, somewhere. Don't touch me. Don't make me hurt. Don't break me.

"Tim, I'm so sorry," Con murmured, and closed the distance between them despite Tim's quick backpedaling. "I'm so sorry." He wrapped his arms around the stiff body, holding Tim close.

It was a long time before Tim began to relax, bringing his arms up slowly and looping them around Con's shoulders. Con held tight when Tim's breathing hitched, tears starting again.

They didn't last long, this time. They were quiet and soft, and faded after just a few minutes. Con released him and stepped back, looking closely at his face.

Tim refused to look up, his eyes haunted, his lips pale. "I hate you," he whispered weakly.

"I know." Con hoped to God it wasn't permanent. Fear spiked through him, and he forced himself to ignore it. Just for now. Just until he knew if this would last. "Come on. I'll get you some breakfast." Slowly, he led Tim over to the couch, sat him down, went into the bedroom and dragged a blanket off the bed.

Tim was still sitting exactly where Con had left him, eyes glassy and skin chalky, hands limp between his knees. Con wrapped the blanket around him, then pressed until Tim lay down, curled on the couch. "Sleep." He knelt to brush hair out of his lover's face. "I'll be here."

Tim looked at him for a long moment, then nodded listlessly and closed his eyes.

Con leaned his forehead against Tim's, praying he hadn't messed things up irrevocably. Then he stood and went back into the kitchen.

***

Tim lay on the couch and stared at nothing, too tired to care, too worn to do anything. The world spun by around him, and he dozed and woke and felt more bruised than he could ever remember feeling before. Like someone had taken a stick to him. He hadn't even felt like this after his parents had died. He'd managed to keep things together then, to bottle up the emotion and move on.

He wasn't moving on, now. At least the tears had stopped.

At some point, he realized he was staring at the television. At explosions and fire and people yelling curse words and shooting guns and doing very unrealistic martial arts. He watched it vacantly, fading in and out of awareness. The knowledge that Con was lying on the couch behind him with an arm around his shoulders, holding him in place, came gradually. Tim shifted back, closer to Con, stealing warmth and comfort. His eyes fell closed, and he rubbed his cheek on the bicep beside his face, the arm propped up to brace Con's head.

"Hey, sleepy," Con murmured, and lips pressed a careful kiss into his hair. "How're you feeling?"

"Worn." The arm under his temple was warm. He stared at the television until his eyelids drooped closed. "What time is it?"

The arm shifted. "Almost two." It shifted back.

"I should eat something." He didn't need to really get sick, despite having a sick day.

"You ate something a little while ago, baby. You hungry?"

Tim frowned. "Don't call me that." He felt Con kiss him again; comforting someone, but Tim couldn't tell if it was him or if Con was comforting himself. "I'm not hungry." And now that he'd been reminded, he remembered eating earlier. Eggs and toast, then some kind of sandwich. "Do I work tomorrow?" He'd been scheduled, he was sure of that.

"No. They said take today and tomorrow off. Hospitals don't like their doctors being sick. And the day after was your day off anyway, so you have a little while."

Tim sighed softly, letting his eyes fall closed, relaxing back against Con. "Good."

Con kissed him again. "Yeah."

Con sat on the edge of Tim's bed, dragging blankets up over the smaller man. "I'm not a baby," Tim groused, closing his eyes and snuggling into his pillow.

"I know." It was easier than arguing. He brushed black hair out the pale face, more for himself than anything. It had been a long day for both of them—for Tim more, certainly, but Con hated seeing anyone hurt. Especially when that someone was so important to him. Especially when he was the cause of that pain.

He just never knew what to *do* when people were sad.

He wanted to curl up around Tim and keep him as safe as possible, but Tim had never actually invited him into his room, much less his bed. He'd stayed there the night before, but that had been a rather extreme circumstance.

"Tim?"

He grunted, eyes firmly shut.

"You want me to go sleep on the couch?" It didn't sound quite as pathetic as, "Can I please sleep here?"

"No," Tim mumbled. "Stay."

Con wondered if what he'd really been asking had been as obvious as Tim's unstated words: "Please don't go." With the emotional walls still broken down, he was terrifyingly easy to read. It was alarming. Tim was supposed to be controlled, mildly sarcastic, unshakeable. He wasn't, now.

The sheets were cool as Con slid into bed, crawling to the open space so he could curl up, Tim's back to his chest, the same way they'd been on the couch for most of the afternoon.

Tim didn't curl back so much as relax into him, everything going soft and a little pliable. Also like they'd been for most of the afternoon. Even exhausted, Con got the feeling Tim wasn't cuddling so much as allowing him to cuddle.

He buried his nose in the soft black strands of hair and drifted off to sleep.

Tim woke to Con's voice, hushed but not quiet enough. "No, Grams, I got it covered. We don't need soup. I have soup here. No, I won't get sick. I dunno, some twenty-four hour bug, I guess. Someone else took my shift, so that's all right. Yeah, okay. Couple of days, maybe? Okay. I love you, too. Bye."

Tim's eyes were open when Con poked his head back through the bedroom doorway. Con smiled at him, and he found himself smiling sleepily back. "How's your grandmother?"

"Worried."

His smile faded. "You didn't tell her...?"

"What, that we had sex, and it actually was earth-shattering, and that's not as good as it sounds?" Con snorted. "No. I said you had the flu and weren't feeling well." He stepped farther into the doorway, outlined by the frame. He looked good, hair still damp from a shower, almost black with water. It curled a little around his neck, dripping onto his snug T-shirt. "Do you want some breakfast?"

Tim closed his eyes so he wouldn't have to look at Con anymore. "Yeah. Thanks." He waited until he heard Con leave, then dragged himself from the cocoon of blankets and staggered into the bathroom in just his boxer-briefs and a tank top.

He looked little. And pale. And littler and paler for having just seen Con, the Muscle-Bound Large Man of Doom, in his doorway. Damn it.

Tim splashed water on his face as if it might magically make a difference. As if it might make the shadows under his eyes go away, or the hint of gray around his jaw fade. His eyes were glassy and weirdly... exposed. He felt naked. He stood for several minutes, trying to make his expression neutral again, but couldn't quite manage it. He went back into his room and donned sweatpants and a hoodie, ignoring the fact that the apartment was far from cool.

He didn't feel any less naked.

Tim still looked awful. Not as awful as he had before, true, but definitely not himself, either. Con turned back to frying eggs, attempting to flip them without breaking the yolks. He succeeded, but only, he suspected, because the yolks were already hard.

The silence hung. He didn't know what to say. Ask how Tim was doing? But that could lead to a really uncomfortable conversation. He could apologize, but he'd already done that.

He put the eggs on a plate and picked up two forks, taking it all over to Tim. He sat down on the couch. "You look better," he said hesitantly, mostly because it seemed the thing to say.

Tim snorted. "Better than what? Dead?"

Sarcasm had to mean he was on the mend. Con smiled. "Better than a zombie, which is how you looked yesterday."

"If this is a pep talk," Tim said dryly, "it's not working."

Con leaned over, ducked his head, and kissed Tim firmly on the mouth. Then he straightened and dug into the food with one of the forks.

"What was that for?" Tim asked after a long moment.

"You needed it." Con ate another bite.

"I did?"

"Yeah." Con smiled, content.

It was another quiet day of movie watching and sprawling on the couch. Tim had never been aware that sprawling could be quite so aggressive, but Con practically made it into a sport. Tim didn't mind. He let himself be shuffled, starting to feel in control of his life again even as he allowed Con to move him wherever was comfortable. Only a few times did he protest; usually with an elbow in the other man's torso.

Occasionally, emotions rose and he found himself tearing up all over again. He turned his head into his lover's chest and tried to breathe calmly, steadily. Sometimes the tears went away, unshed. Sometimes they spilled out, and he found himself shuddering. Those times, Con stroked his back until it passed—a few minutes, that was all, and the familiar exhaustion set in. Numb or drained, he didn't know and didn't care.

By that afternoon, his emotional walls were going

back up, brick by brick—even if they weren't as solid as they had been before. He and Con were in the middle of *The Mummy*—Tim was sure he didn't own this—and completely ensconced on the couch, their legs tangled over and under each other, Tim lying on his back, head on the pillow while Con propped himself up on one arm.

"I love this part," Con said, a grin sliding comfortably over his face.

Tim looked up at him and smiled, laughing softly. "Flesh-eating beetles? Why am I not surprised?"

Con glanced down at him, grin still in place, and paused. Something soft and warm entered his eyes, and he bent to kiss Tim carefully. Full lips brushed against Tim, soothing without demanding anything in return. He relaxed, kissed back, opened his mouth when he felt Con's tongue against his lips. A large palm swept up his torso, skimming over his ribs, down again. Fingers slid under his sweatshirt.

He put a restraining hand on Con's arm and pulled away, pushing into the couch to make the space. "Con—I don't—" He didn't want to have another breakdown. Couldn't stand the thought of more tears, or more strain, or more anything. Not now, when he was finally starting to feel human again.

"I know." Con shifted to nuzzle at Tim's throat.

Tim scowled. He lifted his hand and clocked the side of Con's head.

"Ow!" Con yelped, rearing back.

Tim sat up, tucking his legs close. "I say stop and you don't? What the hell?"

Con rubbed his skull. "You didn't say 'stop,' you said 'I don't.'"

Tim glared furiously. "And you said 'I know.'"

Con had the decency to look abashed. "I just meant... trust me?"

"Trusting you is what turned me into this wreck!" Tim snapped. He regretted it the moment Con flinched, but didn't apologize.

"I have a theory," Con began.

"God save me." Tim wrapped his arms around himself.

Con continued as if he hadn't spoken. "They say that orgasms can trigger emotions you're repressing, right? So you repressed them, and then they all came out, and if you go back to repressing them, then it could happen again, but right now you haven't gone back to it yet, so it should be okay." He smiled hopefully. "Right?"

Tim gave him a dubious look. He wasn't even sure he'd understood what Con was blathering on about.

"It's either try and see if I'm right—see if you haven't had a chance to repress yourself into a sexual mess—or never have sex again."

"I can live with celibacy." The look Con gave him let Tim know that his bluff had been called. He frowned down at the cushion between them. Christ, he just really didn't want to freak out again. Silence stretched, sticky and determined. "Explain again."

Con picked up the remote, turning the television off. "You freaked out—"

"I didn't *freak out*," Tim muttered.

"—because you were repressing, and the orgasm made you stop doing that. But you haven't been bottling the emotions up since then, so you should be fine."

It made a strange sort of sense. He scowled.

"Tim?" The voice was hesitant, unsure. "We don't have to. But it might work."

"Yeah," Tim mumbled. "We could—we could try." But he didn't move. Staring down at the space between them, he heard Con shift. Two hands slid into view across the cushion, followed by a face. Con smiled up at him, leaning in to kiss him softly.

"You wanna be on top? Or you just gonna let me seduce you?" Con asked with a wicked little smile.

Tim found himself returning it reluctantly. "I'm just gonna let you seduce me." It was easier than hanging himself out there, putting himself at risk.

Con didn't seem to mind. He just chuckled deeply, leaning in to brush those full lips over Tim's narrow ones with light, gentle kisses. Tim relaxed slowly, listening to the tick of the clock, feeling Con creep closer. Outside, children shouted. A car started. The blinds clicked together at the window as the breeze picked up.

"I will never hurt you," Con said softly, shifting until he sat close, picking up first one of Tim's feet and then the other, pulling them straight across his thighs.

"I know," Tim said just as quietly, trying to pretend like the words weren't comforting—like he didn't need that reassurance.

"Just making sure." Con put a hand on Tim's hip, sliding up his body. His sweatshirt rucked up, exposing a sliver of pale skin. Tim leaned back a little against the arm of the couch. Con moved with him, wrapping a large, warm hand around the back of Tim's neck before shifting, bending to kiss him slowly. He gave himself to it, shivering when Con pulled Tim's lip into his mouth, sucking gently.

Con's hand slid against Tim's ribs, under his shirt. He lifted his palm, caressing Con's short hair, soft and silky.

Fingers slid high enough to tease his nipple. Tim jumped, muscles tightening. His leg shifted, his foot flat on the couch, toes flexing—anxiety or arousal, he wasn't sure.

"Relax," Con breathed against him, nose edging under his jaw, sliding just a whisper away from his skin. Tim tipped his head back as Con pushed, teeth feathering against his throat. His skin tingled. Con moved out from under Tim's legs, straddling him in one easy motion. Con's hands slipped up under Tim's sweatshirt, skimming along his torso as Con undressed him. He leaned forward, lifting his arms, feeling the material pass over his head. It landed with a soft thump on the floor, and Con curled forward, mouth brushing over Tim's chest.

Tim breathed shallowly, his hands curling around the back of his lover's skull, his fingers threading through the dark hair. Con's lips parted against his skin, warm and damp. A tongue pressed softly, vanishing as Con re-balanced to one side, then laving the bud of a nipple. Tim closed his eyes as heat pooled in his stomach and moved lower.

Con sucked gently, his hands rubbing soothingly up and down Tim's sides. Tim shivered, made a noise— something trapped between a moan and a whimper. His body tensed, hands tightening on Con's shoulders.

What if this didn't work?

"Shhh, it's okay." Con licked softly at the nipple he'd been sucking on. It was hot and wet, and Tim shuddered just before Con rose, licking a trail to his collarbones, kissing his throat. Con leaned an elbow against the arm of the couch, bending to brush his lips against Tim's.

"How do you know what I'm thinking like that?" Tim muttered, both relieved and frustrated. He didn't want anyone to know him that well.

Con smiled, shrugging, his dark eyes warm. He leaned in and kissed Tim softly again, thumb carefully sliding along his jaw. Then Con's hand skimmed down, index finger just ghosting over the center line of Tim's body, across the pale skin, through the thin line of dark hair, over the dip of his belly button.

Con kissed him, his tongue gentle against Tim's lips until he opened, then moving soothingly inside. Tim moaned, feeling heat and the tender movement. Con's fingers pulled at his sweatpants, and a moment later Con broke the kiss, shifting until he could reach down and tug them off.

Tim felt acutely self-conscious, naked on the couch with Con fully dressed over him. Then Con reared back, shimmying out of his shirt, exposing bronzed skin and well-defined muscles.

Tim sat up, firmly pushing nerves to the back of his mind, leaning in to taste flesh. He tugged at the button on Con's jeans until it came free, feeling Con's erection behind his fly. Tim dragged the zipper down. It clicked loudly in the quiet apartment.

Con stood on the couch to get out of his jeans, then dropped back to his knees, one on either side of Tim's hips.

Tim's mouth dried out, his heart fluttering madly against his ribs—too weak to be effective in pumping blood, surely. Con bent, stroking his chest, his hips, the outsides of his thighs. Tim trembled under hands that were calloused and warm.

"Lean back." Breath spilled hot against his ear, stirring up the delicate little hairs there.

He hesitated, wanting—wanting— "No. Sit—back, move, something." He pushed at Con's chest.

Con looked startled, then sat back, expression already falling. "You don't—?"

Tim crawled on top of him, bending to lick the knot of a previously broken collarbone. Con's hands settled on Tim's hips, and Con groaned. His strong fingers dug into flesh and muscle, pulling Tim closer, snugging him right up against Con's thick erection. Tim shuddered, feeling skin slide against skin, hot and silky. He licked Con's ear, pulling the sensitive lobe into his mouth, listening to the other man's breath catch as he thrust up, grinding them together. Tim let go to gasp, wrapping both arms around Con's strong neck, burying his face in hot skin. Con thrust again, pulling Tim's hips in the same rhythm.

Tim tensed, shuddering, breathing ragged. He could feel lust coiling in his stomach, hot and heavy. One of Con's hands shifted, skimming down over his ass, between his legs, down until fingers grazed his testicles, thumb rubbing over them as they ground in together.

Tim bit back a cry, muscles locking, struggling with the urge to back away from the precipice looming before him. If he fell—

Con would catch him.

Con cupped his balls, pinky stroking up the base of his erection, still thrusting together, friction and heat between their bodies, cock sliding hard and soft against his. Tim felt the orgasm build, sharp little nails digging into his gut. He let go. It crashed over him, carrying him up and dropping him down, the world focusing inward for a long, perfect moment.

He breathed, shaky with adrenaline, catching without tears, feeling the pleasure wash through without drowning him.

As it started to recede, Con flipped them. Tim yelped, arms and legs locking around the larger man, and felt Con drive down against him, smearing semen and thrusting hard and fast before he stilled suddenly, his own muscles tensing, his breath hissing between clenched teeth. He shuddered for a long moment, and Tim tightened his legs around Con's waist, pulling him closer, feeling more hot, sticky liquid between them.

Then Con relaxed, falling to one side, nearly pulling Tim off the couch as he rolled. Con brushed Tim's hair out of his face, dark eyes searching. "You okay?"

Tim paused. No tears threatened, no emotions came crashing past walls that shouldn't have been there in the first place. He sighed and relaxed against Con's chest. Handy human pillow. "I'm tired."

He felt Con relax as well, heard the quiet laugh. "That's normal."

"Hmm." Tim closed his eyes, listening to the clock tick on and the blinds click together. Con kissed him, his brow, his closest eyelid, his cheek. He was too warm and too sticky, and semen itched when it dried. He needed to get up so he could go shower.

Con nuzzled his temple, running fingers through his hair.

Okay. He'd stay here for a few minutes. *Then* he'd get up.

Chapter Thirteen

Is Tim at work?"

Con munched a giant bite of pancake and spoke around it. "Nah, he's home sleeping."

"Don't talk with your mouth full," Grams corrected automatically. "Sleeping? Is he still feeling under the weather, then?"

Con shrugged. "A little." He swallowed his bite half-unchewed, winced as it slid down his throat, and added, "But things are better now."

"Maybe I should take him some soup. You're back to work on Tuesday, right?"

"No," Con said quickly, then shook his head and said, "I mean, yes, I'm back to work—but don't take Tim soup while I'm not there, Grams. Okay? Things are better between us. Really. We got some stuff sorted out, and—"

"And you don't want me quizzing him." Slim hands covered in dry skin held her mug carefully, fingers interlaced. "I know. I'm sorry about that."

Con twiddled his fork. "Yeah, me, too." He wished things were better between his boyfriend and his grandparents. "But, for now, just..."

"I'll be good," Grams promised.

Con jiggled his keys, heading slowly up the flight of stairs. It'd be nice if Tim and his grandparents got along. Not that he expected Tim to embrace them fully, since he couldn't quite imagine Tim ever being *excited* to see anyone, but pleasure on both sides would be fantastic, at this point. Especially since his grandparents were still making noises about moving to San Diego—Hillcrest, to be precise. They'd gone to look at apartments.

He paused at the top of the stairs, frowning at the open door to Tim's apartment. He could hear voices from inside, and couldn't imagine who would be there. Tim didn't seem to have a whole lot of friends besides Rick, and that wasn't Rick's voice. Too high. He walked closer, head tipping to listen a little better, not wanting to walk in if it was a bad time.

"I just wanted to make sure you were all right." The voice sounded familiar, but not overly so.

"Well, I am. Now you can go." That was Tim, cool and unruffled like Tim could do so well.

"Can't we have a nice conversation? It's been a while since I was here."

Con hesitated, wondering if he should leave, but not liking the tone of things. Still, Tim could more than take care of himself, and he'd seemed uncertain about letting his coworkers know they were dating. If this guy was from the hospital, and Con just walked in, it would spread rumors fast.

"It's been a while because I don't like you," Tim said. Con smirked. Tim didn't mince words, that was for sure.

"Right. You have a new toy now, right? Is he the reason you're home? You don't look sick. Maybe he doesn't like his little woman out working? He looks like the Neanderthal type."

Con straightened and started for the door. If he was going to be insulted, it was now his business.

"Get out." Tim's voice, cold and hard.

Con rounded the doorway as the man, his back to Con, began with, "Hey, look, I'm sorry, that was out of line. I just wish you'd give us another chance, cutie—"

Tim's eyes flickered up, meeting Con's. The blond between them saw it and turned, his sickly sweet expression vanishing, overtaken by surprising hate. That in turn was replaced by a sneer, but Con remembered the other expression.

"He said, get out." Con stood straight, making use of every inch of his height, shoulders back to seem broader, stretching his shirt over his pectorals. The blond was shorter, closer to Tim's height, and without Tim's compact bulk. Still, Con's gut tensed the way it did when he went out on a call. This was danger.

Peter, Con remembered suddenly. The asshole doctor.

"What are you? His keeper?"

Con was preparing to grab the guy and haul him out the door when Tim did just that, if a little more politely than Con would have.

"Out, Peter." Tim's fingers squeezed Peter's elbow and dragged him past Con.

"Sweetheart, you can't be serious about this guy!" Peter said.

"Whether or not I am, I *am* serious about not being involved with you." Tim gave Peter a little push, forcing him into the apartment hall, and grabbed the door with his other hand.

"You are so ungrateful—" Peter began.

Tim looked astounded. Then he bent and picked up a Tupperware container sitting by the door, thrusting it into Peter's chest. "Go home," he said firmly, and closed the door. He leaned against it for a minute, tipping his head slightly to look up at Con through the shadows of his hair. "Sorry about that."

Con smiled, though he didn't feel amused. "I can't believe you ever dated him."

"Me, neither," Tim muttered. He pushed away from the door to stalk to the kitchen. "I shouldn't have let him in, but he brought soup and I took it and then he just walked in..." His pale fingers scraped through black hair, spiking it upward. "He's just not getting the hint."

It was more than a hint, if you asked Con. He didn't say as much, though, more worried about that hateful expression on Peter's face. "He's not... dangerous, is he? Unstable?"

"Probably unstable." Tim flicked on the tap, water running clear and loud into the sink. "Not dangerous."

Con wasn't so sure. He stepped to the window and pulled the blinds aside, but couldn't see where Peter had gone. Finally, telling himself he was being silly, he dropped the blinds and wandered into the kitchen. He put plates into the dishwasher without really paying attention to them.

"You're feeling better?" It was a silly question; he knew Tim was shoring up his emotional defenses with every hour that passed. The man's skin was starting to have color again, though he was always pale, and his eyes once more carried the self-assurance that was so much a part of him.

He wasn't entirely back to normal. His carefully preppy wardrobe was still in the bedroom, tossed aside in favor of sweatpants and a T-shirt, and he still didn't spend much time meeting Con's eyes, as if locking gazes might give something away.

That was all right. After sex on the couch, they'd done it again that morning—and Tim hadn't been a bundle of nerves, but had happily taken control. The little freak. Con smiled slightly.

"Yeah," Tim said, answering the question Con had

almost forgotten. "I'm feeling much better, actually. Looking forward to work tomorrow." He angled a sly look at Con. "I figure it'll keep me from going stir crazy after so many days off."

Con snorted. "You just don't know how to occupy yourself, that's all."

Tim flicked water at him.

Con blinked, surprised. Then, calm as could be, he filled a glass and tossed the liquid toward Tim.

"Hey!" Tim ducked out of the way *almost* in time. "Dickhead!" A laugh rang out, and he angled the movable faucet up to spray Con.

"You seem happier." Grace looked at Tim curiously as she fell into step beside him, walking down the hall. "You get laid?"

It was always the question she asked anyone who looked better. He should have expected it, shouldn't have reacted. His face remained neutral as he gave her a sharp glance, but the tips of his ears went red. He couldn't quite meet her gaze.

"You did!" Grace crowed. "You totally got laid! That guy who brought you a shirt that day?"

"None of your business," he said firmly.

"Oh, come on! It was him, wasn't it? You're *totally* doing him!"

His face heated. He ducked into the doctors' lounge.

Where Con's grandmother sat, reading a magazine. He froze. For a wild moment, he thought about just leaving. Then Grace followed him in, calling, "Is he hot in the sack? Did you do him or did he do—oh."

The blood that had settled went right back into his face as Mary looked up.

"Can I help you?" Grace asked, unconcerned. "This is the doctors' lounge; if you're waiting for someone, the patient lounge—"

"She knows, Grace." Tim stepped to one side politely so he wasn't blocking the doorway. "This is Mrs. Johnson. My boyfriend's grandmother."

"I *knew*—" Then what he'd said apparently sank in. "Oh." The horror of Mary hearing all of that was almost worth it for the look on Grace's face. "Oh," she repeated, her olive skin going nearly purple. "I, uh, it's nice to meet you. I'll just, uh, go." She backed out of the doorway so fast she nearly tripped on her own feet.

"You enjoyed that." A smile teased the edges of Mary's mouth.

Tim started to deny it, expression all wounded innocence. Then he smirked. Just a little. "Yeah. Can I help you? Nothing wrong, is there?" Part of him hoped so. Otherwise, she was just here to chat. God save him from chatting.

"Well, Con said you were sick and I was forbidden to bring you soup. So, I thought that since you were back to work today, I'd bring it now." She smiled.

Tim was still stuck on the part where Con had 'forbidden' her to do something. "Why were you forbidden?" he asked slowly.

Mary pulled a Tupperware container and plastic bowls out of a paper grocery bag. "Oh, I think he was worried I'd upset you."

"So he was busy trying to protect me?" Annoyance rose. "I don't need him to play guardian!"

Mary looked up. "He's a firefighter, dear. Protecting people is what he does."

"Yeah," Tim said darkly, "and I'm a doctor, but I don't go around randomly giving people physicals!"

There was a beat of silence. Then Mary started to

249

laugh. "Oh, I'm sorry, Tim," she said, her hands on her knees. "But it's just—the image of you—" She laughed harder.

Grudgingly, Tim smiled. When she kept laughing, he finally chuckled. Maybe him molesting people in public wasn't *quite* on par with Con trying to protect him... but still. "Do you want me to heat that?" he asked, when Mary continued laughing.

She waved a hand at the Tupperware; he took the gesture as assent, popping the lid off and sticking it in the microwave. By the time it beeped, Mary had control of herself again.

"I know you don't have long," she said, spooning soup into bowls, "But I thought since you'd been sick..." Tim felt her eyeing him. She handed him a serving, and he sat gingerly on the little couch. "You look remarkably healthy for someone who's been so ill."

Tim's ears went red. "Yeah. Well."

"You weren't really sick, were you?"

He wondered how teenagers ever managed to lie to their parents. He played with his spoon.

"Are you and Conner doing better, then?"

That, he could answer. Tim looked up. "We were never doing badly."

Mary just gave him a look—like she knew *everything*.

"Yes," Tim muttered. "We're doing better."

"I'm glad. I'd hate to think either one of you wasn't happy."

Tim wasn't sure what to say to that. 'Thank you' didn't seem appropriate, but he couldn't think of anything else. Finally, he just set the bowl down on their battered coffee table and smiled apologetically at Mary. "I'm sorry—I didn't realize you were coming today, and I have patients—"

"Yes, of course," she said quickly. "How much longer

are you here for?"

The answer was automatic. "My shift ends at four."

"Then maybe we can go for an early dinner. Just the two of us."

Tim paused, trying to think of a way out. But Con was working, and nothing else came easily to mind. "Sure," he stammered finally, manners overriding his desire for a lie as the silence became awkward. "I can just meet you here."

"Sounds perfect!"

They said their goodbyes, and he fled. Christ, what had he been thinking? He could have just said he was going out with some friends! For a moment, he debated going back and doing just that—apologizing, claiming he'd forgotten.

"So, that's the mother-in-law, huh?" Grace asked, making him jump.

"Yeah." He followed her, tugged away from the lounge door regretfully. "Except I'm not married."

"You get along?"

Tim was pondering a reply when someone else beat him to it.

"'Course not. Look at his face."

He bristled at the second voice, cool gaze swinging around to Peter. "We get along just fine," he said icily.

"Really? You don't look like it. At least my parents wouldn't hassle you." Peter smiled, showing too many teeth, premature wrinkles around his mouth.

"It's not a hassle." Tim lengthened his stride.

Peter kept up as Grace peeled away. Faintly, Tim heard, "Good afternoon, Mr. Tite. What seems to be the prob—" The door swung closed, cutting off the rest of her practiced speech.

"Timmy. What do you see in this guy? He's a fucking hulk!"

Tim slipped into the elevator as people left. Peter's hand snapped out, holding the doors, and he followed.

"Don't you have somewhere to be?" Tim asked darkly.

"Yeah. I need to go up." Peter smirked and leaned back against the wall, uncomfortably close.

Tim's jaw tightened. He was *not* going to give way to this creep.

"Tim, things didn't have to end so badly between us." Peter leaned closer, brushing shoulder to shoulder.

Tim's frayed temper snapped. "Peter, what is the matter with you? I'm not interested!"

"Sure, you are. You're just angry. You have issues, cutie, and no one knows that better than I do."

He turned to stare at the blond, dumbfounded.

"I love you, Tim, I can—"

"You're obsessed with me, maybe." His voice was strangled with anger and disbelief. The elevator door opened, and he stepped out quickly. He didn't bother to turn and look at Peter again.

Mary didn't ask him any questions beyond, "How was your day?" and within twenty minutes Tim found himself starting to relax.

They talked about Con, mostly, and she told him story after story about Con getting himself into one scrape or another.

"Let me tell you," she said as they walked down the boardwalk, the ocean to their right and cars to their left, "we were quite worried when he decided he wanted to be a firefighter. I thought for sure he'd get his hair burned off within the first week."

Tim grinned, stuffing his hands into the pockets of

his slacks. His work clothes were all he had—though, with as much as he'd been dragged directly from work to do things lately, he was considering keeping some extra clothes at the hospital.

"I'm sure he's more careful than that." A group played volleyball down on the beach, voices rising above the surf.

"Oh, if he was aware of how reckless he is, I think he'd be careful." She started to say something else, then shook her head slightly—at herself, Tim thought—and pursed her lips. She turned and smiled at him. "Still, you seem careful enough. Maybe some of it will rub off."

Tim chuckled, mentally reviewing his own actions. 'Careful' was an understatement. About the only reckless thing he'd ever done was fall for Con.

Not that he had *fallen* for the other man. Just—it was nice to think about. Like he could, if he wanted to. But he wasn't going to.

"He was heartbroken after his father went to jail," Mary said, filling the quiet between them. Seagulls wheeled overhead, calling greetings to one another.

Tim frowned slightly, uncomfortable. "I imagine so." He paused, then admitted reluctantly, "I don't remember that, though."

"No, I think you had your own problems at that point." Her smile was soft. "No one could blame you for that, much like I don't blame Con for not remembering your exact emotional state at the time."

"Grieving," he said, deadpan.

Mary looked at him sharply, as if uncertain if he was serious or not. He just looked back at her. "Yes, I'd assume so."

"So, tell me more about Con," he said, shifting the conversation off himself before she could start asking questions. "He grew up in Chicago, right? Why'd you move to Florida?"

She gave a slight smile, as if she knew exactly what he was doing. "Well, Florida's warmer in the winter. We're not as young as we used to be, and I think raising Con aged us prematurely." The last was spoken dryly.

He chuckled. "I imagine." Though, really, as active as Con sounded, it had probably kept them in better shape. He glanced sidelong at Mary. Sun-weathered skin, sagging around the underarms, a little heavy in the middle but skinny elsewhere. She looked her age, certainly, but not decrepit. Her dark eyes—so like Con's dark eyes—were bright and alert.

"Oh, he was probably good for us," she said, as if reading his mind. "It just didn't always feel that way."

The 'ding ding' of a bicycle bell rang across the street. "It probably wasn't easy, taking on a kid when you thought you were done raising them."

She smiled. "It wasn't so bad. We already had experience, and retirement set aside. That just went into a college fund and Sam went back to work. Not with the force, though. He picked up a security job." She turned to look at him, explaining briefly, "He was a police officer. Conner only needing an Associate's degree, rather than a Bachelor's, helped." Then she smiled, quick and bright, and looked at him slyly. "I promised Con I would never tell anyone this, but since you're together..."

Tim lifted his eyebrows encouragingly.

Mary grinned and leaned closer.

Con smiled when he walked in the door to the apartment, seeing Tim curled in the corner of the couch, a book in his hand.

Tim glanced up. His eyes warmed, something fond

tickling the corners of his mouth. "How was your shift?"

"Blissfully uneventful." His overnight bag dropped to the floor. "Except one of the guys started talking about his girl back home... He was the first to die."

Tim gave him an amused look, huffed a chuckle, and went back to his novel. "You weren't working in an army movie, Con. It's the San Diego Fire Department."

Con wandered across the room, sitting down beside Tim. He took Tim's calves and pulled his legs straight, settling them over his own well-muscled thighs. "Then the aliens attacked."

Tim smirked, but didn't look up from his book.

Con began to knead Tim's feet, strong fingers pressing into tissue. "The ninja were fighting with the pirates, though, so we didn't have to worry about them at first."

Without looking up, Tim asked, "What about the cowboys?"

"Ninja and pirates agree, cowboys suck." It earned a laugh from Tim. "But I thought we were done for when Cujo arrived..."

Tim looked up then, face oddly solemn. "Did Captain Tightie Whities save everyone?"

Con paused, mind trying to make whatever leap Tim had just made. "Who?" he asked finally, when he couldn't place the name.

"Captain Tightie Whities. Who wears underwear on his head."

Con groaned, letting his skull fall back against the wall. "Oh, God. How did you find out about that?"

"Your grandmother was happy to tell me." Tim looked back down at his book. Only the slight impression of a smile gave Con any clue that he was having fun with this. "She couldn't remember the theme song, though. Something about Fartman...?"

"I was *six*," Con groaned. "And my dad tanned my hide for that. Grams promised she'd never tell anyone. I had to pay her fifty kisses."

"She said you bent over and put wet farts on people."

Con grimaced. Could this get any more embarrassing?

"And spread your cheeks, even."

Apparently, it could. "Can we never talk about this again?"

"I dunno. I bet you'd look good with underwear on your head. Maybe your coworkers should know what kind of superhero they're dealing with. They might be surprised by your amazing powers of intestinal gas."

Con eyed Tim. The man was still looking mildly at his book, his face completely deadpan. "It cost me fifty kisses to temporarily shut my grandmother up. What will it cost for this to be forgotten?"

Tim put his book down and looked thoughtful. "Fifty kisses might do it."

Con eyed him. "Really?"

Tim tipped his head the other way, gaze drifting over Con. "Fifty very *special* kisses."

Con leaned in, feeling almost gleeful. "Special kisses?" He nipped at Tim's jaw.

"Hm. Not there. Lower."

Con grinned. "Yes, sir."

Chapter Fourteen

Things had settled into a routine. Tim went to work and came home, Con did—well, Tim wasn't sure. Whatever he did when he wasn't at the fire department. Most evenings, he was there when Tim returned. They messed around on the couch or in the bed or sprawled out on the floor—wherever they happened to be. The sex only got better as Tim grew more relaxed, though he started having mood swings he couldn't explain, and found himself thinking about his parents more often than he normally did.

A week into that, he realized he was mentioning them again to Con. He flushed, embarrassed, apologizing though he didn't quite know why.

"Don't worry about it," Con said with a half smile and a shoulder-squeeze. "It's normal."

Tim simply believed him, given that he was the one whose grandmother was a therapist—a fact that had come to light during their last dinner before Sam and Mary had flown back to Florida. Tim had just looked at Con, one eyebrow raised.

Con had squirmed and changed the subject. Tim figured that being grilled by your boyfriend's *therapist* grandmother was worth several days of pampering. He'd gotten it without a complaint from Con, even though he and Mary were getting along after all; Tim even hugged Mary before she left, though it was a little stiff. He didn't have much hugging practice.

Then life had settled in, easy and comfortable. It surprised him a bit, how natural it felt to have Con in his space. He'd always thought that his apartment was sacrosanct; he didn't like to share. But Con wasn't just anyone. He was Con.

Tim sighed and settled more snugly against the muscled torso underneath him. He sat nestled between long legs, which were stretched out around him on the couch. From the corner of his eye he saw an arm move, lifting the remote and changing the channel. Tim just kept reading his book.

"You're off tomorrow?" Con asked idly, voice rumbling through the chest underneath Tim.

He made a noise of assent, turning the page.

"Want to go apartment hunting with me?"

His eyes stopped skimming the words in front of him. "What? Why?"

Con shifted, moving Tim as he did so. "Because I don't want to go by myself." He sounded vaguely amused.

Tim sat up, swinging his legs to the floor, knees draped over Con's thigh. "I suppose that makes sense," he said grudgingly. Then he stood and walked away, upset at the notion of Con leaving. "I mean, you'll want your own space." He stopped talking. It was only discomfort that was making him blather on. Standing by the counter, he glared around the kitchen and tried to find something to occupy himself. His mood, peaceful a moment before, spiraled rapidly into anger. More anger than the conversation warranted. It was understandable that Con wouldn't want to stay here. He tried to take deep breaths and calm down. He'd been overreacting to things lately.

"Is everything okay?" Con sounded alarmed.

"Of course. Why wouldn't it be?" Tim's words were tight, bitten off. He opened a cupboard, looked inside, and closed it.

"Because you're acting like a freak."

"I just thought—" He stopped abruptly, aware of how foolish he'd been. Stupid, it was *stupid* to assume that Con was going to stay. He knew better.

"What?" Con stood, leaning on the other side of the counter, T-shirt snug across his shoulders.

"I just thought you could stay here," Tim muttered. He glowered at the sink, scratching at a stain with his thumb. There was a beat of silence before he glanced up.

Con looked surprised. He didn't seem displeased, but he obviously hadn't been expecting that.

"I mean," Tim continued quickly, feeling foolish, "it just seems easier that way. We already get along all right, and we could split the rent. It'd make for fewer bills." It had nothing to do with wanting Con close. With growing addicted to his smell, his presence. With liking sharing a bed, much to Tim's surprise, and enjoying easy conversation and regular sex. Nothing whatsoever to do with trust and love.

Not love. Falling in love was overrated. He scratched at the stain.

He heard Con move, heard the slightly heavy exhalation, and then felt someone step into his personal space. A thumb traced his cheek. He leaned into it, eyes closing a little.

"It would make me so happy to live with you," Con said quietly, "but not for those reasons."

Tim looked up sharply, unease in his stomach.

"Not so the rent is cheaper," Con said with a melancholy smile. "But if you wanted to live together because you like me... I'd stay."

Tim looked elsewhere, unable to keep looking at Con's

expression. It was dangerous, the way those full lips curved in a humorless smile. The dark eyes carried the knowledge and acceptance that Tim couldn't quite deal with the emotional intimacy that others found so easy.

But Con wasn't asking for that. Not really. Tim didn't have to profess love or even strong like; just a desire for Con to stay. Still, he found himself hesitating, wary of the implications.

After a long moment, Con stepped away. His fingers trailed off the end of Tim's chin, leaving streamers of heat. Tim looked up, saw Con walking out of the kitchen, looking a little sad but not heartbroken. Con understood, in a way most other people didn't, that Tim needed time and space.

"Stay." It was overly loud.

Con stopped and looked up, eyebrows lifting. "Are you sure about that?"

Tim's ears were hot. "I'm sure I want you to stay." He couldn't continue with why. He could, however, say why not. "And not because of bills."

It was enough. Con smiled slightly and nodded. "I'd love to stay. I mean," he grinned, spreading his arms, cocky and self-sure. "This apartment is pretty comfortable."

"And relatively close to the beach." Tim smiled slightly.

Con laughed. "And take-out!"

Tim rolled his eyes, but kept smiling.

"Though, we should probably do something about cooking," Con said thoughtfully as he looked around the kitchen.

Tim turned away, pulling a glass out of the cupboard. "Things are working pretty well so far." He shrugged, running water from the tap.

"Yeah, but..." Con trailed off, then restarted. "You know, if you wanted to take a cooking class I wouldn't mind paying for it."

"Oh, yeah?" Tim said mildly. He turned to face Con, keeping his voice politely curious and his expression bland.

It only seemed to encourage Con, who brightened considerably. "Yeah. Sure. Why not?"

Tim sipped his water to give himself time to think. Con's hope was obviously overriding his common sense. Tim had no compunction about using that. "Those can be expensive," he said thoughtfully. "I mean, the good ones are probably—what? One, two hundred dollars?"

"I wouldn't mind," Con assured him, looking both victorious and magnanimous.

"Oh. Well, neat. In that case, since you have the money to spare, how about you get the take-out for the next few weeks? Until that money's gone." Tim smiled pleasantly.

Con's face fell. He grimaced. "I just seriously put my foot in it, didn't I?"

Still smiling too pleasantly, Tim nodded and went back to the couch and his book.

Tim was standing at the kitchen sink several days later, staring idly at the instructions on the back of a package of frozen perogies. Con stood behind him, his chin on Tim's shoulder, arms around Tim's waist. It took a moment for the man's softly spoken words to penetrate.

Tim blinked. "You want to put your what in my where?"

He felt Con laugh, half nerves and half honest amusement. "I want to fuck you."

"As in," Tim clarified slowly, "your dick in my ass?"

He felt Conner nod.

Tim turned as much as he could with the larger man

pressed against him. Con shifted, and he turned the rest of the way. "Con," he began doubtfully.

"Timmy," Con interrupted, stepping close, pressing Tim against the counter and moving their hips together. "Everything in the world makes you shiver. I think you'll like it."

Tim frowned, embarrassed at his own physical reactions. "Yeah, well, I've *done* prostate exams, and no one ever gets up and asks for a repeat."

Con smiled briefly. "Yeah, and women don't ask for OB-GYN visits, either, yet they like sex just fine."

"Great." Tim glowered. "Now you're comparing me to a woman."

"That's not what I meant and you know it."

"Look," he said quickly, "I've seen you naked and, uh, I don't think it's gonna fit."

"Then we'll stop." Con frowned, ducking his head slightly to look into blue eyes. "Tim, look, I can't tell if you're really worried about size or if you're making up excuses so you don't have to say no. If you don't want to, just say so, all right?"

Tim resisted the urge to squirm. Con had really asked for very little, and Tim *knew* this was a common sexual practice, even knew the mechanics of how and why it felt good. "What if I want to—to top?"

"Okay."

Tim frowned. "Okay? Just like that?"

Con smiled, hands skimming up and down Tim's arms. "It's only fair, since I asked if I could fuck you, that you get to try at least once."

"Once?" He eyed Con.

Con shrugged, giving a lopsided smile. "I'm not a big fan, but if you wanted to do it occasionally..."

Tim paused. Con had done it before? Enough to know he wasn't a fan. Tim's skin went warm, thinking about someone bending over *Con*—His heartbeat picked up. "We could try it." His voice sounded a little strangled.

Con leaned in and kissed him softly. Then again. "We don't have to."

"No. It's fine." Tim felt rigid, though. "I mean, if you've tried it..."

Con leaned in to kiss him again. "I knew this one guy, could get off just from someone fingering him. Nice, gentle strokes..."

Tim swallowed, throat going dry. Con chuckled against him, and he glared up impotently. "Are we going to do this or what?"

"Timmy, you're so romantic." The words were gently teasing.

Tim scowled. "Well," he said finally, deciding to ignore Con, "if we're going to do this I'm not doing it in the kitchen." Before Tim could move, Con reached down and caught his fingers, stepping backward toward the doorway.

"Great. Bedroom?" He pulled Tim relentlessly down the hall.

Butterflies battered inside Tim's stomach, his breath speeding. What, exactly, had he just agreed to?

Then they were in the bedroom, the door closed, and Con was pushing him up against cool wood. He pushed back almost instinctively, only to have the mouth kissing him soften and gentle, hands skimming up and down his arms again.

"Sorry," Con said. "Sorry. Relax. Let me lead, okay?"

Tim nodded, trying to bank his nerves, to keep from taking control just because it was safe and familiar.

"Relax, Tim." Con nuzzled his neck, pushing his head out of the way. "If you're not comfortable, we won't do it. 'Kay?" He kissed the sensitive skin over Tim's jugular, tongue wetting it a moment later.

Tim shivered. "I'm fine." He leaned heavily against the door as Con's hands continued their slow path up and down his arms. His head tipped back, giving Con easier access as his lips and teeth grazed the skin, a subtle dance of nerves and shivers. Con's hands drifted around his waist. Fingers edged underneath Tim's shirt, the pressure just great enough to keep from tickling. Calluses smoothed along his skin and slid up his back.

He sighed softly, seduced despite himself, despite the nerves. Con pressed close, his broad shoulders and strong legs a wall in and of themselves, pinning Tim with size and sheer strength. Tim didn't protest, eyes shuddering closed when Con sucked on his earlobe, tongue running up around the shell of his ear, tracing dips and whorls.

Con stepped back, sliding his hands higher under Tim's shirt before pulling it off and tossing it toward the hamper out of deference to Tim's neatness. Tim smiled briefly, until his mouth was caught in a slow, lingering kiss. Con's thumbs traced the outline of muscle on his torso, up his chest, brushing over his hard nipples. He jumped and leaned into it, sucking lightly on Con's tongue as it slid between his lips. A tiny noise caught in the back of his throat when it pulled away. Teeth nibbled on the line of his jaw, down his throat. Con bit once, sharply, at Tim's collarbone before bending lower.

When Con stooped to suck on a nipple, Tim's muscles tightened clear down to his groin. Con dropped to his knees, his tongue blazing a path down Tim's stomach. Quick fingers undid his pants button, and the sound of the zipper buzzed loudly amid their harsh breathing.

Con's hands tugged at his jeans, sliding both them and his boxers down his legs. A hand on the back of his knee encouraged him to pick his foot up. Balancing with one palm on Con's shoulder, he lifted first one leg and then the other, watching as his clothes were tossed into the hamper, quickly followed by Con's shirt.

"Con—?" Tim began, something a lot heavier than butterflies flitting in his stomach. More like those iridescent Japanese beetles that banged against the window in the summertime.

"Hm?" Con leaned in, breathing against Tim's dick before licking where his leg and hip joined, a hair to one side of his rapidly growing erection.

Tim let his head fall back against the door, anticipation heating his blood. Con's tongue flicked out, teasing his balls, feather-light against his cock. "*Con*," Tim pleaded.

Con chuckled and leaned in, nuzzling. His tongue flicked out again, at the base, then the shaft, never staying long enough for any sort of help. He just left hot, damp places on Tim's skin that prickled when the air hit them.

Then one hand braced Tim's hips, thumbs pressing his erection out of the way. Con took a testicle into his mouth, sliding his tongue softly along it, sucking gently.

Tim buried his hands in Con's soft dark hair, spreading his legs a little for better balance. His muscles tensed, pleasure spilling like light through his bloodstream. He heard a groan and realized it was his own, felt the laugh rumble from Con's mouth to his cock, adding a whole extra level of sensation. Con's hand smoothed along Tim's dick, his mouth shifting to the other testicle to give it the same treatment, enveloping it with heat. Palms slid up and down the inside of Tim's thighs, sparking new shudders as Con fingered the skin just behind Tim's balls before drifting down his thigh again.

"Con," Tim said again, pleading and demanding.

Con laughed and pulled away, licking the moisture off the tip of Tim's cock. Tim jerked at the quick brush of molten wet, gaze snapping down to watch. Con undid his own pants, pulling his cock out, stroking the length of it. He took Tim's head into his mouth, tongue teasing the slit, making Tim shudder. Slowly, Con slid farther down, wetting the shaft before sucking. His lips moved firmly over sensitive skin, the occasional scrape of teeth making it that much more intense. He pumped himself, apparently not in any hurry.

Fuck, Tim was unraveling and Con looked like he was still in easy control. Tim took several deep breaths, trying to get his control back. Con opened his mouth farther and took more in, swallowing against the skin.

Biting back a noise in the bottom of his throat, Tim clenched his hands in Con's hair until he remembered not to. It took a minute.

Then Con pulled off entirely, rocking up to his feet without any effort. He shucked off his pants and underwear, one hand reaching out to stroke Tim's dick once, twice, slick with spit. "Bed." Con's voice was low and throaty. He reached under and gave Tim's balls one last squeeze, then turned and followed his own advice.

Mild anxiety faded to mild nervousness, heightening touch and sensation without crippling him. Yes, it was new, but Con was careful. There was no pressure to go through with anything if he didn't want to. And besides, he was hard. Everything seemed like a better idea when hormones and arousal ganged up on him.

But the walk to the bed was five steps too long. Arousal faded. Nerves tightened. As if aware that just the few steps to the bed had increased Tim's anxiety again, Con reached out and snagged him around the waist, pulling him closer and dragging him onto the blankets. Tim let himself fall, rolling over onto his back so he was looking up at Con. Con dipped his head and kissed him, catching Tim's lower lip between his teeth and tugging.

"Now. Where were we?" he murmured, sliding down Tim's body. Tim saw him grab a tube off the nightstand as he kissed his way down Tim's chest, his torso, his pelvis... And then that talented mouth was back on his cock, hot and wet and tight with suction.

"Con—" he gasped as Con's tongue ran along the flare of his head, tickling at the folds of skin.

Con didn't respond except to suck again, and Tim grasped at his dark hair.

After a moment, Con pulled off, licking one last shiver-inducing stripe along the underside of Tim's cock. His knuckles slid up the back of Tim's thigh, encouraging him to lift his leg a little.

Even through the arousal flush, Tim felt his ears heat.

"Relax." Con kissed the inside of his thigh, fondling his balls with a free hand.

"Aren't I supposed to be on my stomach or something?" Tim shifted when Con pursed his lips and blew a stream of cool air over his wet cock.

"Nah. You're plenty flexible enough for this."

"Oh. I—" The hand on his balls vanished and return a moment later, slick with lube. It wasn't as cold as he'd expected, but it still made his skin prickle. More so when fingers drifted down and began to brush over his hole, back and forth, slowly. "Oh," he said again, but this time his tone was entirely different.

"Relax," Con repeated, hooking the leg he'd encouraged Tim to lift over his own shoulder. The other leg he prodded upward until Tim's foot was flat on the bed.

"I'm relaxed," Tim protested weakly. Despite his words, his toes curled as Con made another pass over his ass.

"Liar. Relax."

Tim took a deep breath, focusing on releasing the tension in his muscles. Then Con licked his dick again, lips sucking just on the flare of the head. Tim groaned, unable to swallow all of the noise, and a finger pressed inside his body.

He tensed, remembered not to, and forced himself to loosen. As large as Con's finger was, it slid in easily enough. Didn't feel too odd; unusual, stretching him, but nothing he couldn't handle. And Con's mouth was doing miraculous things on his cock. The finger pushed in farther, feeling much deeper inside him than he thought a finger would. It shifted, moving in and out carefully, fucking him just a little. He moved, not quite squirming.

"Okay?" Con asked, releasing Tim's dick.

"Yeah." He almost shuddered as cool air hit overheated and wet skin.

"God, you look sexy." A second finger pushing in beside the first.

Tim laughed, feeling anything but sexy with his legs all akimbo and his cock and balls exposed. Then the laughter caught, and he spent a long moment remembering to keep his muscles supple as the second finger stretched him, pressing into his body slowly. "Oh, God." The words were a groan, his breath catching. He couldn't decide if it was good or bad—alien, that was certain. He took a deep breath and made his muscles release, letting Con slide into him a little more easily, trying not to think about fingers opening him up.

"You are sexy," Con insisted as if reading Tim's mind, his voice low and rough. "All still and flushed, with your hands scratching at the sheets."

Tim breathed, mouth open, a little embarrassed and highly aroused just by Con's voice. The fingers pushed deeper inside him, and he spent a long moment focusing on relaxing again when his body insisted on pushing them out. The digits shifted, twisting, stretching him further. He caught a noise in the back of his throat, muscles shuddering as nerves that had never really been used sparked and fired in a confusing array of sensation.

Breath ghosted over the tip of Tim's cock when Con spoke. "But then, I always find something intensely erotic about watching people get fucked." The fingers thrust a little more, and Tim pressed his head back into the pillow, body drawing tight with unexpected pleasure. It felt odd, full, a little stretched. The stroke of it curled into his gut, promising that if he just stopped thinking and felt, he'd enjoy himself.

Con's fingers slid out, and Tim relaxed further, the small war with his muscles fading. Then Con pushed slowly back in, deep and smooth, until Tim felt the pressure of knuckles against his ass. Con twisted his fingers, spread them, stretching Tim.

"Jesus," Tim whimpered, fighting the urge to tense, focusing on the nice parts, the caress of skin against sensitive flesh.

"God, you're sexy as hell." Breath was warm and damp against Tim's cock, tongue flicking out to lick the head.

"Do that again." Tim panted, shifting his hips upward, feeling Con's hand move with them, driving a little more solidly into his ass.

Con licked his cock again, painting a line up the underside of his dick, sucking hot and wet on the head when he got there. Slowly, he lowered himself, taking more of Tim into his mouth, rasping his tongue against the sensitive skin.

Tim groaned and pushed upward as much as he could, only one foot planted on the bed, his other heel digging into Con's back.

Con chuckled, adding another sensation to over-stimulated skin. His fingers pulled out, then pushed in with a third, and Tim went still trying not to tense, to stay relaxed as he was suddenly very stretched.

He made a noise, somewhere between a groan and a whimper, muscles trembling with the inner fight not to clench. Then Con loosened his throat and took Tim all the way in, tongue lapping at the base of his cock.

Tim couldn't decide whether to unravel completely or squirm away from the stretching fingers as they pushed slowly deeper into his body. Con wiggled them, making Tim jump, and then hit—oh, God.

Prostate! his mind cheerfully informed him as his whole body tensed, muscles rippling while his vision went white. He choked off a yell.

Con stopped sucking him, and he could feel the man's dark eyes watching intently as he panted and moved, shuddering under the careful onslaught. The fingers turned, stretching him more, any discomfort overshadowed by the brushes deep inside him that fired bliss through his body.

Then Con pulled his fingers out, leaving Tim oddly empty, still thrumming with leftover shivers.

"Relax." Con braced himself on one arm planted beside Tim's head, Tim's leg still caught over his shoulder. Tim shifted, trying to get more comfortable, and felt the head of Con's cock press into him. He stilled, breathing, the awkward position keeping his muscles from clenching even if he'd been of a mind to go rigid.

"Oh, Jesus fucking Christ." His eyes went wide and his breathing ragged as Con pushed in. Thicker than the three fingers, and sure as hell longer. "Jesus, Con—" he began again, not sure what he wanted to say, not even sure if it was protest or encouragement.

Con looked at him carefully, shrugging so Tim's leg slid down his arm. Then he leaned closer, not thrusting any more, and nuzzled a kiss onto Tim's neck. "You okay?"

He nodded stiffly, and felt Con's free hand wrap around his cock and start to pump. His breath shuddered and he relaxed again, lifting his hands to run them through Con's hair, across the back of his neck. He groaned when Con pushed forward, sliding deeper. It felt unbelievably thick, stroking slowly inside him, pleasant as long as he remembered to stay loose.

"Okay?" Con murmured again, mouth hot and damp on the side of Tim's neck.

Tim nodded again, then took a long, trembling breath as Con pushed the rest of the way in, burying himself deeply. When Con pulled out, he couldn't decide which sensation was better. Then Con thrust again, slowly, long, smooth motions that left Tim gasping in his efforts to stay relaxed as pleasure coiled in his stomach, spreading outward. The next time Con thrust in, he hit that bundle of nerves again. Tim yelled and felt his body contract, heard Con's groan and felt the heat of breath on his neck.

Con rocked back, one hand still sliding along Tim's dick, the other holding his hips and pulling him into the next thrust, cock burying deep in his body.

He scrabbled for some sort of purchase as Con fucked him, picking up speed with each thrust, hitting his prostate and making his vision bright with the feeling. Too fast, now, and his ass was getting sore, but every time Con buried himself entirely it hit just right, and Tim couldn't form the sentences to say slow down, didn't really want to. The stretch was worth the muscle-spasming pleasure of it. His world spiraled down to the hand on his dick and the pulsing points of light every time Con thrust in. He wrapped his feet around the Con's waist, and Con went deeper, pulling a wordless exclamation from Tim.

Another thrust, and another, thick and deep, and Tim felt heat pooling in his cock, his balls tightening in the second before Con rubbed his thumb over the head, stroked his hand down the length, fucking Tim senseless all the while. He yelled hoarsely, legs tensing, inadvertently pulling Con in as orgasm rocked through him like splintered glass and pinpricks of light. He tensed, making the cock buried inside him feel bigger, increasing all the sensations at once.

Orgasm pulsed, waves crashing over him and dragging him along until, finally, he thought he might drown in it. As it slowly faded, he felt Con thrust twice more. He almost winced at the pressure against over-sensitive flesh, shuddering with the contact. Then Con went still, his constricting lungs forcing out a half-gasped sound.

Eventually Con relaxed, breathed, and pulled slowly out. Tim gave a little groan, unable to decide if the removal was pleasure or pain. Con leaned over, forehead on Tim's chest. "Okay?" he asked again, panting.

Tim nodded. "Yeah. Was good." He couldn't think well enough to form complete sentences. Christ, he *felt* like he'd just been thoroughly fucked. A little strange, a little uncomfortable, very stretched, thoroughly sated.

Con rolled over onto his side, tossing an arm over Tim. He leaned in to kiss and nuzzle, lipping at Tim's ear. "Willing to do it again sometime?"

He nodded, let Con snuggle, even moved a little closer. Right then, he didn't mind so much. "We still need dinner." The edge of the sheet was almost impossible to grasp, but he managed it, fumbling it up to wipe off semen before it got hard and itchy.

Con took the sheet, did a more thorough job than Tim would have, and made Tim shiver with leftover sensitivity when he included their genitals. Then he reached back to wipe lube off Tim's ass. "Nap first." Con tucked Tim closer. Tim just let him. "Then shower. Then dinner."

Tim shifted into a more comfortable position, his cheek resting against Con's broad chest. "Okay," he said finally. The shower definitely sounded good. His ass felt wet. It wasn't entirely pleasant. Still, fucking was worth it.

But napping sounded best.

Tim stepped out of the bathroom, trying to get his towel to *stay* wrapped around his waist.

"How do you feel?"

Tim looked up, a smile pulled from him without his say so. "Fine." The towel slid; he grabbed for it, tucking the end under again. "Do I smell food?"

Con nodded, his dark eyes soft, the lines where his dimples lay creasing for just a moment and then smoothing out. "I made you dinner."

"You mean you finished heating the frozen perogies?" Tim asked dryly. Water dripped from his hair down the line of his back.

Con laughed. "I did." He stepped close, leaning down to kiss Tim softly on the mouth. "Mmm. You're all warm, still. Hot shower?"

Tim nodded, Con's face against his, eyelashes brushing his cheek. "It helped the soreness."

The warm presence tucked up close to him was gone suddenly, yanked back. Tim nearly reeled. He felt weirdly bereft. It took him a moment to regain his bearings. He was about to ask what was wrong when he saw the look on his lover's face; Con was stricken.

"Oh, my God," Con murmured. "I'm sorry. I didn't mean to hurt you—"

Tim shook his head quickly, emotions warring between annoyed and concerned. "You didn't. It's okay."

"But if you're sore—"

"*Con.* I enjoyed myself. I didn't ask you to slow down. I didn't think we needed to. Relax. I'm fine." Annoyance was winning.

Con wavered, doubt in his eyes, in the tilt of his brows. "You're sure?"

Tim nodded impatiently. "Look, if we're going to do things that run the risk of hurting, you're going to have to just trust me when I say I'm all right." He eyed Con, who was looking slightly surprised. Tim guessed the other man hadn't thought of it that way. "And I have to trust you," he added, though it seemed obvious to him.

Con nodded slowly. "I do trust you."

"Then stop protecting me. I can protect myself."

Con smiled and took Tim's elbows, stepping in close to kiss him again.

Tim kissed back. Then again. Then a third time. Then he planted a hand on Con's chest and shoved. "Con!" he growled.

Con laughed, face creasing into smile lines. "Sorry. I was just wondering how long you'd let me go for."

Tim rolled his eyes and headed down the hall, catching his towel when it nearly fell off again. "I'm gonna throw some clothes on. Is dinner almost done?"

"It will be when you get your cute ass out here," Con replied happily.

Tim flipped him off, but was grinning as he went through the bedroom door.

"Happy?" The low voice, the breath on the back of his neck, yanked Tim right out of his good mood. He slammed his locker closed and turned, coming nose-to-lips with Peter. The urge to shove him away was almost overwhelming, but he wrestled it back under control—he had to work with Peter, after all.

"It's obvious?" He slid sideways to give himself some

room before starting away.

"You were humming." Peter followed. Of course Peter followed. The dickhead didn't know when to stop.

"Then I must have been happy," Tim shot back over his shoulder, and picked up speed. He *was* happy. Couldn't help it, with everything going so well. Con had dragged a bunch of boxes out of storage and over to Tim's, and they'd realized they needed a bigger place. Con was in charge of apartment hunting when he wasn't working—he was currently, but in general, firefighters had more time off than doctors did. At the moment, Con was at the fire department. He'd been there for almost thirty-six hours, and had another twelve to go. Tim figured they'd get home around the same time.

Not even his nightmares could dim his mood. He tried not to think about the fact that, sometimes, nothing at all dimmed it; it just nose-dived for no apparent reason. He told himself that he was stressed, that it would pass, and shoved down the little voice that whispered it was getting worse.

Fingers wrapped around his elbow, yanking him back just before he reached the door. He took several fast steps to keep his balance, feeling the wall slam into his back.

"I would make you happier." Peter stood too close, breath too hot.

Tim resisted the urge to knee the fucker. He inhaled deeply, forcing his fight-or-flight reaction back. "Get off."

"You lied to me. We had something special, and then you lied to me."

Tim stared dumbly at Peter. "You're an idiot." Civility be damned. "Get off before I call for security." For a moment, he didn't understand Peter's expression. For a moment, the fingers on his arm tightened rather than relaxing, and Tim read anger and intent—

And then the door opened from the other side and they broke apart, Peter taking two steps away.

The doctor who'd entered was an older man, recently transferred. He glanced at them both sharply, then marched past.

Tim took a breath and escaped through the closing door into the public chaos.

Something was going to have to be done about Peter. Tim scowled and tried to let the anger go. He couldn't do anything right now. He wasn't going to make more of a spectacle of himself than he already was, and he didn't want his personal life to become public knowledge in the hospital. It would have to wait. Maybe he'd call Peter later. They could sort this out over the phone.

He shook with anger. He wanted to punch someone. He took another deep breath, focus tunneling downward. The mess with Peter shouldn't cause this much rage. He breathed again.

"Tim!"

He looked up, recognizing more populated corridors. Grace was coming toward him, and a glance back showed Peter nowhere in sight. The hall walls stretched, painted something vaguely pink—supposed to be soothing—and marked at regular intervals with plain white doors. He hated all of it, anger at Peter bleeding irrationally into everything. He hated that, too.

"Tim, are you okay?" Grace asked, reaching him and worriedly searching his face with her eyes.

Tim frowned. "Why wouldn't I be?" His shoulders hunched reflexively. If she was picking up on his mood... He schooled his features to be impassive, straightening up and putting his trembling hands into his pockets. As far as he knew, there wasn't any reason for her to know how angry he was. Mood swing. It was just a mood swing, and it would pass. He'd been having plenty of them, lately.

"I heard there's a fire. Your boyfriend's an officer or a firefighter or something, right? I mean, I heard you on the phone with him the other day..."

Tim paled, anger washed away. "Yeah," he said faintly. "He's a firefighter. How bad—?"

Grace could only shrug, looking apologetic. "It's burned ten acres so far. No casualties... you really hadn't heard?"

He shook his head. "I'm sure he'll be fine." The words were more for himself than for Grace. "He's done this before."

She nodded supportively, still looking pained.

"I have patients to get to," Tim said finally, when Grace showed no inclination to move.

"Oh! Right. Sorry." She stepped back.

Tim smiled faintly at her and continued down the hall.

"How long have you been here?"

Tim's head snapped around, away from the television that was broadcasting news of the fire from the corner of the lounge. He didn't need to look at it to see orange flames eating through trees, scattered teams of firefighters struggling to slow it. He blinked to clear the image, sipping bad coffee out of a Styrofoam cup, and looked at his watch. "Twenty-three hours." If he rounded down by forty-three minutes, and didn't counting the twenty minute nap he'd had somewhere around hour seventeen.

He probably could have gone home—they weren't unusually busy—but there was always work to be done, and the fire wasn't out yet. Here, he didn't have to think about Con. Here, if something went wrong and someone got hurt, he'd know about it right away.

A hand stopped him as he was about to leave the doctors' lounge, with its plain white walls and ugly yellow counter. The lounge was comforting. The hand on his arm, however gentle, was not.

"Maybe it's time to head home."

"I have two more patients to look in on." Fingers pressed into his biceps, holding him in place. He looked up into the grizzled face of Dr. Walen.

"Look in on them. And then go home. You get tired, you make stupid mistakes," the man said firmly, his eyebrows moving up and down his forehead as he spoke.

The eyebrows were fascinating. Tim forced himself to look away. Like big, hairy gray caterpillars, sliding down a slope... He nipped off that train of thought before it could continue. "I'm fine." He willed Walen to believe him.

"Go home," Walen repeated. "We don't need you here making mistakes."

Tim withdrew his arm slowly, not wanting to be touched but not wanting to offer insult, either. Walen was right, as much as Tim didn't want to admit it. "Okay. I'll check on them and go home."

It didn't take him as long to check on his patients as he'd hoped, not even when he stretched it out as much as he could.

The fire, according to the news, was sixty percent contained after burning nearly fifty acres and four houses. No one had called Tim about Con, which could only be good news—assuming they would call at all. Con said they would. Tim had less faith in government agencies.

Con's shift had ended nearly twelve hours earlier, but Tim doubted the man would have actually left. He wasn't even sure how it worked, if Con *could* leave, or if he stayed to fight and they slept in shifts.

He couldn't face going home to an empty apartment and stewing, thinking about the way burned flesh smelled or the screams he'd heard from people who'd been brought in at other times. Burns were among the most painful injuries, and the most resistant to pain killers.

He didn't want to think about any of that.

Two firemen had been taken to a nearby hospital; Tim checked in there before continuing on, telling himself that someone would have called if it were Con. He had to check anyway.

They wouldn't give him the names of the firemen, but they did say none of them were Conner Lemor. It made him feel somewhat better.

Eventually, he ended up going to Rick's dojo.

Rick was in the middle of a class when Tim walked in, tense and tired all at once. Rick looked up, hazel eyes sweeping Tim's slight frame, and issued orders to his students, specific moves to practice until he got back. Then he strode over, long legs eating up the space between rooms. "I heard about the fire. Is everything okay?"

Tim nodded, his gaze sliding over the reception counter, over the colorful pamphlets laid out, over the plastic tree in the corner and the bench seat against one wall. Several parents waited for their kids, one little child playing with cars on the floor at their feet. "I haven't heard anything about Con. I figure that's good news..." He trailed off, too tired to complete the thought, much less the sentence.

"You want to crash in the back?" Rick peered at him closely. "You look like you're about to fall over."

Tim considered it, watching the teenagers idly. Through a wide doorway he could see their backs, and the mirror beyond reflected serious but content faces. "No," he said finally. "I don't think I'll be able to sleep. But if you have extra clothes, I wouldn't mind helping teach...?"

It would keep his mind off of... things.

"Sure. Jay left some stuff here the other night that's less rank than mine. I think he had drawstring pants. You'll have to roll them up, but they ought to tighten enough to fit you." Rick's tone was studiously careful. Tim cringed at the thought of how he must look, to earn that particular caution.

He didn't look up. If he looked at Rick, and Rick looked as wary as he sounded, Tim wasn't sure he'd be able to keep the stress under lock and key. "All right." He walked through the big work-out room, around the mightily kicking students, through the doorway, and down the short hall to the office.

The door swung closed behind him with a nudge from his foot. He pulled his shirt off, tossing it toward the futon as he walked to the tiny television. He turned it on and flipped it to a news station. An anchorwoman was talking about traffic. He flipped channels. The television only got ten stations, and none of them were reporting on the fire. He turned it back to the news and opened the big cupboard that hid the laundry hamper and several shelves. Paperwork shared space with random clothing piled in heaps. Jay's clothes were hung over the edge of the full hamper; Tim pulled out a giant T-shirt and a pair of soft drawstring pants, tossing the T-shirt across the arm of the futon and glancing toward the television again.

Still not talking about the fire. Something about an accident. He didn't care.

He shimmied out of his pants, folding them and laying them on top of his shirt, then stepped into Jay's. They were huge, but he'd expected that. Pulling the drawstring tight made them gather in an uncomfortable bulk around his hips, but he ignored it. Checked the television again. They were talking about the fire.

He stepped to the little file cabinet the television sat on and turned the sound up. The woman was saying it was no longer spreading, talking about the two firemen in the hospital, and the houses that had burned. There was a lot of footage, but nothing close enough to spot Con. Not that it would have been possible anyway with all the gear, but Tim could hope. They switched to the weather.

Tim knelt to roll the cuffs of Jay's pants up until he could walk without tripping, but expected them to unroll right away. He pulled on Jay's shirt, and lost all hope of not looking like a child. The arms went nearly to his elbows, the hem hanging past his hips. He rolled the sleeves until they rested on his shoulders, re-rolled the pant cuffs, and glanced at the news once more.

Commercial break.

Tim left the office, determined not to think about Con out there, breathing smoke and burning slowly inside his flame-retardant suit. Christ. He needed a distraction.

Rick kept half an eye on Tim, watching as the young man wandered aimlessly, fleeing back to the office every few minutes. If the kid was trying not to obsess about the fire, he was doing a miserable job—and was going to run himself ragged.

As the teenagers filed out of the dojo, all sweaty and grinning and talking amongst themselves, Rick glanced over his schedule. The intermediate adult group was next; he could use those.

When Tim wandered out of the office again, Rick waved him over, watching the next batch of students start stretching along the walls. "Think you can manage demos tonight?" he asked idly. He hadn't really been planning on teaching these guys new stuff yet, but it'd keep Tim busy.

"You're not going to do them?" Tim frowned as he re-rolled his pants.

"It's easier to explain things if someone else does. It'd be a help." Rick rubbed a foot over the thin mats, pushing two that had slid out back together.

"Yeah, sure," Tim murmured.

Rick watched him. Tim still wasn't paying much attention, his mind elsewhere. He really shouldn't be playing around with martial arts at all, and looked bone tired anyway. There were purple circles under his eyes, and his skin was pallid. "Unless you wanted to go home and sleep?" Rick suggested hopefully.

Tim just shook his head, a small movement that made hair slip down into his face.

Well, it had been worth a try.

"All right, people," Rick called, getting everyone's attention. "Shall we start?"

He thought up the most difficult things he could teach these students, and then made Tim demonstrate not only those, but what the advanced forms would look like—which included contortions and flips and anything else he could think of. At some point, though, his students had to practice and Tim was able to stop. Rick made sure he was breathing hard and soaked with sweat first, and then started sending him to specific students to help. Then he used him for sparring purposes.

By the time class was starting to wind down, Tim looked ready to fall over. When the kid excused himself to head back to the office, Rick just let him go and finished up the last fifteen minutes.

He started the next class with no sign of Tim, and an hour later finished that one and still hadn't seen the other man. As his oldest students started cleaning up for him, he wandered into the office.

Tim was curled on his side on the futon, hands tucked near his chest, knees raised. Rick smiled wryly and walked over to turn the television off. News. He paused, listening.

The fire was under control, and they were going to allow it to continue to burn in order to clear the brush in the area.

Rick twisted the knob and the screen went black with a pop and a wheeze. He glanced over to see slitted blue eyes peering at him wearily. "Hey, Timmy. Time to go home. You want me to drive you?"

"No, it's fine," Tim mumbled, pushing himself up.

"How long has it been since you were home?" Rick leaned back against the cheap mock-wood desk and folded his arms over his chest.

Tim looked at his watch, blinking slowly several times. "I don't know. More than twenty-four hours. Close to thirty, I guess."

"And when was Con supposed to be home?"

Tim rubbed his face. "Yesterday."

Rick nodded. "Go home, Tim. See if he's there." He watched as Tim sighed, stood, and gathered his things. Rick didn't envy him the drive home.

Anxiety kept Tim awake. He didn't know what he would do if he got back and Con wasn't there. Con's shift should have ended twenty-four hours ago, give or take, but with the big fire... Con could have been hospitalized, and Tim might not even know. They weren't related, and weren't married—not that he wanted to be married right then, not that he knew Con well enough or would ever know Con well enough, and not that he was in love because he wasn't—but there was no reason for a hospital to contact him, at all.

He checked his cell phone messages, even though he didn't have any new ones, as he pulled onto the street his apartment was on. No voicemail. He flipped the cell closed and parked, setting the emergency brake with a yank, almost afraid to look around the small lot.

Then he saw Con's Jeep. Relief flooded him and it was all he could do not to run to the front of the building, then up the stairs and into the apartment. He forced himself to walk, even if it was briskly.

Con was curled up on the couch, asleep. His chest rose and fell, lips slightly parted. Pale yellow light from the streetlamp outside filtered through the blinds, striping his bare chest; he wore only boxers. There was a tensor bandage around one ankle, and scrapes and raw skin up that calf. They glistened wetly; some kind of gel on them, but no cover. Tim let his things slide to the floor, then padded across the room.

Con's eyes opened, focused, and he smiled lazily. "Hey, baby." He turned onto his side, lifting one arm in an invitation.

"You're okay?" Tim trembled as he sat on the edge of the couch, eyes feasting on the large body. He slid his hands over the strong chest, clinical, feeling for bruises or warm spots, checking to see that Con really was whole and unhurt.

"Of course." Con's hand landed on Tim's arm, rubbing up and down soothingly.

"There were two firemen hospitalized..." He shifted down to look over the rest of Con, not bothered that Con's hand had to slip off him in the process.

"Yeah, Matt and Danny. They should be all right; no major damage."

Small raw spots here and there, no worse than a sunburn. Tim started to unwrap Con's ankle, checking it for himself. "What happened?"

"Matt had to go into a house where some idiot had left—"

"No, I mean to you." He had Con's ankle free,

and probed gently at the joint, frowning at the slight swelling.

"Just a sprain." There was a beat of silence. "Tim."

Tim looked up, met concerned eyes and lips pulled into a slight frown. "I'm just making sure you're all right," he mumbled, unable to hold that gaze.

Muscles bunched across Con's stomach, and Con rolled upward. "I'm fine." His big hands caught Tim's face, tugging him away from the sight of the minor burns and scrapes on Con's calf. "I'm fine." As if Tim hadn't heard him the first time. Or maybe just hadn't believed him.

Tim searched his face for any hint of a lie or a truth concealed. When he was sure there wasn't any, he moved, straddling his boyfriend, lifting his hands to run them over Con's broad chest, up heavily muscled shoulders into the nearly-black hair. Con's skin was warm, the heartbeat strong in his neck, as he sat and waited for Tim to come to grips with all of this.

On a soft exhalation Tim leaned forward, finally relaxing, realizing that Con was alive, whole, and mostly uninjured. He settled against Con's shoulder, face turned into the warm neck, the strong heartbeat.

"Oh, baby," Con murmured, rubbing Tim's back, stroking up and down soothingly. "I'm fine. I promise. I didn't mean to scare you."

"You didn't," Tim protested weakly. He breathed in Con's scent, still carrying a hint of smoke. "I was just worried." Worried was totally acceptable. He was only shaking because he was tired. "Now, stop talking." Every time Con opened his mouth, Tim felt like he'd overreacted, and it wasn't a nice feeling.

Con moved, rolling them both until they were lying on the couch again, wrapped up in each other. "When do you have to work?"

Tim looked blearily up at the clock. "Four hours."

"So we have time for a nap."

Tim snorted and buried his face in Conner's neck, feeling broad hands spread over his back. "Yeah. Exactly."

The ground kept slipping out from under him, no matter how hard he struggled. Ahead, people walked without problems, talking and laughing in small clusters.

Tim fought against the earth, shouting for help, but no one saw him. Then the oil started, oozing from the cracks in the unstable sidewalk, leaking out from buildings. He screamed, trying to warn the people ahead that they were in danger, but no one would listen. Nobody heard him.

The ground sucked at his feet. He fell to his knees. Explosions rang out. Everyone just kept walking, oblivious to the fire. He tried to run, to get to the nearest person and drag them down out of the way, but the air was too thick to breathe and the ground just sucked him in again. More explosions blasted. The nearest woman was torn in half. Intestines spread like fat pink maggots across the oily sidewalk. Her mouth worked soundlessly. Tim screamed and struggled to no avail—

There was no in-between time from nightmare to wakefulness; one moment he was dreaming, the next he was lying between Con and the sofa back, Con's big hands on his shoulders, dark eyes searching his face.

"Hey," Con said softly, looking worried. "You okay?"

Tim put both hands on Con's body, thumbs meeting in the hollow between his collarbones, relieved to see he was real and whole and just fine. "Yeah." His voice trembled. So did his fingers.

"You sure?"

Fuck. He was *fine.* "Yes," Tim snapped, sliding his hands up behind Con's neck, nightmare images still dancing through his head. But Con was fine. They were both fine, alive, healthy, and together. He pulled himself close, pressing them chest to chest, burying his face in Con's hair and breathing deeply. He lipped at Con's earlobe, trying to forget the blood and the ground sucking him under, the explosions and the way that woman had looked, torn in half—

He couldn't think about that and stay sane. He sucked hard on Con's neck, grinding against him, his hands sliding down over muscle-sheathed ribs.

"Oh, God, Tim?" The big hands slid around Tim's hips, fingers flexing into his skin.

"Hm?" His mouth was full of warm flesh.

"...Never mind." Con's hands slid under Tim's shirt, pulling it off quickly. They separated long enough to toss the shirt to one side, then Tim leaned back in to tongue a dark nipple, one of his hands going down to fondle Con's dick through his boxers.

Con groaned. Tim could hear it in his bones, deep in his chest. He licked down muscles, sliding his hand through the opening in Con's underwear to feel the satin-smooth head of his cock. It was already hard, balls beginning to tighten. Con's hands were at his waistband, but Tim mostly ignored them, sinking down farther and pulling Con's erection free. He licked the tip, then pulled the head into his mouth, sucking on the flare. Con's fingers threaded through his hair, holding him in place.

He wasn't going to think about explosions or burning or intestines spread across the sidewalk or the way the ground pulled at his feet—

"Tim, you don't have to—"

But obviously, Tim was thinking about *something* other than blowing his boyfriend, or Con wouldn't be so talkative. He sucked, sliding down the shaft, smelling musk and sweat and smoke and the underlying warm-leather scent he associated with the man. Con groaned, and Tim felt it right through his cock. Hands tightened in his hair; he didn't object. He went deeper, trying to take as much as possible, letting it fill his mouth with heat and a vague salty taste.

"Oh, God, Tim, baby—"

That was more like it. He took a little more, wary of his gag reflex but craving the little noises Con made. He wrapped his hand around the bit he couldn't get in his mouth, then started to suck in earnest, sliding up and down Con's dick, tonguing the head. Con's hips came up to meet his mouth, short little thrusts, his hand on the back of Tim's head pleading but not forcing. Con gasped and tensed, and Tim felt semen spill into his mouth, warm and salty and slick on his tongue. He swallowed, dragged his tongue over the underside, licked the head and then Con's stomach, just because it was there.

"Oh, God," Con groaned, and grabbed Tim by the hips, dragging him up and twisting until he could shove Tim back onto the couch.

Tim's heart was still pounding, adrenaline burning off with sex. It picked up speed when Con turned, sliding to the floor, and shoved his way between Tim's knees. Con's hands yanked at his waistband and he realized he'd forgotten to change, was still wearing Jay's clothes. The pants slipped down easily, with minimal wiggling, and Con didn't even bother to pull them past Tim's crotch before leaning in. Tim groaned when Con's tongue swiped the head of his cock, hot and wet and oh so good. The broad palms hooked into the backs of his knees, pulling him forward to the edge of the couch. Con licked again, dark eyes angling upward before he opened his mouth and took Tim's dick in, breath warm and moist in the instant before he sucked.

Tim shuddered, watching those lips wrap around his erection, Con's head sink down on him, just before the man groaned as if it were the greatest thing in the world. The groan vibrated against his flesh, making his breath catch and his muscles tense. Then Con opened his throat and took Tim all the way in, nose brushing black curls, tongue flicking along the underside of his shaft. Tim cried out, fisting a hand in Con's soft hair, strands running between his fingers. He thrust upward before he could stop himself, but Con only hummed and fondled his balls.

Watching Con with his head buried in Tim's lap was almost enough to make him orgasm. When Con swallowed around him, throat constricting, Tim felt his body tighten. He bit back a cry, heat pooling in his groin as he pulled Con's head closer instinctively, coming down his tight throat.

It lasted for a white-hot moment, fading slowly. Con licked, tongue hot and wet and soft against his too-sensitive flesh. Tim gasped and twitched, pulling away slightly, then felt as much as saw Con stand and lean over him. Lips met lips, a tongue flickered over his, and Tim opened willingly.

He tasted Con and something else—oh, God, that was him. The couch dipped as Con put a knee on either side of Tim's hips, hands cradling his head, tongue still fucking his mouth, slow and thorough. Tim groaned softly.

"Good?" Con asked, finally breaking apart long enough for them to breathe.

Tim nodded without speaking.

"You want to talk about it?"

He shook his head, glancing at the clock and wincing. "I should go shower. I have to work soon." But he tipped his head up again, searching out another slow kiss. Con didn't disappoint, tongue sliding hot and wet into his mouth.

After a long moment Con pulled away, sighing regretfully. "Go shower, Timmy. When you get home tonight, I'll even have food."

"Good Mexican?" Tim requested, pushing himself to his feet. Damn, now he was even more tired than he'd been before he'd gone to sleep.

"I will go to Mexico and get it, it'll be that good," Con promised.

Tim gave him a small smile and headed for the bathroom. He paused in the doorway and called back, "Don't call me Timmy."

Con opened the door at the second impatient knock, already annoyed with whoever was there. If dinner burned...

Okay, it was difficult to burn take-out. Impossible, really, since the microwave would stop re-heating at a set time. He really needed to convince Tim to learn how to cook.

The hallway was dim, the man standing there beginning to glower as soon as he saw Con. His scrawny neck arched, trying to look around into the apartment. "I wanted to talk to Tim."

Con stepped to one side, blocking Peter's view. "He isn't here." Tim was showering. If Con listened he could hear it clearly, and knew Peter could, too.

The other man made eye contact for the first time, mouth lifting in a sneer. "His car is in the lot."

"He took the dog for a walk." The lie fell effortlessly from his tongue.

"You don't have a dog." Watery blue eyes focused on

Con for a moment.

Leaning against the doorjamb, Con folded his arms over his chest, effectively blocking the way. "How do you know?"

It was an idle question until Peter looked nervous. Con stiffened.

"Tell Tim I was here," the doctor said superciliously, and strode rapidly down the hallway. Con watched him until he descended the stairs.

"Who was that?"

The voice pulled him around, the sight of Tim in flannel pants and a T-shirt bringing a smile to his face. "Wanna have sex?"

"First, tell me who was at the door. Then sex," Tim laughed.

Con sighed. "You won't want sex after you hear." But at Tim's implacably bland look, he finally said, "Peter."

The bland look gave way to appalled disgust. "Here? What is wrong with that man?" Every muscle now hard, Tim turned and stalked into the kitchen. "Did I tell you he tried to corner me in the cafeteria today? The cafeteria! God!"

Con followed his lover as far as the counter, tension coiling in his stomach. "Tim, maybe we should talk to the police."

Tim shot him a dark look from under the black hair falling over his eyes. "I have to work with him, Con."

"This guy is starting to worry me." Con watched Tim yank drawers open in a search for silverware.

"It's fine." Tim pulled out two plates. "I just—I just need to talk to him." In a mutter, he added, "Yell at him. Make it *clear*. Because apparently he's a moron."

Con stepped around him, opening the microwave and pulling out food containers. "But you've already tried that. You've talked to him, at him, and around him, and he's still not getting it. Maybe this is more serious than him being stupid."

Tim just shook his head, looking immovable. Con hated that look. The smaller man glared at the plates of food, scowl deepening. "We're going to go broke eating take-out."

"I know," Con agreed mournfully.

Tim looked at him with guileless blue eyes. "You should learn to cook."

Tim lay on his side in bed, a book open in front of his face and Con curled around his spine. A broad hand slid idly up and down his ribs and hip, calluses not quite scratching.

"Timmy?" Breath stirred his hair, tickling over his ear.

"Don't call me that." He turned the page.

"Hmm. Tim-mmy..."

He felt Con move, restless, legs shifting against his own while a hand slid down to span his stomach.

"What are you reading?" Con's voice was deep, rough, like liquid sex drizzled over tightening muscles.

"John Grisham." He tried to be interested. He was rapidly losing the battle. That was all right.

"How into it are you?" The hand slid down beneath the elastic of his boxers, rubbing slowly over his cock.

Tim felt his eyes shutter closed, his grip tightening on the pages. "Not that into it." The bed dipped as Con shifted, hips thrusting up against him. Con's lips found his neck and left open-mouthed kisses on already warm skin, a tongue sweeping seductively behind. The hand down his boxers slipped out to tug the material down. The wriggling to get everything off was far from sexy, but still made his skin flush. He knew what followed.

Con snuggled up behind him again, his erection pressing heavy and thick against the back of Tim's thighs, cradled against his ass.

"How's quick 'n' messy sound?" Con purred into his ear, making him shiver.

"Sounds great. Hurry up." Tim closed his eyes to better feel the words over his skin, the muscles flexing in the arm that reached around him and took his dick in hand. Con's fingers were slick with lube, gliding over his flesh warm and easy. He groaned when Con moved closer, the man's whole body grinding against Tim as his hand slid farther down, cradling testicles and spreading moisture over them and Tim's thighs.

"Keep your legs together." Con's cock pressed between his legs, rubbing against his balls.

Tim groaned and felt Con's fingers wrap around his dick again, the rough pads turned erotic by lube. Con fucked slowly, cock sliding between Tim's thighs, against his balls, in a steady rhythm that made his breath catch.

"God, you feel good," Con groaned, hand stroking Tim to the same tempo.

Tim curled his fingers into the sheet, eyes closed and body shoving back, then forward into Con's big hand. He could feel the play of muscles over Con's chest and stomach, the shift of them in his arm, in his legs where they pressed against Tim's. God, the mental image of Con straining forward, the feel of his cock rubbing against sensitive skin, against his balls with every thrust, hand stroking—

Tim shoved back harder. "Faster," he gasped, knowing he was going to come soon, feeling his testicles draw up tight, each of Con's thrusts bringing the image of the two of them to mind.

Con pushed up on one arm, changing the angle

slightly but fucking forward with more strength behind it. Tim could feel the flare of Con's cock head against his balls, against the base of his dick, the hand stroking him tight and hot. Heat started in his groin and spiraled out until, suddenly, it dragged back inward. Tim came with a bitten-off cry, body tensing and pinwheeling into a single bright point. He heard Con come a moment later, felt the wetness on his legs and cock.

Tim was still breathing hard when Con dropped back onto the bed behind him, heaving a deep sigh. "Needed that."

"Yeah." Pleasure faded into heavy-limbed sleepiness. Tim squirmed back, out of the wet spot they'd made, and felt Con shift to give him more room. Fingers stroked his spine, though Tim thought Con himself had flopped to his back a little bit away. Too hot for snuggling.

He breathed deeply, flexing his toes on the exhale, letting his book slide to the floor.

"We should get a puppy."

Tim snapped out of his impending doze. "What?"

"We should get a puppy." Con sounded amused.

Tim rolled to look at his idiot boyfriend. "No," he said in horror.

Con lifted himself up onto one elbow, finger tracing imaginary lines on Tim's chest. "Why not?"

"Because you're *gone* forty-eight hours at a time, and who'll care for it then?" He glared at Con.

Con hesitated, eyebrows climbing. "You?"

"Exactly!" He would have rolled away, but Con caught him, laughing, wrapping an arm around his chest to keep him there.

"C'mon, Tim! Don't you have any parenting instincts?" His dark eyes twinkled, dimples hovering around the sides of his mouth.

"No," Tim answered firmly. "Unlike some other people

in this bed, I have enough testosterone." He wiggled until he could turn away, picking his book up off the floor and flipping it open.

It took him a moment to realize the silence had continued. He turned back. Con watched him thoughtfully.

"I'm just wondering," he drawled, "how many other people you have in this bed..."

Tim stared at him for a moment. Then he turned over and went back to his book, ignoring peals of laughter.

Chapter Fifteen

Tim's good mood lasted, more on than off, for three whole days—despite disturbing dreams one of those nights, and Con being gone for forty-eight hours.

The puppy had come up again. Tim had suggested a scorpion again. He could deal with a scorpion. You didn't have to take it for walks or really even give it attention. It just crawled around and looked neat. Con was considering it, and Tim had agreed to consider a puppy.

Maybe an adult dog. A really old one. One that just slept all day. Or, if Con really wanted to play parent, *he* could quit his job and stay home. The image of Con playing June Cleaver made Tim smirk, lost in his thoughts and imaginings as he hurried down the hospital halls, gaze on his paperwork even though his mind was elsewhere.

"Tim."

He nearly flinched, lifting his gaze to give Peter a black look. Tim stopped moving, forcing the blond to stop as well.

"We need to talk," Tim said in his best annoyed tone.

Peter brightened. "Yeah! Yeah! That's what I've been saying!"

He was *excited* about this? Christ. "After work," Tim added, when it looked like Peter would pull up a chair and start chattering right then. "We can meet at Cuppa Joe's, all right?"

"The site of our first date." Peter was all friendly smiles.

Tim stared at him. It hadn't been a date, and—God! The man was oblivious! "Sure. Now, I have a patient to check in on..."

"Me, too," Peter said, as if just remembering. "I'll see you tonight, then!"

The bells above the door chimed when Tim stepped out of the darkness and into the brightly lit coffee shop. Chalkboards painted red danced along one wall and behind the counter, listing drinks and food and cute little sayings. A woman sat in a beaten-up leather recliner, textbooks spread out on the tables around her. A group of young men hung out by the windows, boisterous and loud. Several were wearing eyeliner, and one kept looking outside, obviously searching for someone. The teenaged girl behind the counter glanced at Tim, then away again, shuffling bottles around.

Peter sat in an empty corner, a paper coffee cup on the table beside him. He brightened and stood when he saw Tim.

It made Tim scowl more. All he wanted was to go home and see Con, trade boring stories about their day and look at pictures of apartments. The thought gave him more comfort than any idea of a typical romance, with dinner and movies and perfection. Con was his best friend and now his lover and—

He was getting melancholy. He tried to shake it off, a little afraid of the yawning ache in his chest when he knew there was no reason for it.

His feet carried him across the room while his mind roller-coasted elsewhere.

"Do you want some coffee?" Peter smiled nervously and started toward the counter.

"No," Tim said firmly. "I'm not staying long."

"Oh, c'mon, cutie, things might go really well." Peter's expression hovered somewhere between a leer and a simper.

"Peter, I just came tonight because you don't seem to be getting this, and I wanted to make it clear. I am *not* interested in you." There. He couldn't possibly be clearer than that.

"Oh, come on, Tim." Watery blue eyes narrowed a little, anger simmering in the gaze. "Just because I made a mistake—"

Tim shook his head once. Black hair fell in his face, and he ignored it. "Whether or not you made a mistake, I'm not interested. I'm seeing someone else now." Someone he desperately wanted to go home to and curl up with, someone who could assuage the threatening darkness he felt.

"You played me, Tim." The words were low, angry. Peter stepped forward. "You *owe* me—"

"I don't owe you anything," he said, trying to keep his calm. "I—"

"You said you loved me!"

He stared, baffled. "No, I didn't."

"You implied it!"

He glanced around, keenly aware that the conversations in the room were growing quieter. The barista was watching them with open fascination.

"We dated, casually, for a couple of months," he murmured, looking back at Peter. "I'm sorry if you read more into that. I am seeing someone else. I'm not interested in you. I don't want to speak to you anymore, and you're not going to change my mind. Leave me alone."

Now Peter would go away.

"We had something." Peter reached out to grab Tim's elbow. "I don't know why you're denying it—"

Tim allowed the initial contact, but the small shake was too much. Anger mounted, seeking an escape. Before he could do more than open his mouth, another voice cut in.

"Hey, man, it ended. Leave him alone."

He glanced sidelong toward the voice, saw one of the young men with eyeliner standing nearby, looking wary and primed all at once.

"Breaking up sucks, but you can at least do it with some dignity." The stranger's eyes flickered nervously between Peter and Tim. His look seemed to ask something—probably 'everything all right?'—but Tim twitched his gaze back to Peter and watched him rather than answering. Part of him hoped Peter would take it a step farther—even just shake him again. Then he would have an excuse to drop the asshole fast and hard. The tile didn't look like it would absorb impact very well.

"Yeah, dude, drink your coffee. Let it alone," another male voice said, not as certain as the first but at least lending his support. Someone stepped up behind Tim, a hand reaching around to settle on Peter's wrist. "It's not worth it."

"Fuck it. Fuck you." Peter snarled the words, dropping Tim's elbow and stepping back. The blond's hands were shaking as he raised them, dragging fingers through his short, spiky hair. "You know what? You're a God-damned asshole. Fucking tease." He inched back to the chair he'd been in, yanking up his coat. "Fuck you, Tim." He turned and stormed out of the coffee house.

Tim took a deep breath, rattled but unworried.

"You okay?"

He glanced at the man next to him, heavy black eyeliner seeming to make him more concerned, black-dyed hair and black clothing highlighted by leather wrist bands and a silver-studded collar.

"Yeah." Tim looked out the window, past the first man who'd spoken. Beyond him, Tim could see Peter get into his BMW and peel out of the lot. "Yeah, I'm fine," Tim said when the other doctor was gone. "He's just a dick. Thanks."

"Yeah, no problem, man." The first guy still looked worried, but headed back to his friends. The man standing beside Tim followed suit.

He watched the parking lot for a moment more, then finally headed out the door himself. He supposed that took care of things.

Con smiled when the door opened, hit 'mute' on the television, and unfolded from his place on the couch. Papers were spread out around him, and a ring-bound map was held open to a specific page simply by being laid upside down along the back of the couch.

"I found some apartments that accept dogs," he said by way of greeting, his smile turning into a grin.

Tim only slanted him an unreadable look, though. A far cry from the 'get real' snort or the ultra-bland look Con expected.

Con sobered. "What's wrong?" Not that anything had to be very wrong lately for Tim to go quiet. Whether it was anger or upset or just plain tiredness, his reaction was always the same: go quiet until he couldn't be quiet any more.

It had started recently, these mood swings that took Tim and washed him along. Con wasn't even sure Tim was aware of them.

"Am I a tease?" Tim's eyes were shadowed.

"What?" Con would have laughed at the absurdity, if his lover hadn't looked so upset. "No, of course not."

Tim didn't seem any happier, and wouldn't quite meet his gaze.

"Hey, baby, what's wrong?" Con trailed Tim as he headed toward the bathroom.

"Nothing," Tim murmured, and closed himself in.

The shower started as Con stood there frowning at the closed door. Eventually, he went back to the couch, turning the sound up on the television again.

Overall, Tim seemed happy. If it weren't for the weird mood swings and the nightmares, Con wouldn't think anything was wrong. But a day didn't go by where one or the other didn't happen, unpredictable and slightly alarming. His own mood now somber, he paged through print-outs for apartments and waited for Tim to get out of the shower.

When Tim emerged from the bathroom, hair still wet and wearing just boxers and a T-shirt—a definite indication that he was toast for the night—he walked straight to the couch and sat, legs curled under him, leaning toward Con. It was as close as he ever came to initiating a snuggle. Con wrapped an arm around his boyfriend's square shoulders and pulled Tim close, the smaller body tucking easily up against him, warm and malleable. *Something* was wrong.

"What happened?" Con asked quietly, turning his head to let soft black curls tickle his nose, smelling shampoo.

"I talked to Peter. He accused me of leading him on. I don't think I did..."

Con tightened his hold, feeling Tim curl farther into him. "No, I doubt you did. Timmy, I really think there's something wrong with him." Every instinct he had screamed it. "Are you sure we shouldn't at least talk to the police?"

"I have to work with him." Anger made Tim's muscles tense. He pulled away, stalking toward the kitchen.

Con sighed. And there was the mood swing he'd grown accustomed to, the one that was making him nervous. "I know you have to work with him," Con said, carefully neutral. "But if we just *talk* to the police, maybe they'll have some ideas—" He stopped at the glare Tim leveled in his direction. "All right. Never mind," he muttered. This couldn't be normal for Tim, these swings from sad to angry to happy to—whatever came next in the emotional alphabet. Surely he'd have noticed them in sixteen years of friendship.

"I'm sorry."

Con glanced up to realize Tim had crept back and was standing near the arm of the couch, looking guilty.

"It's just been a stressful few weeks."

He couldn't argue with that. Leaning back, he smiled an invitation. Tim took it, sliding back onto the couch. Con wrapped an arm around him again, feeling Tim rest his head on one of Con's shoulders.

God, that worried him. Tim shrugged away from arms, didn't tend to cuddle, certainly never did something as snuggly as *leaning* on someone else. "Timmy?"

"Don't call me that." Tim reached one graceful hand out to move an apartment flyer.

Con ignored the protest. "Can I say something without you getting mad? It's not about Peter." That should at least make him a bit happier.

Tim made a small noise of assent, temple rubbing against the cap of muscle on Con's shoulder.

He took a steadying breath, not sure how this was going to go over. "Tim... I know it's been a bad few weeks, lots of things happening, but... is that the reason for your mood? You seem... upset a lot."

There was a beat of silence. "I've been happy."

"You haven't been acting that way. And you've been having nightmares. Is that normal?"

He could almost hear Tim's mind clicking along. "I—I don't guess so." His voice was nearly buried in Con's shirt. "I've just been stressed."

"Totally understandable," Con agreed quickly. "But, y'know, sometimes when people have lots of emotional upheaval—"

"Have you been watching Dr. Phil again?" The words were suspicious.

"No," Con said firmly. "I was raised by a therapist, and I learned a few things. Like, when you have a mental freak-out, sometimes that stuff lasts." It only occurred to him after the words were out that his phrasing might have been bad.

Tim pulled away, turning to look at him coolly. "Mental freak-out?"

"I... shouldn't have said it like that. I'm sorry. But you opened up all that emotion you'd been locking down, and moods swings and nightmares—"

"Mood swings? What, now I'm crazy?" Tim's voice rose. He stood without waiting for a reply, stalking down the hall.

"No, just prickly. Come on, Tim!" Con stood to follow his lover into the bedroom. "I'm worried—where are you going?"

Tim dragged on a pair of sweats, shooting him another dark look. "To Rick's. So you don't have to deal with mood swings."

"Tim," Con said, drawing the name out into a protest. "I didn't mean—"

"I'll be back later." He brushed past.

Con followed him to the living room, and watched him slam out the front door. Well. He'd botched that.

Tim tiptoed into the dark apartment, itchy with dried sweat, anger burned away. Maybe he'd overreacted earlier. It was only fair that Con had noticed his bizarre behavior, and he couldn't keep taking it out on his boyfriend. He hadn't realized how bad it was.

He locked the door, turning the deadbolt as slowly as possible to keep it from thunking. Then he took off his shoes and set his keys down, metal covered with his fingers to avoid a clink. His wallet followed.

No sounds from the bedroom. The least he could do was let Con sleep.

He slipped down the hall and into the room, quietly pulling off his shirt and dropping it in the laundry bin before starting on his pants.

"Feel better?"

The voice surprised him into jumping. His gaze cast around, seeking through the black for Con's face. He could make out the man's shape, but not much else; it was too dark, and his eyes hadn't adjusted yet. "Yeah." He squinted before giving up. "I didn't mean to... to mood swing on you." He grimaced, hoping that had made sense.

Con chuckled. "Yeah, I know. Everyone has bad days." Cloth rustled, sheets and blankets shifting off the big body. Tim saw Con's shadow-shape rise, sitting up in bed. "Are you going to get mad at me if I say I'm still worried?"

He looked away, hooking his thumbs in the waist of his pants, at the small of his spine. "No." He felt more sad than anything. "I'm sorry, Con."

Cloth rustled again. Tim glanced up, saw a big hand lift and ruffle through Con's hair, leaving it sticking out in all directions. "Don't be sorry. It's not like you're doing it on purpose. Is it... because of me?"

Tim's head snapped around, his eyes widening. "No!"

"Wait, think about it." The square shape of his shoulders, outlined by the window, had rounded. "I mean, I basically pushed you into sex, and then the mood swings started, so—"

"Stop." Tim's eyes were adjusting to the dark. He could see Con's head ducked, gaze on his feet. "I think—" He stopped. He didn't want to admit this. Didn't want to admit he couldn't control his emotions. He tucked his hands under his armpits, staring anywhere but at Con. "Maybe you were right earlier. That I let the emotions loose, and I can't seem to get them back under control again." He just wanted them to go away. Go back to the way he'd been. That had been working great.

"What if you talked to someone?" Con asked hesitantly. "Someone else might know—"

Tim glared, knowing full well that 'someone' was code for 'a counselor.' "Don't push," he growled darkly. He wasn't *that* sick.

"Okay, okay." Con lifted his hands in a soothing gesture. "I won't push. Come on, get cleaned up and come to bed."

He woke sobbing. Tim turned his face into the pillow, knowing that it had been a dream, trying to muffle any noise he might make.

Too late. Con's hand rubbed over his back, the man's broad chest pressed against him. He lifted a hand and buried it in the pillow, fingers tightening into a fist.

The terror eased. The dream faded. He remembered the panic, watching people die, struggling to do something while the ground slipped away from under him—and even as he remembered it all, he forgot it.

Tim let the cries ease, feeling anxious and tense from the dream. Con shifted, close against his back as if trying to wrap him up protectively.

They lay there quietly while he caught his breath. Lips pressed against the nape of his neck, warm and slightly chapped.

"Tim," Con murmured against his skin.

He rubbed tears off his face, vaguely embarrassed.

"I'm worried."

He was too tired to bristle.

"This isn't normal." The words were spoken quietly against Tim's flesh, as if that might make things better.

He closed his eyes, stomach knotting. "I'm just stressed." He didn't even believe it himself.

A hand stroked down his arm, though Con could have been soothing either of them. "No one should react like this when they get stressed. And you've been stressed before."

Tim's eyes fell closed. "It's just recently." The words were almost a whisper.

Con laid a soft kiss against his shoulder. "Since I arrived?"

He flinched. "Since... since that day I freaked out."

When Con kissed him this time, it was obviously meant to soothe Tim. "We messed something up in your head, didn't we?"

Tim blinked into his pillowcase. 'We'? Tension unknotted in his chest. Not all his fault. Not that he was crazy. "Maybe."

Con kissed him again, lips against his shoulder blade.

Tim waited for the request again, waited for Con to suggest he go see someone.

It didn't come.

He relaxed further. A shift turned him backward, waiting for Con to move so he could twist around and look up. In the darkness, he couldn't see more than the gleam of Con's eyes. "It's not right," Tim said softly. "Is it?"

He saw Con shake his head, a silhouette above him.

He moved again, sliding onto his back, nearly tucked underneath the broad chest and strong shoulders. Con lay on his side, watching. Tim lifted a hand, tracing firefighter muscles, skimming around the areas he knew were still tender from the last big fire. "Maybe I could talk to... someone."

Con said nothing, just brushed his fingers through Tim's hair, sweeping it back.

Tim sighed and let himself be soothed. He was tired. Tired of waking up scared, tired of the mood swings and the look in Con's eyes, the one that said he was waiting to see what Tim might do. Tired of feeling sick.

"Tomorrow," he said quietly. "I can talk to... to my old intern advisor. She'll have some names, I think." He leaned into the hand brushing his hair back, letting his eyes close. He felt lips, feather-soft, whisper over his brow. Strong hands pulled him closer, pressing him firmly into the cave made between the angle of Con's body and the mattress. Tim grumbled about clingy boyfriends and overwhelming body heat, but didn't move away.

"He said he would." Con peered in the refrigerator door, his cell phone held to his ear with one hand. "I believe him."

"If you pushed him into it—" his grandmother said through the line, louder than she'd normally speak. In the background, he could hear an announcer calling something.

"I didn't push him into it, Grams." The annoyance he felt didn't quite creep into his voice. He didn't think he had pushed, anyway. "Where are you?"

"The supermarket. Are you sure you didn't push? Therapy only works if the person is willing."

Con closed the fridge. "He was willing. Didn't you want this? I'm sure you were telling me it'd be a good idea..." Which wasn't why he'd suggested it to Tim. His grandmother thought everyone should be in therapy, from what he could tell. He looked around the nearly bare kitchen, filling a dirty glass with water and pouring it on Tim's single plant. The plant looked half dead. Too much water or not enough? He couldn't remember ever watering it before.

"Of course I think it'll help. I just don't want to see you arguing."

Con poured a little more water on the plant, then frowned when the dish below it started to overfill. "Listen, Grams, I have to go." He grabbed for paper towels. "I'll call you later, all right?"

"All right," she said, sounding vaguely disapproving. "Papa will want to talk to you. Ed's been suggesting areas to live down there."

Great. "Wonderful. I gotta run. Small kitchen problem. Talk to you later?"

"Of course. Don't burn anything down."

"Very funny," Con muttered to her laughter, and hung up. He blotted up water with his handful of paper towels, then tossed them all in the garbage.

His grandparents' move to SoCal was looking imminent; Papa was talking about coming out at

Christmas to look at apartments. Con smiled reluctantly. As much as they drove him crazy, he liked the thought of them nearby. They were his only family, and he loved them. Almost as much as he sometimes wanted to kill them.

Tim hesitated as he stepped out of the bathroom, towel-drying his hair. Con sat on the couch, flipping through pamphlets and business cards Tim had brought home.

"What are all these?" he asked, glancing up, forms still in his hands.

Tim's ears went red. "Those are counselors. In the area." He lifted his chin slightly as if daring Con to comment.

Con only smiled, and Tim felt his defensiveness melt away.

He continued haltingly, the words coming faster. "Dr. Ferguson said that it's good for doctors to see someone once in a while. Especially to help with stress. 'Cause this is a stressful job." God, he was blathering. He closed his mouth with a click and refused to speak anymore. Con knew all about stressful jobs; his wasn't any easier, even if he didn't work as many hours.

"Smart doctor." Con paused to look at a card. "If you want, I can give you the name of the therapist my boss had me go to."

Tim shifted from foot to foot. "You've stopped seeing him already?"

Con nodded. "He pronounced me fit to leap back into fire again. So if you wanted his number—"

Tim shook his head, just once. "I already called a couple of these ones."

Dark eyes flicked up at him. "Damn. You don't waste time, do you? Once you decide something, you just jump in with both feet." Con grinned. "Brave."

Tim shrugged, embarrassed and self-conscious. "Not really."

"Yes, really." Con stood up, crossing the room and pausing right in front Tim, sliding his hands up and down Tim's arms. "It's one of the many things I love about you."

Tim froze. Con what? When his boyfriend ducked to kiss him, he kissed back more automatically than anything. "Wait." He pulled away. "What?" Then he shook his head sharply. People just said things like that. It didn't mean anything.

But Con was looking at him curiously. Con laughed, and rubbed Tim's arms again. "Timmy. I love you."

Tim pulled farther away. "You—" He stopped, not sure he could continue.

Christ. "You shouldn't say things like that so flippantly," he managed finally, looking warily at Con. "Heck, you did the last time and look at what a mess that created."

Con's smile faded, though he didn't look upset. A little solemn, dimples vanishing. A little thoughtful, dark eyes somber. "I think that mess worked out pretty well, but okay." He nodded slightly, the smallest tip of his head. "Tim? I'm not drugged, and I'm not flippant. I love you." He was serious this time, reaching out to brush the backs of his knuckles along Tim's jaw.

Tim didn't pull away. He stared, half stupefied. And then he realized he couldn't say it back. It was a serious thing, and he just wasn't ready. He looked down, his throat closing as his mood threatened to degenerate into misery.

"No, hey," Con said, as if he were a mind reader.

"I didn't say that to make you say it too, or to make you unhappy. I know you take longer with things like that. And I know that, if you ever do decide you love me back, you'll do it like you do everything else, and I'll be smothered in it."

Tim laughed quietly, looking up through a fall of hair.

"I love you." Con smiled again. "And if you can deal with it, I'm just gonna keep saying it." He leaned in, and Tim tilted his face up for the light kiss. "I've been saying it," Con added against his mouth. "You just haven't heard it."

Tim blinked in surprise, feeling his emotions lighten again. "I—" he began, but couldn't quite force the words out. There was too much going on; he couldn't be certain of what he felt. He shook his head, looking elsewhere.

"Tell me when you feel it," Con said, stepping close and wrapping his arms around Tim. "And not before."

Tim nodded against a broad chest, enjoying the feeling of security. Then he realized he was already warm, and squirmed free. "Jesus, you're the clingiest person in the world," he muttered. But he was smiling.

Rick watched his Little Brother fly through the spar, movements quicker and surer than they'd been in months. Tim twisted through advanced moves, every gesture sharp and fluid at once.

It was good to see. It had been a long time coming back.

There were only five students in Tim's class, and they almost always fell into plain fun before the night was over. Rick broke up the roughhousing toward the end of their hour, sending the group off to grab water and pulling Tim to one side.

"Things better?" he asked, tipping his chin toward the other end of a mat.

Tim grabbed it, wiping his face on his shoulder as he did so, blotting sweat. "Yeah." He bumped the folds of the mat up with his knee and pushed it in.

Rick stuffed it into a closet. "What changed?"

Pale ears turned red. Rick watched with interest. Tim glanced toward his classmates, then grabbed another mat. "I'm... I'm seeing a therapist," he mumbled softly. "And Con's been—" He flashed a smile without looking up, a rare one with teeth. "Great."

Rick's answering smile was softer. "Good." If Tim needed anything, it was some 'great' in his life. "How long have you been seeing the therapist?"

Tim glanced up sharply at his classmates again, but they weren't listening—they were goofing off in the corner, or getting their things. "Just a couple times. About a week." He grabbed another mat, wrestled it into folds, and pushed it into the closet. "The dreams are worse, but he says they'll go away eventually, and they don't seem to bother Con..."

"Good," Rick repeated, grinning. "What changed? One minute you were bottling everything up, and the next you weren't."

Tim shot him a dark look. "I didn't bottle everything—" Then he paused, took a deep breath, and let it out. "Okay. Maybe I did. I just couldn't bottle it up anymore, and then I couldn't control it at all, and Con suggested I talk to someone..."

Tim wouldn't quite look at him. His apparent inability to complete a sentence spoke volumes. Rick reached over, wrapping an arm around him and pulling him into his chest.

"Jesus, Rick—!" Tim said into his shirt.

Rick just laughed, tightened the one-armed hug, and let

go. Now some of Tim's classmates were paying attention, laughing at the two of them. He let the subject drop, aware that Tim was embarrassed and uncomfortable. Maybe someday he wouldn't be, but for now he had enough people picking at him.

A few of the older students, done gathering their things or chugging water, came over to help fold the rest of the mats. Rick gave Tim a brief smile before dropping the subject entirely. Tim smiled back wanly and went to get something to drink.

"Friday, then," Tim agreed, waving as he left the counselor's office. Therapy wasn't as bad as he'd expected. There were rough moments, and emotions that surprised him with their suddenness and intensity. Once he'd gotten used to talking, though, it was easier—and he was starting to understand why he felt like he did, even if he couldn't control it yet.

The mood swings were still in full force, but he was learning how to manage them, and how to explain them to Con rather than freaking out.

He walked out of the building, a nondescript brick box that sat on a corner, filled with various offices, and paused on the sidewalk. He had some errands to run and, if he hurried, he could finish them before Con got back from the fire department.

Tim glanced either way as he crossed the street. He started down the sidewalk, mind on this latest therapy session. It was hard; Dr. Davies wanted to talk about Tim's parents, and Tim didn't want to. It had taken him a bit to admit he was angry with them for dying, which felt stupid, because they hadn't chosen to be hit by a drunk driver, and it seemed like a betrayal. They'd been good parents, and saying anything bad about them hurt.

Still, he had to admit the counseling was helping. The emotions he and Con had unwittingly torn open were starting to heal, rather than getting buried again. Unexpectedly, he felt more comfortable with himself, which made things with Con better.

Just the thought of his boyfriend made him smile. He stopped beside his car and fumbled in his pocket for his keys. Emotions were hard, and the bigger they were the harder they were, but he was willing to admit now—at least to himself—that maybe, just maybe, he was falling in love. God, but that was scary.

Someone stepped up close behind him, and he turned reflexively. Tim didn't catch more than a shape before an arm slammed him into the car. He shoved back, felt pain in his shoulder, a sharp prick, and heard a voice murmur, "It's okay, don't worry—"

Tim swung his elbow around to smash the man in the head, twisting to take him out at the knees. The shape dropped, howling.

Peter.

The world lurched quietly. Tim braced himself, remembering the prick in his shoulder as everything seemed to go drunken. He looked over.

A syringe hung from his shirt, the needle tangled. With shaking hands, he pulled it out. "What did you just do?" he said slowly. Despite his care, the words slurred.

"Don't worry." Peter stood, blood pouring from his nose. "Won't hurt you. S'ketamine."

Ketamine. He didn't have long, then. Less than a minute. And whatever Peter had planned, it wasn't good—not if it involved a heavy sedative.

The ground lurched. He staggered. A hand clamped down on his arm, fingers smeared with blood.

"It's okay, cutie. It'll be fine."

There wasn't much time. He grabbed Peter's wrist, twisting around and snapping the man's elbow the wrong way. There was a sickening crunch, and a scream. He moved again, striking hard and fast as his vision started to blur. He smashed his own elbow into the back of Peter's skull, heard another cry as the body dropped.

Empty streets. Staggering, Tim turned and headed back toward his therapist's office. The ground seemed to careen away. He kept moving forward, unable to feel his footsteps. The curb nearly felled him. He staggered into the street, struggling to tell up from down.

He was beginning not to care. That was the drug, he knew. He didn't care about that, either.

Everything smeared as something cold and hard hit him. Brakes screeched distantly. The world stretched. He blinked. Thunder rumbled in his ears, edging ever slower. Thump-thump. Thump-thump. Thump-thump.

A face blocked out the sun. Worried. Talking. The words made no sense. He stared, fascinated, at the stranger.

The man turned his head. Hair moved. He straightened. Tim blinked, lids swooping down over his eyes. When he opened them again, there were more people. The faint call of a siren. A babble of voices clinging to him.

Tim drifted.

Awareness came back slowly. Con was there. Tim smiled weakly, and only then looked around.

Tan walls. White ceiling. The smell of pine cleaner. The muffled, hollow sound of a loudspeaker.

His tongue felt thick, lips difficult to move. He tried anyway. "'M I at work?"

"Hey." Con spoke with the sort of tone Tim had heard

time and time again from loved ones glad to see patients wake up. "No, you're not at work. Well—you *are* at the hospital. Do you remember what happened?"

He struggled, mind wading through a fog. "Peter..."

"Yeah. He tried to drug you. Serious crazy stalker. The next time I say we should call the police—"

Tim smiled hazily and patted Con with one flopping hand. "S'okay."

"It's not okay!" Con practically squawked.

Tim smiled and patted him again. "S'okay. Why'm I here?"

Con snorted. "You were *drugged.*"

He waved a hand. "Jus' ketamine."

"And you were hit by a car. Thank God it was stopping already."

It was hard to blink his eyes open again—he wasn't sure when they'd fallen closed—and look at Con, but he managed. "Am I okay?" Dimly, he was aware of a hand holding his.

"You're fine."

His eyelids slipped closed. They opened again. "Was he drunk?" That was how things happened, after all. Drunk drivers hit people.

People like his parents.

"No, Timmy. He wasn't drunk."

His eyes slipped closed. "I miss 'em. They were good parents."

He didn't know how much time passed before Con touched him once more. Blunt, callused fingers brushed hair from his temple. "I know."

Time spilled around them, blurred by ketamine. "Bet Peter won' come near me anymore," he said slowly.

There was a snort. "You shattered his elbow and his nose, and gave him a concussion. *And* the cops say that if you want to press charges, he'll end up in jail."

"'Course 'm gonna press charges. Jerk."

A chuckle purred around him.

Half drugged, it was easier to stop thinking about things. To feel, instead. The anger at Peter washed away, and in its place rose anger at his parents. That, too, eased off after a moment, leaving behind grief. He let himself feel it, too woozy to fight, and after a time it passed as well.

Con squeezed his fingers, and stood. "I should let you rest."

Tim startled further awake, looking around wildly for his lover. "Don' go."

Slowly, Con sat back is down. "Okay. It's all right. I'm here."

He relaxed again, falling back into the pillows. "Good." Emotion curled up, filling his chest with a comfortable warmth. "Con," he said sleepily, "I love you."

There was a long beat of silence. Then a rumbling chuckle. "I will be *so* glad when we can both say that without the aid of drugs."

Tim slipped back under.

Epilogue

Bing Crosby crooned about a white Christmas from someone's radio, over the crash of waves and the crackle of a bonfire. Heat spread over Con's face as he stood before the flames. His hands were tucked in his pockets, gaze on the other side of the fire where Tim stood, talking with Rick, gifting the man with a rare, teeth-showing smile. Con was in love. He was so head over heels it wasn't even funny. Life was perfect.

Or would be, if Tim ever admitted to love without being doped up, first. In the months since the accident, he hadn't said it again. Con held to those three little words, spoken absently under a ketamine haze. He wasn't sure Tim even remembered saying them.

The weeks after the kidnapping attempt had been hectic. Police work and lawyers, longer shifts for Tim at the hospital until they'd hired someone to replace Peter. More nightmares. But they'd changed; no longer was Tim unable to do anything while people died. Now they were memories, but memories he grieved openly. The mood swings had begun to abate, and Tim could usually tell when one was coming. His therapist, he'd told Con wryly one night, had given him cookies for making such good progress. Con had laughed.

"Well, son, this might be one of the nicest Christmases

I've ever had," a voice said to his right, and Con turned to smile at his Papa warmly. "Yup. Yup," the man continued, "moving here was the thing to do. I'm just glad Ed could come along."

Con's gaze drifted up, past his grandfather to where his grandmother and Ed sat in matching beach chairs, shoulders covered from the night breeze by a shared blanket, legs warmed by the bonfire. Ed was wearing a skirt, despite the wind. Con thought about pointing out that his grandfather's obsession with Ed the Tranny was a little weird, but... well, it was Christmas. He smiled. "Yeah. That was nice," he agreed mildly. If the man offered him eyeliner one more time...

"Jay just made his night, let me tell you. Spent a good half hour discussing fashion and how long it took to learn to walk in heels."

Oh, *God*, that was just what he needed; Jay convincing the old bugger to hang around more.

"That's nice," Con repeated, though it was getting harder to say. He loved his grandparents, he really did...

"All right, well, I've gotta go break those two up before they start talking about my cholesterol," Papa said, and with a clap on Con's back he left.

Con glanced around at their little party. His family and Tim's; it made for a rather small gathering, an extremely eclectic group, but everyone was getting along and enjoying themselves. He found Tim again with his gaze, smiling at the sight of him, and started around the bonfire.

"Hey, Con," Jay said, waylaying him. "Those people over there—" he pointed out along the beach, dotted with bonfires, "—say the fireworks should start any time. Here." He shoved something at Con, who grabbed automatically.

Sparklers. "Aren't these illegal?" He smiled wryly.

Jay shrugged and grinned, irrepressible. "Don't tell."

"I'm a *firefighter.*" But Jay was already heading off, protest unheard—or ignored. Con reached back, grabbing Jay's elbow to halt him. "Hey. Are you *trying* to get Ed the Tranny to hang out more? He's old, you know."

"*She*," Jay said clearly, "is an interesting person."

"He," Con groused. "Transvestite, not transsexual."

"She," Jay insisted. "She was part of the military, and if she gets the operation there'll be problems with her pension. Don't be so closed-minded, Con." He continued walking.

Con blinked after him. Closed-minded? He was *gay*! He wasn't—

"Hey."

Annoyance vanished at the sound of Tim's voice. "Hey."

Tim leaned up, a hand on Con's elbow for balance. Con tipped his head down and took the offered kiss, thrilled that it was being freely given. In *public*, even.

There was a distant whine and Tim looked up, over the ocean. Con followed suit, and a moment later fireworks splashed across the sky, red and yellow and blue reflected in the water below. Applause smattered across the beach, a staccato burst of laughter from somewhere. Waves crashed.

Tim's compact body tucked in next to Con's. Con smiled without looking down, wrapping his arm around strong, narrow shoulders.

More color splashed across the sky, echoed on the choppy sea, accompanied by little popping explosions. Jay tapped Con on the shoulder and he turned, seeing the lit sparkler. Laughing, and with a vague sense of guilt—if anyone should be upholding fire safety laws, it was him—Con touched his to Jay's, watching it flare to life, bright white, a ground-born starburst. Jay bounded off, spraying sand everywhere, and Con offered it to Tim.

"Wanna light?" Con laughed, lowering his head so he didn't have to shout.

The darkness was broken by more fireworks; green and purple and blue this time. They colored Tim's face, the tips of his mouth curling as he held his sparkler up.

The sticks touched, crackling and flaring at each other as Tim's leaped to life. Con waved his around happily.

"I love you."

Con paused, not sure he'd heard correctly. He lowered his head, leaning down toward his boyfriend. "What?"

Tim looked up, smiling a little, and tucked his mouth near Con's ear. "I love you."

Con pulled away slowly, trying to see blue eyes in the darkness. He couldn't; not quite. Then another set of fireworks shot off, and Tim was there, expression calm, looking vaguely amused at Con's reaction—as if this was perfectly normal.

A grin broke across Con's face. He held tighter. "I love you, too," he said, and then nothing else. He didn't sweep Tim up into his arms like he wanted, or spin him around. If Tim wanted to pretend like this was normal, that was fine with him. He did, however, step behind Tim to wrap his arms around him—careful of their sparklers—and hold him tightly.

Fireworks burst above, bright white and blue and pink. Tim swung his sparkler; Con tossed his into the fire as it burned out, then went back to holding his lover. He could smell Tim, under the smoke and the ozone burn of the show. Soap and mint and shampoo. He tightened his grip and put a kiss in Tim's hair.

"You are way too cuddly," Tim murmured on a small laugh.

Con smiled. "Indulge me. I'm not letting go."

Tim was quiet for a long moment. "I could *make* you

let go."

    Con grinned and tickled him.